SANCTUARY

VOLUME 1

CAT ANDREWS

nine
Beaches
press

Edited by Lopt & Cropt Editing Services

Cover Design by Black Bird Book Covers

ISBN: 978-1-7352404-0-4 (e-book) and 978-1-7352404-3-5 (paperback

For the three men in my life, who have never truly understood my obsession with Jane Austen, but who've always wholeheartedly supported me and my writing endeavors.

Prologue

Beep. Click. Hiss. Beep. Whir.

The soft but incessant noises that surrounded the hospital bed of Fitzwilliam Darcy's wife had become an almost soothing presence. He'd come to depend upon hearing those odd sounds, their steady, repetitive cadence reminding him she was still alive. The smells of the hospital had become familiar too, and although not as welcome as the sounds, they weren't quite as off-putting as they'd been at first.

He sat next to his wife's bed, holding her left hand and rubbing his thumb over the pale band of skin where her wedding rings had been, and his eyes traveled over her battered but slowly healing face.

Just wake up, Anne. Open your eyes.

If sheer willpower on the part of her husband could have forced Anne Darcy's eyes to open, they would have done so two weeks ago when this nightmare began. Parts of that horrible night were still foggy; he'd also suffered some injuries as a result of the accident, and couldn't remember the impact or much of what had followed.

He gently squeezed her hand as tears came to his eyes and he fought to keep them in check. She was so beautiful, even with fading bruises on her face and one cheek still slightly swollen. He knew the creamy complexion beneath the ugly discoloring, the hypnotic violet-blue shade of her eyes underneath their puffy lids, and the color of her hair, like summer wheat…

Will I ever get to touch it again, watch her brush it, watch Jack tangle his hands in it?

Jack. Their little boy who'd turned two just five months ago. What would he do without his mama?

He shook his head and pushed the what-ifs away, concentrating instead on willing his wife to get better. He bent to place a kiss on her hand and lifted it slightly, rubbing his cheek against it before raising his eyes to her face.

"I'm here, Annie," he whispered. "I'm not going anywhere. But you have to do the same. You have to fight hard to stay here with me and Jack."

He stopped when he felt his throat constrict and kissed her hand once more. Hearing movement behind him, he turned to see his in-laws standing in the doorway.

"How is she, Will?" asked Louis, his voice weary.

Will shrugged and stood as they entered the room. "The same. No change."

Louis nodded and wrapped his arm around his wife. "Why don't you go get yourself a bite to eat? Better yet, go home to Jack. We'll stay with Anne."

Catherine nodded and spoke quietly. "Go on, Will, take a break. We'll look after her."

Will shook his head and glanced at his watch. "It's not even dinner-time yet. And Jack's fine, he's with Georgiana." He sighed and felt a wave of exhaustion come over him. "A cup of coffee might be good, though. Can I bring you back anything?" The older couple declined, and after telling them he would return shortly, he kissed his wife's forehead and left her room.

He headed toward the bank of elevators outside of the ICU and was grateful the one that stopped for him on the eighth floor held no other passengers. After entering and pushing the button for the first floor, he leaned against the wall and closed his eyes. Images of his wife immediately flooded his mind, causing tears to pool under his eyelids.

The elevator chimed when it reached its destination, and he took a deep breath, regaining the tenuous hold he had on his emotions. He slowly ambled down the maze of hallways toward the cafeteria and decided to call his sister.

"Hello?"

"Hey, Georgie, it's me," he said quietly. "How are you? How's Jack?"

"We're both fine. How are you? How's Anne?"

"I'm alright. Um, Anne is still the same." Frustration bubbled up in his chest. "It's weird, it's like she's just sleeping, you know? I have to stop myself from shaking her to wake her up."

"It'll happen, Will. She loves you and Jack too much to give up."

"I want to keep hoping, but the doctors...they were so encouraging before, but now I feel like they've become less optimistic. I'm not stupid, I know the longer she's unconscious, the less...the less likely it is..." His voice trailed off as his emotions threatened to take over again.

He cleared his throat briskly and continued on in a low voice. "It's like they're starting to give up, and it's hard. I can only go by what they say." Feeling overwhelmed, he changed the subject. "How's my little man?"

"Oh, he's great," Georgie answered. "Is he always like this? He hasn't stopped moving since he got up from his nap an hour ago."

He smiled as he wandered into the cafeteria, though his eyes were still blurry with unshed tears. "He's pretty busy. If you need to take a breather, just turn on Elmo."

She chuckled softly. "Thanks for the tip. Do you think you'll be home for dinner, or should we eat without you?"

He was torn; he wanted to see his son and hold him and hug him, but he didn't want to leave Anne's side. "Would you mind if I stayed here? Can you stay with Jack a little longer?"

"I told you, I'm here for the duration. I've already unpacked my things in the guest room."

He sighed in relief. "I'm sorry this is disrupting your life so much."

"I'm sixteen, Will. I don't really *have* a life." She paused, and her voice softened. "Seriously, you know I wouldn't be anywhere else."

He felt a rush of affection for his sister. "Thanks, G. I really appreciate it."

They said goodbye and he tucked his phone into his back pocket, determined to push the always-hovering negative thoughts from his mind. He filled a large cup with coffee, and as he stepped up to the cashier he heard a loud page echo through the cafeteria.

Code blue ICU 6, code blue ICU 6.

At first he couldn't process what he was hearing, and he looked at the cashier blankly.

"Wh–what did he just say? Over the loudspeaker?"

The cashier shrugged. "I don't know. I kinda block that stuff out during my shift, it happens so often."

The woman standing in line behind him spoke up. "I think he said they have a code blue in ICU six, but I—"

She stopped speaking when Will suddenly bolted toward the hallway, his coffee tumbling to the floor.

Thursday, July 24
Boston, Massachusetts

Elizabeth Collins sat in the back seat of a police car, watching as its blue strobe lights mixed with the red from the ambulance and danced across the front of her condominium. Silent tears streamed down her face as she wondered how her friend was faring.

I can't believe it's come to this.

She watched as another police car—the one that held her handcuffed husband—slowly left the scene. Someone stepped in front of the window, startling her, and she looked up into the shocked expression of her older sister. A police officer hurried over, clearly concerned that someone was approaching the car, but after speaking with Jane for a moment, he opened the rear door to let her in.

As soon as Jane was inside, Elizabeth fell into her arms, her entire body trembling.

"Shhh, Lizzy. It's okay. Everything will be okay," Jane whispered, holding her sister tightly. "Can you tell me what happened?"

Elizabeth shook her head. "George is hurt, I—I need to make sure he's okay."

The siren on the ambulance sounded, warning the small, curious group of onlookers to move out of the way, and the sisters watched in silence as it sped off down the street.

"I'll find out how he is," Jane assured her. "I'll ask someone, I promise. Are you hurt?"

Elizabeth reached up to touch the back of her head. "J–just here. Bill was pulling my hair." Her bottom lip quivered. "I didn't cry, Jane... I wouldn't let him see me cry." She sat back and took a deep, steadying breath.

"He wasn't supposed to be home; he was supposed to be out of town on business until tomorrow night. I went out for lunch with George...I hardly see him anymore." She shook her head. "He came into the condo, and we were talking in the foyer...I told him I'd decided to leave Bill." She sniffled softly. "He was so relieved."

A tear slid down her cheek, and Jane gently wiped it away. "What happened then?"

"Bill must have been at the top of the stairs listening. He was furious." Elizabeth looked at her sister, fear etched in her expression. "When he came down—I didn't even know he owned a gun, I had no idea—he pointed it at George and then at me. He told George he would never have me, that no one except him would *ever* have me." She sniffled again.

"I've told him over and over that George and I are just friends, but he's never believed me." She reached up to swipe at her wet cheeks. "He grabbed me by the hair and pulled me toward him, and then George yelled and told him he'd had enough and he—he lunged at Bill, but the gun went off..."

"Oh, no," Jane whispered, her eyes wide. "Bill shot him?"

Elizabeth nodded. "George was holding his side, and he was in so much pain, and there was...there was blood everywhere. A neighbor must have heard something because all of a sudden the police were there, but Bill wouldn't let anyone in. He kept saying it was *my* fault George was hurt, that *I* was to blame."

"How did the police get you out?"

Elizabeth stared at her sister. "I told Bill that I lied to George," she finally answered. "I promised him...I swore on my life I would stay by his side, and that we would find a way to get through this mess together."

"Lizzy—"

"I won't stay with him," Elizabeth interrupted. "I can't." She took a deep, shaky breath and looked up at her older sister. In the blink of an eye, her life had spun completely out of control.

"What do I do now?"

One

W ill sat back in the low seat of the ferry, enjoying the warmth of the early morning sunshine. He took a sip of his coffee and cracked open one eye to make sure his five-year-old son was still within sight. Jack was across the deck, holding a cracker high above his head and trying to tempt a seagull to swoop down and take it from his hand. The seagull was teasing him, coming within a foot or two of his small fist before flying higher once again.

"Take it, bird, take it!" Will heard him exclaim.

Jack soon lost interest in the game and tossed the cracker over the side, watching as the seagull dove toward the waves to find the small morsel.

"You almost had him," Will said when Jack came to sit next to him.

"Yeah, almost," Jack responded quietly as he leaned his head against his father's arm. "How much more is the ride?"

"About fifteen minutes or so."

"Will all my stuff be there?"

"I think so," Will answered optimistically. "We haven't caught up to the freight boat yet, so that means it's still ahead of us."

Jack remained silent, and Will wondered if he was feeling anxious about the move. He couldn't blame him—Will was feeling a little anxious too. All Jack had ever known were the sights and smells and sounds of New York City. Things would be different here; he would hear the birds singing, smell the ocean, and see the stars at night. It would all be so new for him.

For both of us.

"Did I tell you Great Diamond Island is filled with lots of kids your age? Especially in the summer?"

Jack nodded. "Mm-hmm."

"There's a big swimming pool and a few beaches, so maybe you can learn how to swim. How does that sound?"

"Good!" Jack raised his head to look at his father, his eyes now lit with excitement. "Can you teach me?"

"Sure."

"Can we build a tree house?"

Will smiled. "We'll have to see what kind of trees are in the yard and make sure there's one big enough."

"If we don't have a good tree, we can just build a fort on the ground."

"A fort would be just as good."

Will thought about the house he'd purchased. He'd taken a gamble as he'd only seen it in pictures. But he'd immediately had the gut feeling that his real estate agent, Madeline Gardiner, could be trusted. She spoke enthusiastically about the house, saying it was a steal at just under a million dollars.

After viewing the dozens of pictures she sent, he had to agree. It was big, but not too much house for him and Jack. The views of Casco Bay from the deck were fantastic, and it had other amenities he loved: a large yard with lots of trees—perfect for forts or tree houses, a home office with views of the bay from every window, and a wine cellar.

They would have neighbors, but the trees provided privacy for the five-acre lot. Madeline and her husband Ed would be close by as well; their home was located just outside of Diamond Cove. They'd lived on the island for twenty years and loved it.

"It will take some getting used to, especially for a city boy like you," Madeline had said to him teasingly. "No cars are allowed, as a rule—only in an emergency or for moving residents on or off the island—but golf carts are okay. There's a market and a couple of restaurants, but the restaurants are only open in the summer. And all of the schools are off island."

Hearing all that made Will think twice. *How will Jack get to school?*

Where will I keep my truck? What if there's an emergency? And golf carts? Really?

Madeline generously offered to help him and Jack adjust to island life. "It's worth every little bit of effort you'll put into it, believe me," she'd declared firmly, and that had sold him.

At the ripe old age of thirty, he was starting over. "It will be an adventure," he'd told Jack just a few days ago. He smiled to himself as he watched his young son walk over to the railing with another cracker.

It certainly will be.

ELIZABETH GRINNED WHEN SHE HEARD A KNOCK ON HER FRONT DOOR. "Come in, Maddie!" she called out as she walked into the living room and smiled at her friend. "I'm almost ready."

"I hope the freight boat is on time this morning. The moving truck carrying all of Mr. Darcy's belongings is supposed to be on it."

"That's right, the wash-ashore arrives today," Elizabeth said, grinning mischievously. "I forgot about him."

"Oh, be nice," Maddie scolded lightly. "You're a wash-ashore too, you know."

"I'm joking, of *course* I'll be nice." Elizabeth turned off her coffee maker and grabbed her backpack and purse. "Ready when you are."

She closed the door behind her and followed Maddie down the stone walkway that led from her small cottage, through the Gardiners' backyard and into their driveway. They climbed into Vixen, Maddie's candy-apple red golf cart, and headed toward the ferry docks.

As they sped along the mostly deserted lane, Elizabeth thought about how lucky she was to *be* a wash-ashore. She'd met Maddie the day after she moved to Portland from Boston two years ago, when she enlisted the friendly real estate agent to help her find a rental that would fit her budget. Unfortunately, the places she could afford weren't in the best neighborhoods, and after nearly two weeks of fruitless searching in and around Portland, Maddie brought her over to Great Diamond Island to show her a small cottage.

Elizabeth was astounded when she heard the cost of the rent, which was well within her budget, but worried that the money spent taking the ferry back and forth would soon eat up any savings she would be lucky enough to tuck away.

"You'll be able to get a resident's pass for the ferry, and it's not too expensive," Maddie had explained. "The cottage is completely furnished, and the utilities cost next to nothing. Cell phone service is very dependable, so you won't need a landline. And if you're careful about not leaving your lights on at all hours, the landlord will pay the electric. All you would be responsible for is the rent and the cable."

Elizabeth fell in love with the cozy yellow cottage and soon discovered that Maddie had conveniently forgotten to mention it was *her* cottage on *her* property. She didn't say a word about it until Elizabeth asked to meet the landlord—and although she was surprised to learn she would be Maddie Gardiner's tenant, it was a pleasant surprise. She'd felt an instant affinity with the petite, gregarious older woman. Maddie's husband Ed was a quiet, unassuming man, his personality quite the opposite of Maddie's, and he'd become a dear friend as well.

When Elizabeth heard the Portland Children's Library was looking for full-time help, Maddie put in a good word for her. That job, along with a part-time gig waiting tables at a local five-star restaurant, helped to pay the bills and enabled her to put some money away. The friendship between the two women had grown steadily, despite the years between them—Maddie was a few years older than Elizabeth's mother—and eventually, Elizabeth had confided in Maddie about her life in Boston and the events that had prompted her to leave.

Now, Elizabeth didn't even bat an eye at the fact that even though she was twenty-six, one of her very best friends was more than twice her age.

"So Mr. Darcy is retiring here?" she asked as they neared the ferry docks.

"I don't think so, he's fairly young," Maddie answered. "I think he's just looking for a change, something new." She cast Elizabeth a sidelong glance. "Kind of like someone else I know."

"Where is he from?"

"New York City."

"Wow, that's a pretty big change. But I'm sure he'll love it here."

They pulled into the parking lot and climbed out of the cart, and Elizabeth watched the passengers disembark from the ferry. "What does he look like?"

"We've never met, so I'm not sure. I've only seen the picture on his driver's license."

Elizabeth was incredulous. "He bought the house without seeing it?"

"He saw all he needed to see in the pictures I sent."

Elizabeth was distracted by the sight of a tall, dark-haired man walking down the long wooden ramp from the ferry. He was smiling and looking down at someone next to him, and soon enough, she could see it was a young boy. They held hands, and the man raised his eyes and scanned the crowd.

"Mr. Darcy!" Maddie called out, waving her hand and walking further ahead.

Elizabeth knew she should be helping Maddie look for Mr. Darcy, but her eyes were still glued to the handsome man. She watched as he waved and then began walking toward Maddie.

Elizabeth's eyes widened. *This is Mr. Darcy?*

"I wasn't sure I would recognize you," Maddie said, smiling widely as he approached.

"You know, I thought about that as we were docking. I was ready to shout out your name if necessary." He grinned and shook her hand. "It's nice to finally meet you. This is my son, Jack. Jack, this is Mrs. Gardiner. She's going to take us to our new home."

Jack held out his hand, his expression serious. "Nice to meet you, Mrs. Gardiner."

Maddie shook his hand solemnly. "It's very nice to meet you too, Jack." She glanced behind her, as if suddenly remembering Elizabeth was there. "This is a dear friend of mine, Elizabeth Bennet. Elizabeth, this is Mr. William Darcy and his son, Jack."

Elizabeth raised her eyes to Mr. Darcy's and was struck by their rich brown color. She smiled brightly and held out her hand. "It's nice to meet you, Mr. Darcy," she said as he gripped her hand lightly. "And you too, Jack." The boy stared up at her with the prettiest blue eyes she'd ever seen. "Welcome to Great Diamond Island."

Mr. Darcy stared at her for a moment before quickly releasing her hand. "Ms. Bennet," he replied with a brisk nod. His gaze lingered on her face until he cleared his throat and turned his attention back to Maddie. "Um, where's the freight boat?"

"It's there, I see it," Maddie said, pointing further down the docks. "Why don't we hop into Vixen and head down that way?"

"Vixen?" he asked, eyebrows raised.

"Oh, that's my ride," Maddie said with a grin, and then leaned close to him. "Sexiest little golf cart you'll ever meet."

"I've yet to meet a sexy golf cart," he said, smiling slightly.

"See? The fun is already beginning!"

"I—I should board the ferry," Elizabeth interjected. "I don't want to be late for work."

"Oh, of course," Maddie answered, turning to her. "Are you going to the picnic tonight?"

"I'm not sure. It's Charlotte's birthday, so I might spend the night at her place. I won't know until later."

"Well, have fun if you stay, but please be careful."

"I will." She turned back to Mr. Darcy and Jack. "Nice to meet you both. Enjoy the island." Once again, Mr. Darcy only nodded.

She said goodbye to Maddie and then boarded the ferry, taking her usual seat on the top deck. She leaned on the railing and watched as they climbed into Vixen, Jack sitting in back and Mr. Darcy folding his tall frame into the front seat. She lost sight of them as they headed to the freight boat, so she turned around and settled into her seat.

She thought about his greeting. *Ms. Bennet.* Obviously he wasn't the overly friendly sort. He seemed approachable enough when he greeted Maddie, though he probably felt as if he knew her already, just from talking to her on the phone; she had the knack of making anyone feel like an old friend.

As much as she tried to pretend his response to her introduction didn't bother her, it did. She felt brushed off, but told herself he was probably just another uptight wash-ashore. They were a dime a dozen, and too many of them assumed their status followed them to the island like a second shadow.

He'll be in for a rude awakening when he finds out otherwise.

Mr. Darcy was forgotten by the time the ferry docked in Portland, and Elizabeth shouldered her ever-present backpack and prepared for the one-mile trek to work. She enjoyed starting her day with a walk, and only drove in the winter when it was very cold. She kept her car at the parking garage next to the ferry terminal, as the city gave long-term parking discounts to the Casco Bay island residents. It was worth the small fee to have it when she needed it.

Her cell phone rang, and she smiled when she saw who it was. "Good morning, Jane," she answered cheerfully.

"Hey, Lizzy! Did I catch you at a bad time?"

"No, I'm just walking to work. What's up?"

"Not much, I just thought I'd call and check in. We haven't talked in a bit."

"You're checking up on me?"

Jane laughed. "Not checking *up*, checking *in*. There's a difference."

"Hm. Maybe a small one," Elizabeth conceded. "I'm fine, things are really good."

Jane had always been Elizabeth's staunchest ally. They were only fifteen months apart and were best friends as well as sisters. There had been some tense moments between them when Elizabeth had decided to leave Boston, but Jane finally came to understand that her younger sister needed to go somewhere new and start over. Elizabeth knew that deep down, Jane had only been concerned and wanted to keep her close by.

"How's Stuart?" Elizabeth asked.

"Oh, he's fine. He's...he's good." Jane sighed. "He's just...Stuart. Unflappable, imperturbable Stuart."

Elizabeth giggled. "What does *that* mean?"

Stuart Carver was Jane's boyfriend of nearly a year. He was a nice man, divorced—and eighteen years Jane's senior. That had surprised Elizabeth at first, but she could see why Jane liked him. He was well-educated and attractive, in a bookish kind of way.

"Oh, I don't know what it means," Jane answered, sounding flustered. "I just feel...I don't know. Things are weird lately, like we're not clicking or something. We're not fighting, it's just...it's like he's here, but he's not."

"Okay, so what are you going to do about it?"

"I don't know," Jane answered. "I care about him, I really do. He's reliable, sweet, cute—"

"Is he a man or a puppy?" Elizabeth teased. "It sounds like you need to talk to him."

"I know, and I will. Eventually. And what about you? Are you dating anyone? Dipping your toes in the water?"

"Huh. No toe dipping here. I haven't found any waters worthy of my toes."

Jane laughed lightly. "Seriously, have you met anyone?"

"Sure, I've met lots of people. Just no one I'm interested in dating."

"You've got to put yourself out there, it's the only way to get past everything," Jane advised. "Not every man is like Bill Collins. *Or* George Wickham."

"No, you're right," Elizabeth countered quickly, "there are a bunch of Stuart Carvers out there too."

"That's not fair, Lizzy," Jane grumbled. "Stuart's not a bad guy. A little too set in his ways maybe, but he's nice."

"And sweet and cute, I know. Leave it alone, okay?"

Jane huffed. "Fine."

"Fine. So how's everyone else? How's Dad?"

"He's okay, but he misses you. He always asks when you're coming home, and now I don't even bother answering. I just shrug."

"I miss him too. I call him all the time, but he never asks *me* when I'm coming home."

"That's because he knows you'll tell him the truth. He asks me because he knows I won't say what he doesn't want to hear."

Elizabeth's eyes teared up, and she quickly changed the subject. "How's our little sister?"

"She's great. Now that she's about to graduate from college, the reality of heading out into the world is finally sinking in." Jane laughed. "Sadly, we might have to drag her kicking and screaming from her little pink bedroom. As much as she tries to come across as this worldly, experienced girl, I think she's terrified of venturing out on her own." She paused. "Do you think you'll come for her graduation? It's only a week away."

"I don't know," Elizabeth answered vaguely. "I'll try. It's a possibility."

"Lydia would be thrilled, and so would Mom and Dad." Jane's voice softened. "You can come home. There's nothing to be afraid of."

"I know that," Elizabeth responded quickly. "And correction—Dad and Lydia would be thrilled. Mom? Not so much."

"Come on, Lizzy," Jane argued, "you know that's not true."

Elizabeth slowed as she neared her favorite bakery and inhaled the mouth-watering scent of freshly baked bread that wafted out to the sidewalk. Unable to resist, she asked Jane to hold on as she stopped and ordered a blueberry muffin to go.

"No, I *don't* know that," she continued as she stepped back out into the sunshine. "For some reason, Mom doesn't want to face reality. Well, not *my* reality."

"She had a soft spot for Bill."

"Apparently, it was a bigger soft spot than the one she has for me," Elizabeth responded, feeling a swell of frustration. "And I really don't want to talk about this right now."

"Okay." There was a long pause before Jane spoke again. "I saw George the other night."

Elizabeth's heart skipped a beat. "You did? Where?"

"I was out with Stuart. We went for a drink, and he happened to be sitting at the bar."

Elizabeth frowned. "How is he? How did he look?" she asked, then silently cursed her curiosity.

"Honestly? He was hammered and had some skank hanging all over him."

"Did he see you?"

"Yes. He smirked and looked away, which was fine with me. He didn't give me the time of day."

Elizabeth remained silent, prompting Jane to speak again.

"Don't do this, Lizzy. You did everything you could for him, and he took total advantage of you. You don't owe him *anything*. You never did, and he had no right—"

"Stop! I'm fine," Elizabeth interrupted. "I just didn't expect to hear his name." She sighed when her sister remained silent. "Honestly, you just caught me off guard."

"I'm sorry," Jane responded sympathetically. "I shouldn't have said anything, I just...I get so mad when I think about all the crap he pulled. He's such a jackass."

"You're right, he is," Elizabeth agreed. "I kind of pity him now. He wasn't always a jackass."

"He wasn't, but the way he changed—none of what happened was your fault. You know that, right?"

"Yes, I *do* know that. Of course I know that."

"Are you sure?"

"Yes, I'm sure! I'm okay, Jane, truly." Elizabeth glanced up and saw she was standing in front of the library. "I'm here."

"I'll let you go, but *please* call Lydia this week to let her know if you'll be at graduation. She would love it."

"I know. I'll think about it, okay?"

"Okay, good enough." Jane paused. "Are you sure you're alright?"

"Jane!"

"Okay, okay, I'll leave it alone. Bye, Lizzy, have a good day. Love you."

"Love you too. Bye, sis."

Elizabeth tucked her phone into her purse and walked up the wide granite steps that led into the library, her thoughts already on next weekend. Images of George Wickham floated into her mind, and she forcibly pushed them away, determined to forget him and the pain he'd so callously inflicted.

It's all in the past, she thought, lifting her chin. *I have a new life now.*

WILL GLANCED UP AT THE CEILING OF HIS NEW HOME, LISTENING AS JACK raced around the second floor. The moving company had finally finished bringing everything into the house, and now there were boxes upon boxes waiting to be unpacked and pieces of furniture begging to be arranged in every room.

"Well, I think Jack definitely approves," he said to Maddie as he toured the first floor with her.

"I had a feeling he would," she responded, smiling widely.

Will was beyond pleased with the house; the pictures she'd sent hadn't done it justice. There were windows everywhere, flooding the home with natural light and warmth. The soft colors on the walls contrasted nicely with the dark wood floors, and the arched doorways of the kitchen and living room were unique.

They headed upstairs, where they ran into Jack as he came tearing down the hallway.

"Dad, can I show you the room I picked out for me?" he asked, out of breath and red-cheeked from running around.

"Absolutely, lead the way."

Maddie chuckled, and Will understood why when Jack led them straight to the master bedroom. "I hate to break it to you buddy, but I think this is my room," he said, trying to contain his laughter.

Jack's face fell. "Why is it your room?"

"Because it's the master bedroom."

"What does that mean?"

"It means it's the master's bedroom, and that's me. Parent and master."

Jack frowned. "But sometimes Mrs. Reynolds calls me Master Jack. So I'm a master too, right?"

Will heard Maddie's muffled laughter and fought to keep his expression sober. "Well, that's just a nickname," he explained. "Since you're still too young to be called *Mister* Darcy, she calls you Master Jack."

"So why can't I have a master's bedroom?" Jack pressed.

Will grinned. "Why don't we talk about this later? We should let Mrs. Gardiner show us the rest of the upstairs."

Jack shrugged. "'Kay."

He wandered off down the hall, and Will shook his head in bemusement.

"He's a clever one, isn't he?" Maddie asked.

"You have no idea. He can talk me into a corner like you wouldn't believe."

She laughed. "Maybe I can persuade him to focus on another room. The one at the opposite end of the hall has something I think he'll like."

Jack had already discovered it on his own. "Whoa, Dad, look at this! A secret room!" Another doorway hidden in the wall led to a separate, small space.

"Wow," Will answered. "I think I'll let you have that master bedroom after all. I'll take this one."

"No, Dad, this one's good for me," Jack insisted. "You can have the master's bedroom."

"I don't know, we might have to arm wrestle for it."

"Aw, c'mon Dad, I really want this one. Please?"

Will sighed dramatically. "Alright, you win. I'll take the other."

Jack's face lit up. "Thanks."

He disappeared into the small room, and Will nodded toward the doorway. "What's it for?" he asked Maddie.

"I have no idea. It could have been a walk-in closet, but it's odd that there are windows, and the ceiling seems too low. Maybe it was just used for storage." She shrugged. "I knew it would appeal to him. What boy wouldn't like to have a secret room?"

"I'm glad you knew about it, or I'm sure I would have ended up in here," Will said with a laugh.

They left Jack upstairs and headed down to the basement. Will was impressed by the wine cellar; each of the four storage areas held 125 bottles and could be programmed to maintain different temperatures.

"This is incredible," he said, eying the space. "The former owners must have had a taste for wine."

"They did. I'm sure they'll be happy to learn the new owner has the same taste."

"My wife loved a good wine. I couldn't tell the difference between a five-dollar bottle and a five-hundred-dollar bottle, but she tried to teach me," he said, smiling softly. "How to look at it, smell it, taste it, how to detect all those subtle flavors and scents that are all locked into it...it's like an art."

"It is." She paused for a moment, a brief look of confusion settling across her features. "I didn't realize you're married, Mr. Darcy."

"I was. My wife passed away."

"Oh, I'm–I'm so sorry, I had no idea..." Her voice trailed off, and it was obvious she was disconcerted.

"Its fine, Maddie," he responded gently. "I had no reason to mention it before. It happened a few years ago." He offered her a reassuring look; the last thing he wanted was to make her feel badly. "Honestly, it's okay."

And it *was* okay. He could talk about Anne now and be reminded of her without those cold feelings of loneliness and grief stealing over him. He'd had to learn to overcome them, for Jack's sake. Over the past year or so, Jack had begun asking to look at pictures of his mother. At first, Will found it impossible to look at them with him—it was too painful. But eventually the pain began to lessen, and with it, his sorrow.

Looking at the pictures made Jack even more curious, and he'd begun asking questions about his mother as well. Usually they were simple questions, like what her favorite color was or what foods she liked or didn't like, but sometimes he'd ask something that would knock Will for a loop.

"Did she smell like flowers?"

That innocent question had sent Will's mind reeling. It was a long moment before he was able to respond, overwhelmed as he'd been with memories.

"She smelled like the prettiest flower you've ever seen, Jack," he'd finally answered.

It was Jack who'd pulled Will out of the well of grief he'd been drowning in. If it hadn't been for his son, *living* for his son, Will was pretty sure he'd have died right along with Anne. A piece of him had, he knew, but there was still plenty of life left to live; it had just taken him some time to realize it.

Will spoke again, hoping to restore the easygoing banter between them.

"I have two requests. First, you have to stop calling me Mr. Darcy and start calling me Will. Second, you need to point me in the direction of the finest wine shop in Portland so I can start stocking up."

Maddie brightened. "I know just the place. There's a small shop called Casco Wine and Cigar…"

Their conversation continued as they headed back upstairs, and she reminded him about the picnic taking place later that evening.

"It's held the first Saturday of June as an official kickoff to summer," she explained. "It would be the perfect opportunity for you and Jack to meet some of the locals. I'm sure there will be plenty of kids for him to play with."

"I don't know," he said, rubbing his forehead distractedly. "Jack's going to be exhausted by dinner. And I have so much unpacking to do."

She raised her eyebrows. "Does it all have to be done today?"

"Well no, but I wanted to make a good start."

"Unpack what you need for tonight, that's all you should worry about today," she advised. "The picnic will save you from making a trip to the store to get some dinner. I'm making my homemade fried chicken, and would be happy to bring along enough for the two of you. I could introduce you around to some of the other families—" She stopped suddenly and shook her head.

"I'm sorry, I'm being pushy. You can tell me to be quiet, you know." She smiled contritely. "I wouldn't be offended. But please consider joining us. It's just down at the parade grounds, not too far from here."

"You're not being pushy at all, and your offer of fried chicken may persuade me." His stomach rumbled hungrily at the thought of it.

"Good enough. Elizabeth may come too, if she doesn't stay in Portland."

He nodded. "Okay. Can I let you know?"

"Of course! And if you think you might want to purchase a golf cart, you can talk to Ed. He'll be able to help you find one."

"Great. Where are the parade grounds?"

"It's the park in the middle of the cove. We passed it on the way here."

"Right, I remember."

"And on that note, I won't bother you any longer. I'm going to head home and get to work on that chicken."

"Thanks for everything, Maddie." He walked her out the front door and onto the large porch. "I really appreciate everything you've done."

"No thanks necessary. We take care of each other on this island; you'll find that out soon enough. I hope to see you at the picnic. Five o'clock sharp!"

"I'll call you," he responded, watching as she climbed into Vixen.

Jack came dashing out the front door. "Bye, Mrs. Gardiner! Thanks for the house!"

Will heard her laughter as she drove away. "You're welcome, Jack! See you soon!"

Will gave Jack the go-ahead to start unpacking his toys and watched him run back into the house and up to his room. He sat down on the top step of the porch and surveyed the property around him, and his mind drifted back to his conversation with Maddie.

Elizabeth may come too, if she doesn't stay in Portland.

He lay back on the wooden floor and stared up at the beadboard ceiling, suddenly feeling fatigued.

He'd acted like such a jerk when he met her. The way she'd looked at him with those big brown eyes, and when she shook his hand… He'd felt a subtle but certain flare of awareness.

But being the socially inept idiot he was, he hadn't known how to react, and so he'd done what he always did when he felt awkward —clammed up.

He shook his head ruefully. *It's a great defense mechanism, and I've mastered it.*

He thought again about the picnic—the call of Maddie's fried chicken was hard to resist. He could go and meet a few people, even if it was just so Jack could make some friends.

Maybe Elizabeth Bennet will stay in Portland and save me from looking foolish again.

He stood and went back into the house, calling out to his son as he walked upstairs. "Hey Jack, what do you think about going to a picnic?"

Two

T he sounds of laughter and exuberant shouting drifted across the park, and Will smiled as he watched Jack run around with a group of kids he'd just met. He was pretty sure a few were Jack's age, and they were playing as if they'd known each other for years.

Maddie had been busy introducing Will around, and everyone was kind and welcoming. Ed Gardiner talked to him about what to expect from island life and offered to take the Darcys on a tour the next day. Will readily accepted; he needed to get a feel for the island and learn where things were located.

They talked about golf carts too, as Will had already decided he would need one. Jack mentioned he wanted a black one with racing stripes and "big fat tires" and pipes in the back that shot flames—to which Will responded that he thought Jack was getting the cart confused with the Batmobile.

Maddie hadn't been telling tales about her fried chicken—it was delicious, and the Darcys dug in enthusiastically, comfortably situated on a blanket Maddie brought along for them to use. She'd also brought fresh biscuits, still warm from the oven, and homemade potato salad.

Will noticed a couple walking across the expansive lawn of the parade grounds. They were both tall and blonde and looked to be around his age.

Maddie saw them as well. "Oh, the Bingleys are here. I'll introduce you." She waved, motioning for the couple to come over and join them. "Charles and Caroline grew up on the island," she explained. "I was hoping they would come tonight."

The couple made their way over to the small group, and Will stood as Maddie made the introductions.

"Great to meet you, Will! Welcome to the island," Charles Bingley said warmly, extending his hand.

"Thanks. Nice to meet you both as well," Will said, first shaking Charles's hand and then Caroline's. "This is my son, Jack."

Charles held out his hand toward Jack. "Hey, Jack, how are you?"

Jack shook Charles's hand shyly but managed to look him in the eye. "I'm good." He turned to look at his father. "I'm done eatin'. Can I go play again?"

"Go ahead. Just stay where I can see you, okay?"

Jack agreed and bolted off to join the other kids.

"So Will, are you the one who bought the Millers' place?" Charles asked.

"That's me."

"I just love that old house. Always have," Caroline said. "The views of the bay are fabulous."

"They are. We just arrived today, so I haven't had much of a chance to appreciate them, but what I've seen so far is great."

"Where are you from?" she asked.

"New York City."

Her eyes widened. "And you moved here? That's quite a change of pace."

"It was long overdue."

"How old is Jack?" She sat down on a blanket she'd brought with her, and then took some food and a beer from the cooler and handed it to Charles.

"He's five." Will watched as his son ran around with the other children, chasing after a soccer ball. "Looks like he'll have plenty of playmates."

"There are loads of kids on the island, especially in the summer," she told him.

"That's what I've heard." Will glanced at the Bingleys. "So you both grew up here and then ended up marrying and settling here?"

Charles choked on his beer, and Caroline burst out laughing, as did Maddie and Ed.

"I suppose that when I said the Bingleys are here, I should have clarified that they are the Bingley *siblings*. Brother and sister, not husband and wife," Maddie said, still laughing.

Will felt his cheeks heat. "Sorry. I just figured…" Everyone was laughing, so he gave up trying to mumble an apology and joined them. "Alright, no more trying to embarrass the new guy."

"Sorry. We're so used to everyone knowing us," Caroline said. She caught Will's eye and smiled sweetly. "It's an easy mistake to make, I suppose."

He grinned and held her gaze for a moment before looking away, still feeling the flush on his cheeks. He turned to look at Charles, but his attention was diverted by the bottle of beer leaning against the cooler. "Is that a local brew?" he asked, nodding toward it. The label was roughly adhered and unreadable.

Charles held up the bottle proudly. "Can't get any more local than this!"

Caroline rolled her eyes. "Don't get him started," she said, before turning to talk to Maddie.

"This is my own beer," Charles told Will, "brewed right here on the island. It's an IPA. You a beer drinker?"

"I like my craft brews. You got an extra one in there?" Will asked.

"Absolutely." Charles reached into the cooler and pulled out a pair of cups and two more beers, handing one to Ed and one to Will, along with a bottle opener. "Let me know what you think—and I want an honest opinion. No trying to be polite because you're the new guy."

Will smiled as he slowly poured the beer, careful not to disturb the sediment at the bottom of the bottle, and then took a small sip. His eyes widened. "This is excellent." He took another sip, a longer one this time, and nodded his head appreciatively. "Where do you make it?"

Charles grinned. "In my backyard shed."

Caroline leaned toward Will. "You'll know which house belongs to Charles, because the lawn mower, the gardening tools, and everything else that belongs in the shed are in his backyard."

Will smiled. "This is really good. Have you tried to market it?"

"Without the ability to mass-produce, it's kind of pointless. My shed isn't exactly suitable for large-scale production." He shrugged. "I managed to run some plumbing out there and get it pretty well set up for a small operation."

Will was impressed. "Is this your only style?"

"No, I've got a few. A stout, a dark lager, a blonde ale, and this IPA. I need to work on the stout, it's not quite where I want it yet. The others, though...they're pretty good. Of course, that's just my opinion."

"No," Ed interjected, "that's *everyone's* opinion. Charles hasn't made a beer I haven't liked—the stout included. Lucky for me, I get to be a taste-tester."

"When's the next batch due?" Will asked.

Conversation was interrupted by the sound of a child crying, and Will looked up to see Jack rushing toward him, his small hands covering his nose and mouth. He handed his beer to Charles and quickly went to his son, squatting down in front of him.

"What happened?"

Jack sniffled. "I got hit with the soccer ball," he answered, his voice muffled by his hands.

A little boy ran up next to Jack. "Sorry, Jack, I wasn't aimin' for your face." He turned to look at Will with wide eyes. "I didn't mean to hit him."

"It's okay. Accidents happen." Will slowly pulled Jack's hands away. His nose was bleeding, and his upper lip was already beginning to swell. Caroline walked over with some ice wrapped in a small towel.

"Here you go, Jack. Hold this to your lip." She squatted down next to Will and gently held the ice to Jack's mouth, and although he winced and pulled away at first, he finally allowed her to place it against the tender spot. "Hopefully he didn't cut the inside of his lip. You should check to make sure."

Jack shook his head. "I didn't cut my lip, just my nose is bleedin', but I think it stopped."

"I want you to sit for a few minutes anyway," Will told him.

"Aw, Dad, do I hafta? I wanna go play again."

"You can in a little while. For right now, I want you to sit and hold the ice to your lip. Okay?"

Jack frowned. "'Kay."

Caroline and Will stood, and she smiled. "I hate to say it, but it's probably the first of many. I'm surprised my parents didn't have their own boat to take us back and forth to the mainland. It seemed like Charles was getting hurt every other day of the week, and we were always making trips to the emergency room or some doctor or another."

After a few minutes, Will sent Jack back to his friends, telling him to take it easy and that they'd be leaving in about half an hour.

"He looks exhausted, but he's being a trouper," Maddie observed.

"I'm wiped out, so I'm sure he is too," Will said. "But I wanted to give him the chance to meet some kids."

"Sam Grady is the boy who kicked the ball. I think he's about the same age as Jack. His parents are there." Maddie pointed to a couple on the other side of the picnic. "They're a nice family."

Will nodded. "Good to know."

They sat for a while longer, discussing everyday things and answering Will's questions about the island and the Portland area. He learned there was a children's museum on the mainland, which he looked forward to visiting with Jack. Maddie also told him about several programs the public library hosted during the summer.

"I'll ask Elizabeth to get you some information," she told him. "She works in the children's library, so she's familiar with the schedule."

"That would be great, thanks."

"I guess she decided to stay in Portland tonight with Charlotte." Maddie grinned and shook her head. "Those two are a force to be reckoned with when they're together."

Out of the corner of his eye, Will saw Caroline roll her eyes. It was meant to be discreet, he was sure, but he noticed it.

Jack came ambling over to the group slowly. "I think I'm ready to go, Dad." He sat in Will's lap and yawned widely as he leaned into his father's chest.

Will glanced at his watch and saw that it was almost seven o'clock. "I think I'm ready to go too, kiddo. It's been a long day." He lifted Jack from his lap and stood. "What time does the tour bus leave tomorrow, Ed?"

"You tell me. My day is wide open, so it's up to you."

"How about ten? Too early?"

"Not at all. I'll swing by and pick you up."

Will reached to shake his hand. "Great, I'll see you in the morning." He turned to Maddie. "Thanks again for dinner, it was fantastic." He nudged Jack a little, subtly encouraging him to remember his manners.

"Thanks for the chicken, Mrs. Gardiner," Jack said, yawning again.

"You're both very welcome," Maddie answered. "Go home and get a good night's sleep."

"We will, thanks."

"I'll get you over to my place sometime to try the stout," Charles said, rising from the blanket to shake Will's hand.

"I'd like that, Charles, thanks." Will turned to Caroline. "Thank you for helping out with Jack. I appreciate it."

"Oh, it was nothing. I'm glad he's okay."

After saying a final good night to everyone, Will walked away with Jack perched high on his shoulders.

Within an hour of arriving home, Jack was asleep, tucked into bed after taking a quick but needed bath. Will had showered as well, and then they settled into Jack's bed to read his favorite book of the moment, *Where the Wild Things Are*. Jack had struggled valiantly to stay awake, but lost the battle with exhaustion about eight pages in. After turning on a nightlight, Will kissed him on the forehead and left the room, leaving the door ajar in case he woke during the night.

After a few moments of lying on the couch and soaking in the silence, Will glanced at the clock and saw it was almost nine. He got up and went into the kitchen, retrieving his cell phone from the counter.

I should call Georgiana.

He'd promised he would, so he grabbed a bottle of water from the refrigerator before heading back into the living room. He rang her number, and after only a few rings, she picked up.

"Hi, Will!"

"Hey, Georgie."

"I was hoping you would call. How did everything go? How's the house?"

The excitement in her voice made him smile. "Everything went smoothly, and the house is incredible. You'll have to visit soon. Once I'm unpacked, that is." He looked around at the boxes stacked in the living room and grimaced. "It might be a while."

She laughed. "Just let me know when you're ready, and I'll be there. How's Jack?"

"He's great. I was worried he might not be able to fall asleep in his new room, but he crashed hard. He met a bunch of kids at a picnic, and they ran full tilt for a couple of hours."

"You went to a *picnic*?"

"Yes, we went to a picnic," he repeated, noting the disbelief in her voice. "My real estate agent told me about it and offered to feed us, so we went."

"Thinking with your stomach, as usual."

"It was worth it. I met a few people, and Jack made some friends. He got nailed in the face by a soccer ball, but he's no worse for it."

"Aw, poor kid."

"He's okay," Will assured her, and then sighed heavily.

"What's the matter?"

"Nothing, I'm just tired."

"Are you sure?"

"Yeah." He paused for a minute as his thoughts began to race and a rush of anxiety shot through him. "Did I do the right thing, G? Bringing him here?"

"You're his father," she responded softly. "Only you know that for sure."

"I know." He paused. "I'm just tired, that's all. I think the long day is catching up with me." He took a sip of water and wished it was something stronger.

"You're probably right," she agreed. "Try not to overthink things. You don't have to be on the phone with me, you know. I just wanted to know when you got settled, that's all."

"I'm far from settled." His eyes traveled over the boxes again.

"But there's no rush, right? Don't put so much pressure on yourself."

"I know."

"One thing: will you call Mrs. R soon?" she asked. "I'll let her know I heard from you, but I'm sure she'd like to hear from you too."

"Of course. I'll call her tomorrow." The last thing he wanted was to worry Alice Reynolds.

Georgiana's voice softened. "What about Dad? Are you going to call him?"

Will's eyebrows rose. "No. You can tell him I made it here, but I'm not calling him."

"Will—"

"Georgie, please. I'm way too tired to have this conversation, alright?" he said, his voice clipped.

"Okay. Go to bed and get some sleep, and I'll call you in a couple of days."

He frowned. "I'm sorry, I didn't mean to snap at you, I'm just...I'm tired."

"I know, it's fine. I'll talk to you soon, okay?"

They said their goodbyes, and after hanging up, Will closed his eyes and recalled the last conversation he'd had with his father.

"You're taking him away from everyone and everything he knows. His legacy is here, *Fitzwilliam, not in the backwoods of Maine. This is his life. This is where he belongs."*

"His legacy? My God, Dad, he's only five years old! Give him a chance to be a kid before you start jamming the Darcy legacy down his throat."

"Do you think he'll truly be happy away from here? Away from all of us?"

"Yes, I do. If I'm away from here, I'll be happier. How can I be a good father to him if I'm not happy?" He paused and lowered his voice. "He's my son, and I'll be damned if I'll let you or anyone else question my abilities and decisions as his father."

"That's not what I'm doing."

"Yes, it is! You're trying to make me doubt myself. Two years ago—hell, even a year ago—it might have worked. Not now."

"You don't have to leave New York to be a good father."

"I disagree. I have to leave New York—the people, the places—I have to leave them behind."

"The people? Including me?"

"Yes, Dad, including you. Especially you."

He'd felt a twinge of remorse at the look on his father's face when he'd flung those last words, but he'd needed to speak the truth. His father had immediately fired back, declaring right then and there that Will would be cut off if he went through with his "preposterous idea."

Leave it to my father to react with a financial threat.

It didn't matter, anyway; he had plenty of money, enough that he wouldn't have to work another day in his life if he didn't want to. Wise investments made over the past eight years, plus money bequeathed to him by his grandfather, *and* the inheritance he'd received from his mother's estate, had left him quite wealthy.

His father just didn't understand. Will grew up the same way Jack was going to grow up: motherless. Granted, Will had lost his mother at an older age—he was eleven, while Jack was only two—but the last thing he wanted was for Jack to have the life Will had had after such a tremendous loss. In fact, he would do everything in his power to make sure it didn't happen.

Including moving my son to the backwoods of Maine.

ED GARDINER ARRIVED AT THE DARCYS' PROMPTLY AT TEN ON SUNDAY morning. Jack sprinted outside, looking forward to another ride in the flashy red cart.

"Can I sit in the front, Dad?"

"Not today. I need to talk to Mr. Gardiner, so it'll be easier if I'm up front." Jack frowned, and Will ruffled his dark hair.

"I'll tell you what," Ed said to Jack. "I'll take your father to the important places first, then we'll head down to the docks. If it's okay with him, you can switch seats with him once we get there."

Jack's face lit up as he looked from Ed to his father. "Can I?"

Will grinned. "Sounds reasonable."

Ed took the scenic route, taking them outside of Diamond Cove to show them a couple of the beaches—the island had five in total—and the community swimming pool. Jack was pleased to see a spectacular playground in a large expanse of grass right next to the pool.

"Is that where I can learn how to swim?" he asked, staring at the glimmering water.

"I can teach you in the pool or the ocean. Your pick," Will responded.

"I pick both!" Jack answered, smiling widely.

There were tennis and basketball courts, a gym, and duckpin bowling in a beautifully restored turn-of-the-century bowling alley, which also housed an arcade and billiard room. Just outside the gates of Diamond Cove stood a small art gallery and an even smaller museum dedicated to the history of the cove. Ed also told Will about the small shuttle that served the island and took people to and from the ferry.

The general store was a beautiful old brick building. "That's where the locals go to socialize," Ed explained, chuckling. "All the old-timers who are still around sit at the picnic tables and talk about the good old days. How are you in the kitchen?"

Will raised his eyebrows. "Um...alright, I guess. I'm not bad with the basics."

"What do you say, Jack?" Ed asked, glancing over his shoulder quickly. "Is your father a good cook?"

"Yeah, he's good," Jack replied earnestly. "But sometimes he burns stuff."

They laughed, and Ed continued. "If you're ever in need of a quick dinner, the general store is the place to go. They have all kinds of prepared foods and the best homemade ice cream around. As far as groceries go, you can get your staples there, but most people shop off island. There are a couple of grocery stores in Portland that provide once-a-week delivery service to the islands, if you want to take advantage of that. You just have to meet the freight boat when it docks."

Will nodded. "Good to know."

The more he saw and heard, the more confident he felt about his decision to move. It would be a much simpler way of life. *This is what we need.*

As they headed down the narrow lanes, Ed told Will more of the history of Diamond Cove. Will was surprised to learn it was originally built as an artists' haven, housing the likes of Henry Wadsworth

Longfellow—a Portland native—and Harriet Beecher Stowe. Eventually the government took over the property and constructed Fort McKinley. The fort had been an active military base until just after World War II, at which time it was closed down and the buildings completely abandoned.

Someone had conceived the brilliant idea of investing in the land and building a gated community overlooking the bay. Most of the original buildings stood and were still used, although many had been heavily renovated. The barracks had been transformed into elegant town homes, and "officers' row" was now a beautiful tree-lined lane, dotted with stately homes.

They sped away toward the docks where Ed pointed out one of the two restaurants on the island—aptly named Island Jewel—and informed Will that it was only open from May until October.

"Maddie mentioned that," Will said.

"Once fall arrives, you'll be amazed at the drop in the island's population. The last census showed us hovering at right around one hundred full-time residents."

"Really?" Will asked, pleasantly surprised the number was that low. He grinned to himself.

Paradise.

SUNDAY MORNING WAS AS BRIGHT AND GLORIOUS AS A SPRING MORNING IN Maine could possibly be. Elizabeth lamented this fact as she sat on the ferry heading back to the island, feeling a bit hungover. On any other day she would have been sprawled out in her seat, soaking in the sunshine.

Not today.

Today, she slid as low in the seat as she could and adjusted her dark sunglasses, praying that a giant cumulus cloud would come along and blot out the sun.

She could only imagine how Mary was feeling this morning. Innocent Mary, one of her co-workers at the library who rarely drank alcohol yet thought that going out with the girls to celebrate Charlotte's twenty-fifth birthday "sounded like a hoot."

It was a hoot alright.

Elizabeth usually drank beer or wine, but last night, Charlotte had persuaded her to drink cocktails with hard liquor—and bizarre names. *I can't believe I asked that bartender for a Sex on the Beach.* She shook her head. At the time, it had seemed hilarious; today, not so much.

When the ferry docked, she roused herself and shuffled off, ready to make the walk home and go straight to bed. She was heading across the small parking lot when a high-pitched horn sounded behind her. She spun around and saw Ed sitting in the driver's seat of Vixen.

Ahh, a ride. A happy thought—until she noticed his passenger.

"Hello, Elizabeth!" Ed called out. "Going home?"

"Making my way, slowly but surely."

"Hop in, I'll give you a lift."

"Thanks." She smiled as she walked toward the cart and glanced at Mr. Darcy, who seemed to be staring at her—though it was hard to tell as he was wearing sunglasses as well.

"Good morning," she mumbled. His response was entirely predictable; no attempt at a smile or a "good morning" in return, just that damned nod. She sat in the back next to Jack, suddenly wishing she'd refused the ride.

"Dad, you said we could switch when we got to the docks," Jack piped up. "Can I sit in the front now?"

Mr. Darcy turned to his son. "Sure, come on up."

Elizabeth watched as he got Jack settled before climbing into the back seat. The golf cart was fairly wide, but when he sat down, he was shoulder to shoulder with her. She observed him discreetly and again noticed his height—his knees were practically drawn up to his chest. He rested his hands on his thighs, and she couldn't help but notice how large they were. He had short dark hair and a drop-dead gorgeous profile.

Thankfully, Ed chose that moment to jumpstart the conversation, interrupting her scrutiny. "I've been giving Will and Jack a tour of the island," he said jovially. "Trying to fill them in on some of the history."

She smiled. "That's nice."

Jack turned around and peered at her from the front seat. "You live here too?"

She nodded. "I do."

"Where?"

"Sort of near you. I live in Mr. Gardiner's guesthouse."

"Did you live here all the time?"

Her brows furrowed. "Do you mean when I was little?"

"Yeah."

"No, I grew up in Massachusetts."

"Where's that?"

"Oh, it's not too far away."

"I lived in New York. That's far away."

She smiled. "Farther away than Massachusetts, that's for sure."

What a cute kid. She noticed his father shifting his legs and fidgeting next to her, rubbing his palms on his thighs.

"You know, Will," Ed said, "if you want to learn the ins and outs of Portland, Lizzy would be a great tour guide. I think she's done more walking in that city in the two years she's been here than I have in my entire life. What do you say, Lizzy?"

She grimaced. *Thanks for putting me on the spot, Ed, that's what I say.*

Instead of speaking her mind, she dredged up what she hoped would pass for a polite grin. "Sure." She cast a sidelong glance at Mr. Darcy, just in time to see him frown. "If you need help finding your way around, I guess I could help you."

"No, thanks. I—I don't think we'll need help. I think…um, Jack and I can find our way around just fine." He cleared his throat. "We don't need any help. No help needed."

She rolled her eyes. "Whatever," she muttered under her breath, wincing slightly when she saw him suddenly turn toward her.

Conversation ceased, and when they pulled up in front of the Gardiners' house, Elizabeth climbed out of the cart and grabbed her belongings.

"Enjoy the rest of the tour." She tried to sound cheerful and purposely directed her comment to the occupants of the front seat.

"See you later, Lizzy," Ed said. "I might come over later to fix that faucet."

"No rush," she replied before smiling at Jack. "'Bye, Jack. Have fun checking out the island today." She looked at Mr. Darcy, and although he seemed to be staring at her from behind his sunglasses, he remained completely stone-faced.

Her smile faded from her lips, even though she tried to keep it pasted there. "Have a nice day, Mr. Darcy." She paused—*wait for it*—and there it was.

The nod.

"Ms. Bennet."

MONDAY ENDED UP RAINY AND COOL, AND WILL WAS GRATEFUL FOR IT; IT gave him no excuse to avoid the boxes scattered throughout the house. He and Jack walked to the market to grab a few things that would tide them over until they could shop in Portland tomorrow, and then with Jack's help—using the term loosely—Will managed to tackle their bedrooms, the living room, and the kitchen. He also set up his office and called the cable company to inquire about television and Wi-Fi.

Jack spotted the photo albums that held the pictures of him with his mom, and they decided he should keep those in his bedroom so he could look at them whenever he wanted. The albums had been kept in a box marked "Anne," which also held their wedding photos and other keepsakes from their time spent together—things that had no meaning to anyone except Will.

Eleven years, reduced to one box.

He still thought of her often, though the consumptive sorrow and paralyzing grief that had gripped him for the first year or so after her death had lessened tremendously. Memories of her still snuck up on him, especially when Jack made a particular facial expression or when he said or did something that struck Will as funny. Jack had her eyes, that odd but mesmerizing shade of violet-blue, and when they crinkled at the corners, he was definitely his mother. Sometimes those eyes would remind him of the enormous loss they'd suffered, and for a brief moment, the sorrow and grief would return.

He placed the box in the office for the time being but already decided he wouldn't unpack it, knowing there was a difference between remembering someone and having reminders of them everywhere. He would always remember Anne, but he felt that having things that belonged to her scattered throughout the house wouldn't be healthy. And he had Jack, after all—he was the greatest reminder of her and their life together.

Both Darcys slept soundly that night, and the following morning found them headed to Portland on the ferry. Jack was restless and eager to explore, and after spending the previous day in the house, Will was starting to feel antsy as well. "We need to get the lay of the land," he told Jack.

He soon spotted Elizabeth Bennet sitting a few rows away from them. Her face was tilted up toward the sun, and for a long moment, his gaze was riveted to her. His eyes wandered over the line of her throat and down her arm to her hand where it was draped over the back of the seat next to her. Her hair was a dark, rich brown, spilling down in soft waves and shining brilliantly in the sun. His gaze traveled to her legs, clad in capris that bared most of her calves. She had them stretched out, ankles crossed and resting on the row of seats in front of her. They weren't especially long, but they were shapely and not too muscular...

He suddenly realized what he was doing and dragged his eyes away, clearing his throat self-consciously as he turned to his son...who was also staring at her.

"That's the lady we know," Jack said, lifting his arm to point her out. "Ms. Bennet."

Will reached up and quickly lowered his son's hand. "Don't point, it's not polite."

"We should say hi."

"Um, not right now. She looks tired. Plus, we really don't know her well enough to go and talk to her."

Jack stared into his father's eyes. "I didn't know any of the kids at the picnic but you told me to go an' talk to them anyway."

Smarty pants. "That's different. Kids are different from adults."

"How come?"

"Well, it's easier for kids." Will hoped he sounded reasonable. "It's important for you to meet other kids so you have friends to play with this summer and when you go to kindergarten."

"But you gotta have friends too."

Will chuckled. "I do. I met Mr. Bingley and his sister, and I know Mr. and Mrs. Gardiner too. And I talked to Sam's parents when we were leaving the picnic."

Jack glanced over to Elizabeth again. "How come Ms. Bennet's not your friend?"

"It's not that she's *not* my friend, I just haven't talked to her much." *Because when I do, I end up behaving like an idiot.*

"She's sittin' by herself. We can go talk to her right now."

"No, we'll stay here." Will checked to see how close they were to land. "It looks like we'll be docking soon anyway, just another ten minutes or so."

At that moment Elizabeth sat up and stretched, and Will watched as she turned in their direction. Jack noticed as well and immediately began waving.

"Hi, Ms. Bennet!"

Three

Elizabeth was surprised to see Jack Darcy waving to her from across the long expanse of seats between her and where he sat with his father. She smiled and waved back, although his father remained stone-faced, leading her to believe he wasn't quite as happy to see her.

She watched as Jack turned to his father and, after a short conversation with him, came walking across the deck to her.

"Hi, Ms. Bennet," he said, smiling at her.

"Hi there, Jack. Where are you off to today?"

"We're goin' to the store to get some food and stuff. Where are you goin'?"

"I'm on my way to work."

"Oh. Where do you work?"

"At the library." Once again, she was struck by the beautiful blue shade of his eyes. "Do you have a car in Portland?"

He nodded. "My dad has a truck, but he said we're gonna walk today 'cause we need to lay on the land."

She was momentarily confused. "Oh, do you mean get the lay of the land?"

"Yeah, get the *lay* of the *land*," he repeated. "It means we need to find everythin' so we don't get lost."

"Right. Do you have a map?"

He shrugged. "I dunno."

She reached into her backpack and pulled out an old, worn map. "Tell your dad he can use this one. It's the best. I've written on it a little, but it's still in good shape."

Jack looked down at the map and then back up to her. "Can you show me where the library is?"

She looked over the map with him, showing him where the ferry would dock, where the library was, and the location of the children's museum. He pointed at certain things and asked what they were, and she was happy to explain as much as she could to him.

The ferry docked, and Elizabeth watched as Jack's father slowly made his way over to them.

"Good morning," she said to him with a smile.

"Good morning."

His dark brown eyes were focused on her, and she was grateful when Jack pried his father's attention away from her.

"Dad, Ms. Bennet is lettin' us use her map. She said it's the best," he said happily, holding up the dog-eared paper.

"That's not necessary, Jack. We can buy one when we get off the boat."

Jack frowned. "But she showed me everythin' on *this* one, and now I know where we hafta go."

"But she might need it."

Elizabeth shook her head. "It's fine. I haven't used it in ages."

Will turned to Jack. "I'm sure there's a store near the dock that sells them."

"Aw c'mon, Dad, I wanna use *this* one," Jack pleaded. "We can give it back when we're done."

"Really, Mr. Darcy, it's just a map," Elizabeth interjected, inwardly rolling her eyes. "Please take it. You can return it if you want, but it's really not necessary."

"Okay, fine, we'll use the map," he responded tersely. "Let's go, Jack. Everyone's getting off the ferry."

"'K. Thanks for the map, Ms. Bennet."

Elizabeth bent toward him slightly. "You're very welcome, Jack." She glanced back up at Mr. Darcy. "Enjoy your day in Portland."

He nodded. "Thank you."

She watched as he quickly herded Jack in front of him, obviously hoping to get a good distance ahead of her. *That's fine with me.* The last thing she wanted was to end up walking with him through the streets of Portland.

"I JUST DON'T GET IT," ELIZABETH SAID, SHAKING HER HEAD AT Charlotte Lucas. The two women were enjoying lunch in the shade of a massive elm tree outside of the Portland Children's Library. "But I guess I don't really care."

"Maybe you *should* care. Maybe you rocked his world a little," Charlotte replied around a mouthful of chicken salad. "Maybe he's so astounded by your beauty that he can't think straight around you."

Elizabeth laughed. "Fat chance. I think he's just not very nice. Not to me, anyway. He's perfectly friendly to Ed and Maddie, but Maddie helped him find the house and Ed gave him a tour of the island. He kind of *has* to be nice to them, right?"

Charlotte shrugged. "I guess. Why did he move here?"

"I don't know."

"And he has a kid?"

Elizabeth nodded. "Yes, Jack. He's adorable."

"Wife?"

"I have no idea."

"How could you have no idea? Didn't you check for a ring?"

"No! Why would I do that?"

"You mean to tell me"—a smile slowly spread across Charlotte's lips —"that you sat shoulder to shoulder with this man, checking out, in your own words, how *tall* he is, how *hot* he is, and when you saw him again on the ferry, you never looked for a ring? Oh, please. I call bullshit."

"It didn't even occur to me! I have no interest in—in *that*," Elizabeth stated. "And there's no way to miss how hot he is. I'm not blind, for Pete's sake. But checking for a ring is pointless."

"It's *not* pointless." Charlotte sighed and turned serious. "You have to start thinking about getting out there again. And I'm not talking about this Darcy guy anymore, forget about him. But it's time for you to move on."

"I *have* moved on," Elizabeth responded firmly. "How can you even say that? I've put everything behind me. But moving on doesn't have to include getting into another relationship." She shrugged. "I'm happy as I am. I have my friends and my family, I love my job, and I love where I live. I'm *happy.*"

Charlotte smiled softly. "I know you have all of those things, and you're very lucky. But someday you might feel like you're missing out on something. That will be the test, I suppose."

"The test?"

"Yes. Letting yourself fall for someone."

Elizabeth shook her head. "I don't need *someone.*" Her eyes narrowed as she glared at Charlotte. "And aren't *you* the pot calling the kettle black! Where's *your* someone?"

Charlotte rolled her eyes. "I'm not the someone type. Wait, I take that back. I *am* the someone type, I just don't want the same someone all the time." She winked, making Elizabeth laugh and lightening the conversation.

"Can you honestly tell me you haven't been interested in any guy for more than a one-night stand? You haven't wanted to go further with any of them?"

"No. I'm not into the whole relationship thing."

"Ha. Now *I* call bullshit. And if you can say *you're* not into the whole relationship thing, why can't I say the same?"

"Because I know you, and you are *sooo* a relationship person." Elizabeth remained silent, and after a moment Charlotte continued, sounding contrite. "I'm not trying to be intrusive. I'm sorry if I got carried away."

Elizabeth shook her head, staring out toward the bay. "I just can't imagine going through all of that again, just to try and attain some… some elusive *thing* that only exists in fairy tales. I know some people find it, and I thought I had it once, but I was so wrong. I don't want to make that mistake again. I'm happy, right now. My life is wonderful, *right now.*" She paused and took a bite of her sandwich before continuing. "Do you think there are degrees of happiness?"

Charlotte shrugged. "I don't know. I suppose there could be."

"Can someone say, 'I'm really, really happy, but I'd be even happier if...'?"

"Oh, of course," Charlotte agreed. "There are definitely people who think like that, people who always want more. The grass is always greener, as the saying goes."

"Well then, I must be okay," Elizabeth said, a small smile on her face, "because I never think like that."

WILL AND JACK SPENT A FUN BUT EXHAUSTING DAY EXPLORING THE STREETS and sights of Portland. Will was pleasantly surprised and pleased with the seaside city; it offered what any large city would offer but on a much smaller scale.

The first thing they did was stop at one of the grocery stores to shop for food. Will knew the freight boat would bring his groceries over later in the day, so he wanted to get the shopping out of the way while Jack was feeling energetic. He bought enough to stock them up for at least a week and knew he would use grocery shopping as an excuse to regularly visit the city.

Jack was impatient to see the children's museum, so it became their primary destination after they left the grocery store. After spending over an hour there but still only seeing a small portion of it, Will paid for a membership; he knew it would be a place they would return to again and again.

They spent a little more time wandering around, using the map to find bookstores and toy shops and restaurants to try. They strolled the cobblestone streets of Old Port, and the East Coast Lobster Shack was their choice for lunch.

The elementary school wasn't within walking distance, so Will promised Jack they'd check it out the next time they came to Portland. Ed had mentioned an old military fort on Cape Elizabeth that he thought the Darcys might like to see, so Will thought he would combine a trip to both places.

He made some phone calls when they returned home. The first was to the school district's office so he could begin the process of enrolling

Jack in kindergarten, and the second was to a local pediatrician's office. As the injury at the picnic had shown, it was important Jack have a doctor nearby.

They headed down to the docks later that afternoon to pick up their groceries from the freight boat—courtesy of Ed Gardiner and Vixen— and then went home to put everything away. Ed told Will about an island resident who was looking to sell one of the two golf carts he owned and promised Will it was in excellent condition.

"It's nothing like Vixen, here," Ed said, patting the golf cart's roof and laughing. "It's just a two-seater, but it's a nice one just the same. I think you'll like it." He agreed to take Will to the seller's house the following day so he could see the cart.

The Darcys curled up on the couch to watch a movie after dinner, but it didn't take long for Jack's busy day to catch up with him. Will shut off the television and gazed down at his sleeping son, who was completely stretched out on top of him. He lie there for a long while, enjoying the feel of his son's warm body, the sound of Jack's steady breathing the only noise in the room. Will wrapped his arms around him, hugging him tighter, and kissed the top of his head before carefully rising and carrying him to bed.

THE NEXT MORNING FOUND THE DARCYS STANDING WITH ED AND A MAN named Tom Ingram in the driveway of Tom's home, checking out the golf cart that was for sale.

"It's very…yellow," Will said politely.

The most hideous shade of neon yellow I've ever seen.

"It was my wife's cart, but seein' as her eyesight's gotten so bad, she don't drive her much anymore. Yellow's her favorite color."

Jack tugged on Will's arm. "Can we paint it black and put stripes on it?"

"First I have to decide if I'm going to buy it."

"Well now, just take her for a little drive if you want." Tom pressed the key into Will's hand. "She runs damn near perfect."

Will looked at Jack and wiggled his eyebrows. "Hop in, co-pilot."

"Yesss!" Jack exclaimed, pumping his fist.

They took a short drive around the neighborhood, and Will agreed with Tom—the cart ran perfectly. They headed back to the house, and Will promptly told Tom he wanted to purchase it. Tom named his price, Will wrote the check, and the cart was theirs.

"Woo-hoo!" Jack cheered excitedly. "Now we can drive all over the island. Can we go to the beach today?"

"How about the pool instead?" Will suggested. The air was still a little cool for the beach, but the pool was heated and would be much warmer.

"Yeah! The pool is good too."

Tom thanked Will, and the two men shook hands before Tom left them to go back into his house. Will stood and talked with Ed for another moment.

"Okay, who can I get to paint this thing?" Will asked, gesturing toward his new ride. "I can't drive around in a cart this color."

Ed chuckled. "I'd ask Charles. He does anything for anyone on the island. Jack of all trades, master of none, you know the saying. I'm sure he could take care of it for you." Ed wrote down Charles's number and gave it to Will, and the men parted ways.

After arriving back home, Will called Charles and explained the situation—and the color—of the golf cart.

"I know that cart well," Charles said, laughing. "You can see it coming from a mile away."

"Do you think you can paint it?" Will asked.

"Sure, I've painted a few carts. I even painted Vixen for Maddie a while back. She insisted on having a bright red cart. What color are you thinking?"

Will cleared his throat. "Well...um, can you do it black with racing stripes?"

"Racing stripes, huh?"

"For Jack. He also wants pipes that shoot flames."

Charles laughed. "I can't help you there. Sorry."

Will grinned. "Yeah, I guess the racing stripes will have to do. Hey, how's that stout coming along?"

"Funny you should ask, I just brewed some yesterday. When it's ready, you'll be the first to know. Actually, you'll be the second, after Ed. I still think it needs work, but we'll see how it turns out."

"I'd be more than happy to be your guinea pig, believe me."

"I'll remember that. So what are you up to today? Do you want me to get going on the cart right away?"

"Jack and I were going to head to the pool for a little while," Will told him. "I didn't think you'd be able to do it so quickly."

"I don't have much else going on right now," Charles explained. "I have an appointment in Portland later with Maddie, but I have time to get at least one coat on it and maybe a second coat tomorrow."

"Sounds good. Are you looking at property in Portland?"

"Yeah, Maddie wants me to take a look at a building that's empty. It used to house the Portland Head Brewery." He sighed. "She knows I've always wanted to open my own place, but the right spot just hasn't come along."

"What happened to the Portland Head Brewery?"

"I don't know, they just went under. Truthfully, I didn't like their beer much."

Will laughed. "Of course you didn't."

"Seriously. I'm not just saying that because I make beer."

"I believe you," Will replied, still smiling. "So, where am I delivering my cart?"

Will wrote down directions to Charles's home, and after he and Jack changed into their swimsuits and grabbed towels and drinks, they headed out. On the drive over, Will thought about the few conversations he'd had with Charles and realized he felt very comfortable with him. He had an easygoing personality and an open and affable nature that Will appreciated and perhaps envied a little.

It only took a few minutes to get to Charles's house, as he lived just outside of Diamond Cove. Will's jaw dropped when he saw the size of it; it was easily twice the size of his own home.

Charles came out to greet them, bounding down the steps of the massive front porch with a big smile on his face.

"Hey, Will. Hey, Jack." He shook Will's hand and gave Jack a high five. "Why don't I give you a lift to the pool in the cart? Then I can bring it back here to get started."

"Sure." Will glanced at the house again. "This is a beautiful place, Charles."

"Oh, thanks. It's where I grew up. That house over there," he said, pointing to another home Will could barely see across the yard and through some trees, "is my sister's house. After my parents died, we split the property, and she built her own place."

"So you've always lived here?"

"No, I lived in Portland for a little while. I moved back to the island after my parents were killed in a car accident. I didn't want the house to just sit here empty, but I didn't want to rent it out or sell it either. It means too much to me."

Will's heart skipped a beat. "Your parents were killed in an accident?"

Charles nodded. "Drunk driver on the Maine Turnpike."

Jack looked up at Charles. "My mom died in a car accident too. I was little."

Charles's eyes flew from Jack to Will. "Oh man, I'm sorry. I had no idea. I wouldn't have mentioned—"

"Don't worry about it," Will interrupted. "It was a few years ago. It's okay."

Charles reached out to grip Will's shoulder in a show of understanding. "Time heals all wounds. It sounds cliché, but it's true."

Will nodded. "I'm slowly finding that out."

THE POOL WAS NEARLY EMPTY, THOUGH JACK WAS HAPPY TO SEE HIS NEW friend Sam Grady there. Will talked with Sam's mother, Sarah, and after exchanging telephone numbers for future playdates, he ventured over to a quiet corner near the shallow end of the pool and placed their things on two side-by-side lounge chairs.

Jack wanted to swim so Will went in with him. They played and splashed for a while, tossing a ball back and forth with Sam, until Will decided it was a good time to start teaching Jack the basics of swimming. Will held him afloat, showing him how to move his arms and kick his legs. By the end of the short lesson, Jack had mastered the doggy paddle and was very proud of himself.

Sam came trotting over to the edge of the pool and squatted down.

"Hey Jack, my mom's takin' me to the playground. Do you wanna come?"

Jack turned to his father. "Can I?"

Will glanced over to Sarah. "You're okay with that?"

"Of course. Sam's been dying to play with him since the picnic. It's no trouble at all."

Jack was out of the water in a flash with Will following behind him. He helped Jack dry off, and then helped him with his shirt and the straps of his sandals. Catching his son's eye before he bolted off, Will reminded him to be polite and listen to Sam's mom.

"I will, Dad. Bye!" Jack responded, before heading over to a smiling Sam.

"Thanks, Sarah," Will called out, and she waved in response. He watched as the two boys ran across the grass ahead of her toward the playground. *How easy it is for them.*

He donned his sunglasses and sat down in his chair, and immediately spotted Caroline Bingley strolling across the grass toward the pool enclosure, talking on her cell phone as she walked.

She's attractive. Tall, blonde, blue-eyed... He almost laughed out loud when he had the random thought that she was his type. *That's a joke.*

The truth was, he had no type; his type had been Anne. Yes, Anne had been blonde, though a darker blonde than Caroline. And their eyes, though blue, were not at all alike.

She spotted him, and he realized she'd probably noticed him staring in her direction, so he looked away. She headed over to him, a smile lighting her face.

"I heard you were down here," she said, approaching Will's chair. "I stopped at my brother's house to say hello, and he was just starting to paint your golf cart."

"Ah yes, my very yellow cart. How does it look?"

"It kind of resembles a large bumblebee right now. I can't believe you bought Eunice Ingram's cart! You could seriously damage your retinas if you look at that thing for too long."

He chuckled. "Yeah, well, now you know why your brother offered to paint it right away. There was no way I was turning him down."

"He'll do a good job." She glanced around the pool area. "Is Jack with you?"

"Yes and no. We swam for a little while, but he decided to ditch me and head to the playground with Sam Grady. I think they've hit it off despite the soccer ball incident."

"The Gradys are nice people. They moved here when Sam was just a baby." She looked at the empty chair on the other side of Will. "Do you mind if I join you?"

"Of course not," he answered, gesturing toward the seat.

He watched as Caroline placed her bag down and removed her sunglasses. She slowly shimmied out of her shorts and then raised her arms to remove her tank top, revealing a body displayed to full advantage in a black bikini. He turned away, feeling a slight surge of discomfort.

"Ooh, it's still a bit chilly for sunbathing," she said softly as she spread out her towel and then stretched out on the chair. "The water must be cold."

"Actually," he began, mortified when it came out as croak. He cleared his throat and tried again. "Actually, it's not bad. Jack and I swam for a while. The water is crystal clear."

"The island association changed it over from chlorine to salt a few years back. Best thing they ever did."

He nodded. "It's great."

It was silent for a moment as they reclined in their chairs, soaking up the sun, until she spoke again.

"So, Will…"

"Hm?" he responded without opening his eyes.

"What do you like to do for fun?"

"Fun?"

"Yes. What do you do to cut loose?"

He turned slightly to look at her and saw that she'd rolled to her side and was resting her head in her hand.

"I mean, it's obvious you work out," she went on, her eyes traveling slowly down his body and up to his face again. "You don't get to look like you do by sitting on a couch all day."

"Sitting on a couch all day is pretty impossible when you have a five-year-old boy."

She smiled. "True. Jack must keep you busy. But there must be *other* things you like to do; maybe we have something in common, something we could enjoy together. Oh, what about wine?"

"Wine?"

"Yes. You have that wonderful wine cellar, and I have quite a few lovely bottles at home. Maybe I could bring a bottle or two over to your place some night? You know…for a private tasting?"

He watched as she shifted on the chair and stroked one foot lazily along her other calf. There was no mistaking her suggestive tone, and his eyebrows rose behind his sunglasses. He felt his face heat, and when he opened his mouth to respond, not a word came out.

Thankfully, he heard Jack's laughter and turned to see him and the Gradys walking back to the pool. He smiled as he watched Jack and Sam talk animatedly, laughing and looking as if they'd been best friends for years.

Once inside the pool area, Jack trotted over to Will. "Can we go back in?"

"Sure. Can you say hello to Ms. Bingley? You met her at the picnic, remember?"

Jack turned to her and smiled. "Hi, Ms. Bingley."

"Hi, Jack. How's your lip? All better?"

"Yeah, it doesn't hurt anymore." He looked at his father again. "Can we go in now?"

Will rose from his seat. "Alright, let's go. Excuse us," he said to Caroline.

An hour later, Will was feeling thoroughly waterlogged, though Jack and Sam were still going strong. Caroline remained in her chair, stretched out on her stomach, and Will was in no hurry to rejoin her.

Something had changed with her, he could feel it. He felt like a bug under a microscope, and it vaguely reminded him of how he used to feel when he lived in New York, though not to the same degree. There, he'd felt like the proverbial goldfish in a glass bowl—no privacy, every aspect of his life discussed and dissected by family and strangers alike. It was one of the reasons he left; he refused to let his life become fodder for speculation.

This new feeling with Caroline was unfortunate, because he'd found her somewhat easy to talk with—unlike Elizabeth Bennet, who somehow managed to turn him into a fourteen-year-old boy whenever she was in the immediate vicinity. Granted, he'd never been especially verbose around people he didn't know well, but he turned into a bumbling fool around her. *A rude, bumbling fool.*

He swam into the deep end of the pool and rested with his arms stretched out along the edge, watching as Jack and Sam played together in the shallow end. His attention was diverted by the sound of a cart zipping up the lane toward the pool. He could hear laughter over the low hum of the motor and was pleasantly surprised to see Maddie behind the wheel of Vixen, her passenger none other than the object of his thoughts.

ELIZABETH GROANED WHEN SHE SPOTTED CAROLINE BINGLEY IN ONE OF the lounge chairs at the pool.

"What was that for?" Maddie asked as she pulled to a stop in the parking area.

"Caroline is here." Elizabeth's eyes lit on Jack, and she grinned. "And there's Jack, which means..." Her voice trailed off as she searched the pool area again. "Yes, there's his father."

"Will's a nice man, isn't he?" Maddie asked.

Elizabeth shrugged. "I have no idea."

"What do you mean?"

"The few times I've seen him, he's barely spoken to me," Elizabeth explained. "He just seems very...standoffish, I guess. I don't think he likes me very much."

Maddie rolled her eyes. "Don't be ridiculous, how could he not like you? He doesn't even know you."

"Well, he's not very friendly to me. Jack is adorable, though." Elizabeth smiled. "He sat with me on the ferry for a little while yesterday; we looked at a map of Portland together. He's a smart little boy."

They both watched as Will exited the pool, water dripping from his body. Elizabeth couldn't help but notice he was in fantastic shape as he walked over to his chair.

"Ugh, of course he's with Caroline," Elizabeth said flatly. "She doesn't waste any time, does she?"

Maddie frowned. "She asked about him after he left the picnic the other night. I tried to be circumspect with my answers, but I couldn't lie to her; she would have found out soon enough."

"Found out what?"

"That he's a widower. His wife died a few years ago."

Elizabeth's face fell. "Oh, that's awful. Poor Jack."

"I know, it's very sad. I'd hate to see Caroline get her hooks into him." She paused. "I think that might be why he moved here. I think he needed a new beginning with his son. And what better place to begin again than on our lovely island, right?"

Elizabeth nodded thoughtfully. "True. I speak from experience." She climbed out of the cart. "Thanks for the lift. Oh, tell Charles I said good luck. I hope it works out for him."

Despite her admitted dislike of Caroline Bingley, Elizabeth was very fond of her brother. Charles was one of the first friends she made when she moved here, and she'd instantly felt at ease with him. About two months after she was settled in, he'd asked her out on a date, but she'd turned him down; she hadn't felt that way toward him, and the last thing she wanted to think about back then was dating. Even so, they'd become great friends.

"Are you working at Trinity tonight?" Maddie asked before Elizabeth walked away.

"Yes. I'll stay at Kate's and go to the library from there in the morning." She glanced at her watch. "I'll probably only stay here for an hour or so, then I'll have to get home and get ready."

Kate O'Leary had also become a good friend since Elizabeth moved to the island. Kate had been friends with Charlotte for many years, and now the three women were very tight and spent a lot of time together.

Kate was also a server and back-up bartender at Trinity, and had helped Elizabeth immensely when she'd started working there.

"Ed and I are overdue for a nice dinner out," Maddie said. "Maybe I'll persuade him to take the ferry over and meet me there after I finish up my business with Charles."

"If you do, make sure you get a table in my section."

"It's a date. See you tonight!"

Maddie sped off, and Elizabeth made her way into the pool area, walking toward the opposite end from where Will and Caroline sat. Before she could get too far, she heard a familiar voice call out.

"Hi, Ms. Bennet!"

She turned to see Jack waving at her from the shallow end, so she approached the side of the pool and squatted down as he paddled over to her. Sam swam up alongside him, and both boys looked up at her with smiles on their faces.

"Hi, Jack. Hi, Sam. How's the water?"

"It's good," Jack replied. He lifted one hand and examined his fingers closely. "My dad said I'm a prune 'cause I've been in so long." He held his hand up for Elizabeth to inspect. "See?"

She furrowed her brows as she pretended to inspect it closely. "Hmm, you are a little bit wrinkly. How about you, Sam?"

Sam looked at his hand. "I'm a prune too."

"My dad taught me the doggy paddle. I'm gonna learn how to swim this summer," Jack said excitedly. "We're gonna come to the pool a lot, but I wanna swim in the ocean too."

"I bet you'll learn very quickly."

"How come you're not at the library?"

"I work at my other job today."

"You have another job too?"

"Yes, I work at a restaurant."

"Are you a chef?" Sam asked.

She chuckled. "No, I'm a server. I bring the food to the customers after the chef cooks it."

"Oh. Are you coming in the water?" Jack asked.

"Maybe. I think I'll just lie in the sun for a little while first."

"Okay. If you come in, you can swim with us," Jack offered.

Elizabeth smiled. "Thanks."

She stood and walked away, feeling a sudden wave of sadness for Jack, who would never know his mother, and for the mother who would never get to see her little boy grow up.

WILL SAT UP IN HIS CHAIR AND DISCREETLY WATCHED FROM BEHIND HIS sunglasses as Elizabeth chatted with Jack and Sam. Once again, he had the thought that she was very pretty, but not in a blatant, knock-your-socks-off way. Even so, something about her understated beauty appealed to him on a deeper level, making him feel off balance.

He watched as she walked to a chair at the opposite end of the pool area and pulled off her T-shirt and shorts. Her hair was tied back in a long ponytail, and she wore a simple one-piece navy blue suit. Will found himself begrudging that it hid more than it revealed, though he appreciated what it did show. She had a very nice figure, curves in all the right places... He shook his head, determined to stop his thoughts from meandering in that direction. *Again.*

Caroline rolled onto her back and cleared her throat. "You've met Elizabeth, I presume?"

He nodded. "I have. We've run into each other a couple of times."

"She's a wounded creature, that one. Ran away from a nasty husband or something like that." She rolled her eyes. "I can't stand when people feel the need to play victim or wallow in some great tragedy in their lives just to gain the sympathy of others."

Will's brows knit together as he looked at Caroline. He knew she'd lost her parents, and he was a little shocked by her comment. It was reminiscent of a few heated conversations he'd had with his father and his cousin Richard, and he suddenly felt defensive for himself *and* for Elizabeth.

"How long do you think is an acceptable period for a person's past to haunt them?" he asked, his voice flat. "I mean, does it depend on what it *is* that's haunting them? Or is there just an expiration date for those types of feelings?"

It was obvious she was taken aback by his response, and she shook her head. "I don't mean any offense, of course, it's just...well, I know her story, and obviously you don't. She used to live in Boston, and—"

"I'm not interested," he said, cutting her off. The last thing he wanted was to hear Elizabeth Bennet's tale of woe; he had his own to deal with. "I'm sorry, I don't mean to be rude, but whatever happened to her is none of my business. We all have pasts; we all have things that linger. I don't need to know what those things are for her."

Caroline's eyebrows rose. "Fair enough."

He watched as Elizabeth rose from her chair and walked toward the ladder that would put her into the deep end, and was appalled when Caroline leaned in close to him before waving and calling out to her.

"Hello, Elizabeth!"

She waved in return before climbing into the pool. Jack noticed her as well and called to her from the shallow end, where he sat on the wide steps with Sam.

"Ms. Bennet! Are you comin' down here?"

Will watched as Elizabeth slipped under the water and swam the entire length of the pool, finally surfacing directly in front of the two boys and causing both of them to burst out laughing.

"Dad, can you come back in?" Jack yelled to his father. "Ms. Bennet's swimmin' with us."

"Sure."

He stood and strode over to the pool, walking down to the deep end so he could swim straight to the boys, just as Elizabeth had. Caroline rose and walked to the side of the pool, lowering herself to sit on the edge of the shallow end and letting her feet dangle in the water.

"That's a lovely suit, Elizabeth," she said loudly.

"Oh, thanks," Elizabeth answered, before turning back to Jack and Sam.

"I think I had one similar to it in high school," Caroline noted, an edge of ridicule in her tone.

"This one actually *is* from my high school days—lucky for me, it still fits. You probably outgrew yours, huh?"

Will coughed into his hand and cast a sideways glance at Elizabeth, and they shared a small grin. Despite her pink cheeks, her brown eyes were bright with amusement.

"Well, Jack, I think it's time you and I headed out," he finally said. "You're turning blue."

Jack held his arm out in front of him to examine his skin closely. "Am not. But my hand is really wrinkly now." He held out his hand, and Will grabbed it before hauling Jack up against his chest. He lowered himself under the water so that he could put Jack on his shoulders, and when he stood again, Jack squealed with laughter.

"I'm the tallest one here! Sam, Ms. Bennet, look at me!"

"Wow, you *are* tall," Elizabeth replied, smiling up at him.

"I forgot to tell ya we used the map you gave us," Jack told her. "We didn't even get lost one time!"

"That's great! It's pretty hard to get lost in Portland anyway."

"Um, I didn't know you'd be here. I—I would have brought it with me," Will stammered.

"I have plenty of maps, Will," Caroline chimed in. "Why don't you swing by and pick some up? Maybe we can enjoy that bottle of wine we discussed."

He grimaced slightly. "Um, thanks, but I think we're all set."

His turned to Elizabeth, and she shook her head slightly. "I told you, you can keep it. It's not a big deal, I don't use it."

"No, I don't want it. I mean, we don't...we don't need it. But...but thank you."

She shrugged. "Okay."

He needed to leave before he embarrassed himself further. He walked carefully up the steps and out of the pool, then lowered Jack to the ground so they could gather their things. Before they left, Will went over to Sarah to ask where Sam would be attending school and was pleased to hear the boys would be enrolled together at Portland Elementary. They briefly discussed working out some type of arrangement for the ferry, agreeing to revisit the idea again before the end of the summer.

"Say goodbye to Sam and his mom," Will told Jack, "and Ms. Bennet and Ms. Bingley."

"Bye, Sam! Bye Sam's mom! Bye Ms. Bennet an' Ms. Bingley!" They started to leave the pool area when Jack suddenly tugged on Will's hand. "Wait, I forgot to tell Ms. Bennet somethin'!"

Will turned to watch his son run back to the pool.

"Ms. Bennet, we got a golf cart! It's yellow, but Mr. Bingley's paintin' it black and it's gonna have racing stripes and maybe pipes that shoot out flames and my dad said it will kinda be like the Batmobile."

Elizabeth's eyes widened and she laughed. "Wow, that sounds fantastic! You'll have the fanciest cart on the island."

"Yeah, it's gonna be better than Vixen, I bet." He turned back to Will. "'Kay, Dad, we can go."

Will rolled his eyes dramatically. "Yes, sir."

Their cart would be at Charles's house at least until tomorrow, so they walked home at a leisurely pace. Jack was a bundle of energy, talking about every little thing that had happened today, but Will knew that when they got home, Jack would eat his dinner, take a bath, and be out like a light.

Jack eventually became less chatty, giving Will time to reflect on something he figured out while at the pool but hadn't wanted to dwell on at the time. Initially, his reaction to Elizabeth had puzzled him; he'd allowed himself to acknowledge she was pretty, but there was something else, an underlying factor that caused him to fumble and stutter when he was around her.

I'm attracted to her.

He'd been able to talk with Caroline, and for the most part, he didn't feel awkward or uncomfortable—not until this afternoon. Yes, she was beautiful and would probably be considered stunning by some men. She was attractive, but he wasn't *attracted*. It was as if she was trying too hard to capture his attention.

Funny that Elizabeth wasn't trying at all, but here he was, feeling things—slight as they were—that he hadn't felt in years. There was just something *there*, something in her eyes…something that drew him in.

It was disconcerting, recognizing these feelings for what they were. It didn't feel right to him, the direction his mind had taken. It felt a whole lot wrong, actually. He hadn't felt this way about anyone, hadn't had such an instantaneous response to someone since…well, since Anne.

One thing was for sure—he would have to talk to Elizabeth and apologize for being so impolite, especially since she'd been so sweet to Jack and had tried to be friendly during their few brief exchanges.

Tomorrow.

He'd brushed off Jack on Tuesday when he'd asked to go to the library because he hadn't wanted to bump into her. But maybe they could go there tomorrow and check the place out, and if he happened to see her, he'd be ready with something witty to say.

He shook his head.

Me? Witty? Good luck with that.

Four

As it turned out, Will never made it to Portland on Thursday, as Sarah Grady called in the morning to ask if Jack could spend the afternoon at their house. She offered to pick him up after lunch, but Will figured he should learn the route, since it would probably be the first of many trips to their house. Sam ran outside to greet them as they walked up the driveway, and Sarah asked Will in. He met Sam's older sister Jessica, who appeared to be in her early teens, and also had the pleasure of meeting the family pet—a huge Great Dane named Maximus. Will stayed for a few minutes and then located Sam and Jack in the family room, playing with a train set.

"I'll see you later, Jack. Remember your manners."

Jack glanced up at him before returning his attention to his friend and the trains. "I will. Bye, Dad."

He called Charles after leaving the Gradys' to get an update on the golf cart. Charles told him to head over, so Will walked out of Diamond Cove and toward Charles's house.

As he ambled along, taking in his surroundings and enjoying the peace and quiet, he found himself falling more in love with the island. He'd chosen Maine randomly; at the time, it had seemed the antithesis to everything about New York. He'd stumbled across Great Diamond accidentally, and it seemed perfect—an idyllic spot removed from the craziness of the city, yet still with enough of a city life in reach.

He arrived at Charles's house and heard the low hum of music coming from the backyard. He went around back and saw Charles in a paint-spattered T-shirt and shorts, slowly walking around the cart and inspecting it closely, and Will called out to him.

Charles turned around and smiled. "Hey, Will! What's up?"

Will's eyes traveled over the cart. "This looks excellent!"

"Thanks. Take a look at the striping I picked out."

Will walked closer and saw the stripes were actually made up of red, orange, and yellow flames that widened as they reached the back of the cart. He smiled widely. "That's perfect. Jack will love it."

"Oh, these too." Charles pointed to the back of the cart. "They're just for show, but they make the cart look pretty mean."

Will laughed out loud when he saw the fat chrome pipes Charles had attached to the underside of the back end of the cart. They looked like real exhaust pipes and gave the cart a little bit of an attitude.

"Jack will flip when he sees those!" He pulled his wallet from the back pocket of his shorts. "How much do I owe you for everything?"

Charles shook his head. "You don't owe me a thing."

Will's expression sobered. "Come on, I'm not letting you do all this for free. No way."

"Consider it my welcome gift for you and Jack," Charles insisted. "It was fun and took no time at all."

"No, you need to take something for it. I can't have you doing work for me for nothing."

"I don't need the money."

"Funny, I don't either," Will argued, "so you would be helping me out by taking some."

"Nope, sorry. Hey, that place I checked out with Maddie yesterday has some possibilities."

Will recognized the abrupt change of topic for what it was, but let it go. Still, he glared at Charles before answering. "Really?" he asked, tucking his wallet away.

"Yeah. It's perfect, actually. The tanks and brewing system are in good shape, the kitchen has new appliances, and the restaurant itself is clean and modern. And it isn't huge, which is nice. The bar is pristine."

"What are you going to do?"

Charles shrugged. "I don't know. Maddie told the bank I'm interested and pushed the fact that I'm a local boy, which they like. I just have a lot to think about. It's a huge investment."

"Do you have a business plan?"

"Um...yes?"

Will laughed. "Your answer isn't supposed to sound like a question."

"I figured that."

"What are you doing right now?" Will asked. "Jack will be at Sam's for a couple of hours. I could help you with some things."

"Do you know about that kind of stuff?"

Will nodded and pursed his lips. "Yeah. A little."

"Up for a beer while we talk?"

Will smiled. "Always."

Charles went into the house to get a pad of paper and pens and a couple of beers, and the two men made themselves comfortable outside on the deck. Nearly two hours later, they hadn't moved much at all and were on their second beer.

Will made a list of things Charles needed to do before he even thought about buying or investing in any type of business and went over each item one by one. First, a business plan—other than Charles stating "I want to own my own brewery"—had to be written up. Charles hadn't thought it necessary, but Will stressed the importance of having a formal plan in writing; it helped to have every step mapped out clearly.

"You need something describing what you would like the business to be, what your goal is. You should write up a sales strategy, a marketing plan, and a projected profit and loss statement." He paused to take in the baffled look on Charles's face. "And you'll need to figure out what your operations cost will be. For example, are you brewing all the beer yourself, or will you bring in someone to help you, someone who has experience as a brewer? Plus, you'll need additional staff and an idea of the capital needed to cover everything." He hesitated again, watching as Charles's face fell further. "If you plan on doing remodeling—new tables, chairs, flooring, paint, even plates and glasses—things like that will add up."

Charles groaned and lowered his head to the table. "Shit."

Will chuckled. "It's not that bad. I can help you with everything."

Charles lifted his head. "You would do that?"

"Sure, why not? You can consider it payment for painting my cart."

Charles laughed. "I have a feeling I'll be the one making out in this deal."

They were interrupted by Caroline's voice coming to them from across the yard.

"Hello, boys," she called out, waving as she came closer. "What are you two up to? No good, I assume."

"Just having a beer and relaxing. Will's giving me some business tips," Charles answered, leaning back in his chair and folding his hands across his stomach. "What are you up to, sis?"

"I was bored and thought I'd wander over. How nice to find you here, Will." She placed her hand on his shoulder.

Will waited for her to remove it, but she left it in place. "I came to check out my cart. I think I'll be driving it home today. It's almost dry." He glanced at his watch and stood, causing Caroline's hand to drop. "If you think it's ready, I should get going. I have to pick up Jack."

"It should be all set," Charles said. "Can we get together again soon and start working on some of this stuff?"

"Absolutely," Will said, excited at the prospect. "I think I'm heading into Portland tomorrow with Jack, but I'll be around tomorrow night if you want to come by."

"That works."

"In the meantime, start gathering some of the information we talked about. Even if it's just rough figures, it's something to start with. Don't worry about getting everything perfect right off the bat. You have to look at it as a work in progress."

Charles shook his head. "Man, I'm gonna owe you for this. I'll be painting your whole damn house before you know it." They both laughed. "Give me a call when you're back from Portland tomorrow."

"Sounds good."

"I'm heading to Portland tomorrow morning myself," Caroline said lightly. "Maybe I'll see you and Jack on the ferry. What time are you heading over?"

"I'm not sure yet."

"Where will you be going?"

"I think we'll just be exploring the city again. No set destination in mind." *Except for the library.*

"I'd love to show you some of the sights, if you don't mind having a third...?"

Will read the expectant look on her face. "Actually, I'd rather spend the day with Jack. Nothing personal, we just need the time together."

"Oh, that's fine. I just thought I'd offer. If you change your mind, give me a call. I've got some business to take care of in Portland, so just let me know."

Will nodded. "Thanks." He glanced toward Charles. "Talk to you tomorrow. Thanks again."

"No problem. See you tomorrow."

JACK'S REACTION TO THE DARCYS' NEW GOLF CART WAS COMICAL: HIS JAW dropped and his eyes opened wide, the only word coming out of his mouth a very quiet "wow."

Will thanked Sarah, and as soon as they were out of the Gradys' yard, Will drove as fast as the little cart could go. They spent nearly an hour cruising around the island, past the beaches and down by the docks before heading home.

At the end of their driveway, Will pulled Jack up onto his lap and let him steer the cart while Will controlled the pedals. Jack giggled the entire time, the contagious sound making Will laugh. He drove all over the lawn, but he was having so much fun Will didn't have the heart to stop him.

After parking behind the house, they walked inside together. Will could barely keep up with Jack's excited chatter as he climbed up onto a stool at the kitchen island.

"We played with the trains for a long time, Sam has lots of trains, and then his sister Jess came and played a fun game with us but then we went outside 'cause Sam has a climbing thing that has a fort at the top. I told him me an' you are gonna build a fort too or a tree house and he said he would help us and maybe his dad would too."

"That's nice of Sam to offer up his dad's help," Will said, thinking a busy attorney who only had weekends off was not going to give up one to work on a fort or a tree house.

"We got bored in the fort thingy, so then we played with Max. He's huge, Dad, did you see him? Sam said he's the biggest dog on the island, but I think maybe he's the biggest dog in Maine or even New York."

"Yeah, he's pretty big."

"Sam's mom let us have a snack and I had chocolate chip cookies but she asked me if I was al–al—if I could eat the stuff in the cookie and I said I could 'cause I eat cookies all the time and she said she shoulda asked you but I told her it was okay and chocolate chip was my favorite and we got to dip 'em in milk."

"Sounds delicious," Will replied as he walked around the kitchen, putting on some water to boil for pasta and taking a jar of sauce from a cabinet. "Pause for a second—meatballs or no meatballs?"

"Meatballs, please. And then we went down into the basement 'cause he has a whole room down there with a ping-ping table—"

"Ping-pong," Will corrected him, grinning as he took meatballs from the freezer.

"That's what I said, ping-pong, and we tried to play but I wasn't good at it so we went back upstairs and went back outside."

Will raised his eyebrows. "Is that it?"

Jack nodded and took a deep breath. "Yeah, that's it. Then you came to get me. Our cart is the best on the whole island, even if the pipes don't have flames comin' out."

"I don't know if the other people on the island would like it if flames shot out," Will explained. "And what about a name for that thing? That's your job."

"I already have a name, it's the Batmobile," Jack said, looking at Will as if he had three heads.

"Oh, that's right. The Batmobile."

"Yeah, I'm Batman an' you're Robin."

Will grinned. "An unstoppable pair."

"Yup. An unsobbable pair."

Later that night, once Jack was tucked in, Will sat down at his desk and called Georgiana again. He was surprised at how much he missed her. Although they hadn't lived under the same roof in a long time, he was used to seeing her frequently, even when she was busy with school. She'd been a lifeline for him after the accident, always there to help with Jack while Will kept a bedside vigil at the hospital. After Anne died, Georgie had been the one who'd kept Will glued together as best as she could, and they'd grown even closer.

She was all grown up now, something that had happened seemingly overnight. She understood things, understood feelings, *his* feelings, even when he couldn't put them into words.

When she didn't answer her phone, he decided to give Mrs. Reynolds a call. Georgiana wasn't the only person whose company Will missed; while Alice Reynolds was technically an employee of the Darcy family, working as both a housekeeper and a nanny, she was so much more than that to him. She'd been there to provide comfort and love when he'd been trying to cope with the death of his mother, she'd given support and strength during the family trials and tribulations that had surrounded his relationship with Anne, she'd celebrated the birth of Jack with them, and she'd provided strength and a shoulder to cry on when Anne had been taken from them.

A smile broke out on his face when he heard her voice on the phone.

"Hello, Alice."

"Fitzwilliam! How are you?"

"I'm great. How are you?"

"I'm well, thank you. How's my little prince?"

He chuckled. "Sound asleep. I don't think he's ever slept as well as he has the past five nights. He just conks right out."

"It's all that fresh air, I suppose."

"He's getting plenty of that."

They talked for a while about Jack and his new friend Sam, and he told her about the other people they'd met since arriving on the island and the things they'd been doing to keep themselves busy. He also asked about her health, as he knew she'd been having some trouble with one of her hips for a while and had been having a difficult time getting around. Over the past year or so, he'd been encouraging her to retire, but she wouldn't hear of it. Her life had revolved around the Darcy family for so long, it was impossible for her to imagine a life without them.

But there were no more kids to nanny for, hadn't been for a long time, and he knew there was very little cleaning or cooking to do for his father as the man was hardly ever home. Still, the Darcy home was *her* home as well, and she wasn't about to change that now. That was one thing he could commend his father for—providing a home for and taking care of Alice, long after her services were actually needed.

"When are you coming to visit me?" he asked.

"Oh, Maine is much too far for me to travel. I hope you'll come back to New York for a visit."

"I will. Um, probably not for a while though." *I'm in no rush.* "Georgiana is itching to get up here...maybe you could join her. It's really not too far at all."

"Oh, well... When is she going?"

"We haven't discussed details yet. Why don't you talk to her, and the two of you can figure out some dates? My calendar is pretty wide open."

"I imagine so, what with no job and all."

"Alice—"

"I just worry about you becoming bored and restless," she explained, interrupting him. "You become very cranky when you have nothing to do."

He chuckled. "I *like* having nothing to do, at least right now." He thought of Charles. "Anyway, I found a little project to keep me busy. I'm helping a friend with a business venture."

"Oh—a friend?"

He smiled at the curiosity in her voice. "Yes, a friend. Charles, the guy I just told you about."

"Oh."

He detected a note of disappointment. "Alice, I've been here for six days."

"I know, I'm sorry. I did sound a bit eager, didn't I? I just want to see you happy again, that's all."

"I know you do, and I'm getting there. This place is growing on me. It's like I was meant to be here." He leaned back in his chair and stared up at the ceiling. "The house, the island, Portland... I feel relaxed. I'm starting to feel like myself again." He reached up with his free hand

and dragged it through his hair. "And no, I'm not getting soft or going crazy, so don't say it."

"I wasn't going to say a thing," she answered. "I'm thrilled for you, Fitzwilliam. I know you were questioning your decision right up until the day you left New York, and I'll tell you again what I told you then —you're doing the right thing at the right time for the right reasons."

He felt an unexpected wave of relief wash over him. "You did tell me that, didn't you?"

"I did, and I'll tell you again, anytime you need to hear it."

"Thanks, Alice."

"You're welcome. Now, I can tell you're tired, I can hear it in your voice. Go and get some rest. And be sure to give that handsome boy of yours a kiss and a hug from me, alright?"

"I will. I'll even take a share for myself."

"There's plenty for both of you," she replied, laughing quietly. "Good night, Fitzwilliam. Thank you for calling."

"Good night, Alice."

He hung up and let out a lengthy sigh. *The downside of moving,* he thought. *Being away from Georgie and Alice.* But they weren't so far away, and Portland had an airport, after all. He was sure he could convince them to fly here, maybe in a couple of weeks. Even though Jack hadn't mentioned it, Will knew his son missed both women as much as he did.

His thoughts turned back to Georgiana. If she'd answered her phone, he might have broached the topic of Elizabeth with her...or maybe he wouldn't have, as there wasn't much to say. Still, he was curious to hear her thoughts. Maybe he just needed someone to tell him he shouldn't feel guilty about having feelings for a woman—even if those feelings amounted to little more than curiosity at the moment.

Actually, he already knew what Georgie would say; she would tell him it was okay, and that even the *slightest* bit of curiosity was a sign he really was healing. She would tell him Anne would want him and Jack to be happy, first and foremost, and not dwell in the shadow of her ghost.

Even so, hearing it was one thing—believing it was another.

ELIZABETH CALLED LYDIA WHILE WALKING TO THE LIBRARY ON FRIDAY morning to let her sister know she would be in Boston the next day for graduation. Lydia was ecstatic and promised to pass on the news to the rest of their family. Elizabeth smiled at her excitement and realized she truly was looking forward to seeing everyone again.

As she strolled into work, she instantly felt herself relax. The children's library was located in the large, glass-fronted portion of the building that housed the Portland Public Library. She loved it here amongst the shelves of books and playful learning atmosphere.

By two o'clock, a fairly large group of kids had assembled, as Friday's story hour was quite popular among the four-to-seven-year-old set. Elizabeth would often be the one who read to them; it was one of the best parts of her job. She loved the expressions on the kids' faces as she narrated the story, changing her voice to suit each character, and watching as the kids became completely engrossed in the tale.

Today she was reading *Blueberries for Sal*, one of her favorites. Parents ushered their kids to sit on the large circular rug and then retreated to the rear of the room to lounge in the colorful, overstuffed furniture, usually burying themselves in their smart phones or talking quietly until story hour was finished.

As the kids started to settle, she heard a voice from her left.

"Hi, Ms. Bennet."

She turned and saw Jack Darcy sitting in the sea of children scurrying about and trying to get comfortable or find friends to sit with.

"Hi, Jack, how are you?" she answered, smiling down at him.

"I'm good. I didn't know you're gonna read."

"It's one of my favorite things to do. I'm glad you came."

Her eyes left him, and she quickly scanned the room. She found his father standing against the wall in the back. He was looking at his phone but glanced up for a moment, his eyes instantly locking with hers. To her surprise, he offered a small smile and a wave, which she returned.

"Are you exploring more of Portland today?" she asked Jack.

"Yup. We're gonna go look at my school after this. My dad showed me pictures of it on the computer but he said we should go an' see the real thing."

"That's a great idea."

"I hope it has a good playground."

"I'm sure it does."

She gently shushed the kids and asked them to sit, and once they were settled, she launched into the tale with enthusiasm. Occasionally, she would glance up to where the parents were gathered, and inevitably her gaze would land on Mr. Darcy.

He wasn't looking at his phone or engaged in conversation with anyone; every time she looked at him, he was looking at her. She began to feel a bit self-conscious, and more than once, she stumbled over the words in the second-grade level book, causing a warm blush to spread across her cheeks.

His stares were a bit unnerving, even though he remained, for the most part, completely expressionless. Sometimes it almost looked as though he was smiling a little, but mostly he just stared, and for the first time she could remember, she was relieved when the story came to its conclusion.

She went behind the circulation desk to sit at her computer, doing her best to focus on an acquisitions list. As the parents began to collect their kids, she risked another look around the large room and saw Jack and his father talking near the small wooden playhouse located in the far corner. She saw Jack nod his head at whatever his father was saying before he ventured into the playhouse with some other children. And then she noticed—with no small amount of trepidation—that Mr. Darcy was heading her way.

He came to the counter and cleared his throat before he spoke. "Hello, Ms. Bennet."

Elizabeth, who'd been studiously trying to ignore his approach, pasted a smile to her face as she turned to look at him. "Hello, Mr. Darcy. How are you?"

"I'm—I'm well, thanks. You?"

"I'm fine, thank you." They lapsed into silence, but he was still looking at her in that way he had...and Lord, he had the darkest eyes she'd ever seen. "Um, is there something I can help you with?" she asked, unsure of whether he really needed something or was just going to stand there and stare at her for the rest of the afternoon.

"Oh, yes. Sorry. I have…I have a few books I need, and I was wondering if you could help me locate them. I have a list." He retrieved something from his shorts pocket and cleared his throat again. "Um, here." He unfolded the slightly wrinkled paper and smoothed it on the counter in front of him.

She rose from her seat and walked toward him. "I'd be happy to help. These are books you would find here, in the children's area?"

"Um, yes."

She picked up the paper and looked at the titles he'd written down. The first was *A Little Book of Manners for Boys*. Her eyes moved to the next. *How to Be a Friend: A Guide to Making Friends on the Playground.*

Her brows pinched together in a frown. *Does he really think Jack needs books like these?*

The third book was simply titled *Sorry!* and before she realized it, she was shaking her head, enough that he noticed.

"Is—is there something wrong?" he asked quietly. "Don't you have them here?"

"I…well, possibly," she answered hesitantly as she looked up from the paper, subconsciously noting she only reached his shoulder. "It's just…these are strange books for Jack to be reading. He just…he seems so well-mannered and polite. I can't imagine he needs them." Her eyes widened in mortification. "Oh, no…did I say that out loud? I apologize," she offered sincerely. "It's none of my business."

"No, it's fine. Really," he responded earnestly, his voice low. "I'm glad you think he's well-mannered and polite. I think so too." He cleared his throat again. "These are for me."

She stared at him for a moment, unsure if she'd heard him correctly, before breaking into soft laughter. She tried to stop it by covering her mouth with her hand and it took a few seconds, but she managed to control it enough so she could speak again. She was relieved to see he was grinning as well.

"You're going to read *A Little Book of Manners for Boys*? Aren't you a bit too old for that?"

"Well, apparently not," he answered seriously. "I've always heard you're never too old to learn new things, and it seems I could use a lesson in manners and how to make friends…and how to apologize."

His eyes were intent on hers, and it finally dawned on her that he was trying to apologize to her in his own odd, amusing way. She felt a blush creeping onto her face again, and couldn't think of a single thing to say in response. Luckily, he spoke and relieved her of the responsibility.

"I've been really unpleasant to you, and I can't apologize enough," he went on. "Jack thinks the world of you. You've been so nice to him, and I've been…not so nice."

"Jack is very sweet."

He turned away from her, his eyes searching for and finding his son. "He is, isn't he? He's a great kid, though I'm probably a little biased." He smiled as he turned back to her.

She was taken aback by that smile and the dimples that peeked out along with it, and she was struck again by how handsome he was. "Well, you have every right to be, Mr. Darcy."

"Please, it's Will." He grimaced. "It makes me feel old when you call me Mr. Darcy."

She laughed lightly, feeling a bit more comfortable now. "Well, no more Ms. Bennet then. It's Elizabeth."

"Okay." He paused. "Can I ask you something, Elizabeth?"

"Sure." She felt an unexpected thrill at the sound of his deep voice saying her name.

"Do you ever wish you had a second chance to meet someone again for the first time?"

"Is—is that what we're doing?" she asked softly.

He smiled again, dimples and all, and her stomach did a funny little dance that she felt all the way down to her toes. Instead of answering her, he held out his hand.

"Hi, my name is Will Darcy. It's nice to meet you."

She grinned and took his hand, holding it lightly. "Hello, Will. I'm Elizabeth Bennet. It's nice to meet you too."

Five

W ill left the library feeling as if something off-kilter had finally been set right. At the very least, he felt more confident that the next time he and Elizabeth ran into each other, he would be capable of having an intelligent conversation without tripping over his words.

One can always hope.

He'd only planned a brief visit to the library, but Jack begged to stay when he saw Elizabeth was going to read. Will had readily agreed; it gave him the chance to observe her. She was in her element, her eyes bright with enthusiasm and the smile on her face completely genuine. He found himself unabashedly staring, and it was obvious she was aware of his gaze; her cheeks flushed, and she glanced at him every now and again. He didn't want to make her uncomfortable or self-conscious, but he couldn't take his eyes off her; he tried more than once to focus on something else, but his gaze always wandered back to her.

They talked a bit longer after reintroducing themselves, and he asked if he might see her on the ferry. She told him she was staying overnight in Portland and then driving to Boston the next morning to attend her younger sister's college graduation. Not wanting to push anything—and not really sure what he would be pushing anyway—he told her that maybe he would see her around the island, and they'd bid each other goodbye.

Now, he slowly pulled his truck up in front of Jack's new school. Jack immediately spotted the playground and asked if he could get out to play.

"Sure, but we don't have a lot of time," Will told him. It was all Jack needed to hear; he was off like a shot, sprinting across the grass toward the swing set. "Fifteen minutes, then we need to leave to catch the ferry," Will called out, trailing after him.

"'Kay!" Jack grabbed a swing. "Hey, Dad, can you push me?"

"Sure." Jack chatted about the school, staring at the building and asking his father which room he thought might be the kindergarten room. Will had to force himself to pay attention to his son, as his mind kept wandering to a certain librarian with a contagious smile and a pair of bright brown eyes.

Jack tired of the swings and persuaded Will to join him on the seesaw. It turned out to be quite a feat; in order for Jack to go up high, Will had to practically pull his knees up to his chin, which made his son laugh hysterically. After a few more minutes of silliness, they headed back to the truck.

"I told you Mr. Bingley was coming over tonight, right?" Will asked as they walked side by side.

Jack nodded. "Uh-huh. You're gonna do some work."

"Just for a little while. We'll have time to play a game or something after dinner before he comes over."

"'Kay. What are we havin' for dinner?"

"How about pizza?" Will suggested. "I heard the market has really good cheese pizza."

Jack's eyes opened wide. "Yeah, pizza! Maybe they have the peproni you like."

"I bet they do. We can eat right there at a picnic table if you want."

"Yeah, kinda like eatin' out."

Will smiled. "Exactly."

The ferry ride back to the island was relaxing. The sinking sun was still shining brightly, and the breeze felt refreshing. Jack rested against Will, content to sit and talk about his new school and their visit to the library.

"Can we go again?" Jack asked. "I like the little house inside. It's neat."

"Sure we can." Will's thoughts traveled to Elizabeth again. "Maybe we'll stay longer so you can pick out a book."

"Okay. Ms. Bennet's nice, an' she reads good. I like the way she does the people." Jack looked up at his father. "Maybe we can go when she's gonna read again."

Will nodded, wrapping his arm around Jack's shoulders and kissing the top of his head before pulling him tighter to his side. "I think we can do that."

AFTER DINNER, WILL AND JACK HEADED HOME AND PLAYED UNO UNTIL Charles came over. Will turned on a movie for Jack so he'd be occupied while the men talked business.

"I think I managed alright with these things," Charles said, handing Will a stack of papers as they sat at the kitchen table. "I may need your help with some others."

Will glanced at the papers, all handwritten and full of ink blots and words that were crossed out and scribbled over. He turned the papers this way and that, trying to make heads or tails of them, then shook his head. "Don't you have a computer?"

Charles nodded. "How do you think I was able to come up with this stuff? I researched everything online; I was up most of the night."

"Okay, so… Why didn't you type everything and save it on your computer?"

"Because I can't type."

"I hate to break it to you, but you can't write either."

"Shut up," Charles responded, giving him a friendly shove. "I know its chicken scratch, but if I had to type all that…well, I wouldn't be here. I'd still be home, typing."

Will chuckled and turned on his laptop. "We need to clean this up a little."

He read over what Charles had come up with so far, encouraging him to delve deeper with some aspects of his plans while restructuring or correcting others. He was impressed with what Charles had accomplished in such a short period of time. Besides writing an executive summary and a company summary, he'd also firmed up his product line and mapped out a management plan, including a basic framework for personnel he would need to hire.

"This is really good work. You got a lot done," Will told him.

"Thanks."

"What did you get stuck on?"

"Um, the whole part about market analysis and sales strategy kind of threw me," Charles answered with a frown. "I don't have a head for that stuff, I guess."

"Lucky for you, I do," Will said.

"Oh yeah? Is this what you used to do? Or what you do now?"

"Um, *used* to do. Have you ever heard of Darcy Marketing Group?" Charles shook his head and shrugged.

"It's my father's company and one of the premiere marketing firms in the country. Eventually, it was going to be mine."

"*Was* going to be yours? What happened?" Charles asked, before holding up a hand. "Wait, forget I asked. It's none of my business."

"No, it's fine. I wanted to leave New York, my father didn't want me to go, and that's how he retaliated against me. It's not the first time. I piss him off, he fires me, and then he cuts me off. It's a vicious cycle of dysfunction."

"And you're okay with that?"

"I don't have much of a choice."

"What about your mother, what does she think?"

"She died when I was eleven."

Charles's eyebrows rose. "Oh, man."

Will grinned. "If she was alive, she would have kicked my father's ass a long time ago." He paused. "It's taken a long time, but I feel like I finally have a good grasp of what's most important, and it's not DMG or money. That's where my father and I see things differently."

"I know what you mean," said Charles. "Losing someone makes you rethink things. It's a pretty harsh awakening, isn't it?" Will nodded his head slowly. "How long were you married?"

"A little more than two and a half years, but we'd been together since high school."

"Wow. That's unusual."

Will shrugged, and his eyes softened. "If you'd known Anne, you wouldn't think that. She was pretty great."

"Does Jack ever ask about her?"

"Sometimes. We look at pictures together." Will's eyes strayed toward the living room. "It must be like reading a story for him, like she isn't real or something." It was quiet for a moment, both men lost in their own thoughts until Will spoke again. "You said you were twenty-four when your parents died?" Charles nodded. "How old were they?"

"My dad was fifty-four, my mom was fifty. They were hit by a drunk driving the wrong way on the Maine Turnpike. They both died instantly." His eyes dropped to the stack of papers in front of him. "The bastard who killed them lived, of course. He got a year in jail and lost his license, which didn't stop him from driving again anyway. He ended up getting in another accident, but that time he only killed himself."

Will shook his head in disbelief. "Unreal, isn't it?"

"Completely. How…what about Anne?"

"We were hit by someone who blew through a red light." He swallowed heavily. "We were coming home from a party. Jack was supposed to be with us, but Anne got a sitter at the last minute. She wanted to have a date night." He smiled sadly, remembering their discussion about it but not really remembering anything about the party or the accident itself. "She was in a coma for a couple of weeks, but…" His voice trailed off and he looked up at Charles. "Her body couldn't handle the trauma. She was twenty-six."

"Were you hurt?"

"I got a little banged up, but Anne took the brunt of it." He sighed. "I was a mess. Um, mentally. The months after her death are a complete blur."

"Did you ever go to a support group or anything?"

"No, I couldn't. I didn't want anything to do with that stuff."

"Me either. Caroline tried, but she gave up. We were each other's support, I guess."

"I have a sister too. Georgiana. She's a lot younger than me, but she was a lifesaver. I had to keep going for Jack. I lost my wife, but he lost his mom."

They fell silent again, and Will shook his head before lightly banging one fist on the table. "Alright, enough of this gloomy shit. We have a business to plan."

Charles nodded. "You're right. Let's get back to work."

ELIZABETH FELT A SWELL OF ANXIETY AS SHE DROVE THROUGH THE familiar streets of Lexington and turned into the driveway of her parents' home. She pulled alongside Jane's car, grateful her older sister was already there. The house looked the same, with its manicured lawn and vibrant tulips and daffodils lining the driveway and walkway. Brilliant red azalea bushes adorned the beds along the front of the house, and the stone steps that led to the front door held pots of colorful geraniums. Her father loved to garden, and Elizabeth knew that when she walked around to the backyard, she would see even more evidence of his green thumb.

She hadn't been home since Christmas nearly six months ago, and that visit hadn't been pleasant; her father kept insisting she move back home, and her mother had nagged her incessantly about anything and everything. It hadn't been a very merry holiday, and she'd stayed away since then, keeping in touch only by phone.

The side door to the house opened, and Jane stepped out onto the small porch. "Lizzy! I was hoping you wouldn't get caught in traffic." The sisters rushed toward each other and embraced tightly. "I can't believe I haven't seen you in four months."

They walked into the house arm in arm and headed for the kitchen.

"Where are Mom and Dad?" Elizabeth asked.

"Dad drove Lydia into Boston," Jane answered before glancing at the clock on the wall. "He should be back soon. Mom is relaxing on the patio."

Elizabeth sighed. "I guess I should go say hi." She looked at Jane pleadingly.

Jane grinned. "Yes, I'll come with you."

Fran Bennet was dressed in a lightweight lavender robe and slippers and was seated in a wicker chair, sipping tea and staring out at the backyard. She turned when she heard the slider open. "Oh, you made it!" She set her cup on a small table and rose from her seat. "I just knew you wouldn't disappoint Lydia. She'll be thrilled to see you." She gave Elizabeth a brisk hug. "How was your drive?"

"It was fine."

"That car of yours is holding up?"

"I barely use it, so yes, it's running great. I usually walk everywhere anyway."

Mrs. Bennet rolled her eyes. "Oh, you and your walking. You should be thin as a rail with all that walking you do." She reached up to squeeze her middle daughter's cheeks. "Not quite, hmm?"

Elizabeth sighed. "Gee, thanks, Mom."

Jane winked and grinned. "You look fabulous, Lizzy. Island life agrees with you."

"Oh, and city life is suddenly horrible? Boston air isn't good enough?" Mrs. Bennet asked both girls, shaking her head. She turned to Jane. "Next thing we know, you'll be running off to join your sister on that ridiculous island."

"Can we go get ready?" Elizabeth cut in, already dying to get away from her mother. "I have my dress and bag in the car."

"Are you staying overnight?" Jane asked.

The sisters walked into the house while they talked, leaving their mother outside to finish her tea.

"I don't know. What's the plan for after? Is there a party or anything?"

"Lydia is having a few friends over. Dad is cooking on the grill, burgers or steaks or something. You know Lydia, she won't stick around for long. She'll want to go out and hit the clubs." Jane shrugged. "I don't blame her. She's worked hard the past four years."

"Can you believe it? She's actually graduating. Didn't we have a bet about that?"

"We did," Jane said with a smile. "I owe you fifty bucks."

The sisters retrieved Elizabeth's things from her car, then returned to the house and headed upstairs. Thirty minutes later they were ready, and when they went downstairs, Elizabeth saw her father standing in the kitchen.

"Hi, Daddy," she said softly, her face breaking into a broad smile as she went to hug him.

David Bennet wrapped his daughter in his arms, holding her tightly. "Hello, sweetheart." He kissed her cheek. "I've missed you."

"I've missed you too. How are you?"

"Oh, I'm fine." His gaze swept over her and then moved to Jane, and he smiled. "You both look lovely."

"Thanks," the sisters said in unison.

Elizabeth had to agree. Jane, in all her golden splendor, looked fabulous in a pale blue sundress that brought out the color of her eyes, her long blonde hair swept up high on her head. Elizabeth had opted for a similarly styled dress in navy blue but left her dark hair tumbling down in soft waves to the middle of her back. They were the same height, but Jane was slimmer, almost waifish; Elizabeth's curves were slightly more generous. Both women had gone through phases when they were younger of being envious of the other's appearance. Lydia was a mixture of her older sisters: she had Jane's blue eyes but Elizabeth's build and long, dark hair.

"Really, Dad, you're feeling okay?" Elizabeth asked with concern.

Her father had been rushed to the hospital with chest pain in early March, and the fear was that he'd suffered a heart attack. Elizabeth had been ready to head to Boston immediately, but Jane called and told her not to come, as it hadn't been a cardiac issue after all. Even so, she worried about him.

Mr. Bennet looked at her and smiled. "I feel wonderful. It's my favorite time of year, you know."

"I can tell you've been working outside," she said. "The yard looks gorgeous, everything is in bloom."

Mrs. Bennet came into the house from the backyard. "Yes, everything is in bloom, including my allergies." To prove her point, she sneezed loudly. "These flowers will be the death of me."

Mr. Bennet grinned at Elizabeth and shrugged, his eyes lit with humor.

"And how are you, Lizzy?" he asked. "How's the library?"

"It's great."

"And the restaurant?"

"Very busy. The tips are fantastic."

Mrs. Bennet huffed. "I wish you wouldn't wait tables, Elizabeth. It's no job for you."

"It's the perfect job for me," Elizabeth reasoned. "I work with my friends, I get to be social and meet people, and I make good money."

"Let's not have this conversation again, okay?" Jane interjected. "Mom, unless you plan on attending Lydia's graduation in that lovely robe, you need to get moving."

Mrs. Bennet glanced at the clock. "Oh, dear, we need to be there in an hour. David, you too! Let's go, you need to get into your suit."

BY FIVE O'CLOCK, THE BENNETS WERE BACK AT HOME AFTER THE commencement at Bunker Hill College, and the party was in full swing. There were a dozen or so of Lydia's friends scattered here and there around the backyard. Elizabeth and Jane were putting assorted appetizers onto platters while Mr. Bennet manned the grill. Mrs. Bennet was the consummate hostess, checking on each guest and ensuring all were enjoying themselves. Elizabeth glanced up when she heard the slider open and smiled when Stuart Carver walked in.

"Hey, Stuart," she said quietly, nudging Jane.

Stuart smiled in return. "Hello, Elizabeth. Nice to see you."

"Nice to see you too."

Jane walked over to him and stood on her tiptoes to kiss him, holding his shoulders for balance. One of his hands went to her waist and squeezed lightly before sliding down a bit to rest on the curve of her hip.

Elizabeth looked away, giving them a moment of privacy. She felt like she owed it to Jane to get to know Stuart a little bit better, and maybe today, she would have the chance. Glancing at them again, she saw him smile at Jane and caress her cheek with his free hand.

"You look good enough to eat," he murmured, obviously intending the comment for Jane's ears only.

Elizabeth's mouth nearly dropped open.

Jane playfully slapped his chest. "I'll remember you said that later," she said, laughing up at him.

"I'll go help your Dad on the grill," he told her with a wink.

"I'm sure he'll enjoy your company." After Stuart went outside, Jane glanced at her sister's face. "What's that look for?"

"'Good enough to eat'?" Elizabeth whispered, giggling.

Jane colored. "You heard that?"

"I most certainly did. What happened to unflappable Stuart?"

"We had a heart-to-heart last weekend after I vented to you on the phone."

"What did you say to him?"

"Just that lately, when we've been together, it's like he's not there," Jane explained. "He's off in his own world, completely preoccupied. I told him I thought he was losing interest."

"And what did he say?"

"That he's been distracted at work. There's been talk of a layoff, so he's worried about that. I told him he needed to confide in me about those things instead of just shutting me out." She sighed. "In any case, he apologized."

"That's good." Elizabeth knew Stuart was a staff manager at one of the major teaching hospitals in Boston and imagined it could be a stressful job. "I'm glad you guys talked."

"Me too. It's been better this week, but I *still* think something else is going on. I don't know, it's just a feeling I have."

The subject of their conversation came back into the house. "Um, I have to go," he said hastily.

Jane frowned. "What do you mean you have to *go*? You just got here!"

"I know, but there's something going on at work. Some of the staff is threatening to walk out... I have to go now, I'm sorry."

Jane pursed her lips as she stared at him for a moment. "Fine," she finally said, crossing her arms over her chest. "I understand."

Stuart approached her and planted a quick kiss on her lips. "Pass on my congratulations to Lydia. I'll try to come back, but I don't know how long I'll be there."

"It's alright," Jane said quietly.

He looked at her and pouted. "I'll make it up to you, I swear."

She nodded. "Just call me or text me later, okay?"

"Of course." He leaned in for another kiss, this one a bit longer than the first. "I'm sorry." He turned to Elizabeth. "It was good to see you, Elizabeth. Take care."

"You too, Stuart."

The moment he was out the door, Jane turned and looked at her sister, mouth drawn into a tight line and eyebrows raised.

"You don't believe him, do you?" Elizabeth asked.

Jane shook her head. "Nope."

BY NINE O'CLOCK, THE PARTY HAD ENDED AND EVERYTHING HAD BEEN cleaned up. Lydia had already left with her friends, and Elizabeth was debating whether or not she wanted to make the drive back to Portland. The alternative—staying here—wasn't very appealing. Jane offered to put her up for the night, but Elizabeth didn't want to be in the way if Stuart came calling, so she decided to suck it up and stay with her parents.

When Jane was ready to leave, Elizabeth walked her outside. They promised to talk soon and hugged tightly before Jane got into her car and drove off. Elizabeth was turning back to the house when she heard a deep voice call out to her from the street.

"Hello, Lizzy Collins."

She spun around, recognizing the voice instantly. "George?"

He stepped out from the shadows in front of the neighbor's house and walked toward her, stopping when they were only a few feet apart in the driveway. Her stomach lurched, but all she could do was stare; he was the last person she expected to see.

"Oh, that's right—its Lizzy *Bennet* again, isn't it?" He smirked at her. She remained silent, and he leaned forward until his face was just inches from hers. "Cat got your tongue?"

The pungent smell of alcohol wafted over her, and she took a step back. "I—I'm just surprised to see you."

He glanced at the Bennet home. "I figured you'd be here for Lydia's graduation, so I took my chances." His eyes went back to hers. "I wanted to see you."

"Well you've seen me, so now you can leave." She turned and took a step toward the house, but he was faster and moved in front of her.

"Come on, Lizzy. I'm sorry I startled you." His demeanor softened as the words rushed out of him. "Don't go yet. I didn't come here to cause trouble, I swear. I just want to talk to you."

"You're drunk," she stated.

"No, I'm not, not really. I've only had a few drinks." He sighed heavily. "Can we just talk for a minute?"

"No. I have nothing to say to you." She took a step around him, but he reached for her arm, holding it firmly.

"Wait, you don't have to say anything. I'll do all the talking."

"Let me go, George. I'm not interested in anything you have to say," she said calmly, though her anger was beginning to rise. She wasn't afraid, but she had no desire to speak with him.

He released her arm and held up his hands, shaking his head. "I just want to talk to you, I want to explain—"

The front door opened, and Mrs. Bennet stuck her head outside. "Elizabeth? What are you doing out there?" she called out loudly. "Who's that with you?"

Elizabeth lifted her chin and stared directly at George. "It's no one, Mom. No one important." His face fell, and she felt a tiny bit of remorse, but it was gone as quickly as it came.

"Is that George Wickham?" Mrs. Bennet asked, her voice rising more. "What is *he* doing here?"

"Go back inside, Mom."

"I told you to stay away from him. Did you tell him to come here?" her mother asked, her tone accusatory. "He's nothing but trouble; how many times do you need to learn that lesson? If your father finds out—"

"Mom, *please* go back inside. I'll be there in a second, alright?" Elizabeth's voice was firm as she glared at her mother. The funny thing was, her mother despised George Wickham just as much as she did but for completely different reasons.

"If you're not in this house in five minutes, I'm sending your father outside."

The door slammed, and it was quiet again.

"I'll leave," George said, shaking his head. "I shouldn't have snuck up on you, but I knew you wouldn't see me if I asked."

"You're right, I wouldn't have. And why do you think that is?"

He wouldn't look her in the eye, staring instead at some point over her head. "I told you I was sorry, Lizzy. I made a mistake. What do you want from me?"

"Nothing, George. I want *nothing* from you, except for you to leave me alone," she answered in exasperation. "After everything I went through with Bill...you said you'd be there for me, but you weren't. You made things worse." Tears pricked her eyes, but she held them back. "I can't do this with you. Not now."

"Then when?" he asked, his voice rising slightly. "When are you finally going to forgive me? I love you, you know I do. It's always been you."

"You don't love me, George. It's *never* been me." She shook her head in disbelief as she turned away from him and walked toward the house. "You don't even know what love is."

Six

E lizabeth smiled as she tiptoed past Lydia's bedroom on Sunday morning, unsurprised her sister was still asleep; she'd come home late and had woken Elizabeth, saying they needed to catch up.

"Lydia, it's two o'clock," Elizabeth had said, her voice froggy. "Don't you want to go to bed?"

"No, I'm wide awake. I've been dancing for hours. C'mon, Lizzy, we never get to chat anymore."

"Alright. Let's go downstairs and have some tea." Elizabeth got up and dug around in her bag for a pair of shorts to put on with the T-shirt she'd worn to bed while Lydia changed into her pajamas.

They made their way to the kitchen, treading carefully on the creaky stairs so as not to wake their parents.

"Where did you go tonight?" Elizabeth asked, yawning as she put the kettle on the stove.

"Where *didn't* we go is the better question! We went everywhere. It was so much fun."

"You didn't drive, did you?"

"No, but I only had a couple of beers. I didn't want to be hung over this morning."

Elizabeth lifted the kettle from the stove as it began to whistle and poured them each a cup of tea, and they sat at the small kitchen table talking in hushed voices. "So what are your plans now?"

Lydia sighed. "I don't know. I think I just want to have fun this summer. I'm going to look for a real job, but I feel like this is my last summer to be a kid and goof around." She paused. "Is that a bad thing, to want to have a little fun one last time?"

Elizabeth smiled at the finality in her sister's tone. "No, of course it isn't. And it's *not* the last time you'll ever have fun. Mom and Dad aren't pushing you out the door, so just enjoy the next few months. You're the last one at home, after all." She laughed quietly. "They're going to get on each other's nerves *so bad* when empty nest syndrome sets in."

They both giggled at that.

"I'm a little scared, I guess," Lydia confessed quietly. "This is the real deal. Life starts now."

Elizabeth remembered feeling that way when she graduated from college, but she'd been with Bill back then, and it had seemed so much easier. Moving to Portland and starting over had been a far scarier step.

"You should come to Maine this summer," Elizabeth encouraged her. "Jane is visiting soon. You could come with her."

Lydia smiled. "I'd like that. I'm sorry I've never visited before, it's just…I've always felt kind of in the middle—"

"You don't need to explain," Elizabeth interrupted. "I know Mom would give you a hard time."

"Dad still thinks you belong here and that you'll come back. Mom's still pissed at George."

"And me," Elizabeth reminded her. "She's not pissed at Bill, though. Never Bill." She shrugged. "She'll get over it." She paused to sip her tea. "I don't know how to convince Dad I'm not coming back. It's obvious how happy I am—why wouldn't he want me to stay in a place that makes me happy?"

"Because he wants you to stay in a place that makes *him* happy. Right here in Lexington. Like, you should just buy the house next door."

Elizabeth chuckled and shook her head. "It's not going to happen. I love Portland too much."

"I can't wait to visit. Any hot guys?"

Elizabeth's mind immediately conjured up Will Darcy's face, and she felt herself blush. "Um, yes. Plenty."

Lydia's eyes narrowed. "Why are you turning pink?"

"It's the tea. It's hot."

"Mm-hmm," Lydia murmured over the rim of her tea cup. "No one specifically came to mind?"

"Nope."

"Liar."

Elizabeth laughed before quickly changing the subject. "So, um… George showed up after you left."

Lydia gasped. "He did?"

"I was out front saying goodbye to Jane, and all of a sudden he was there."

"Ugh. I told him not to come by."

Elizabeth's eyes grew wide. "What do you mean you *told* him not to come by? Have you been talking to him?"

"He came into the coffee shop a couple of weeks ago," Lydia explained. "He asked if you were coming home for my graduation, and I told him I wasn't sure yet. I *also* told him to stay away because I knew you wouldn't want to see him."

"Well, he didn't listen," Elizabeth stated, feeling stirrings of frustration. She looked closely at her sister. "You're not becoming too friendly with him, are you?"

"No! He comes into the shop once in a while. We make small talk, that's it."

"You don't tell him things about me, do you?"

"Like what?"

"I don't know, *anything*," Elizabeth responded, her voice rising slightly. "I don't want him to know a single detail about my life."

"If he wanted to know about your life, he could just go to Maine and find you. He knows you moved to Portland." Lydia paused. "Do you think you'll ever be able to be friends with him again? He seems genuinely sorry."

Elizabeth's faint irritation grew into full blown annoyance. "What makes you think he's genuinely sorry? What have you two talked about?"

"Nothing big, Lizzy, geez! He's mentioned you a few times, and he always seems sad. I feel kind of bad for him."

"Don't let him fool you. I thought I knew him, but he proved me so wrong. He's very good at manipulation."

"Maybe he's changed."

Elizabeth stared at her for a long moment. "You're right, he very well may have changed," she said softly. "But even if he has...it doesn't erase what happened. It can't. That's just the way it is."

"What *did* happen? You've never talked about it with me."

Elizabeth sighed heavily. "It's a long story."

Lydia shrugged. "I'm not going anywhere."

Elizabeth wavered, unsure whether she wanted to rehash everything. *But why not? Maybe Lydia needs to hear the truth about him.*

"Alright. I'll tell you," she said, rising from the table, "but it's going to require another cup of tea." She put more water in the kettle and turned on the stove, then leaned back against the counter and looked at her sister.

"Everything changed after the shooting. You know what happened that day, right?"

Lydia nodded, her attention completely focused on her older sister. "Bill saw you with George, he thought there was something going on, and he totally freaked and shot George."

Elizabeth chuckled. "That's the gist of it, I guess. George was in the hospital for over a month," she went on, growing serious again. "I took care of him when he got out. He has no family—his mom died of an overdose when he was nineteen, he doesn't know his father, and he has no brothers or sisters. So he really only had me."

"I remember you were at his place a lot."

"I was. I did everything for him. Cleaning, laundry, grocery shopping, cooking, driving him to appointments... It got to the point that between taking care of him, dealing with Bill's trial, and holding down a new job—plus going to counseling—I was physically and emotionally exhausted."

"You had a lot on your plate," Lydia said softly. The tea kettle started singing again, and she rose to carry her mug to the stove. Elizabeth poured for both of them and they sat down again.

"I did, but I never thought twice about it," Elizabeth continued. "I felt like I was doing the right thing, what I was *supposed* to do. George wouldn't have been in that situation if it hadn't been for me, right?" She shook her head as she thought back to those days. "I felt guilty.

Responsible. And then I started to feel...other things. Different things."

"Love?"

"I wasn't sure what it was. Affection, tenderness... I'd had a huge crush on him in high school, and we were already so close. We had a great friendship. Well, I *thought* it was a great friendship. But I wasn't sure if what I was feeling was genuine, or if it was the guilt and responsibility disguised as something else." She paused and stared down into her tea. "One night about four months after the shooting, I had a total meltdown. I was completely exhausted and so confused. I didn't know what to do, what to feel... I just knew I didn't feel like myself."

"What about Bill?"

Elizabeth looked at her sister. "What about him?"

"Did you still have feelings for him?"

"Sure—loathing, anger, fear—I could go on and on. Any good feelings were thoroughly obliterated by him during our one year of marriage, believe me."

"He was a bastard, huh?"

Elizabeth nodded.

"What happened after the meltdown?"

"George asked me if I wanted to be with him. He told me it was what he'd always wanted."

"Did you believe him?"

"I wanted to. Part of me was thinking he was finally saying the words I'd waited forever to hear."

"Did you become a couple?" Lydia leaned on the table and rested her chin in her hand.

"Sort of, but...it wasn't something where one day we were friends and the next day we were more. It didn't happen that way. It very slowly grew into this little...fledgling romance, I guess."

"Aww."

"No *aww*. There was nothing *aww* about it. He knew I needed to go slow and that I couldn't just go barreling into a relationship, especially a physical one. I'd only ever been with Bill, and I was just getting out of *that* mess of a relationship. I wasn't ready to go charging into another."

"Smart."

"That's what I thought. And I still wasn't really sure how I felt about George. We'd been around each other so much—was it just comfort and convenience? Was it guilt, or were my feelings real? I was still so confused." She paused. "George was patient for a little while, but then we argued one night, and he said something horrible to me..." Her voice trailed off as she remembered his words and the coldness in his blue eyes.

"I took a bullet for you, Lizzy. The least you could do is fuck me."

"What did he say to you?" Lydia asked.

"It doesn't matter. I walked away, but he kept calling. When I wouldn't answer his calls, he blew up my phone with texts. First he was angry, then he resorted to making up excuses, and then he just kept apologizing and begging me to come back, telling me he didn't know what he was saying. And stupid me, I believed it." She shook her head. "I explained how I felt, and he said he got it. He said he would be patient because I was worth it. And I believed him."

"Did you...did you ever...?"

"No, we didn't. I couldn't. I would try, but I always ended up pushing him away. I wasn't at the same place he was, mentally. To him, sex wasn't a big deal. He thought because it was me and him, it would be easy. But for me, sex was the biggest deal in the world. I'd had horrible experiences with Bill..." She looked down at her tea again. *I can't go there with Lydia.* "But it wasn't just that. The reasons it wasn't a big deal to George were the same reasons it *was* a big deal to me. Does that make sense?"

Lydia frowned. "I'm not sure."

"It was *because* it was me and because it was *him*," Elizabeth continued. "I thought it was a huge step for us, so for me it wasn't easy at all. It seemed like such an enormous risk, physically *and* emotionally, and I was still trying to find my way after everything with Bill." She sighed and shook her head. "It just...it wasn't easy. I wasn't ready."

"So what happened?"

"He lied. Just weeks after that conversation, after telling me he understood and would wait, I stopped by his apartment one afternoon. He was in bed with some blonde chick."

Lydia's jaw dropped. "Are you serious?"

"Completely serious. I left and drove straight to Jane's. I was such a mess by the time I got there, I'm surprised I didn't wreck the car on the way over."

"Jane must have wanted to kill him."

"She did! I practically had to physically restrain her from going to his apartment. She kept saying she was going to cut his balls off." Elizabeth could smile about it now, but back then she was shocked and hurt.

Lydia chuckled. "Sounds like Jane. Did you ever talk to George again?"

"Yes. After a week of more phone calls and more texts, I caved. I shouldn't have, but as long as he kept hounding me, I couldn't get past it." Elizabeth shook her head. "He had excuses, but then it all came down to blame."

"Did he try to blame you?"

Elizabeth nodded as her mind traveled back more than two years to that rainy Friday in January; her recollection of that day and his words were still incredibly sharp.

"What did you expect me to do?" he yelled. "Wait until you deemed me worthy enough to sleep with?"

"That's not what this is about," she responded quietly, refusing to yell. "We've both been through a horrible trauma, and I want to make sure that these feelings we're having, that I'm having, aren't because of that. And you know about Bill... It's never been about you being worthy enough, don't you dare say that to me. You know what this is about."

"Oh, that's right," he went on sarcastically, "put it all on me, make me look like the bad guy. But the thing is, if it wasn't for you I wouldn't be in this mess to begin with, all scarred up and in pain. You're here all the time, cooking, cleaning, taking care of me like I'm a child! I saved your life from that crazy bastard you married, and this is how I get repaid? I get a maid? Oh, I forgot. You feel guilty, right? You feel bad for me? Yeah, you feel bad, alright, but only bad enough to do anything for me but sleep with me. No, no sex with George, it just doesn't feel right."

She blanched as he mocked her feelings. Too shocked to respond, she could do nothing but stand there and let him carry on.

"You come over here, playing the loving girlfriend and winding me up tighter than a drum, and all I get is a big red stop sign every single time." His blue eyes were bright with anger as he spoke, his voice low and scornful. "Don't you think you owe me something more than that? It's your fault that it's come to this. You know that, right? Don't you want to fix it?"

She finally found her voice. "Isn't that what the blonde was for?"

He smirked. "She's been helpful. At least she's always been willing. She does have that going for her."

Her mouth gaped. "Wh–what does that mean? This wasn't the first time?"

He had the audacity to laugh. "The first time? God, Lizzy, are you really that naïve?" He shook his head, and his voice softened slightly. "Look, I really care about you, and I want to make this work, but I need things. More than what you're giving me. I can't live like this."

She swallowed thickly as she felt the color drain from her face. She understood exactly what he was saying. "In order for us to–to move forward, I need to sleep with you, have sex with you, and satisfy your needs. That's what it all comes down to, right? I need to–to repay you, is that it?"

He looked at her for a long moment. "It sounds kind of cheap when you say it like that, but yes." He shrugged nonchalantly. "I feel like you're already mine, anyway. You're damaged goods, just like me." He paused and shook his head sadly. "Don't you get it, Lizzy? No one else is ever going to want you."

The memory of that conversation made Elizabeth's stomach turn, and it took a few seconds before she realized Lydia had said her name. "What? I'm sorry, I got lost there for a minute."

"I was just asking what he said to you." She reached out to gently grasp Elizabeth's wrist. "If you don't want to tell me, it's okay."

Elizabeth let out a deep breath. "He just said some horrible things, and I couldn't...I couldn't forgive him and be with him anymore, not even as a friend. It wasn't just what he did. The things he said to me were far more hurtful than any of his actions."

Lydia tilted her head and frowned. "I'm sorry, I didn't mean to upset you. And I want you to know, I haven't said *anything* about you when he asks. I really haven't." She held Elizabeth's eyes. "Why did he come last night? What did he want?"

"To say that he's sorry and to find out if I've forgiven him yet. And he told me he loves me, which is too ridiculous to even contemplate." Elizabeth sighed. "I don't believe him, of course. I don't trust anything he says."

"But what if it's true? What if he *does* love you and didn't realize it until after you were gone?"

"He doesn't love me. If he did, he never would have treated me so poorly. Besides, it's too little, too late. I don't love him. I don't even want to be friends with him. I was so confused back then, everything was so messed up in my head. He knew it, and he took advantage of that. It took a while, but I realized I never loved him, not in that way. I'd been letting guilt and responsibility muck up my feelings, and it confused me even more. It wasn't love at all."

"Not like when you were in high school?"

"A high school crush isn't real love. I grew out of it."

"And then you met Bill."

Elizabeth gave a short, sarcastic laugh. "Yup, I met Bill. Lucky me." She rolled her eyes.

"Boy, your track record with men sucks." Lydia's eyes suddenly widened, and she clapped a hand over her mouth.

Elizabeth burst out laughing, and when she stopped, she took a deep breath. "Oh, it certainly does, Lydia. It certainly does."

Elizabeth was relieved to depart Lexington on Sunday morning. Her mother and father had cornered her at the breakfast table, demanding to know why George Wickham had shown up the night before.

"I don't know why he came," she told them calmly, "because I sure as hell didn't invite him."

Mrs. Bennet shook her head. "That man! I suppose ruining your marriage wasn't enough for him! He had to ruin your sister's graduation celebration too?"

"What did he say, Lizzy?" her father asked, his concern for his daughter clearly written on his face.

"That's between me and George. It's nothing for you to worry about."

"I wish you lived closer so we could keep an eye on you."

Elizabeth sighed deeply. *Here we go again.* "I don't need you to keep an eye on me, Dad. I'm a grown woman."

"It's just that you're so far—"

"One hundred miles, give or take a mile or two, isn't that far," she gently interrupted him. "I'm not moving back to Lexington. *Or* Boston. End of discussion."

"But it was supposed to be *temporary*," Mrs. Bennet whined. "You were only going for a little while, to—what did you say back then?—to 'get your head together.'"

Her mother was right, that *is* what Elizabeth had told them, but she'd only said it to appease them; she'd known even then that she wouldn't come back. "I know, Mom, but I didn't expect to fall in love with Portland and the island. I'm staying there. I've made wonderful friends and have two great jobs. It's my home."

Her father turned away, his gaze focused on the slider and the backyard beyond. "As long as you're happy, Lizzy. That's all we truly want." He looked back to her with a touch of sadness in his eyes. "I just wish you could be happy here."

To her father's credit, he understood what Elizabeth had endured at the hands of her husband during their brief marriage. He also had a vague understanding of George's betrayal and the pain he'd caused, though she'd never gone into the specifics of what had happened; she felt it was more information than a daughter should share with her father.

Elizabeth's mother, on the other hand, steadfastly believed George had been the catalyst in the downfall of Elizabeth's marriage. Elizabeth had repeatedly tried to explain what her marriage had been like, but her mother had either chosen not to believe it or was too blind, even now, to see the truth. Elizabeth had eventually given up trying to explain, realizing the futility of trying to defend herself and her choices.

The conversation at the breakfast table waned after that, and Eliza-beth went upstairs to pack. It was nearing eleven-thirty, and she wanted to be back in Portland to catch the two o'clock ferry home.

Her parting was somber at best. She hugged her father tightly and almost became teary. She *did* miss him—missed his wit and presence and spending time with him—but not enough to give up her life in Maine. The look in his eyes told her he finally understood his favorite daughter was gone for good.

"Will you visit again soon?" he asked quietly.

"I'll try to come over the summer, but you and Mom can always come to visit me too. I don't have a spare room at the house, but there are some wonderful hotels and inns in Portland. I'm sure you'd love it."

Mrs. Bennet chimed in. "Oh Lizzy, you know your father shouldn't be driving such long distances. It's just too far for us to go."

"Take a bus or fly," Elizabeth suggested. *Always with the excuses.* "There's an airport in Portland. I could pick you up."

"Nonsense. If you want to see us, you'll have to come here. That's the way it should be—children are supposed to visit their parents, not the other way around."

Elizabeth rolled her eyes. "Okay, Mom. Whatever you say." She gave her mother a brief hug. "I'll call you soon."

With one last apologetic glance at her father, she was out the door.

During the drive back to Portland, she thought about how she felt when she'd spoken to Lydia about George. It was a relief to recognize the anger and hurt she'd held onto for so long had faded, though she knew she would never be able to forgive George and let him back into her life. Too much had happened between them; in his own way, he'd become another incarnation of Bill.

It wasn't too long after that final conversation with George when she'd decided she needed to leave Boston. She remembered a college friend mentioning how great Portland was, so she started to do more research on the city. Once the trial ended and her divorce became final, she was gone. *No looking back.*

It had been a risk to move without having a job lined up, but she'd squirreled away every penny she'd made for almost a year and added it to the meager amount she'd managed to save while married to Bill. Luckily, Maddie had come through for her, and everything else had magically fallen into place—except for her self-esteem and happiness. Those things took much longer to bloom again, but she felt as though she was finally getting back to being herself.

She sighed as the familiar sight of Portland's skyline came into view and knew it would only be another fifteen minutes or so before she would be parking her car in the garage.

Home sweet home.

"I THINK IT'S PERFECT," WILL SAID TO CHARLES AS THEY LOUNGED ON A bench near the docks, waiting for the ferry to arrive to take them back to the island.

"Do you think it's big enough?" Charles asked, looking over some notes he'd made while he and Will had visited the potential site for Charles's brewery. "I don't want a huge place, but I don't want a little hole in the wall either."

"It's a good size, and the glass wall behind the bar makes it look even bigger."

"Yeah, I like that." Charles glanced up from his papers. "What time do you need to get Jack?"

Will checked his watch. "As soon as we dock. It was nice of the Gradys to take him for a few hours, but I don't want to take advantage."

"Why don't you bring him over for dinner? We'll throw some burgers on the grill."

Will slunk down low on the bench, resting his head on the back of it and stretching his long legs out in front of him. He cast Charles a sideways glance. "Don't you have a girlfriend or something?"

Charles laughed. "What the hell does that mean?"

"I don't know, you're always hanging around on the island. What do you do for fun?"

"I come here."

"I always see you on the island."

"You've been living here for, like, five minutes."

Will chuckled. "But you're always home."

"I come to Portland at night," Charles replied without hesitation. "I have my fun, don't you worry about me."

"So...you stay overnight?" Will asked, curious about his new friend.

"Yeah. A couple of nights a week, usually."

"Where do you stay?"

"None of your business," Charles responded with a grin.

"Okay, I get it," Will said, laughing again.

"I have friends I crash with."

"Female friends?"

"Occasionally. You should come with me some time," Charles suggested tentatively. "I'll take you to some of the local spots."

"I'm home with Jack every night, so I wouldn't count on that." The last thing Will wanted to do was experience the bar scene.

"You need to find a babysitter," Charles suggested. He set his papers down and stood up to stretch.

"Like you just said, I've been living here for five minutes. It's too soon to put Jack with a sitter."

"I bet the Gradys' daughter would do it. I think she's old enough."

"I'll take that into consideration."

"Well, look who it is," Charles suddenly called out. "Hey there, Lizzy."

Will stood up so quickly he nearly tripped over his own feet. He turned, and yes, there she was. Elizabeth Bennet. Walking toward the bench.

"Hi, Charles." She smiled brightly. "Hi, Will."

Will smiled in return and was horrified when he felt his face flush. "Hi–hi, Elizabeth."

Her eyes went back and forth between the two men. "Are you guys heading back to the island?"

"Yes, we just finished looking at some property in Portland," Charles answered. "Looks like I might be opening that brewpub after all."

"Oh Charles, that's fantastic! I knew it was only a matter of time before you found the right place."

Charles went on to tell Elizabeth all about the property while Will stood there, silent but transfixed, unsure of what to say or do. He could only stare at her, taking in her expressive eyes and the way they were lit with happiness for Charles. She asked a lot of smart questions and he was relieved when Charles answered them, enabling him to remain tongue-tied a bit longer.

Eventually she turned her attention to him. "Did you have a good weekend?"

He nodded. "Um, yes. It–it was great. Jack and I went to visit his–his school, after we left the library on Friday."

She grinned. "I told him I was *positive* it would have a great playground. I hope he wasn't disappointed."

"No, no, not at all. He was really excited about it. Um, how–how was your sister's graduation?" he asked, embarrassed he couldn't stop stuttering.

"It was very nice, thanks. I'm glad I went, but I'm happy to be back home."

The ferry docked and they all boarded together. They sat at a table, and Will remained mostly silent as he watched Charles interact with Elizabeth. They were so comfortable with each other, so *familiar*. The thought made him withdraw further, and by the time the ferry arrived at the island, he felt sullen and irritable.

"Hey, what are you doing tonight?" Charles asked her as they disembarked.

"Nothing, really," she responded. "I need to sleep. My sister kept me up until all hours this morning."

"Why don't you come over for dinner? Will is coming over with Jack. I'm going to throw some burgers on the grill."

Will's eyebrows raised. *I don't remember saying we were coming over.* He turned to Charles, who was smiling oddly. "I have to see how tired Jack is first."

"Oh, come on. The kid's gotta eat, right?" Charles slapped Will's shoulder. "Burgers at my place. You in, Lizzy?"

"Sure, why not? Do you want me to bring something?"

Charles grinned. "Just your pretty little self."

She rolled her eyes. "I'll bring a bottle of wine too."

"Sounds good. Hey, you want a lift? Will's cart is parked over there." Charles pointed across the small dirt lot. "It's only a two-seater, but you can sit on my lap." He winked and smiled broadly, causing her to laugh and Will's eyes to widen.

"Oh, you'd like that, wouldn't you?" she replied saucily, lifting one eyebrow. "Thanks, but I'll pass. I need the walk after that drive. What time tonight?"

"Well, Will has to get Jack, so how about in an hour or so?"

"Sounds good. See you then."

They all bid each other goodbye, and Charles turned to Will as they walked to the cart.

"What's the matter?"

"Nothing," Will said, a bit rougher than he intended to.

"Do you mind that I invited Lizzy?"

"It's your house, why would I mind? But I didn't say I was coming over."

"Come on, it's early. Jack will be fine."

They arrived at the cart and climbed in. Will focused on driving, staring straight ahead and remaining silent.

"So she's pretty, huh?" Charles asked.

"Who?"

"Lizzy."

"You mean Elizabeth?"

Charles grinned. "Yes, Elizabeth."

Will cleared his throat. "I guess."

Charles's eyes widened. "You *guess*? You couldn't take your eyes off her when she showed up, and you blushed like a teenage girl when you were talking to her. *And* you kept looking at her ass when we were boarding the ferry."

Will shot him a quelling look but remained silent.

"So, you *guess*?" Charles repeated.

"Okay, yes, she's pretty," Will admitted, feeling his cheeks warm again. "Do you have a point? Or are you busting my balls for the hell of it?"

The teasing tone left Charles's voice. "I just noticed *you* noticed, that's all. I'm sorry if I went too far."

Will sighed, feeling a bit badly he'd snapped. "It's fine, you didn't go too far. I *was* looking at her. She's…she's just…I don't know. I don't know *what* she is, I don't know *what* I think." He shrugged, feeling flustered all over again.

"She's pretty," Charles stated simply, "and she's unattached. I used to have a thing for her when she first moved here. Asked her out on a date and everything."

Will did a double take, making the golf cart swerve as he glanced at Charles. "You asked her out? Really?"

"Really. She shot me down, which is a good thing. She's a nice girl. Not that I'm not a nice guy, but we're better off as friends. She's like a sister to me now."

Will nodded, and after thinking for a moment, he became sure of two things: The first was, yes, Elizabeth Bennet was very pretty. The second was that he knew, without a doubt, that the feelings he experienced when he looked at and stood next to her were not the least bit brotherly.

As Elizabeth walked home from the ferry dock, she thought back to her conversation with Charles and Will. Well, her conversation with Charles, that is, as Will had remained mostly silent. *What a difference between them!*

Charles Bingley was all brashness and flirt, and with his shoulder-length blond hair, baby blue eyes, and surfer-boy good looks, he could get away with it. He'd dated her friend Kate for about eight months, but when Kate decided she wanted more of a commitment, Charles had backed off. Even so, they'd remained on good terms—it was impossible to dislike Charles—and Elizabeth considered him a good friend. *How he and his sister came from the same parents is beyond me.*

Will Darcy was a completely different animal, and as her mind traveled to him she felt an odd thump in the pit of her stomach. She'd already decided he was one of the most gorgeous men she'd ever laid eyes on. But where Charles was outgoing and flirty, Will seemed introverted and a bit intense. He still appeared uncomfortable around her, even though they'd broken the ice so nicely on Friday. His charming, unique apology and his honesty about his actions and behavior made her see him in an entirely different light.

When he'd asked her if she ever wished she had a second chance to meet someone again for the first time, it had hit a soft spot, and she knew why; it was completely genuine.

As she turned to walk up the short driveway that led to the Gardiners' home, she remembered what Maddie had told her about Will when they'd gone down to meet him at the docks the day he'd moved here. Maddie said she thought he was looking for a fresh start —but knowing what she now knew about his wife, she wondered if he was running away from his grief. He seemed withdrawn, but after such a tremendous loss, who wouldn't be?

She remembered feeling the same way herself not too long ago. She certainly wasn't comparing what she'd gone through to what he'd endured, but even so, she'd felt so…off-course. It was like she'd been adrift in the ocean with nothing to anchor her in place.

Moving to Maine had changed all of that. She was proof of the healing properties that seemed to be incorporated into the island air, and the restorative power of good friendships with kind, generous people. Charlotte, Kate, Mary, Charles, and of course the Gardiners— they were all so new to her life but had enriched it immensely. They'd all contributed to the healing of her mind and especially her heart.

With that thought, she promised herself she would try to draw Will out of his shell and wouldn't let his silence deter her. She could see he and Charles were becoming good friends and thought that Charles's inability to be anything but an extrovert would encourage Will to relax a little bit and let his guard down.

Will may have moved here looking for an escape, but he has the chance to gain so much more.

"ONE HOUR!" CHARLES YELLED FROM HIS FRONT PORCH. "YOU'D BETTER be here if you want some of that stout!"

Will waved back over his shoulder, shaking his head as he drove away.

By the time they'd reached Charles's house, Will had managed to steer the conversation away from Elizabeth, but Charles had *also* talked him into coming for dinner. Will knew Jack would be excited; he was a social kid who enjoyed being in the company of others, children and adults alike. *If social skills are passed through genes, Jack definitely inherited his from his mother.*

As he headed to the Gradys' house, he let himself think of Anne. He missed her, but the feeling of not being able to live without her, of feeling as though he was suffocating and couldn't possibly carry on, had disappeared. He *had* proven he could live without her and carry on; he'd had no choice in the matter.

Things had shifted. Now, it was more the companionship he missed, and knowing the person you loved was waiting at home for you. He missed *being* that someone as well. The emotional and physical intimacy, the security, the feeling of belonging and the sharing of desires, dreams and fears—all of that had been wrapped up in her. He missed her, but he missed everything she'd represented in his life as well.

He thought of Elizabeth again and his ridiculous behavior on the ferry and then thought ahead to dinner. They were actually going to eat together; they weren't riding the ferry or seeing each other for five or ten minutes in passing. He felt a twinge of nervous anticipation in his stomach, and he shook his head. *I can't be nervous. It just won't do.*

Taking a deep breath, he vowed to be more open and outgoing. If he wanted to feel comfortable around Elizabeth—or around *any* new people, for that matter—he would have to push his personal boundaries a little. He wanted to have friends here, wanted to have people around him who he cared about and who cared about him and Jack. He'd found someone like that in Charles; he already sensed the bond he was forming with his new friend would be one that lasted a lifetime.

Being easy and open didn't come naturally to him, but he would try. He would make the effort to talk, smile, and laugh more. Enjoy his life. *Live* his life. Starting tonight.

Seven

"Is there gonna be other kids at Mr. Bingley's?" Jack asked his father as they drove toward Charles's house.

"I don't think so, bud. You're it."

"Oh."

"Sorry about that. I think it's just the two of us and Ms. Bennet."

Jack's expression brightened. "I like Ms. Bennet."

One corner of Will's mouth lifted. "I can tell."

"Do you like her now, Dad? Are you friends?"

"Well, I never said I *didn't* like her," Will refuted. "And I think we're friends."

When they turned into Charles's driveway, Will noticed Vixen already parked there.

"Mrs. Gardiner's cart is really cool," Jack said as he walked around it. "It fits more people than ours."

"But since it's just you and me, two seats are enough, right?"

Jack nodded. "Right."

Will reached into the Batmobile and grabbed a plastic bag he'd placed between the seats. He'd stopped at the market and bought scallops, shrimp, a package of bacon and some cocktail sauce, thinking it wouldn't be polite to show up empty-handed. Scallops wrapped in bacon and shrimp cocktail were easy enough to throw together.

They rounded the corner into Charles's backyard, and Will was happy to see Maddie seated at the table with Elizabeth and Charles.

"Hello, Will! Hello, Jack!" she called out, smiling widely.

Will and Jack smiled in return and waved as they walked toward the deck. "This is a pleasant surprise," Will said to her. He said hello to Elizabeth as well, smiling at her as he set the bag on the table.

"Oh, I'm not staying long," Maddie explained. "Ed sent me on a mission to procure some stout from Mr. Beer here." She elbowed Charles lightly. "I thought I might as well sample some of Elizabeth's guacamole. I can't resist it."

Charles ruffled Jack's hair. "Glad you guys could make it."

"Thanks for having us. Um, I brought some shrimp and scallops and bacon," Will said, gesturing to the bag.

"Good man!" Charles stood up from the table. "What are we doing with them?"

Will's eyebrows rose. "I assumed we would eat them?"

Elizabeth laughed lightly, and the sound immediately drew Will's eyes to her. He found himself grinning stupidly in response.

"I mean, *how* do you want to cook them?" Charles asked, glaring comically at Elizabeth.

"Oh, I don't know," Will answered as he leaned against the railing. He watched as Jack started a conversation with Elizabeth and Maddie. "How do you usually cook them?"

"How about throwing them on the grill?" Charles suggested.

"Sounds good to me." At the moment, he was more interested in watching Elizabeth as she talked with Jack.

"I think I have some toothpicks in the house, we can use them to secure the bacon." Charles got up from the table to walk inside.

"Okay," Will said, keeping his eyes on Elizabeth and Jack.

"What else did they have there?" she was asking as she leaned toward Jack, listening attentively.

"There's a jungle gym an' swings an' some seesaws," Jack answered. "My dad went on a seesaw with me. It was funny. He's too tall."

She glanced at Will and smiled. "I'm sure he is."

Will spoke up. "I think I bruised my chin with one of my knees."

Elizabeth and Maddie laughed, and Elizabeth turned her attention back to Jack. "Did you do anything else?"

"Naw, we didn't have enough time, but we're goin' back another day. Right, Dad?" Will nodded. "He said we can go to the library again too. Are you gonna read?"

"I will if I have enough time, but I can't promise."

"Okay. My dad's a good reader too. He can read if you can't."

"Whoa, Jack, please don't volunteer me for anything," Will said, chuckling lightly.

"But you do all the voices an' stuff really good too, just like Ms. Bennet."

"Now *that* I would pay to see," Maddie teased.

"Me too." Elizabeth grinned widely. "We're always looking for volunteers."

"I'll keep that in mind." Will smiled back at her and momentarily forgot how to breathe. It was amazing how her eyes lit up when she smiled; he didn't think he'd ever seen brown eyes quite like hers.

Charles came out of the house. "I couldn't find toothpicks, but I have these." He handed some long metal skewers to Will. "Have at it."

"Do you have butter and garlic?" Will asked.

"Sure. Follow me."

"Sorry, I should have asked before." Will followed Charles through the sliding door and into the kitchen. "I need a small saucepan too."

"Hey, I apologize if Jack is bored," Charles said as he unhooked a pan from the rack hanging over the center-island stove. "I don't have a lot of stuff that would interest a five-year-old kid."

Will shrugged and set the skewers on the counter. "He'll be fine. He brought some things to keep himself busy."

Charles's eyes suddenly opened wide. "Oh, wait, do you know what I *do* have?" He handed the pan to Will and rubbed both hands together excitedly. "I have a serious squirt gun arsenal." He wiggled his eyebrows before retrieving the butter and fresh garlic. "Can he get wet?"

"I don't mind if he doesn't mind," Will said, placing the pan on the stove.

"Great. I might have to challenge him to a battle." Charles opened the refrigerator and took out a bottle of his home-brewed stout and handed it to Will, along with a pint glass. "I'm going to dig up those squirt guns. I think they're in the basement."

Charles disappeared down the hall, and Will opened and slowly poured the dark liquid into the glass. When he took a sip, he was astonished, once again, at just how good it was. After taking another long sip, he dropped some butter in the pan and began searching for a garlic press. The sliding door opened, and he smiled when Maddie poked her head in.

"I'm heading home. Where did Charles disappear to?"

"He's in the basement looking for squirt guns."

"That man refuses to grow up," she said with a laugh. "Tell him I said goodbye and I'll give him a call tomorrow morning. We have another meeting with the bank."

"You do?"

"Yes, I think we're moving forward. Charles told me you've been helping him—it's very nice of you. He's wanted to do this for so long."

"I'm happy to help. He's got some great ideas, he just needs to flesh them out a little more."

"You're certainly getting him to do that. If you could only teach him how to type!" She rolled her eyes, making him laugh. "I'm off with my stout. Enjoy your dinner."

"Bye, Maddie. See you soon."

A moment later, Will heard Charles coming down the hall toward the kitchen. "Maddie just left, she said she'll call you in the morning. Do you have a garlic—" Glancing up, he froze mid-sentence. "Are you serious?"

He looked at the brightly colored plastic squirt guns Charles held in his arms. There were six of them, and they were *huge*.

"Cool, huh? Oh, if you were about to ask me for a garlic press, I don't have one. Just smash it on the cutting board over there."

He went out the slider, and Will knew the squirt guns were a hit when he heard Jack's loud "wow!" Not a moment later, the door opened again and Elizabeth came in, carrying her glass of wine. She closed the door firmly behind her before looking back outside.

"Leave it to Charles to have squirt guns," she said, grinning a little.

Will looked up from the garlic clove he was about to annihilate and smiled at her. "You're safe in here. But Charles wouldn't squirt you anyway."

She raised a brow at him. "You want to bet?"

He laughed. "Maybe not."

She walked around to the other side of the island. "What are you making?"

"Oh, um, just a little something to put on the scallops before I grill them. Some melted butter with a little bit of garlic. Nothing fancy."

"Sounds delicious. Are you putting it on the shrimp too?"

He shrugged and took another sip of his stout. "I could if you'd like. It would probably taste pretty good." He cleared his throat. "So, do you like this stuff? Shellfish?"

She nodded as she sat down on one of the tall stools. "I like everything. I'm easy to please."

"Me too." He smashed the garlic with the flat side of a carving knife and slowly scraped it off the board and into his hand before dropping it into the melted butter.

He was trying his best not to stare at her, but it was difficult. She was dressed in faded jeans and a simple V-neck, long-sleeved top in a deep burgundy color. Her hair was loose around her shoulders, and he'd noticed her bare feet when she walked into the house.

"Um, I need to get the scallops and shrimp, they're outside," he said, his voice hoarse. "I'll put them on the skewers in here."

She smiled. "You'll be safer. Do you need some help?"

"No, thanks. I'll be right back."

He walked outside and was immediately assaulted by streams of water. Caught by surprise, he yelled and started laughing, scrambling for the bag before sprinting back inside the house. The last thing he heard was Jack's hysterical laughter before he closed the door firmly behind him.

Sighing loudly and still laughing a little, he turned to put the bag on the counter. Water was dripping from his face and hair, and the front and back of his sweatshirt were soaked. He glanced at Elizabeth and saw she was covering her mouth with one hand, obviously trying not to laugh.

He held his arms away from his body. "I'm wounded, and you're giggling," he said indignantly.

She burst out laughing, and just as it had before, the sound brought a smile to his face. It was a natural, uninhibited laugh that brightened her eyes even further, and he knew right then that he wanted to make her laugh as often as possible.

"I should have taken you up on your offer and let *you* get everything," he teased. He glanced outside again and saw Jack running across the backyard with one of the squirt guns, chasing Charles and having a ball.

"I'm glad you didn't. I'll grab you a towel, I think I can probably find one." She rose from the stool and disappeared down the hallway. She was back in an instant and handed him a towel. "I don't know how much good it will do, because the minute you go out there again, they're going to nail you."

He smiled down at her as he dried his hair a little and wiped his face. He detected the faint scent of something slightly floral, perhaps her shampoo or perfume. "I know. Next time, you're going with me."

"Deal," she answered, grinning up at him before going to sit down again.

He turned to the cabinets and took a deep breath as he began searching for a platter, determined to calm his racing pulse.

ELIZABETH WATCHED AS WILL SLOWLY AND METHODICALLY TRIMMED A piece of bacon before wrapping it around a scallop and threading it onto a skewer. He repeated the process with the rest of the scallops, brushed them with the butter and garlic mixture, and then set them on the platter before turning to the shrimp.

She examined his hands as he worked. They were large and definitely those of a man who hadn't done much manual labor. Even so, they were masculine and strong, and when she found herself staring at them a little too long, she forced her eyes away and took a sip of her wine, trying to ward off the warmth that was spreading across her cheeks.

He was focused on getting the shrimp onto the skewers, his eyelashes lowered and throwing spiky shadows on his cheeks, and she looked at them with envy. His thick, dark hair was cut moderately short but had a little bit of a wave to it, falling across his forehead as he worked. Her gaze traveled over his face, admiring its strong features, and then dropped to his pleasantly full lips. She could see the resemblance now between father and son; Jack's face was basically just a smaller, younger version of Will's, the major difference being the color of their eyes.

Conversation had ceased, but the silence wasn't uncomfortable —*she* wasn't uncomfortable, anyway, and he didn't appear to be either. She remembered what she'd told herself about trying to draw him out a little, and she cleared her throat.

"So, you're from New York City?" She didn't want to ask questions that were too invasive and figured it was a safe one to start with.

He nodded as he slid the last shrimp onto a skewer. "I am."

"It must seem awfully quiet here. Portland doesn't exactly compare."

"No, it doesn't. But Portland is…" He shrugged. "I don't know. It's nice. I like it, more than New York."

"Really?" She tilted her head and looked at him curiously. "Why is that?"

"Because it's quiet, especially on the island," he answered, his eyes on hers. "I wanted to move to a place where I could hear myself think. That's hard to do in New York."

He'd finished preparing the food, but she pretended not to notice. "I grew up in Boston. Well, just outside of Boston, in Lexington."

"Is it noisy there too?" he asked, a small smile on his lips.

She nodded slowly and took another sip of wine. "Too noisy, too…everything."

"This island is like a little haven, isn't it? I can't believe it isn't swarmed with people." He carried the saucepan, cutting board, and dirty utensils to the sink and began washing everything.

"We'll have a mini population explosion in a week or two, but it never gets very crowded." She paused for a moment and stared at the muscles of his back and shoulders as they moved under his sweatshirt. "What did you do in New York? For work, I mean."

He finished washing everything and turned to look at her, drying his hands on a dish towel as he leaned back against the counter. "Um, I worked for a large marketing firm there."

"You don't work for them anymore?"

"No, I was let go."

Her eyes widened. "You were fired?"

He smiled. "Don't look so shocked. It wasn't the first time."

"Oh." She frowned. "It–it wasn't the first time you've been fired from a job? Or…it wasn't the first time you were fired from *that* job?"

"That job."

"Sorry, I'm confused. How do you get fired more than once from the same job?"

"It's possible if your father is the owner of the company and can't make up his mind whether or not he wants to keep you on the payroll." He took a long sip of his beer.

"Ohh, now I understand. I think."

"It's pretty straightforward," he explained. "Anytime I do something that upsets him, he fires me, but then he eventually rehires me. When I told him I was moving to Maine, I was canned. Again."

"That's not very fair."

He shrugged. "That's my father."

"So what are you going to do? For work, I mean. Are you going to look for a job here?"

"Right now, I'm going to help Charles get his brewpub off the ground."

"What about after that?"

He released a long exhalation of air. "Honestly? I just want to spend the summer playing with my kid."

WILL GLANCED OUT THE WINDOW OVER THE KITCHEN SINK AND THEN turned back to her. "So, are you a *real* librarian?" he asked, pushing away from the counter and lifting the platter. "C'mon, we can go out now. They're taking a break."

"What do you mean, a *real* librarian?" She rose from the stool and her hands went to her hips.

He grinned at her defensive posture. "I mean, do you have a degree in Library Science? Or do you just happen to work at the library?"

"I studied Library Information Systems, I have a bachelor's, and I'm a *real* librarian."

He opened the sliding door, and she walked through it ahead of him, carrying her glass of wine.

"Is the stereotype about librarians true?" He enjoyed watching her color rise, and his lips twitched when she set her drink down on the table and spun to face him, hands propped on her hips again.

"What stereotype?" she asked, brows furrowed. "That all librarians are high-collared, buttoned-up prudes? We all wear glasses and buns and frown and say *'shhh'* constantly?"

He set the platter down, unable to hide his smile. "Well, obviously, that's not the stereotype I was referring to."

He waited until she figured it out and saw her face flush even more. Her mouth dropped open, and he started to panic, thinking he'd overstepped—until she started laughing.

He laughed with her, but then truly *did* panic when he realized he was flirting. At least, he thought he was. *I'm not really sure.*

Charles overheard and ambled over while Jack ran around the backyard, aiming at imaginary objects with a squirt gun. "I believe he's talking about the *sexy* librarian stereotype," he teased, wiggling his eyebrows as he stepped up onto the deck. "Underneath all those buttoned-up, high-collared blouses are little tigresses waiting to break loose and extend their claws." He leaned close to Elizabeth and growled playfully.

She shoved him away and rolled her eyes. "Oh, please."

"Let me guess," he went on. "It's Mary. She's the tigress, right?"

She laughed. "Mary? No, she's more like the *other* stereotype." Her eyes widened. "Oh no, see what you're making me do?" She looked at Will. "I'm talking about a coworker I love to death. She's a wonderful person."

"You didn't say anything bad. I'm sure she's very nice," he offered, still trying to figure out if he was flirting.

"I'm going in to get changed," Charles said. "Get that grill warmed up, will ya?"

Will lit the grill and then looked at her. "I'm sorry, I–I hope I wasn't out of line. With the stereotype thing. Um, I wasn't...I was just kidding."

She smiled softly. "I know you were. I've developed a pretty thick skin, so no worries there."

He looked at her thoughtfully. *How could someone like her need a thick skin?*

The conversation he'd had at the pool with Caroline suddenly came back to him. She'd mentioned something about Elizabeth having a "nasty husband."

After a moment, she lifted one eyebrow playfully. "I feel like I'm under a microscope."

He looked away. "I'm–I'm sorry. I have a tendency to stare."

"Yes, you do."

Thankfully, she didn't seem put off by it. "I was just thinking about…well, nothing, really." He cleared his throat. "But you're very easy to stare at." His heart pounded in his chest as he said the words, and he was satisfied when he saw her blush again.

Yes, I think I'm flirting.

"Oh. Um, thank you," she answered, looking away from him.

"You're welcome." He took a deep breath and reached for the platter, suddenly feeling a bit awkward. "Time to put these on." He saw Jack refilling one of the squirt guns and called out to him. "Hey buddy, how wet are you?"

Jack stopped what he was doing and looked down at himself before answering. "A little."

"Why don't you give the squirt guns a rest for now?"

"Aw, Dad!"

"Just for a little while. I'd like you to be dry when we sit down to eat."

"'Kay," Jack agreed grudgingly. He set down the squirt gun and walked up onto the deck, taking a seat next to Elizabeth.

Will felt his son's sweatshirt. "I think you're just a little damp, it won't take your shirt long to dry. Your hair is another story," he said, rubbing his son's head playfully.

"What's that green stuff?" Jack asked, pointing to the bowl in the middle of the table.

"It's called guacamole," Elizabeth said. "I made it myself."

He wrinkled his nose. "Is it made of broccoli?"

She grinned. "No, it's made with avocados. Want to try it?"

Will lay the scallop skewers on the grill to cook while watching Jack out of the corner of his eye. He could see Jack was debating what to do, and although Will knew he was usually game for trying new foods, this particular food being green was a serious obstacle. Finally Jack took a chip, dipped it, and took a bite. The look on his face said it all.

"No?" Will asked, trying to refrain from laughing at the grimace on Jack's face and watching as he shook his head brusquely. "Napkin?" he offered, and this time he did laugh when Jack nodded, eyes wide. He very quickly took the napkin and expelled the contents of his mouth into it.

He turned to Elizabeth and shuddered. "I don't think I like it."

She smiled and handed him his drink. "Well, you tried it. That's what counts."

"Why don't you go into the house and throw that away?" Will said, pointing to the napkin. "Grab the towel on the back of one of the kitchen chairs to dry your hair a little."

"'Kay." Jack went inside, returning quickly with the towel and with Charles right behind him.

"Ahhh, smells good, my friend, smells good! Who needs another drink?"

Will glanced around. "I think I left mine in the house."

"I'll get it, I need to go in anyway." Elizabeth rose and disappeared inside.

"Dad, can I get my backpack out of the cart?" Jack asked.

"Sure, go ahead." He opened the grill cover and turned the scallops before putting on the skewers of shrimp.

"So?" Charles asked once they were alone.

Will closed the grill cover and turned to look at him. "So...what?"

"You and Lizzy seem to be getting along very well."

"Does that surprise you?"

"No, not at all." Charles paused. "You and I have had some bad shit happen to us, huh?"

Will nodded. "Other people have been through worse, but yeah, we have."

"Lizzy's had some bad shit happen to her too. She's been through a lot."

Will looked at him closely. "Is there a reason you're telling me this?"

He knew she was about to walk outside, but he wanted to know what had happened to her. That day at the pool when he'd spoken to Caroline, he'd remarked that everyone had things that linger, and he hadn't wanted to know, then, what those things were for Elizabeth— but now he wanted to know so badly he could practically taste it.

"I just think you should be aware she's been through some things, that's all." Charles's eyes were focused on Will's.

Will nodded in understanding. *Be careful, tread lightly.* "I just want to be her friend. That's all."

"I didn't say you wanted anything more, did I?" Charles raised his eyebrows. "Don't look so nervous. Just enjoy yourself. Get to know her and see where it goes."

Jack walked back into the yard just as Elizabeth came outside. She handed Will his beer, and as he took it from her, their fingers touched, and a warmth immediately flared in his hand.

"Thank you," he said, looking down at her.

She smiled up at him, her cheeks once again a lovely shade of pink. "You're welcome."

He turned back to the grill to hide his discomposure, and Charles's words came back to him.

Just enjoy yourself. Get to know her and see where it goes.

A SHORT TIME LATER, EVERYONE WAS RELAXING AFTER FINISHING OFF THE last of the appetizers. While still wary of the guacamole, Jack heartily indulged in the scallops and shrimp.

"Bacon, butter, and garlic. What more do you need?" Charles said, laughing as he watched Jack grab the last scallop.

Will lifted his empty pint glass. "Beer."

"I'll get it, I need more wine anyway," Elizabeth said, polishing off her glass.

"No, I don't want you to wait on me again. I'll get it, and I'll pour you another glass." He removed the empty platter from the center of the table and carried it and her wine glass into the house.

He set the platter on the counter, and after pouring Elizabeth's wine, he looked out the window over the sink and watched Charles and Elizabeth chat with Jack. His son had just pulled a Transformer from his backpack and was trying to show Charles how it changed from a flashy sports car into a menacing robot.

He felt more relaxed than he'd felt in a very long time. He enjoyed sitting with Elizabeth, listening to her talk and enjoying the melodic sound of her voice. She was left-handed, and since she was sitting to his right—and he was right-handed—their arms bumped occasionally. He didn't mind it, nor did he mind the floral scent he'd detected earlier drifting over to him when she turned in his direction or moved her hair a certain way. Her hair was beautiful—long and thick, a deep shade of brown with strands of lighter colors here and there. He'd leaned back in his chair at one point and observed the way the curls and waves tumbled down her back, and he'd wondered if it was as soft as it looked.

He'd sat up quickly, unprepared to let his imagination get the best of him—at least not here. His attraction to Elizabeth was growing; it would do no good to deny it, and really, did he need to? Just because he was willing to acknowledge it didn't mean he would act on it.

Shaking himself out of his reverie, he pulled two bottles of beer from the refrigerator, picked up Elizabeth's wine glass, and headed back outside. Charles was standing and talking to Caroline, who was making her way across the backyard.

"Hello, everyone," she said as she stepped onto the deck, smiling pleasantly. "I smelled something delicious and had to come over to investigate."

Everyone greeted her as she made herself comfortable at the table, and she leaned toward Jack.

"What do you have there? A robot?"

"Sorta. It's a Transformer named Bumblebee. He's my favorite in the Autobots."

"Well, I can see why. He looks very cool."

Charles went into the house to get the burgers, and when he came back out, he spoke to his sister. "You staying for dinner?"

"I'd love to, if you don't mind. Do you have any turkey burgers? Or veggie burgers?"

Charles looked at her as if she'd lost her mind. "No, I have real *beef* burgers. Pure cow. If you wanted girly food, you should have brought it with you."

She rolled her eyes. "So how did you all end up here for dinner?"

Will noted the way her eyes had settled on Elizabeth. "We were all on the ferry together this afternoon. Charles invited us over."

"I took Will to look at the site for the brewery," Charles added. "I wanted to see what he thought of the place." He placed five burgers on the grill and closed the cover.

"And?" Caroline asked, her eyes shifting to Will.

"I think it's great," he answered honestly. "Excellent location, good size, and very clean. I think a brewpub would do well there."

"That's good to hear," she responded. "Maybe it won't be a waste of our father's money after all."

"Caroline, stop. Not now," Charles warned, his voice low.

"The quality of your beer will bring the beer lovers in, that's for sure," Elizabeth offered. "I think it's going to be a huge success."

Caroline narrowed her eyes at Elizabeth. "Oh, *you* think it's going to be a huge success? Do you have your finger on the pulse of Portland?"

"No, but I know this is something Charles has always wanted," Elizabeth stated plainly, "and I know him well enough to know he'll bust his hump to make it successful."

"Thank you for that vote of confidence, Lizzy." Charles walked around the table, lifted her hand, and planted a very loud kiss on the back of it. "It's nice to know I have friends backing me up," he said pointedly before making his way back to the grill.

"You know you always have my support, Charles," Caroline went on, "but this has seemed like wishful thinking for so long. I'm just not sure you know what you're doing."

"He knows what he's doing," Will chimed in, "and I agree with

Lizzy. Um, Elizabeth." He cleared his throat. "Charles has what it takes to make it successful. He'll do just fine."

"What's a brewpub?" Jack asked.

"It's a kind of restaurant," Will answered. "Mr. Bingley is going to open one in Portland."

"Are we gonna eat there?"

"I'm sure we will."

"A pub isn't really an ideal place for a child," Caroline said offhandedly.

"Of course it is, it's going to be a *family* place," Charles told her. "I want people to come for the food and the atmosphere as much as for the beer and the *incredibly* handsome owner."

Elizabeth and Will laughed, while Caroline just rolled her eyes again. "Do you hear him?" she asked, sounding exasperated. "These are the answers I get."

"Maybe I'd answer you seriously if you actually *took* me seriously."

The humor had clearly left his voice, and Caroline shook her head before rising from the table. "I'm going to get something to drink, does anyone need anything?" Everyone answered they were all set, so she went into the house without saying another word.

Charles flipped the burgers and then turned to face the table. "Sorry about that."

Will shook his head. "No need to apologize." He was feeling a little sorry that his friend had been put on the defensive by his sister.

"I didn't realize Caroline was opposed to this," Elizabeth said.

"She isn't, really." Charles sighed. "She just...she doesn't have a lot of faith in me. Granted, I haven't exactly been overly motivated for the past few years, but things are different now. I know what I want to do. I was just waiting for the right opportunity."

"I know what you mean," Will said. "I've dealt with enough business owners starting from scratch to know a success story when I see one. You're ready for this."

Charles smiled. "Thanks, man."

Caroline came back outside with a glass of wine. "I helped myself, I hope you don't mind," she said to Charles.

"That's Lizzy's wine."

She turned to Elizabeth. "Oh, I'm sorry."

"It's fine," Elizabeth said. "I brought it for everyone. Um, I brought a salad too. I'll pull it out of the refrigerator and get some utensils and plates."

Will looked at her hopefully. "Do you need some help?"

"No, thanks. I'm all set."

She lay her hand on his shoulder as she rose, only lifting it when she moved away from the table. He felt the warmth of it long after and felt ridiculously buoyant over the intimate, familiar gesture.

"Is the burgers almost done?" Jack asked, intruding on Will's thoughts. "I'm hungry."

"Coming right up, Jack-o," Charles answered. "Do you want cheese on yours?"

"Yeah!"

"How about 'yes, please'?" Will reminded him quietly.

"Yes, please, Mr. Bingley," Jack repeated.

Elizabeth came out of the house with her hands full, and Will rose to help her. He looked down at the large bowl of salad as he took it from her hands.

"Girly food," he whispered conspiratorially, making her laugh softly.

After the plates, utensils, and rolls were passed out, Charles served the burgers and everyone sat down to eat. Caroline asked Charles more questions about the site for the pub, but it wasn't long before her attention shifted to Will.

"You must really miss New York." She smiled warmly, focusing her blue eyes on him. "Portland is just so dull and uninspired, especially during the winter. New York must be amazing! The city that never sleeps, right? I don't think you'll be half as entertained living here."

"I think I'll be just fine," he responded. "From what I've seen so far, Portland has a lot to offer." He noticed Elizabeth nodding. "Plus, there's a lot to do outside of the city. I can't wait to go camping with Jack."

"When are we gonna go?" Jack asked excitedly. "I forgot about it."

"When it gets a little warmer. Maybe in July or August."

"You have to go to Acadia," Elizabeth said, turning to Will. "It's just beautiful, and it's only about three hours north of here."

"Have you been?"

"Yes, a couple of times with Charlotte and Kate." She laughed. "We have so much fun, and we really rough it. Tents, sleeping bags, and a portable gas stove, that's it. Completely back to nature."

"How do you shower?" Caroline asked, looking mildly horrified.

"Um, we don't. We're only there for a few nights, and we swim, so..." She shrugged. "It's just us girls, so we don't worry about it. We're thinking about going back again this year."

"Do I get to skip my bath when we go?" Jack asked, obviously thrilled at the notion.

Will laughed. "It's a good possibility." He turned back to Elizabeth. "I'll have to look into it a little more."

"I have some pamphlets and a map you can borrow," she said, smiling cheekily, "but I *will* need them back."

He grinned. "Thanks. I'll see that they're returned in one piece."

Caroline cleared her throat. "How *is* Charlotte? And John, of course."

"They're both doing very well. John especially," Elizabeth answered.

Caroline smirked. "I'm sure."

"He's actually made junior partner at the law firm," Elizabeth went on. "New office, big raise... He's doing really, really well. Climbing right up that corporate ladder."

"Oh, that's wonderful," Caroline said, her smirk fading.

Will watched the interplay between the two women and sensed some tension.

Elizabeth looked around at the empty plates. "Well, I'll clear the table if everyone is finished."

"I'm full," Jack groaned, rubbing his stomach.

Charles rubbed his hands together. "Too full for round two of our battle, Jack?"

"No way, I'm ready." Jack bolted out of his seat and ran straight for the squirt guns with Charles right behind him.

Elizabeth stood. "The deck is off limits to the water battle! *No* squirting the ladies!" she called out before walking to the door and going inside.

"Yes, no squirting the ladies," Carolyn echoed. She turned to Will and smiled. "I can think of far better ways to get wet, can't you?" she asked him quietly.

"Um...I'm just...going to stick with a squirt gun," he answered, and quickly stepped off the deck.

ELIZABETH KEPT HERSELF BUSY IN THE KITCHEN, GLAD CAROLINE HADN'T offered to help. It was obvious she knew nothing of John's recent success, and Elizabeth enjoyed getting a little dig in on her friend's behalf.

She watched through the window as Will, Charles, and Jack chased each other around. Will pulled Jack aside to whisper in his ear, and not a moment later they were ganging up on Charles. The boyish laughter she could hear coming from the three of them made her chuckle.

Her awareness of Will had deepened during dinner, and she decided it was partly due to their earlier conversation. She felt as though she'd been given a clearer glimpse into who he was. Besides that, his tall, broad frame was very appealing to her...and at one point, she'd laid her hand on his shoulder.

What was I thinking when I did that?

The answer was apparent; she wasn't thinking, she was just doing.

And then he'd called her *Lizzy*. It was obvious it wasn't done on purpose; he'd stumbled and corrected himself, and it was a good thing he hadn't looked at her right then because her cheeks had surely been as pink as a grapefruit. But it had rolled off his tongue so easily, as if he'd *always* called her Lizzy—as if they knew each other well enough already.

In a way, I suppose we do. Both had been through trials and tribulations, and both had come to Maine to heal and regroup. Could she help him to do that? Could they help each other? Her friends had been such a huge support system to her when she'd moved here; could she be a support for Will?

She realized she *wanted* to be that person for him. She didn't want him to rely on Charles or, God forbid, on Caroline; she wanted him to rely on *her*. She shook her head, thinking it was completely absurd for her to feel this way—but absurd or not, it was how she felt.

After finishing up the dishes and wiping down the counter tops and stove, she made a quick trip to the bathroom and then went back outside. She was immediately caught in the line of fire between Jack and Will as they squirted each other from opposite sides of the deck, narrowly missing Caroline.

They stopped, and Will was obviously stifling his laughter as he walked onto the deck and apologized profusely. He reached for the towel hanging over the back of one of the chairs, the same one he and Jack had used, and approached her as she stood with hair and face dripping. Charles was laughing hysterically and congratulating the Darcy men on their impeccable aim, and even Caroline was snickering.

"Sorry, Ms. Bennet," Jack yelled from the lawn before turning to run after Charles.

"I'm so, so sorry," Will said through twitching lips as he handed her the towel.

She began to reach for it, but quickly grasped the squirt gun instead. It slipped from his hand easily, and she spun and moved away from him, squirting him as she stepped off the deck. He was caught off guard and could only throw up his hands to block the water as he laughed.

Charles immediately launched an attack on Elizabeth, encouraging Jack to do the same. Will ran from the deck and grabbed a new weapon, quickly filling it at the faucet. Within minutes, all four were laughing and thoroughly soaked.

AFTER A CEASE-FIRE WAS FINALLY CALLED, WILL TURNED TO LOOK AT Elizabeth and immediately appreciated the view. Her damp shirt clung to her body, accentuating her curves. He dragged his eyes away and forced himself to pay attention to Jack, who was now completely drenched.

Caroline called out from the deck. "I can't believe three grown adults—and I use the term *very* loosely—are running around and squirting each other. Maybe bathing suits would have—"

"Lighten up, Caroline." Charles shot her with a steady stream of water, laughing as she sputtered and shrieked, and followed her movements as she tried to escape the spray by darting into the house.

"I don't think Ms. Bingley wanted to get wet," Jack observed.

"I don't think she did either," Will agreed, laughing a little.

Charles grinned. "It's okay, Jack. She'll live."

Will's eyes went back to Elizabeth, and he watched as she loosely crossed her arms over her chest.

"Well, I think this may be the end of the evening for me," she said, her cheeks pinking. "It's a little too chilly to sit around in wet clothes."

"Yeah, for us too," Will echoed.

"Aw, do we have to go? I want to battle some more," Jack said.

"This is what I'll do, Jack," Charles said. "You pick out four squirt guns and take them home. That way, you and your dad can battle anytime you want. And if I'm ever at your house, or if your friend Sam comes over, you'll have enough for everyone. Sound good?"

"Yeah! Thanks, Mr. Bingley!" Jack ran over to the pile of bright plastic and began choosing which ones he wanted to take home. Charles helped him sort through them and showed him which he thought were the best.

Will approached Elizabeth as she stood on the deck, trying to dry off with the towel Will had offered to her before she stole the squirt gun out of his hands.

"Do you want a ride home?" he asked quietly.

"Oh, um… Where would I sit?"

"I'll let Jack drive, you can sit on my lap."

She looked up at him quickly, her mouth gaping in surprise until she laughed.

"It didn't work for Charles, but I thought I'd give it a try." He grinned mischievously. "Seriously, you can drive, and Jack can sit on my lap, or I can drive, and he can sit on your lap. Either way works."

She tilted her head. "Okay."

Caroline came out of the house then, a little damp and carrying a newly refilled glass of wine. "Does anyone else want anything?"

"No, thanks. We're actually going to head out," Will said. "It's getting chilly, and we're all soaked. Jack needs a bath." He looked down at himself. "I think I do too."

"Oh, I thought we could all enjoy an after-dinner drink," she whined.

"Maybe another time."

Elizabeth, Jack, and Will thanked Charles for dinner, said their goodbyes, and headed to the golf cart. Jack stopped suddenly and turned to Will. "Dad, I forgot my backpack!"

"Hurry up, go get it," Will told him. While Jack ran to the backyard, Will put the squirt guns into the back storage area and then held up the key. "Who's driving?" he asked Elizabeth.

She grinned and swiped it from his hand. "Me. You can have all the pleasure of your water-logged son sitting on your lap."

"Gee, thanks." He cleared his throat. "So, um, do you have a busy work week ahead?"

She shrugged. "It's not too bad. I have Wednesday off from the library, but I have to work at Trinity that night."

"Is that the restaurant in the old church?" he asked, trying to recall what he'd read about it.

She nodded. "It's absolutely beautiful."

"I'll have to check it out sometime. Do you work there a lot?"

Before she could answer, Jack came flying around the corner with his backpack and watched as she climbed into the driver's seat. He turned to look at his father. "You're lettin' Ms. Bennet drive?"

"Sure, why not? Climb up." Will patted his legs.

Once Jack was settled, Elizabeth maneuvered the cart down the driveway and out onto the narrow lane. The ride was mostly silent, with Jack occasionally commenting on the water battle. They all agreed it was a lot of fun but better suited for warmer weather.

Will discreetly observed Elizabeth as she drove, and he distinctly remembered how it had felt when she'd placed one hand on his shoulder tonight. Just the thought of it made his face warm, but he liked it.

And that's it, he realized. *She's making me feel things again.*

He was physically attracted to her, but there was more to it than that. The fact that he felt comfortable enough with her to share a little bit about himself was no small thing. She was quick to smile and laugh, and he enjoyed making her do both for purely selfish reasons.

And he appreciated the way she'd stood up for Charles. He hadn't known Charles for very long, but he agreed his new friend was smart and had determination in spades, and Will was confident he would be successful.

Beyond that, it was the way she interacted with Jack and the way she'd cut loose and played with them tonight. Everything about her seemed to draw him in, and right now it all felt good. She made *him* feel good, and although he had no idea what these feelings would lead to or whether they would lead to anything at all, he had no desire to fight them.

WILL HAD BEEN QUIET FOR MOST OF THE RIDE, BUT ELIZABETH HAD COME to realize he just wasn't much of a talker at times. They arrived at the Gardiners' home, and he glanced around when she pulled into the driveway.

"Where's your house?" he asked as they climbed from the cart.

"Oh, it's back there. See the footpath?" It was still light out, but her home was hidden from view. "It leads back to my ridiculously huge house."

Will raised an eyebrow. "Huge?" They both walked around to the front of the cart.

She laughed. "I'm kidding. It's only *slightly* bigger than the Batmobile. I love it though. It's cozy." He smiled but remained silent. "So, um, I have Wednesday off, like I said. I was wondering if maybe you and Jack would like to go to the pool? Or to the beach?" She ignored the flutter in her stomach.

"Yeah, can we, Dad? I wanna go to the beach," Jack chimed in from the front seat of the cart.

"Sure, that sounds great," Will answered. "Um, I can swing by and pick you up if you want. If you don't want to walk. If it's...if it's too far to walk. I don't know which beach, or–or where they are, or..." He looked away from her and took a deep breath before offering her a sheepish grin. "Would you like me to pick you up, Elizabeth?"

She laughed lightly. "That would be perfect. How about eleven?"

"Eleven is fine. I'll see you then."

Her stomach bottomed out when he smiled, showing his dimples, and she felt her face flush as she continued to stare up at him. "Great, I'll see you then. Um, both of you." She turned to Jack. "Good night, Jack."

"Bye, Ms. Bennet. See ya later."

She looked back up at Will. "Good night. Thanks for the ride home."

"You're welcome," he answered softly. "Good night, Elizabeth."

She watched as he climbed back into the golf cart and drove away.

Wednesday can't come soon enough.

Eight

E lizabeth was in a pleasant haze when she walked into her house. She'd enjoyed herself tonight, especially the time she'd spent talking with Will, and even now, she still had a ridiculous grin plastered to her lips.

Her cell phone rang, pulling her from her thoughts, and she smiled when she saw who it was.

"Hey, Jane!"

"Oh, I could kill him, Lizzy. I could kill him! That lying, cheating son of a bitch!"

The pleasant haze evaporated. "Oh no. What happened?"

"Stuart didn't have to go to the hospital last night, it was a total lie. All of it! Being distracted because of work, the talk of a layoff...not a word of it was true! He confessed everything, he said he couldn't take it anymore and didn't want to hurt me or–or *her* anymore."

"Her who? Who is her?"

"His ex-wife! Can you believe it? They've been divorced for six years. *Six years!* How can you go back to someone after being divorced from them for *six years*?"

"Is he really getting back together with her?"

"Yes," Jane answered, sounding calmer now. "They're reuniting. He said they ran into each other and ended up having coffee. He's been seeing her for two months, and I had no idea. They were married young, and it didn't work out, but now..." She sighed, all traces of anger gone. "Now they want to make it work. He said he's *always* loved her, even when they weren't together. He's always thought about her but was afraid to reach out." She groaned. "He said she's his soul mate."

"Ohhh," Elizabeth responded, cringing a little.

"Yeah. Ohhh."

"What did you say to him?"

"I wished him the best and said goodbye. What else could I say? What do you say to a guy you've been dating who says he's found his soul mate, and it isn't you?"

"So...are you upset? I mean, I can tell you're angry, but are you broken-hearted? Or just mad that he was cheating?"

"I'm upset he was cheating, of course, but I think I'm madder at myself for not figuring it out sooner."

"He was really good at hiding it."

"He was good at *lying*. Too good." Jane paused. "I wonder if she knows about me."

"You're not going to do something crazy like find her and tell her, are you?"

"No, I wouldn't do that. I'm done with him. I just wonder if she knows, if he was honest with her as well." Jane took a deep breath. "It really doesn't matter now, I guess."

"You're right, it doesn't. And I know just what you need to forget about him."

"I can only imagine."

"Come visit me," Elizabeth suggested. "We'll go out and have some fun."

"You know what? I think I will. School is out on Thursday. How about if I come on Friday?"

"That's perfect! Only...I have to work at the library on Saturday." Elizabeth thought for a moment. "Maybe I can get Mary to switch weekends with me. I'll talk to her tomorrow."

"That would be great. How long can I stay?"

"As long as you want."

Jane chuckled. "Maybe I'll find a nice young man to take my mind off of Stuart."

"If you're thinking like that, I'd say your mind was already off of him."

"Yeah, I guess it is. I'm fine, I really am. I'm just embarrassed."

"Well I'm glad you're not sobbing into the phone."

"Nope, no sobbing."

"Good." Elizabeth paused. "So guess who showed up after you left Mom and Dad's last night?"

"Who?"

"George."

"*What?* What did he want?"

Elizabeth told Jane about George's brief visit and went on to tell her about her conversation with Lydia as well.

"Do you think I should be worried about Lydia talking to him? She says it's usually just polite conversation, but I don't know. I don't trust him, and I would hate to see Lydia get fooled by him. He can turn on the charm."

"She's a smart girl," Jane responded. "Hopefully she'll ignore him or leave it at being civil, and that's it."

Elizabeth sighed. "I hope so." Will popped into her head then, and she almost told Jane about him, but wasn't quite sure what to say. She decided to keep mum, figuring Jane would have the opportunity to meet him when she came to visit.

"Well, I'm going to run," Jane said. "I'm going to the gym before it closes. I need a good long workout. We'll talk this week once you've figured out your schedule."

"Sounds good. Keep your chin up, Jane."

"Oh, it's up. Thanks for letting me vent."

"Anytime. Love you, sis."

"Love you too, Lizzy. Bye."

Elizabeth's thoughts soon returned to Will, and she realized she'd wanted to do more than talk about him with Jane; she'd wanted to *gush* about him.

I like him. Probably more than I ought to at this point.

She swallowed nervously, unsettled by the way her stomach fluttered at just the *thought* of liking him. But she didn't think he was completely immune to her, either; she heard the way he tripped over his words and noticed the way he stared at her, and how he sometimes looked as though he didn't know what to do with himself when he was near her.

She couldn't help but wonder… *Is he thinking of me too?*

~

AFTER SHOWERS AND BATHS WERE TAKEN, WILL AND JACK SAT DOWN ON
the couch to watch television before bed.

"Can we watch a movie?" Jack asked.

Will glanced at his watch. "It's almost eight, are you sure you can
stay awake?"

"Yeah, I can. Can we watch *The Lion King* again?"

"Sure." Will was doubtful Jack would stay awake for the whole
movie, and within thirty minutes of starting it, Jack was out cold. Will
slowly lifted him and carried him up to his room, and he woke when
Will lay him in bed.

"Dad, the movie isn't done yet," he mumbled, half asleep.

"I think it's done for you. You can watch it tomorrow night, okay?"

"'Kay. Night, Dad."

Will bent to kiss his forehead. "Good night. Sweet dreams."

He went back downstairs and grabbed his cellphone, then walked
out onto the deck and settled himself into a chair, staring out into the
pitch black night.

His mind was full of Elizabeth and had been since he dropped her
off, the image of her smiling face and the sound of her laughter
dancing through his mind. He was already looking forward to
Wednesday, though it seemed ages away. He was hoping to run into
her again before that.

With another sigh, he pushed all thoughts of the pretty brunette
from his head and called Georgiana. She answered on the third ring.

"Hi, Will!"

He smiled. "Hey, G, what's up?"

"Not much. I just got home. I went to a matinee with some friends,
and then we went to dinner."

"What'd you see?"

They talked for a while about the movie, her friends, and what her
plans were for the summer. She asked about Jack, the island, the
people, and what he'd been doing to keep busy.

He told her about Charles: how he'd immediately felt at ease with
him, and told her about Charles's plans to open a brewpub and what

had happened to his parents. He mentioned Elizabeth too, only saying he'd had dinner with her and Charles and Charles's sister.

Georgiana laughed when he mentioned the squirt gun battle. "You sound so relaxed," she noted quietly. "And happy."

"I am. It's nice here. The whole vibe is so laid-back. And it's not just the island, Portland is the same way. It's a great little city with its own pace."

"Sounds perfect. What does Jack think?"

"He loves it. He hasn't mentioned New York at all. Not once."

"Wow," she replied softly.

"I don't mean you, Auntie G," he told her, detecting the sadness in her voice. "He talks about you and Alice a lot. He already asked when you're coming to visit, so I know he misses you. He just doesn't miss the city."

"What about his Grampa?"

"He hasn't talked about him at all."

"Has Dad called you? Have you called him?"

"No and no."

"You Darcy men are ridiculously stubborn, do you know that?"

"Don't put me in the same category as our father, Georgie. We are completely different, you know that better than anyone."

"In some ways you're just like him, whether you think so or not. Why don't you just call him?"

"Why? So he can berate me and make me feel guilty about removing the Darcy heir from his proper home?" He felt his annoyance growing. "No way."

"He misses Jack."

"If he misses Jack, he should call him. Dad is the only grandparent Jack has ever really known, and despite everything, I've *never* told him he can't speak to his grandson or have a relationship with him. What I won't let him do is control our lives. That's what he was trying to do, and that's why I left." He paused and took a deep breath, lowering his voice. "He had my mind so twisted up, I didn't know what the hell I was doing. He hasn't called because he knows he was wrong. He screwed up, and he knows he'll have to own up to it. It's as simple as that."

"That's not true," she replied, her voice rising. "He hasn't called because..." She sighed. "I don't know why he hasn't called."

"He doesn't want to admit he brought all this on himself, *that's* why. If there's one thing I've learned about Dad, it's that he's an expert at living in denial. I know it's hard for you to see it, but you have a different relationship with him. Hopefully you'll never know what it's like to make a decision he doesn't like or, God forbid, fall in love with someone he doesn't approve of. *That's* when his true colors come out, and *that's* when he throws around his ultimatums."

He took a deep breath, once again trying to calm down. The last thing he wanted was to upset his sister, though he had a feeling it was probably too late to worry about that.

"I just hate that things are this way between the two of you. Have you talked to Richard?"

"No, not in a while." He didn't want to think about his father *or* his cousin, and the many ways they'd betrayed him and interfered in his life. "I don't want to deal with that stuff, not right now. I need to get settled and be present for Jack. I couldn't do that in New York. Richard and Dad and I will get things straightened out eventually." *Maybe.* "Right now, I just need to breathe a little and focus on my son."

"I just miss you, Will. I wish everything was okay *now*," she said, her voice soft.

"I'm sure it won't be like this forever. And I miss you too." It had been the two of them for so long. They'd stayed close, even after he married Anne, and leaving New York made him feel as if he were abandoning her.

"When can I come to visit?" she asked.

"Whenever you want, as often as you like. You don't need an invitation, the door is always open. Just call and tell me you're on your way."

"How about this Saturday?"

"Seriously?"

"Yes. I want to check out this island."

"I would love it, and Jack will flip, you know he will. Please come." He was grinning now, his mood completely altered.

"Alright, it's settled."

"Stay as long as you want, okay?"

She laughed. "Watch what you say. I may never leave."

"I wouldn't complain, and neither would your nephew."

"Sure, that's what you say now. Alright, Saturday it is. I'll check out flights and call you tomorrow night, okay?"

"Okay, I'll talk to you then. Bye, Georgie. Love you."

"Love you too. Bye."

He stayed on the deck a bit longer, his heart still beating heavily in his chest. How could he make Georgie or anyone else understand how it felt to be around Robert Darcy, to lose control of his own life and that of his son's?

It was like drowning or being smothered. Suffocated.

Yes, Jack was the Darcy heir, but always, first and foremost, Jack was his son.

My son.

THE LIBRARY WAS USUALLY BUSY ON MONDAYS, AND ELIZABETH WAS thankful for it. Charlotte stopped by, and they went to a nearby café for a quick lunch. She wanted to hear all about Lydia's graduation party, but there really wasn't much to say, especially since Elizabeth had already decided not to tell her about George's sudden appearance. She knew Charlotte would be concerned and would have a million questions, and honestly, Elizabeth didn't want to talk about him anymore.

Charlotte had become her closest friend and was the only person in Portland—besides Maddie—who knew every sordid detail about Elizabeth's past. The day that Kate had introduced them, Elizabeth was fairly sure she'd embarrassed herself by unabashedly gawking. Charlotte was tall and stunning, her beautiful chestnut-colored skin accented by a pair of deep green eyes; but it was her long, jet-black braids streaked with blonde and the bright, colorful tattoos that adorned her arms and shoulders that had commanded Elizabeth's attention. She soon learned that Charlotte was the owner of a tattoo shop in Portland and was widely considered the best tattoo artist in the city. She'd noticed Elizabeth staring and had assured her she was quite used to it. They'd hit it off immediately—although Charlotte *still* hadn't been able to persuade Elizabeth to get a tattoo.

Kate and Mary only knew that Elizabeth had been married, it hadn't been pleasant, and she was now happily divorced. It's not that she didn't trust them enough to confide in them; she just didn't feel the need to show off the skeletons in her closet to everyone she knew.

Charles knew only slightly more than Kate and Mary. As they'd become closer, she shared some things with him just as he'd shared things with her about the loss of his parents. He didn't know every last detail about Elizabeth's life, but he knew she'd been married to a controlling and abusive man who was now in jail.

Smiling, she remembered what Charles's final words had been on the subject of her marriage: *"He was a real prick, Lizzy, but not all guys are pricks. Some of us are pretty cool."*

"So nothing exciting happened?" Charlotte asked her now. "No one went streaking across the stage? No one got hammered and threw up in your father's rose bushes?"

Elizabeth laughed. "No, nothing like that happened."

"Did your mother drive you nuts?"

"She wasn't bad. I think she and my Dad are finally beginning to realize I'm not moving back to Lexington."

"Wow! It only took them two years to figure it out."

"We Bennets are quick," Elizabeth replied, and they both laughed. "Oh, guess who I had the pleasure of dining with last night?"

"Who?"

"Caroline."

"Ugh, really?" Charlotte answered with a sneer. "You actually shared a meal with her?"

"Not by choice. She just kind of…showed up."

"Where were you?"

"At Charles's house, having dinner with him, Will Darcy, and Will's son."

"Mr. Stick-Up-His-Ass Darcy?"

Elizabeth giggled. "Yes, but he doesn't have a stick up his ass. He's just quiet."

"How did you end up having dinner with them?"

Elizabeth recounted how she bumped into Charles and Will while waiting for the ferry Sunday afternoon.

"So you *must* know if he's single or not by now."

"He's single."

"Ha! I bet you fifty bucks Caroline will try to sink her claws into him. Does he have money? That would be a huge factor."

"Well, he's not working at the moment."

"Oh, he's unemployed?" Charlotte stuck her nose in the air playfully. "That won't sit well with her, unless he's independently wealthy." She stared at Elizabeth.

"What are you looking at me for? I have no idea if he's wealthy or not." Elizabeth thought about the house he'd purchased and how much it had been listed for. "It doesn't matter. He's a nice guy."

"Is he divorced? Is there an evil ex-wife looming somewhere?"

"He's actually a widower."

Charlotte frowned. "Really? Do you know what happened?"

Elizabeth shrugged. "I have no idea. Charles might know, but I don't want to ask him." She glared at Charlotte. "Why are you grilling me?"

Charlotte took a sip of her water and grinned mischievously. "Because the entire time you've been talking about him, you've been turning pink."

Elizabeth clapped her hands to her cheeks. "I have not!"

"Yes, you have. So when are you going to see this *quiet* guy again? And by the way, it's always the quiet ones you have to watch out for. You know that, right?"

"I *didn't* know that, and I don't *need* to know that, and I'm going to see him Wednesday," Elizabeth said in a rush of words. "We're going to the beach."

"Just the two of you?"

"No, of course not. Jack will be with us."

"But no other *adult* people?"

"You mean like chaperones?" Elizabeth flinched when Charlotte slapped her arm. "No, no other adults. Just us."

Charlotte slowly chewed and swallowed before speaking again. "So...do you like him?"

Now Elizabeth could *feel* her face turning pink, and she could tell from the look on Charlotte's face that she noticed it too.

"I do. I mean, not like how *you* mean. He's–he's nice. Like I said, he doesn't say much, but he's sweet, and he has a good sense of humor." Her mind traveled back to the previous night. "He has a gorgeous smile and these amazing dimples..." Her voice trailed off, and she realized too late that she'd said more than she should have.

"So Mr. Stick-Up-His-Ass has now officially become Mr. Dimples? Mr. *Amazing* Dimples?" Charlotte laughed when Elizabeth stuck out her tongue, but then grew serious. "Really, Lizzy, I'm glad you like him." She shrugged. "You never know what can happen, right?"

WILL BOARDED THE FERRY WITH JACK ON TUESDAY MORNING AND immediately began scanning the seats for Elizabeth, remembering she'd been on this same trip last Tuesday.

It seemed more crowded than usual, but he spotted her sitting inside at a table. She looked every inch the professional in a light gray skirt and lavender blouse. Her hair was down, falling in waves around her face as she studied some papers laid out in front of her.

"Hi, Ms. Bennet," Jack said as they got closer.

She looked up. "Oh, hi, Jack!" Her eyes moved to Will, and her smile grew. "Hi, Will."

He grinned, pleased with his stroke of luck. "Good morning."

She gestured to the empty seats at the table. "Do you want to join me?"

Will glanced at the papers in front of her and could clearly see they were work-related. "You look busy. We don't want to bother you."

She shook her head. "I'd love the excuse to avoid this stuff, believe me. We have meetings on the second Tuesday of every month, and usually Mary and I alternate. This would have been her Tuesday, but we made a schedule swap, so I got stuck with the meeting."

"Lucky you," Will responded as he and Jack sat down.

"Where are you off to today?" she asked, smiling at Jack expectantly.

"Um, we're goin' to get food, and then we're goin'…" He frowned and looked at his father. "Where are we goin' again?"

"I'm not sure. Maybe the museum again, though I don't want to ruin that with overkill. We might head out to Fort Williams."

"Oh, I love it out there," she told them. "It's in Cape Elizabeth, did you know that?"

"I do. Must be a lovely town." He chuckled a little when she blushed.

"Goddard Mansion is there. It's basically a ruin, but you can walk around and look inside. There are lots of trails too. It's one of my favorite places to go when I want to get out of Portland and into the woods. The lighthouse there is just beautiful." She glanced out one of the ferry windows. "It will probably be crowded today, with the weather so perfect."

Will watched her as she talked, becoming more and more mesmerized as she went on enthusiastically.

"Can we climb up in the lighthouse?" Jack asked.

"No, but there's a museum. They have a lot of really cool things."

"You should come with us!" Jack turned to look at his father. "Can Ms. Bennet come?"

Will smiled, staring at her intently. "Sure. If she wants to play hooky, she's welcome to come along." He held her gaze steadily and waited for her to look away, but she didn't.

"I wish I could," she said quietly. "I'd like nothing better. However, I *do* have a responsibility to my job, so I have to go to work."

"Maybe you can go with us another day," Jack said.

"Good idea," Will chimed in, before she could answer for herself. She smiled at him but didn't say anything, and he felt himself blush. "I mean, if you want to."

"I would enjoy that."

He cleared his throat. "So, you mentioned your sister's graduation went well?"

They spoke a little about the graduation ceremony, and when she mentioned Jane's upcoming visit and how much she was looking forward to it, he began to say something about Georgiana but stopped himself. She looked at him curiously, and he shot a sidelong glance at Jack.

She changed the subject, asking him more questions about Charles's pub, and he filled her in on some of the details. Jack rose from the table and walked over to one of the open ferry windows, pushing his face out into the morning sunshine.

"Were you going to say something to me before about your sister?" Elizabeth asked quietly.

Will smiled and nodded. "She's coming to visit on Saturday, but Jack doesn't know. Georgiana wants to surprise him."

"Oh, that's great! How long is she staying?"

He shrugged. "I have no idea. I think she's coming to check up on me." He turned to watch Jack again.

She followed his eyes. "Sisters are good for that. Jane does it all the time." They were quiet for a moment. "You know, he doesn't have to call me Ms. Bennet unless you really want him to. I don't mind if he calls me by my first name."

He turned to her. "It's fine with me if you're comfortable with it."

"Most of the kids who come to the library call me Ms. Elizabeth, but Elizabeth is fine."

He stared at her. "Charles calls you Lizzy."

She arched an eyebrow. "I believe you did too, just the other day," she teased.

"Yeah…that was a little slip."

"It's fine, I like it. Most of my friends call me Lizzy."

"Lizzy suits you, I think." He smiled softly, unable to pull his eyes from hers. "I like it too."

Will was busy packing a cooler for the beach on Wednesday morning when his phone rang. He hesitated when he saw it was his father, unsure if he should answer. After another two rings, he did, but only because he'd told Georgie he would let his father talk to Jack whenever he wanted. *Maybe that's why he's calling.*

Taking a deep breath, he picked up the phone and said hello.

"Hello, Fitzwilliam," Robert Darcy responded quietly. "How are you, son? How's Jack?"

"We're both fine." Will's guard lowered slightly when he heard the hesitancy in his father's voice.

"That's good, I'm glad to hear it. You've gotten settled in alright?"

"Mm-hmm, just fine."

"How does Jack like his new home?"

"He loves it." The subject of their conversation wandered into the kitchen, so Will went out to the deck and closed the door behind him. "I don't think he misses New York at all." He leaned against the railing. "I don't miss it either."

"I'm sure you don't." His father sighed loudly. "Listen, I just wanted to let you know you've proven your point. You're your own man, I see that now. You don't have to go running off to show me you're capable of controlling your life."

"You see that I'm my own man *now?*" Will repeated incredulously. "Gee, thanks, Dad." He felt a spike of annoyance but remained calm. "And is that what you think I've done? Run off? Do you think this is some kind of temper tantrum? This move wasn't something I spent five minutes thinking about despite what you believe. It's not me stomping my foot and pouting."

"It certainly appears that way."

"I don't care how it *appears*," Will said angrily. "Unlike you, I couldn't care less about appearances. And that drives you crazy, doesn't it?"

"Don't try to get a rise out of me, Fitzwilliam. It won't work. And as much as I'm enjoying this conversation," Robert said with quiet sarcasm, "I'd like to end it and talk to my grandson. If I'm allowed, that is."

"I've never said you couldn't talk to him, you know that as well as I do." Will paused and shook his head, trying to rein in his anger. "I'm sure he'd like to say hello."

He walked back into the house and found Jack sitting on the living room floor in his bathing suit and a T-shirt, playing with his Transformers.

"Hey Jack, Grampa's on the phone. Do you want to say hi?"

Jack nodded. "Okay."

Will handed him the phone and stepped to the back of the room. He could only hear one side of the conversation, but knew what they were talking about by Jack's answers.

His mind wandered to Elizabeth when he saw it was nearing eleven. He realized he was going to be late and lamented the fact he'd never asked for her phone number. His attention snapped back to Jack when he heard her name.

"Her name is 'Lizabeth, she's really nice," Jack said. There was a brief pause, then he giggled a little and looked at Will with wide eyes. "Nope."

Will walked over to Jack and held out his hand. "Say goodbye to Grampa."

"I gotta go, Grampa. Bye." He handed the phone to Will.

"Why don't you put on your sandals so we can leave, okay? And maybe one last trip to the bathroom?"

"Okay."

"I have to get going," Will said to his father after Jack left the living room.

"Yes, I heard you're going to the beach with *Elizabeth* today. A new friend?"

Will closed his eyes. "Yes. And if you're going to dig for information, at least have the decency to ask me and not your grandson."

"What does she do for a living? Or does she just latch onto rich men?"

Will felt an immediate rush of anger and bit back the four-letter word on the tip of his tongue.

"She's a stripper."

He felt a surge of satisfaction at the heavy silence on the other end of the line even though he knew it was childish.

"Don't toy with me, Fitzwilliam."

"Maybe I'm not."

"You would never lower yourself."

"According to you, I did that when I married Anne," Will reminded him. "What makes you think I wouldn't do it again?"

"I just want to make sure you're not doing anything that will cause you pain or embarrassment."

"No, you want to make sure I'm not doing anything that will cause *you* pain or embarrassment. Don't worry, Dad, Elizabeth is a fine, upstanding librarian. Is that better?" He gave another short laugh. "I don't even know why I'm telling you, it's really none of your business how I spend my time and who I spend it with."

His father's voice was somber. "You've certainly made that clear." He paused for a moment. "Well, have fun at the beach. And enjoy Georgiana's visit."

"I'm sure we'll have a great time. We miss her."

"She misses you too. We all do," his father said.

A tense, uncomfortable silence fell until Will spoke again.

"Like I said, I need to get going. Goodbye, Dad." He heard his father's heavy sigh.

"Goodbye, Fitzwilliam."

As Will drove to Elizabeth's house, he was preoccupied by the conversation with his father and what had followed. Jack had been antsy and impatient to leave, and Will had snapped at him—something he never did. It brought tears to Jack's eyes and made Will feel lousy. To top it off, he was running late and had no way of contacting Elizabeth.

He'd knelt down on the floor and apologized to Jack, explaining he was upset about something else and had wrongly taken it out on him. Will almost felt like crying himself when Jack wrapped his arms around his neck, hugged him, and told him it was okay. Will was so choked up from both the stress of the phone call and the words of forgiveness spoken so easily by his son, he was unable to respond. He just hugged Jack tighter and waited for the emotions to loosen their grip.

He shook his head when he glanced at his watch and saw it was almost eleven-twenty. *I should have called Charles or Maddie and asked for*

Elizabeth's number. He turned into the Gardiners' driveway and not seeing her there, he parked the cart.

"Don't touch anything," he instructed Jack. "I'll be back in a minute."

Following the walkway, he went into the backyard and was astonished by the sight of the small yellow cottage tucked toward the back of the property. It truly looked like something out of a fairy tale; flowers surrounded it, and its bright, sunny color lent to its fanciful appearance, as did the section of it that resembled a miniature lighthouse.

He knocked at the screen door and was relieved when she answered right away.

"Good morning," she said brightly, beaming at him.

Her grin was contagious, and he instantly felt some of the morning's stress melt away.

"Good morning. I'm sorry I'm late, it was…it was unavoidable. I got tied up on the phone with my father, and then I realized I had no way to get in touch with you, and then I thought I should have called Charles or Maddie to get your number, but by then—"

"Will, it's fine," she said, and reached out to place her hand on his arm. "Forget it. Things happen."

He breathed an audible sigh of relief, and she looked at him with surprise.

"Did you really think I would be upset?" They stepped outside, and she locked the door behind them.

He shrugged. "I don't know. I hate being late for things, especially important things." He picked up the beach chair and a small cooler she'd placed on her porch, and she lifted a brightly colored beach bag and slung it over her shoulder. They headed down the path toward the driveway.

"A day at the beach isn't *that* important," she said teasingly, eliciting a grin from him as they walked.

"It is to me."

She stopped them in the middle of the path and turned to him with an outstretched hand. "Where's your phone?"

He set the chair and cooler on the ground and reached into the pocket of his swimsuit, then handed his phone to her. He watched as she examined it closely, brows furrowed, and after pressing a few buttons, she smiled and handed it back to him. He immediately went to the E's in his contact list but found nothing.

"I don't see your name," he said, slightly puzzled.

She grinned and started walking again, leaving him to follow her. "It's under L."

He chuckled and quickly caught up to her. They rounded the corner of the Gardiners' house in time to see the golf cart moving swiftly backwards, a terrified-looking Jack behind the wheel.

"Dammit." Will dropped the chair and cooler and sprinted the short distance to the cart. He was able to stick one leg in and apply the brakes, bringing it to a jarring halt. "What happened?"

"I–I was just playin' with the wheel, turnin' it and stuff, an'–an' movin' the–the shifter thingy," Jack answered with wide eyes. "It started movin' an' I didn't know how to make it stop."

"Didn't I tell you not to touch anything?" Will asked calmly, refusing to lose his temper again.

"Yeah."

"Why didn't you listen to me? You could have driven into the Gardiners' carport and caused a lot of damage and gotten hurt." He spoke firmly but quietly. "When I tell you not to touch something, it means *don't touch it*. Okay?" He nudged Jack over into the passenger's seat and drove the cart back into the driveway.

"Okay. I'm sorry, Dad."

Will sighed and squeezed Jack's shoulder before walking over to Elizabeth, who'd hung back a bit. "Sorry about that." He picked up the things he'd hastily set down and stored them in the back of the cart with her beach bag.

Elizabeth turned to Jack. "Good morning, Jack."

"Hi, 'Lizabeth," he answered, slightly subdued. "Are you gonna drive today?"

"I think your dad should since he needs to learn the way to the beach. Unless you would rather sit on his lap instead of mine?"

Jack shrugged, still frowning. "I can sit on your lap."

They all climbed in, and once Jack was settled comfortably, Will headed out onto the lane.

"So where are we going?" Will asked, glancing at Elizabeth. She looked pretty in a pair of white shorts and a short-sleeved pink top, her hair pulled back into a ponytail. Unfortunately he couldn't see her eyes; she wore a pair of large sunglasses that completely obscured them from view.

"I thought we'd go a little out of the way, if you don't mind. Indian Cove Beach is on the northwestern part of the island. It's scenic, and there's good protection from the wind."

"Great. Um, I packed some food for us." He'd been so out of sorts from his father's phone call and from snapping at Jack, he'd nearly left the house without the cooler.

"I packed a few things too. We'll have a feast."

As they drove along, she told them a little bit more about the history of the area. It was a good ten minutes before they arrived at the beach, and as soon as they parked, Jack leapt from Elizabeth's lap and ran for the sand.

"Hey, hold on a second. You have some stuff to carry," Will called out to him. Jack abruptly stopped and came running back. "Here's your bucket, your backpack, your towel, and your chair."

Jack juggled everything and still managed to run to the sand. Elizabeth laughed as she watched him go.

"The beach is a novelty," Will explained. "He's never been."

"Never?"

He thought for a moment. "Well, that's not exactly true. He went when he was about a year old. We were on Cape Cod." He turned to her. "Sort of near your old stomping grounds."

She nodded. "I spent some time on the Cape when I was younger. We rented a house there for a week every summer. It's a beautiful place, isn't it?"

"It is, from what I can remember. I've only been the one time. Jack has seen pictures of it, but I suppose it doesn't compare to having actual memories of it." He pulled everything else they'd brought from the back of the cart, and between the two of them, they managed to carry it all onto the sand. "Where should we sit? Do you think we'll be able to find a spot?" He looked around with a frown on his face. "It might be tight."

She laughed. "I don't know. How about over there?" She pointed to a spot directly in the center of the beach.

He smiled, and they walked to the spot she'd pointed out, in the middle of what was actually an empty beach. The rocky walls of the cove were dark, almost black, contrasting starkly against the bright blue-green of the water.

"I can't believe no one else is here," he said, gazing at the picturesque scenery. "It's beautiful." Jack was already wading in the water and kicking up the spray.

"I bet the pool is packed," she replied. "It's still a bit chilly for the beach, but even when it's hot, this one doesn't get very crowded. It's kind of out of the way. Most people like to go to Diamond Cove Beach; it's closer to the store and the docks." She shrugged as she looked out at the sea. "I like the scenery here better."

Will watched her as she took in their surroundings. His gaze traveled from her face to her neck and then to her shoulder, where he could see the strap of her bathing suit peeking out from under the wide neck of her shirt.

He realized, then, that she'd completely erased his father from his mind. She was like a balm, wiping away his anger and stress as swiftly as his father had brought it on.

Without thinking, he reached up and lightly took hold of a lock of her hair that had come loose from her ponytail and was lifting in the breeze, and he gently wrapped it around his finger. "I like the scenery here too."

Nine

E lizabeth turned her head slightly. "Wh–what are you doing?" She faced him fully and her eyes latched onto his.

"I–I'm not sure." He played with that one lock of hair for another moment before releasing it and dropping his hand. "I shouldn't have done that, I'm sorry." He pulled his eyes from hers and let out a ragged sigh.

"No, it's–it's okay," she said softly.

His eyes flew to hers again, and it seemed a dozen thoughts went through his mind in the space of a heartbeat. He wanted to do more than touch her hair—he wanted to run his fingertips along the curve of her cheek to feel the softness of her skin. He wanted to press his mouth to hers, curious if her lips were as soft and lush as they appeared.

He swallowed roughly, knowing his desire was about more than the tactile and physical. He wanted to make her laugh, just to see her eyes sparkle again. He wanted to talk to her, confide in her, share himself with her, and he wanted her to do the same with him. He wanted to know all there was to know about Elizabeth Bennet.

It hit him so swiftly and with such magnitude that he couldn't speak. Instead he pulled his eyes away from hers again and anxiously dug the toes of one foot into the sand. He focused on Jack and watched as he ran up and down the shoreline chasing seagulls.

She reached out and placed a hand atop one of his, her touch light. "What's going on in there?"

He sighed and threaded their fingers together, unable to speak. His grip tightened slightly and she returned the pressure, sending an unexpected but welcome surge of warmth through his body.

His eyes went back to hers, and she smiled. "Should we sit? We can set up the chairs and put out the blanket."

He nodded and reluctantly released her hand. They placed their chairs side by side, and then Will set up Jack's chair while Elizabeth spread out the blanket. When everything was arranged, they sat down and silently absorbed the sunshine and scenery.

Jack came sprinting back to them with a wide smile. "The water's cold!" he called out excitedly, focusing on his father. "Are you gonna swim?"

Will grimaced. "Can I see *how* cold it is first?"

"Yeah. I wanna make roads for my trucks, can you help me?"

"Sure, I'll be down in a minute. Go ahead and get started without me."

"'Kay." Jack dug into his backpack, gathering several trucks and a plastic shovel into his arms before heading down to the water's edge. Will watched as his son chased another seagull before dropping to his knees in the sand to start digging.

When he turned back to Elizabeth, he noticed her eyes were fixed on him.

"You stare too," he said quietly.

"I'm an observer."

"Is that what you call it?" He smiled when she nodded and then cleared his throat. "So tell me how you met Maddie. You seem close."

"We are. When I moved here a couple of years ago, I contacted the real estate agency Maddie works for because I was staying in a motel and needed a place to live. She became my agent, and I guess our friendship grew from there." She grinned. "I think she began to feel a little protective of me. She would take me to apartments in different parts of the city, but then she would say, 'Oh, you can't live here, this isn't the right place for you.'"

She laughed lightly. "She brought me over to the island one day to show me the cottage. I fell in love with it immediately, and *then* I found out she and Ed owned it. Now I consider her one of my very best friends. Ed, too."

"Why didn't she just show you the cottage to begin with?"

"She wasn't sure I would be happy living on the island. Once she got to know me a little better, she changed her mind." She arched an eyebrow at him. "And now I have a question for *you*. How is it that you bought a house without even seeing it? I mean, except in pictures."

"They were really, *really* good pictures," he answered and smiled when she laughed. "Maddie was so sincere about the condition of the house and how well it had been taken care of. She didn't sound like someone who was just out to make a buck." He shrugged. "I fell in love with it. The style, the view…" He grinned. "The wine cellar."

"That wine cellar is pretty famous in these parts, though I've never seen it myself. It's kind of legendary."

"You're more than welcome to come over and check it out, though right now it's completely empty. I have yet to buy a single bottle." He sighed dramatically and frowned. "It's kind of pathetic."

She laughed. "Yes, it is. You have to go to Casco Wine—"

"—and Cigar, I know. Maddie told me all about it. I'll get there at some point."

"You must really love wine if the cellar was a selling point."

"That, and the home office, which"—he laughed a little—"I won't be using much, since I don't have a job. I *do* like wine, although it was my…it was Jack's mom who was the real wine lover."

"I love it too, but I know absolutely nothing about it. I usually pick bottles with pretty labels."

He chuckled. "You're not alone. I found out during a wine tasting that's how most people pick their wines. If the label is pretty or the name is clever and the price is right, they'll buy it. Maybe I'll swing by that store on Friday and pick up a few bottles."

"You should. A few bottles a week, and before you know it, you'll have a stocked wine cellar. What about your sister, does she like it?"

"She's only nineteen. Well, almost twenty. Still not legal though."

"Is she your only sibling?"

"Yes. She's eleven years younger, but we're close. She was a surprise for my parents. My mother was told she couldn't have any more children after me."

"Wow. I suppose it was a good surprise though."

"I'm sure it was," he answered vaguely. "So, um, what made you decide to be a librarian? I'm curious because you're the only one I know personally."

"Are you making fun of my career choice?"

He laughed and held his hands up. "Not at all. I think it's great you're a librarian. It's an admirable profession, and it must be very… exciting." He laughed again and leaned away from her when she narrowed her eyes at him. "Seriously, I think it's great. Obviously you enjoy books."

"I'm an avid reader, but that's not the only reason I chose to go into that *admirable* profession." She rolled her eyes. "When I was growing up, I loved going to the library to do research for book reports or science projects. Even in high school and college, when I had access to a computer, I still went to the library to look up things." She paused. "The smell of it, the hushed sounds… I love it all. Now I get to help people who need information or want to immerse themselves in the perfect book. I enjoy when the kids come in from the schools and when I get to read for story hour. I love to witness the excitement of reading take hold in a child. It's very rewarding for me." Her cheeks suddenly pinked. "Sorry for rambling."

"You weren't rambling. Loving what you do is huge, isn't it? I would hate to be stuck in a job I disliked but had to keep for one reason or another."

"Me too."

"Do you like working at the restaurant just as much?"

She nodded. "I like being social and chatting with the customers who come in, meeting new people, and serving them a fantastic meal. I work with a great group, and we have a lot of fun."

"Fun is good."

"It's very good." She tilted her head and looked at him. "What about you? You said you worked for a large marketing firm owned by your father?"

"That's right."

"And he fired you."

"Yes."

She frowned. "That's too bad."

"It is and it isn't. I really liked my job, and I was looking forward to running the company someday." He paused. "But I didn't like having someone trying to control my life." He shrugged and rose from his chair. "I'm going to go dig some roads with my kid. Did you say you have to work tonight?"

"Yes." She glanced at her watch. "But it's only twelve-thirty now, and I don't need to be home for a couple of hours. Go have fun. I'll soak up some sun."

A LITTLE WHILE LATER, SHE WAS LYING ON HER STOMACH ON THE BLANKET, using her folded clothing as a pillow so she could watch Will and Jack play down at the waterline. She thought about what he'd said earlier about someone—his father, she assumed—trying to control his life. She'd blanched a bit when she'd heard that, knowing all too well how it felt.

She'd let Will and Jack play alone for a while, but then she walked down to see the elaborate system of roads they'd constructed. She didn't want to intrude on their father-son time, but any worry about that disappeared when Jack pushed a dump truck into her hands and told her she was in charge of hauling lumber—or, as it were, a few small pieces of driftwood.

Will and Jack decided to go for a swim, but Elizabeth opted out, stretching out in the sun again instead. When Will pulled off his T-shirt and tossed it onto the sand, it definitely caught her attention. He was in good shape, and the sight of him in only his swim trunks kept her eyes glued to him until he finally dove into the water and disappeared under the waves.

Sighing, she glanced at her watch and noticed it was almost one-thirty. If she was going to make the four o'clock ferry, she would need to be home by three to shower. She turned her head sideways and closed her eyes, resting her cheek on her makeshift pillow.

Not a moment later, the sound of Jack's laughter and Will's deep voice caused her to lift her head and look for them. They were coming up the beach, Jack riding on his father's shoulders, both of them soaking wet. Elizabeth watched as Will spoke quietly to Jack, to which Jack responded with an enthusiastic nod.

Suddenly they were looming over her and shaking their heads, spraying droplets of cold water everywhere. She squealed and jumped up from the blanket.

Jack was pleased with their prank and laughed hysterically as his father set him down in the sand.

"Gotcha, 'Lizabeth!" He grinned from ear to ear.

"You got me good," she agreed, laughing with him. "How could you swim in that water? It's ice cold."

"It's not so bad after you're in for a bit," Will answered. "The numbness eventually goes away." He grabbed a thick towel and wrapped it around Jack, then took another for himself.

"Yeah, it's not so bad," Jack repeated. "I can hold my breath under the water now."

"I can see that." She ruffled his wet hair and smiled at his excitement. "Pretty soon you'll be swimming like a fish."

"Yup, pretty soon." He turned to his father. "Can we eat now? I'm hungry."

Will nodded. "I'm hungry too."

They sat on the blanket and had a small feast, just as Elizabeth predicted. She'd packed fresh fruit and assorted cheeses and crackers, and Will brought sandwiches and drinks. Jack was curious about the black rocks that lined the cove, and Elizabeth was happy to tell him what she knew.

"Those rocks are part of something called the Cushing Formation. It's a big pile of rocks formed by a volcano a long time ago. It's even older than dinosaurs."

"Wow, that's pretty old." He took another bite of his sandwich as he listened.

"All those rocks are under Casco Bay, which is where the water for this beach comes from." She paused for a moment, popping a grape into her mouth. "When you were at the lighthouse yesterday, did you see the cliff the lighthouse is on?"

Jack nodded. "Yeah, it's big. But you can't climb it."

"It's too dangerous. All of the rocks in that cliff are part of the Cushing Formation too."

"Oh. Why are they black?" he asked, his violet-blue eyes focused on her.

"I bet if you looked at them closely, you would see lots of different colors. They only look black from far away."

Jack stared at her as he swallowed the last bite of his sandwich. "You're smart 'cause you work at the library, huh?"

She laughed. "I'm sure that's it. I've learned a lot working there."

He turned to his father. "Can I go look for some black rocks near the water?"

"Sure, but stay where I can see you."

"'Kay." Jack hopped up from the blanket, grabbed his bucket, and ran down toward the surf.

Will had been content to let Elizabeth and Jack carry the conversation. He was surprised Elizabeth knew so much about the scientific history of the island and supposed some of it did come with the territory of being a librarian.

"That was pretty interesting, what you told him," he said before eating a strawberry. "I didn't know about the rocks."

"I get asked about them a lot at work, so I did a little research. There's more to it, but that was my standard answer for a five-year-old."

They both watched Jack as he wandered down the beach, occasionally picking up a rock or a shell and looking it over before either dropping it into his bucket or letting it fall back to the sand.

Will turned to Elizabeth, his eyes skimming over her lightly. Her one-piece suit did very little to hide her curves, as he'd already noticed that day at the pool. He saw her lips turn up at the corners.

"Now *you're* staring," she said quietly, although her eyes were focused on Jack.

"I've said it before, you're easy to stare at." He was pleased to see her face pink slightly, and before he could overthink it, he reached to take her hand and rested their entwined fingers on the blanket between them. "Can I tell you something?"

She turned to look at him. "Sure."

"Charles told me you've been through some things." Her eyes widened. "He didn't tell me anything more specific than that, I promise."

She nodded, her brown eyes glued to his.

"And I'm sure you've been told a few things about me and Jack, right?"

"Yes," she whispered.

"I figured that." He lightly squeezed her hand. "It's funny, but when I'm around you...I forget about those things."

He turned to see Jack slowly walking down the beach. "Like this morning...I was on the phone with my father, and I was angry when I got off the phone. And then to make matters worse, I snapped at Jack, *and* I was running late. But we're here enjoying the day...and all that other stuff has just disappeared. I'm almost convinced the entire conversation I had with my father is a figment of my imagination."

When she didn't respond, he looked at her and continued. "I feel very comfortable around you, is what I'm saying...or trying to say. I feel like I can...like I can let my guard down with you, like I've known you for longer than I have. Does that make sense?"

"Yes." She smiled softly. "I feel the same way. Now that you actually *talk* to me, instead of all that nodding and frowning."

He groaned and fell backward onto the blanket, using his free hand to cover his face. "I can't apologize enough for that. I've read all the books on that list. I've learned my lessons." He sat up again and smiled widely. "I really was a jerk, wasn't I?"

She shrugged teasingly. "You weren't *that* bad."

"You're being too polite. I was *bad*."

"Okay, you're right. You were," she agreed, laughing a little. "You just glared at me, and I couldn't figure out for the life of me what I'd done to antagonize you."

"You didn't do anything, it was all me." He sighed and looked into her eyes. "Even then, I knew there was something about you... I just didn't know how to deal with it."

"And now you do?"

He grinned and shook his head. "No. I've just decided to quit trying to figure it out."

She smiled widely. "Good plan."

Jack ran up the beach to them, ending their conversation, and after giving their clasped hands nothing more than a cursory glance, he dropped down onto the blanket to show them the loot he'd collected. Will reluctantly released Elizabeth's hand to hold the treasures Jack was pulling from his bucket.

Elizabeth looked on, occasionally adding a comment or two if she knew anything in particular about a piece of rock or a shell. After a little while, she glanced at her watch and grudgingly noted it was nearing three.

After looking at everything in Jack's bucket, Will sent him back down to the water to pick up the rest of his toys. He rose from the blanket and offered a hand to Elizabeth as she stood, lingering for a moment before slowly releasing her hand. They packed up their belongings and the remnants of their picnic, and when they were finished, he turned to her.

"So, um, what's your schedule like for the rest of the week?"

"I work tomorrow and Friday, and then Jane comes on Friday afternoon. I was able to switch my work schedules to have some time off while she's here. How about you?"

"I think Jack and I will just hang around the island tomorrow. Maybe I'll see if he wants to have Sam over. We'll be in Portland on Friday, and I told him we could stop in for story hour."

She smiled brightly. "I told him I'd try to read again, so hopefully I can squeeze it in. Although according to him, you're more than qualified to take my place."

He chuckled. "Oh no. I'll leave it to the professionals, thanks."

"When does your sister arrive?"

"Saturday morning. Jack is going to be so excited to see her."

"I think Jack's not the only one."

He laughed. "No, he isn't. I'll be happy to see her too." He paused. "Maybe I'll have a cookout on Sunday. You could come over with Jane, and I could invite Maddie and Ed and Charles. If–if you and Jane don't have plans, that is."

"That sounds like fun."

"Okay. Good. I'll give Charles a call, and maybe you can mention it to Maddie and Ed? I'll call them too, but can you just give them a heads-up?"

"Sure."

"I'm ready, Dad, I got all my stuff," Jack said as he trudged across the sand. "Can I take the shells and rocks home?"

"Sure, we can put them on the deck."

"'Kay."

No one said much on the way home, and Will wondered if Jack had dozed off on Elizabeth's lap. He was leaning back against her, his head tucked comfortably under her chin, and the sight of him snuggled there made his heart lurch.

When they arrived at the Gardiners' house, she lifted Jack from her lap so she could climb out. Will parked the cart, reminding Jack not to touch anything, and grabbed Elizabeth's cooler and chair. He walked her to her door, and after setting the chair and cooler down, he dusted the loose grains of sand from his hands.

"Well," he said as he stared down at her, "thanks for a great day."

She smiled. "I had fun, thanks. Too bad I have to go to work, or we could have stayed there all day."

"Another time?"

"Definitely."

"Great. Um, I guess I'll see you soon," he said, his eyes glued to hers.

"Mm-hmm, soon. Probably Friday, right?"

"Oh, yeah. Friday. Right. At the library."

She suddenly rose up on her tiptoes to kiss his cheek. Her lips were warm and she smelled like sunscreen, and his heart thrummed in his chest.

"Bye, Will. Thanks again."

He smiled before he took her hand and squeezed it lightly. "Bye, Elizabeth."

He turned to walk down the path, unable to erase the smile from his face.

∽

AFTER HIS BATH, JACK IMMEDIATELY FELL ASLEEP ON THE COUCH. WILL took a quick shower and then woke him up a little while later, and they agreed on a plan for dinner: breakfast. They indulged occasionally, and this time Jack picked pancakes.

"Can we have chocolate chips in 'em?" he asked as he stirred the batter.

"I don't think we have any."

"Darn."

"Sorry, pal. I'll put it on the shopping list. Oh, hang on..." Will opened the refrigerator. "We have chocolate syrup. What do you think?"

"Yeah! That's good."

Will was doubtful but went along with it anyway. He poured the batter into perfect circular shapes on the griddle and handed the bottle of chocolate syrup to Jack, who proceeded to make smiley faces and squiggles in all of them.

"See? It works." Jack smiled at his handiwork and helped to flip the pancakes, Will's larger hand clasped over his smaller one on the spatula handle.

"Perfect," Will said when they were done. He grabbed plates and served up the pancakes, then took the maple syrup from the cabinet. They went outside to the deck, and after Will went back in to pour them each a glass of milk, they settled down to eat.

"Dad, these are awesome," Jack said, his mouth ringed with chocolate. "We should have pancakes with chocolate syrup in 'em all the time."

Will handed him a napkin. "Once in a while is alright, I think."

After dinner was finished and the kitchen cleaned up, they headed to Jack's room to play with his Matchbox cars. Even though it was only a little after seven, Jack yawned frequently and his eyelids began to droop.

"What do you say, buddy, ready for bed?" Will asked.

Jack nodded. "Yeah, I'm tired. Can I leave all the cars set up like this?"

"Sure. Just be careful when you get up in the morning; it hurts if you step on them." Will had learned that lesson the hard way.

"'Kay. I'm gonna go brush."

He was back a few moments later, and Will tucked him into bed.

"Are you still mad?" Jack asked quietly as he stared up at his father.

Will was confused until he remembered the incident with the golf cart. "No, I'm not mad," he replied gently, seating himself on the edge of the bed. "I was before, a little bit. But you know why, right?"

"Yeah," Jack whispered, nodding slightly. "'Cause I touched the shifter thingy."

"Well, it was more because you didn't listen to me. I know it's just a cart, and it doesn't go very fast, but you still could have been hurt."

Jack looked down at his blanket and chewed on his bottom lip for a moment.

"Your mom used to do that."

Jack's eyes rose back to his father's. "Do what?"

Will reached out and gently tapped Jack's lower lip. "Bite her lip when she was thinking about something. What are you thinking about?"

"Are we gonna go to the library on Friday?"

"Of course. Do you still want to?"

Jack nodded. "I thought 'cause I got in trouble, you might say no."

Will sighed. "Do you promise not to touch anything in the cart again?"

Jack stared at his father seriously. "I promise."

"Alright then, case closed. We'll go to the library on Friday, okay?"

A smile brightened Jack's face. "'Kay."

Will leaned down to kiss his forehead. "Sweet dreams, buddy. Love you."

"Love you too, Dad. Night."

"Good night."

Will rose from the bed and turned off the light on the way out. As he made his way downstairs and into the living room, he heard the ringing of his cell phone and picked it up when he saw it was Charles.

"Hey, Charles."

"Will! I just wanted to call and give you the good news. I'm officially a business owner!"

Will smiled. "Congratulations, that's great!"

"Thanks. I couldn't have done it without you." Charles sighed loudly. "I can't believe I actually *own* the place. I'm looking forward to getting in there and tearing it apart—did you see the booths? All those tacky colors? Man, I'm going to love ripping it up."

Will chuckled. "See if there's anything that's salvageable before you go crazy. You never know."

"I will. I had big dreams of going in there with an ax and just demolishing the place, though the bar is okay."

"It is—"

"But I don't want to keep it, I want to build a huge mahogany bar. That's what I've always envisioned."

"I could see that. It would change the look of the place. You could make it *look* upscale without it really *being* upscale."

"Right. I want it to be classy, but warm and welcoming too. And I need to think of a name. I have a bunch of ideas written down, I just have to narrow it to one. Hey, what are you doing right now?"

"Talking to you. Sitting on my couch."

"Where's Jack?"

"He's sound asleep. We spent a few hours at the beach today, and it wiped him out."

"I'm on the ferry headed back to the island. Can I stop by for a celebratory beer?"

"Absolutely. I think I have a few stashed away."

"I'll stop and get some from my house. I'll be there in less than an hour."

True to his word, Charles was there in forty-five minutes, toting a six-pack of his home-brewed blonde ale. Will shook his hand and congratulated him once again, genuinely pleased by his new friend's success.

After cracking two beers, Will slapped Charles on the back as they stood for a moment in the kitchen. "Why do I get the feeling you've been celebrating a little already?"

Charles grinned crookedly. "I don't know, why do you get that feeling?"

"Well, unless you've started wearing perfume..."

Charles had the decency to blush, and his smile grew wider. "I paid a visit to an old friend after I left the bank, that's all."

"Does this old friend have a name?"

"Yup."

"And you're not going to tell me? It's not like I'll know who she is."

"She's an ex-girlfriend. Kate. She and Lizzy are good friends."

"She doesn't *seem* very ex-ish," Will noted, his interest piqued.

"She is. But sometimes, you know, we hook up." Charles shrugged. "Not all the time, just once in a while."

"Friends with benefits, is that what it's called?" Will asked. Despite the fact he'd been with only one woman in his thirty years, he wasn't ignorant of how things worked in the singles world—he only knew he didn't want to be a part of it. In that respect, he was fairly old-fashioned.

Charles laughed. "Yeah, that's it. She's a friend with benefits. I mean, I really like her. She's smart and funny and unbelievably gorgeous. She looks like a typical Irish lass with beautiful fair skin and freckles and deep red hair and green eyes that are just..." His voice trailed off, and he sighed and shrugged again. "She wanted the whole commitment thing, wanted us to live together, and...I don't know. I chickened out."

"Chickened out?" Will repeated, eyebrows raised.

Charles shrugged again. "Yeah. It was getting too serious too fast. When she started talking about shacking up, it freaked me out." He paused for a moment. "I guess it doesn't make much sense to you, considering you married your high school sweetheart."

"Yeah, Anne and I were together for a long time." His brows drew together in puzzlement. "But when you wanted to celebrate today, you went and found Kate, right?"

Charles groaned. "Yeah, I did. *Please* don't psychoanalyze me."

They moved outside to the deck and sat at the table, the only light coming from inside the kitchen. "I'm not analyzing you, I'm just making an observation." Will smiled as he thought of Elizabeth. "I'm an observer."

"Yeah, you're an observer alright," Charles agreed. "You know how I know that? It's because I saw you *observe* Lizzy's ass when we were getting on the ferry on Sunday, remember? And then you *observed* her during dinner at my house, and then you *really* observed her when her shirt was wet and plastered to her body after our little squirt gun fight. And as a matter of fact, you drove her home, and you never said a word to me about it."

"There's nothing to say." Will took a sip of his beer, grateful the darkness hid his heated face. "I drove her home and dropped her off. That's it."

Charles squinted at him. "Mm-hmm."

"Oh, by the way," Will said, changing the subject, "I think I'm going to have a cookout or something on Sunday. My sister is flying in on Saturday, so I thought I would have a few people over."

"Cool, I'll be there."

"Good. Um, I was thinking of inviting Caroline," Will said, but then quickly wondered if that was a wise idea.

"I'll let her know. You don't need to call her." Charles sighed. "She already has all kinds of ideas in her head about you."

Will's eyebrows flew up. "What kinds of ideas?"

Charles rolled his eyes. "C'mon, Will. She's a single woman, and you're a single guy."

"I am," Will acknowledged haltingly, his voice low. "I'm a single guy." He shook his head. "It's funny, I've never thought of myself that way. I mean, I know I'm not married anymore, but..." He shrugged. "I don't know, it just sounds weird."

Charles looked at him sympathetically. "Not to be crass or insensitive, but Caroline doesn't care *why* you're single, she just cares that you are. I love my sister, but I wouldn't recommend her as a girlfriend." He grinned when Will laughed. "Just let her know you're not interested. Be blunt. She'll get the hint."

"Thanks for the tip."

"Lizzy, on the other hand..." Charles grinned. "I would recommend *her*."

"Based on what? Didn't she shoot you down?" Will teased.

"She did, flat out. But she's a great girl, and she's not as...what's the word I'm looking for?"

"Hungry?"

Charles nearly spat out his beer and coughed loudly. "That's a good one, but not what I was going for."

"Mercenary?"

Charles snapped his fingers and pointed a finger at Will. "Yes, *mercenary*. That's it. She's just a genuine, down-to-earth, sweet person."

Will reached up to scratch his head, then dragged his hand down over his face. "We spent the day at the beach."

Charles's eyes widened. "Who is *we*?"

"Jack and Elizabeth and me."

Charles leaned forward. "How the hell did this come about?"

"When I drove her home from your house, she asked if we wanted to go." He shrugged. "Simple as that."

"So?"

"So what?"

"So what happened? Did you rub lotion on her back?" Charles waggled his eyebrows. "Or any other body parts?"

"No, I didn't rub lotion on her back or *anywhere*," Will said, shaking his head. "We hung out. We're just friends."

"When's your next date?"

"It wasn't a date."

Charles grinned again. "Okay, so when are you going to *ask* her on a date?"

"I'm not…we aren't…it's not…" Embarrassed, Will stopped talking and let out a long exhale. "We're just friends," he repeated, his voice low.

"Well, you couldn't be friends with a nicer person." Charles smiled and reached across the table to cuff Will's shoulder. "Except me, of course."

Elizabeth's mouth dropped open as she looked at Kate. "Again? This is getting to be a habit, don't you think?"

Kate glanced around to make sure they weren't overheard by any of their coworkers. Trinity was due to open shortly, though they wouldn't see patrons start to trickle through the doors for another hour or so.

It was once a church but had been converted years ago into one of the premier spots for fine dining in Portland. The beauty, unique atmosphere, and incredible cuisine drew throngs of people through its doors every night.

"It's only happened a few times," Kate said. "And it's not like we hate each other. We're still friends."

"With benefits."

"Yes, but at least I know him. I know his history, and I'm comfortable with him. And honestly? The man is a sex machine."

Elizabeth closed her eyes and shook her head, trying to blot that image of Charles from her mind, but she was also laughing. "Ugh, Kate, TMI!"

Kate giggled. "I know, but he's amazing, and even though we're not a couple anymore, he still makes me feel...special. It's not just wham, bam, thank you ma'am. He stays, we talk and laugh and have fun... It's almost like we're still together."

Elizabeth looked at her friend closely. "Are you still in love with him?"

Kate sighed. "I don't know. Maybe. I still don't understand what happened with us. I mean, I know what he told me, but I just...I don't see it. We were so *good* together. We're *still* good together. I think he's just skittish, or maybe he feels like he needs to sow his oats or whatever. But he's thirty-one. You'd think he'd be ready to settle down." Her lips twisted into a frown. "Or maybe he *is* ready, and I'm just not the one he wants to settle down *with*."

"But he wanted to share his good news with you first, didn't he?"

"He also wanted to get laid."

"I think there's more to it than that," Elizabeth reasoned. "This was something important to him. He wanted to celebrate with someone, and he picked you. You didn't have to sleep with him."

"I know. It just kind of happened." Her eyes scanned the restaurant. "Anyway, he's really excited about everything." She laughed. "He wants us to work for him. He said he's determined to steal us away from this place. I told him no way." She looked at Elizabeth. "Oh, who is Will?"

Elizabeth's eyes widened slightly. "Will?"

"The guy who helped Charles with all the business stuff? Charles told me you know him."

"He's just a–a guy. He moved to the island not too long ago." She cleared her throat. "Um, yes, he did help Charles. He used to work for a marketing company in New York before he moved here, so I suppose he knows a lot about…business. So, yeah. That's who Will is."

"He's nice?"

Elizabeth grinned softly and nodded, her hands smoothing over her apron as she steadfastly avoided meeting Kate's eyes. "He's very nice."

"Is he single?"

Elizabeth rolled her eyes. "You sound like Charlotte."

"Is he single?"

Elizabeth sighed. "Yes. A single dad. He has a five-year-old son named Jack."

"Ugh, baggage."

Elizabeth put her hands on her hips and looked at Kate, her eyebrows knit together. "Jack isn't *baggage*, he's a sweet little boy."

"Ooh, getting defensive?" Kate smirked. "Hmm."

"I'm not…I'm not getting *defensive*, I just…I don't think it's very nice to call a child baggage, that's all."

"Is he divorced?"

"No, he's…his wife passed away. I don't know the specifics."

"Oh, geez. That's awful. How well do you know him?"

"Not very. I saw him at Charles's house Sunday night, and I've seen him a couple times on the ferry…we bump into each other." She swallowed. "We went to the beach today for a little while."

Kate's eyebrows rose high on her forehead. "You went to the beach with him today? Just the two of you?"

"Well, Jack was with us." She kept her eyes focused on the restaurant as she felt her cheeks heat, aware Kate was watching her closely.

"You're not telling me everything, are you? I just told you all my woes about Charles, and you're buttoning up. What's going on?"

Elizabeth closed her eyes briefly. "There's really nothing to tell, but...I like him."

"You like him?"

"Yes. He's a nice guy, kind of quiet...but he's smart and funny and incredibly sweet with his son." She sighed. "And he's tall and absolutely gorgeous."

She paused as a fleeting image of Will in his bathing suit passed through her mind.

"This is going to sound childish compared to what you just told me about your afternoon with Charles, but...he held my hand today at the beach, and it felt nice. It felt...I don't know. I don't know *how* it felt. I mean, we're just starting to get to know each other..." She glanced at Kate and saw the way her friend was studying her. "This probably sounds ridiculous to you."

Kate's face softened. "It doesn't sound ridiculous at all. Do you think I don't remember what it felt like when Charles held my hand for the first time?" She reached to squeeze Elizabeth's hand. "You haven't shown interest in anyone since you moved here, so I know this is a big deal for you."

Elizabeth started to speak, but Kate cut her off. "I'm not jumping the gun, okay? It's just a friendship at the moment, right?"

Elizabeth nodded.

"That's great. Would you be happy if it grew into something more?"

"I–I don't know. I think it's too early to think about that. Plus, I have no idea what he's thinking." *And I don't want to get my hopes up.*

"He held your hand, didn't he? Little things can mean a lot."

"I guess."

"Just do one thing for me, okay?"

Elizabeth hesitated. "Okay."

"Promise me you'll leave yourself open to the possibility of something more. I know your marriage sucked, but if Will is as nice as you say, don't talk yourself out of anything. Let the chips fall where they may."

Elizabeth shook her head slightly and looked away from Kate's hopeful expression. Just the thought of something more with Will made her stomach tumble.

"Okay," she finally said. "I'll keep myself open to possibilities." Kate beamed at her and wrapped an arm around her shoulders, and Elizabeth took a deep breath.

Let the chips fall where they may.

Ten

E lizabeth sat behind her desk at the library and sighed when she glanced at the clock. *It's five minutes later than the last time I looked.* Time seemed to be crawling, and she knew why—she was anticipating her lunch date.

No, not date, she reminded herself, *just lunch.*

Will had called her last night to ask if she'd like to have lunch with him and Jack before story hour, and she'd immediately said yes. They'd chatted for a little while—he'd asked about her day and she'd asked about his time spent with Jack and Sam. He had a couple of humorous stories about the boys' escapades and told her they'd indulged in a pretty competitive squirt gun battle. He'd also mentioned that Charles had officially bought the spot in Portland for his pub, and she'd told him she'd already heard the news. They only talked for five minutes or so, but her grin stayed in place until she fell asleep.

As it grew closer to lunchtime, her stomach began to flip nervously. She sat at her desk, repeatedly tapping a pencil on the blotter until Mary came up behind her and took it out of her hand.

Elizabeth grinned at her sheepishly. "Sorry." In lieu of having no pencil to tap, she clasped her hands together and forced them to stay in her lap.

"What's going on?" Mary asked in a whisper. "You've been a nervous bundle of energy all day. It's driving me crazy."

"I have *not* been a nervous bundle of energy," Elizabeth refuted. "You're exaggerating."

"I beg to differ." Mary pointed to the paperclips scattered all over Elizabeth's desk. Most of them had been bent and twisted from their original shape, and those that weren't rendered unrecognizable were linked together in a long chain. "You are the most organized person I know, but right now your desk looks like the aftermath of an explosion at a paperclip factory."

Elizabeth gathered all the clips together and swept them into a drawer. "Don't you have a list of people to persecute for their overdue books or something? I promise, I'll sit—"

She halted mid-sentence when she saw Jack walk into the library with his father in tow. Her eyes traveled over Will, taking in the way his blue polo shirt enhanced the darkness of his hair and eyes. He wore gray shorts and a pair of startlingly white sneakers, and she watched as he glanced around the library. When his gaze finally came to rest on her, the smile that broke out on his face put her heart—and her stomach—into overdrive.

Mary turned to see what had arrested her coworker's attention. She discreetly tapped Elizabeth on the shoulder as Will approached. "Elizabeth Bennet, who is *that*?" she murmured under her breath.

"A friend," Elizabeth answered quietly, keeping her eyes on Will. "We're having lunch." She rose and exhaled anxiously, grabbing her purse and looping it onto her shoulder before looking at Mary with a bright smile. "Back in an hour."

"Wait, no introduction?"

"Maybe when we get back. Bye."

Elizabeth walked out from behind the desk and didn't miss the way Will's eyes quickly traveled over her. She'd dressed up a bit today, wearing a navy blue skirt, a white sleeveless blouse, and her navy heels—but repeatedly told herself it was *not* because of her lunch date.

Just lunch. Not date.

Her heels gave her a little extra height, but she still only reached his shoulder. "Hi," she said, feeling slightly breathless as she stared up at him.

"Hi, yourself." His gaze roamed over her face and hair before stopping at her eyes, and he smiled. "You look nice."

"Thank you," she responded as her face warmed. "Um, do you have a preference for lunch?"

"Is there a McDonald's here?" Jack asked as he tugged on her hand. "I haven't had chicken nuggets in a really long time."

Will shook his head. "I don't think so."

"Actually, there is," Elizabeth said, "but it's not close enough to walk to."

"Darn," Jack said. "Can we go another day?"

"Sure," Will told him before turning to Elizabeth. "I don't have a preference, and Jack will eat a sandwich or some soup. Is there a café or a deli nearby?"

"I know just the place."

They stepped out into the bright sunshine and headed down the sidewalk with Jack walking between them. Elizabeth looked down in surprise when she felt Jack's small hand take hold of hers, and saw he was holding his father's hand as well. He sauntered along, hopping over the cracks in the sidewalk and holding their hands as if he'd done it a million times before.

It was a short walk to the café, and Jack released their hands and wandered around, looking at all of the colorful paintings on the walls while Will and Elizabeth read the giant chalkboard menu.

After they ordered, Elizabeth offered to split the check, but Will wouldn't hear of it.

"*I* invited you to lunch with *us*, what kind of guy would I be if I made you pay?" He shook his head, looking at her as if she'd gone crazy, and she couldn't help but laugh a little.

It was a beautiful day, so they chose to sit outside on the patio. It was surrounded by tall hedges, and each picnic table was shaded by a colorful umbrella. It didn't take long for their food to arrive, and Will's mouth dropped open comically when the server placed his burger in front of him.

Jack giggled. "That's a huge burger, Dad." The server placed his grilled cheese in front of him, and his face lit up. "I didn't know it had fries!" He happily started munching away, leaving Will and Elizabeth to talk a little more.

"When is your sister due in?" he asked.

"Good question. Knowing her, she'll just show up." Her eyes widened as she reached for her purse and pulled out her cell phone.

"Sorry, I just realized I haven't checked to see if she's texted me at all."
She looked at the screen and giggled. "Oops," she said, tucking away
her phone.

"Oops?"

She nodded. "She's due in around 1:30, which is now. I'm supposed
to work until five, but maybe I'll leave early if it's not too busy."

"What's your sister's name again?" Jack asked around a mouthful
of gooey cheese.

"Jane," Elizabeth answered.

Jack nodded and went back to watching the sparrows hopping
around under the tables, searching for crumbs.

"If she doesn't want to get together on Sunday, it's okay," Will told
her quietly. "I thought about it and realized the last thing she'll probably want to do is hang out with a bunch of people she doesn't know."

Elizabeth arched an eyebrow. "Are you rescinding your invitation,
Mr. Darcy?"

He grinned. "No, of course not. I want you to come, but I don't
want you to feel obligated. Especially if your sister isn't up for it."

"I'm sure she'll be fine with it. What would you like me to bring?"

"Oh, um...nothing," he answered, staring into her eyes.

"I have to bring *something*, I can't show up empty-handed," she
insisted. "Especially since I'm bringing a guest."

"Alright, well...the guacamole you made the other day was great.
Would you mind making it again?" They both laughed when Jack
scrunched up his nose. "Don't worry, you don't have to eat it," Will
told him.

"Anything else?"

He tilted his head. "Surprise me."

She smiled. "I just might do that."

They finished their meals and left the café, and this time Jack
walked ahead of them, still studiously avoiding the sidewalk cracks.

"Do all kids do that?" she asked, leaning in toward Will as they
walked. "It's like they know they're supposed to skip over the sidewalk cracks."

"It's funny, I don't think I've ever played that game with him," Will
said.

She looked up at him, her eyes wide. "I'm–I'm sorry, that was insensitive of me. I wasn't thinking about…about the rest of it, the rhyme." *Step on a crack, break your mother's back.*

"No need to apologize," he assured her, lightly bumping her arm with his. "He's just keeping himself occupied." She looked away, but he touched her hand, tugging on her fingers a little before weaving them loosely with his. "Elizabeth, it's fine. You don't have an insensitive bone in your body."

She was about to respond when she heard a familiar voice.

"Lizzy! There you are!"

She looked to her right and saw her sister sitting on a bench in front of the library, basking in the sun. Jane stood and quickly walked toward them, and Elizabeth felt Will's hand slowly slip from hers. The two women embraced as if they hadn't seen each other in ages, when it had actually been less than a week.

"Hi, Jane! I'm sorry, I didn't get your text until just a little while ago, and I'd already left for lunch."

Jane waved a hand, brushing her off. "That's okay, I've only been here for twenty minutes or so. I've been people-watching." She turned to Will and smiled, holding out her hand. "Hi, I'm Jane Bennet."

"Oh, sorry. Jane, this is Will Darcy and his son, Jack," Elizabeth said. "This is my sister Jane."

Will shook her hand and smiled. "Hi, Jane. Nice to meet you."

"You too." Jack offered his hand as well, and Jane shook it lightly. "Nice to meet you, Jack."

"Nice to meet you." He looked up at Elizabeth. "Is it almost story hour?"

Elizabeth glanced at her watch. "Oh! It is, and I haven't even picked out a book yet. I hope Mary took care of that." She looked at Jane. "I'll try to get off early, but I have to read first. I hope you don't mind."

"Of course not, I knew you had to work. I'll find something to keep me busy." She grinned mischievously. "Maybe I'll come in and see if I can make you laugh while you read."

"Hmm, maybe I'll help you," Will chimed in, speaking to Jane but looking at Elizabeth.

Elizabeth groaned and shook her head. "If you make me laugh, it will get the kids laughing, and then it will *all* go downhill from there. Please restrain yourselves."

"Yes, mother," Jane replied. "Actually, I might browse in some of the shops. I'll come back in an hour."

"Great idea," Elizabeth said. "Go spend some money. I'll see you in a little while."

Jane turned to Will and Jack. "It was nice to meet you both. Enjoy the rest of the day."

"Thanks, nice to meet you too," Will said.

Jane walked away, and Elizabeth turned back to Will with a grimace. "I just realized I never thanked you for lunch." She shook her head. "I'm normally not this forgetful. Or rude! I'm sorry." He smiled down at her, and suddenly it felt ten degrees hotter outside.

"You're welcome," he said, his voice low. "Will you please stop apologizing?"

"I'm sor—" She laughed as she realized what she was about to say, and his smile grew as he laughed with her. *Oh, those dimples.* "Okay, I'll stop."

"Get in there and hypnotize the kids for an hour. I'll talk to you after."

"Okay." She looked down at Jack, who was starting to fidget. "Thanks for having lunch with me, Jack."

He grinned. "You're welcome."

"Make sure you sit up front, okay?"

"'Kay."

She looked at Will one last time. "Thanks again."

He rolled his eyes. "Get in there!"

She walked into the library feeling as though she was floating in the clouds, until the sound of two dozen chattering children very quickly brought her right back down to earth.

ELIZABETH TALKED WITH WILL AND JACK FOR A FEW MINUTES AFTER STORY hour ended, well aware of the curious looks she was garnering from

Mary. She finally caved and introduced them, and could see a glint of humor in Will's eyes; undoubtedly, he was remembering the teasing conversation they'd had at Charles's house about librarians.

She was grateful Jane hadn't come back yet; she would have questions, and seeing Will again would only add fuel to the fire.

Will seemed hesitant to leave, but he finally gave in to Jack's persistent hand-tugging; he was anxious to get to the lumber supply company to order wood for the fort they'd decided to build.

He took her hand and gave it a light squeeze before saying goodbye, and she watched as father and son walked down the sidewalk toward the waterfront. Will glanced back, and when their eyes met, they both smiled. She gave a slight wave, and he returned it before hoisting Jack onto his shoulders. Watching his affection toward Jack made her heart melt a little, and she continued to watch them until they were out of sight. She felt a light tap on her shoulder and turned to find her sister standing behind her.

"What are you staring at?" Jane asked, peering down the street.

"Oh, um, nothing. I was looking for you, actually."

"And here I am." Jane smiled and raised an eyebrow. "So, you weren't watching Mr. Tall, Dark, and Dreamy as he walked away? Because I certainly was."

Elizabeth sighed. "Can we go back in? I still have a little work to do."

"You can avoid my question right now, but you have some explaining to do, little sister."

"Fine, but later. Over drinks?"

"Sounds perfect."

An hour later, the sisters made their way down Fore Street and into Bull Sweeney's. It was one of Elizabeth's favorite pubs, mostly because it was old and unpretentious. The owners had remodeled the upstairs dining room, making it lighter and brighter, but the downstairs bar still had dark wood paneling, exposed brick, and slightly lopsided stools.

"How was the drive up?" Elizabeth asked after they settled in at the bar and ordered their drinks.

"It was fine, no traffic at all. Traveling in the middle of the day makes a huge difference."

"How are Mom and Dad?"

Jane shrugged. "They're okay. Mom is devastated that Stuart is no longer in the picture, but she'll get over it."

Elizabeth nodded as the bartender set their glasses of wine in front of them. "She always does."

"Dad seems more resigned to the fact you're not coming back to Lexington."

"That's good." Elizabeth sighed a little. "I don't know why he was holding on so tightly. You're nearby, Lydia is still home... It's not like we all flew the coop at once."

"But you're his favorite, Lizzy. You always have been. He doesn't have the intelligent conversation with Mom or Lydia that he has with you. You're a lot like him." Jane grinned. "I'm afraid I don't compare either."

"You're just as capable of intelligent conversation as I am. And so is Lydia! She's just not as interested in making it, I suppose." They both chuckled. "Speaking of Lydia, have you talked to her at all this week?"

Jane shook her head. "We've texted a few times, but that's it."

"I wonder if George has stopped into the coffee shop again. I hope she took what I said seriously."

"I'm sure she did."

"Have you talked to Stuart?"

"No, but I don't expect to. There's nothing else to say, so why bother?"

Elizabeth looked at her sister closely, but didn't see any signs of distress. "And you're sure you're okay with everything, with the way it ended?"

Jane took a sip of her wine. "Well, I would have preferred he didn't cheat on me, obviously, but I've thought about it more... If his ex-wife really *is* his soul mate, how can I begrudge him that happiness?"

"I'm glad you're not a wreck over everything. I would hate to see you heartbroken."

"I'm good." She looked at Elizabeth with penetrating blue eyes. "So, are you ready to talk?"

Elizabeth groaned, knowing what was about to come. "Talk about what?"

"Who. Talk about *who*."

"You mean Will who?" Elizabeth asked innocently.

Jane rolled her eyes. "Yes, of course I mean *Will who*. Anything you want to tell me?"

"We're just friends."

Jane laughed. "Friends don't hold hands when they walk down the street. Try again."

Elizabeth felt her face color. "We're really just friends. I–I think we both feel a little something more, but we haven't done anything about it."

"Do you want to?"

"I don't know. I think…I think I might."

"Oh, I love it when you're so decisive and confident," Jane teased. "Okay, start from the beginning. Tell me all about him."

Elizabeth told her sister what she knew of him and talked about the time they'd spent together, from their inauspicious first meeting on the dock to their lunch today. Images of him floated through her mind as she spoke.

"He's just…nice," she finally said. "He makes me laugh, though sometimes he's quiet. I would never call him an extrovert." She shrugged. "I think he's just trying to find his way with his son."

"Wow," Jane responded, studying her sister closely.

"I know. But like I said, it's just friendship."

"And you don't know how his wife died?"

Elizabeth shook her head. "No, we haven't talked about it."

"Has he been in any relationships since then?"

Elizabeth's brows came together and she took a sip of wine. "I don't know. I get the impression there hasn't been anyone, but I could be wrong."

"And he said he's comfortable around you?"

Elizabeth nodded but said nothing.

Jane smiled softly. "The way he looks at you… I was watching when you were going into the library for story hour."

"You were spying on us?"

Jane rolled her eyes. "Stupid question, of course I was! You were holding his hand. I had to watch. It's my sisterly duty."

"Ha." Elizabeth paused and then smiled coyly. "So how did he look at me?"

Jane burst out laughing, and Elizabeth joined her. "He just—he couldn't take his eyes off of you, and he had a little smile on his face... He looked kind of smitten."

"Smitten?"

Jane nodded. "Smitten."

Elizabeth sighed. "I'll take smitten."

WILL FINISHED HIS PHONE CALL WITH MADDIE, GLAD TO HEAR THAT SHE and Ed would be able to come on Sunday afternoon. She'd asked if he and Jack had enjoyed the beach on Wednesday, so he knew Elizabeth must have said something to her about them going together. He didn't get the impression Maddie was prying; if anything, she seemed interested in knowing what he and Jack thought of the cove.

He walked to the kitchen table, where Jack was studying the blueprints for the fort. "This is gonna be awesome, Dad. Me an' Sam are gonna have a club."

"What kind of club?"

Jack shrugged. "I dunno, we didn't think of one yet."

"Well, we probably won't get started on it right away." He didn't want to undertake a project like this while Georgiana was here—especially since he was no handyman.

Jack looked crestfallen. "Why not? I thought we were gonna do it tomorrow!"

"We can't. The wood won't be delivered until Tuesday."

"Oh yeah. So can we start it the next day?" Jack asked, his expression hopeful.

"Sure."

"Maybe Mr. Bingley can help us."

"Mr. Bingley just bought a restaurant, so he's going to be pretty busy. I'm sure you and I can handle it on our own." He didn't feel nearly as confident as he sounded.

Jack looked at his father, then back at the blueprints, then back at his father again. "Maybe Mr. Gardiner can help. He's never doin' anythin'."

Will laughed. "I'm sure Mr. Gardiner is busy. But that's not a bad idea, maybe I'll ask him. They're coming over for dinner on Sunday."

"Oh. Is anyone else comin'?"

Will nodded. "Elizabeth and her sister, Mr. Bingley and maybe Ms. Bingley too… And how about the Gradys? I was thinking of calling them to see if they wanted to come."

Jack's face lit up. "Yeah, that would be awesome! Can Sam sleep over? He wants me to sleep at his house too."

Will thought again about Georgiana's visit. "Maybe not Sunday night, but another time for sure, okay?"

"'Kay."

"We have the whole summer for sleepovers."

"Yeah, I know."

Will nodded toward the blueprints. "You keep studying that and let me know when you have it all figured out. I have to call Auntie G, okay?"

"'Kay. Can I talk to her when you're done?"

"Sure." He walked into his office and shut the door so Jack wouldn't hear them discussing Georgiana's travel plans. She answered her phone right away, and Will immediately sensed something was wrong.

"It's nothing," she told him. "It's just—it's Dad, that's all."

"What'd he do now?"

"Can we talk about it when I see you? I don't want to get into it right now."

As much as he wanted to pry it out of her, he respected her wishes. "Alright, we'll talk tomorrow night. When are you flying in?"

She gave him her itinerary and offered to take a cab from the airport to the ferry terminal.

"You're not taking a cab," he insisted. "I'll pick you up."

"No, that will ruin the surprise! If you go to the airport, Jack will know something's up. Just let me take a cab from the airport to the docks, and then I'll take the ferry over and meet you on the island."

He hesitated. "Are you sure? How about we meet you at the docks in Portland?"

"Will! Can we do this my way? Please?" she asked pointedly.

He chuckled. "Alright, you win. We'll be waiting for you in the Batmobile."

"The what?"

He smiled. "You'll see."

ELIZABETH AND JANE GIGGLED AS THEY SAT TOGETHER ON THE LAST FERRY of the night, headed back to the island. They'd ended up having dinner with Kate and Charlotte, and it had been a laugh a minute. They'd drawn the attention of three young men—four attractive women out on the town on a Friday night and obviously having a great time had a way of doing that. After saying goodbye to Charlotte and Kate—who were still embracing the flirtatious attention from the men—the sisters slowly worked their way to the docks and found seats on the top deck of the ferry.

"Ohhh, I'm going to regret this tomorrow," Elizabeth groaned, kicking off her heels and placing her feet on the back of the seat in front of her. "I shouldn't have had that last drink. You're a bad influence."

"I am no such thing. You sucked that drink down willingly," Jane argued. "I can't believe we almost forgot to go to the garage to get my bag from my car! Do you know how annoyed I would have been if we'd gotten all the way over to the island and I realized I didn't have my toothbrush?" Jane stretched out her legs alongside Elizabeth's.

"I have extras."

Jane wiggled her eyebrows and looked at her sister. "Maybe you'll need one for someone else sometime soon, hmm? Mr. Tall, Dark, and Dreamy perhaps?"

Elizabeth rolled her eyes. "Please don't go there. I am *so* not ready to go there."

"Oh please, you can't tell me you haven't gone there in your head already."

"No, I–I haven't. I'm attracted to him, but no, I haven't gone *there*." She sighed and then grinned. "But even when he holds my hand, it's like I'm hyper-aware of every point of contact between his skin and mine. I've never felt anything like that before."

Jane smiled. "It's nice, isn't it? Does your stomach get all flip-floppy too?"

Elizabeth giggled. "Yes." She grew serious and her eyes wandered up to the sky, taking in the canopy of stars above them. "I really like him, Jane. As little as I know about him, I just—I have a good feeling. I think he appreciates life a little more than other people might, you know? He doesn't strike me as someone who would play games. He has Jack, after all. Jack is the center of his life."

Jane was quiet for a moment. "Of course Jack is the center of his life, that's the way it should be," she finally said. "But that doesn't mean he doesn't have room for someone else." She wrapped her arm around Elizabeth's shoulders, and they leaned their heads together. "If you like him, just go with it. See where it takes you. Leave yourself open to what-ifs."

"You sound like Kate. She made me promise to be open to possibilities."

"Kate's a smart girl," Jane continued. "I told you he looked smitten. If he hasn't been with anyone else, if you're the first since his wife, then I'm sure it's a big deal for him." She paused. "I know you haven't been with anyone else since Bill—unless you count George," she grumbled, "so I know it's a big deal for you too."

"George and Bill are in the past," Elizabeth said firmly, sitting up and turning to look at her sister. "I'm not going to let them control my future. I refuse to let that happen."

Jane smiled softly. "I'm glad to hear you say that."

Elizabeth sighed and sat back in her seat. *And I'll keep saying it, until I finally believe it.*

"WHAT ARE WE WAITIN' FOR, DAD?" JACK ASKED HIS FATHER AS THEY stood next to the Batmobile, parked at the docks on Saturday morning. "Are they bringing the wood today so we can build the fort?"

Will smiled at the expectant look on his son's face. "Not today. Um, I just thought it would be fun to people-watch for a little bit." The ferry had docked, and the passengers were slowly disembarking. He smiled when he caught sight of Georgiana's long blonde hair. "Look at all the people coming to the island and see if you can pick someone out who you could tell me a story about."

Jack sighed impatiently and stared at the crowd. "How am I s'posed to—"

His words stopped, and Will knew he'd caught sight of Georgiana. He watched Jack's expression as his son's mind raced to confirm what his eyes were seeing. When he realized it was truly her, his face exploded in a huge smile and revealed dimples that matched his father's.

"Auntie G! Auntie G!" Jack yelled excitedly as he ran toward her. Georgiana saw him coming and squatted down to wrap him up in her arms. She squeezed him tightly until he struggled to pull away. "Why are you here?"

"I came to see you! Are you surprised?"

"Yeah, I am! Wait till my dad sees you! He's gonna be surprised too!" He spun around and looked at his father, who was slowly walking to join them. "Dad, look, it's Auntie G! She's surprisin' us!"

Will chuckled as Georgiana stood, and he hugged her tightly. "Wow, this is a great surprise," he said, kissing her cheek and then looking at Jack.

Jack eyed him suspiciously. "You knew she was comin', huh?"

Will nodded. "We wanted to surprise you. I guess it worked."

"Yeah, it worked," Jack responded happily. "I'm surprised."

"I'm glad," Georgiana said, ruffling his hair.

"Are you stayin' for a long time? Are you gonna stay at our house?"

"Yup, I'm staying with you. But I don't know how long I'll be here. Maybe a week?" She glanced at Will.

"I told you, you're welcome to stay as long as you want," he said quietly.

She nodded. "Okay."

Georgiana loved the Batmobile and found it amusing that golf carts were the main form of transportation on the island. Will loaded her suitcase into the back and they headed away from the docks. He pointed out a few things to her as they drove along, telling her some of the history of the island.

"Hey Dad, look. Is that 'Lizabeth?" Jack asked, pointing ahead of them from his seat on Georgiana's lap.

"I think it might be," Will answered, his eyes now glued to the two women walking towards them from far down the lane. "We'll see when we get a little closer."

Sure enough it was the Bennet sisters, walking with beach bags slung over their shoulders.

"Hi 'Lizabeth!" Jack called out.

"Hi, Jack. Hi, Will," Elizabeth answered, smiling at them.

Will greeted both women and introduced them to Georgiana. "I take it you're headed to the beach?" he asked.

"We are," Elizabeth answered. "We're going to Diamond Cove."

"I thought you liked the view from Indian Cove best?" Will asked, his attention now completely focused on Elizabeth. He smiled when he saw her face flush.

"It's a little too far to walk," she told him with a grin. "Not all of us are spoiled enough to own a flashy cart."

"Ah, jealous of the Batmobile, are you?" he teased. "I'm sorry I don't have the space, I would offer you a ride."

"I think we can manage."

"Enjoy it. It's certainly a perfect beach day." He hesitated but kept his eyes on hers. "Um, see you tomorrow?"

She nodded. "See you tomorrow."

They said goodbye and Jack chatted as they drove away.

"That's 'Lizabeth, she's really nice. She works at the library and she's really good at readin'. One time we had a squirt gun battle at Mr. Bingley's house and Dad squirted her on accident and she got him back really good. We went to the beach with her the other day, the one that Dad said. She told me all about the black rocks. Sometimes we sit with her on the ferry if we see her and she ate lunch outside with us yesterday."

Will felt Georgiana's eyes on him as Jack told her all about their new friend, and knew that the more Jack spoke about Elizabeth, the more Georgiana's curiosity would be piqued.

I'll get the third degree at some point.

They pulled up to Will's house a few minutes later, and Georgiana gasped. "Oh, Will, this is just gorgeous! Look at that porch!" She climbed out of the cart and looked around in awe. "It's beautiful."

He moved to stand next to her. "It is, isn't it?"

She inhaled deeply. "It even smells good!"

He laughed. "According to the real estate agent who sold me the place, there will be flowers everywhere soon." He nodded toward the door. "Come on, I'll give you the tour."

A bit later, after enjoying a light lunch and a full tour of the house, they sat outside on the deck. Georgiana sipped from a glass of water and Will had a beer, while Jack played on a tire swing that hung from the solid branch of a huge oak tree in the backyard.

"Jack is happy," she stated quietly, watching Jack as he spun around in lazy circles.

"He is," Will agreed. "He's already made a friend, Sam, who lives nearby. Um, he might be coming over tomorrow afternoon with his family. I hope you don't mind, I invited some people over for a cook-out. Nothing big, just a few friends. I thought it would be nice for you to meet them."

She smiled. "That sounds great."

"You'll like Charles, he's…well, he's the total opposite of me." He laughed a little. "He talks constantly and he's always in a good mood. He's opening a business—I told you about that—so I've been helping him get his footing." He held up his glass. "This is his beer, actually."

"Who else is coming?"

"Maddie, who was my real estate agent, and her husband Ed. Charles might bring his sister, Caroline. And you met Elizabeth and her sister Jane. Jane is just visiting for a few days, I think." He cleared his throat. "Like I said, a small group. I haven't exactly been going crazy with the socializing."

"I'm actually impressed you've met that many people already."

He rolled his eyes. "I'm not a hermit, you know."

"I know. It's just that you haven't made an effort to get out much. Not in a long time."

He shrugged. "It was too hard in New York. Everyone already knew me, knew Anne...knew *everything*. It was overwhelming."

"Have you told anyone here what happened?"

"Charles knows. His parents were killed by a drunk driver."

"You told me about that. It's horrible," she said softly.

"Yeah, it is. So he knows about the accident and all that. I haven't talked to anyone else about it, though I'm pretty sure they all know I'm a widower." He shook his head. "God, I hate that word. It makes me feel old." He sighed. "They all know I lost my wife."

"But it's okay that they know, right?"

He nodded. "It's not a secret."

"Jack seems to like Elizabeth."

He grinned and picked at the handmade label on the beer bottle. "Yeah, she's, um...he likes her. Mm-hmm."

"It sounds like you see a lot of each other."

Here come the questions. "Um, yeah, we–we see each other. Around. Occasionally."

"At the beach, on the ferry, at story hour, at lunch..." Her voice trailed off and when he lifted his eyes to hers, her mouth dropped open. "You are *blushing!*"

"I am not," he responded quickly. "It's the beer, it's strong."

"Bullshit."

"Georgie!"

"Sorry, but that's a crock. What gives?"

He paused for a moment. "Nothing. Nothing gives. We've spent some time together. She's nice, Jack likes her—"

"Oh, *Jack* likes her. Hmm, okay, now I understand."

"Georgie, please."

She immediately stopped teasing and looked at him seriously. "I'm sorry Will, it's just...I haven't ever seen you flustered over anyone before. Except Anne, but I was too young to remember much of that."

"I know. Anne is the only person I've ever *been* flustered over, as you so eloquently put it, so how do you think *I* feel?"

"I'm sorry if I made it worse."

"You didn't make it worse, because it couldn't *be* any worse," he said quietly. "I'm just now getting to the point where I can talk to her without tripping over my words."

It fell silent as he took a moment to gather his thoughts, his eyes focused on the glimmering bay beyond the trees.

"She's very nice, and we get along well," he finally said. "I like spending time with her and getting to know her. She's easy to be around. I don't feel self-conscious, or like I have to be someone I'm not…" He looked at his sister. "I *like* her. And when I'm not spending time with her, I *want* to be spending time with her."

"It feels weird, though," he continued quietly. "It all comes back to what I said to you before, about being a widower. It's not like I went out and got a divorce. I didn't choose to end my marriage; the choice was made for me." He swallowed roughly. "It's hard to just become unmarried, you know? And it's hard to admit I might have feelings for someone else. I don't—I don't feel guilty, or at least I'm *trying* not to feel guilty, but it feels odd. Anne is still there—she's still a part of me, and I see her in Jack every day. How do I let myself feel for someone else when I still love the little parts of Anne that I see in my son? Do I just push all those feelings away and pretend they don't exist anymore?"

Georgiana shook her head slowly. "I don't think you have to push those feelings away or pretend they're not there," she began, "because I think a part of you will always love Anne."

She reached out to squeeze his arm lightly, silently urging him to look at her.

"*You* have to accept that. And if you find the right person, someone who loves you enough, she'll be able to accept it too. I think Anne will always occupy a space in your heart, but I also think that when the time comes, there will be lots of space for someone else. Does that make sense?"

Will nodded as he stared at his sister. Deep in his gut, he *knew* she was right, but even so, he needed to talk about it.

"Where do you see this going with Elizabeth?" she asked. "Or is that too much to even think about right now?"

He shrugged and went back to picking at the label on the bottle. "I don't know. To be honest, I haven't thought beyond the next time I'm going to see her."

"Have you thought about taking her out on a date?"

He shook his head. "No, that won't work. How can I? I have Jack, and he goes with me pretty much everywhere. And I'm not complaining. I just don't have any other options yet."

"If you *could* take her out on a date, would you ask her?"

"Probably." He thought about how nice it would be to take Elizabeth out. Maybe they'd go to dinner and take a walk on the beach, just the two of them. He looked at Georgiana and nodded. "Yeah, I would. I would ask her out. I don't know if she would say yes, but I would ask."

"Oh, come on! I only met her for five minutes, and even *I* know she would say yes."

"How could you possibly know that? You barely spoke to her."

She sighed and rolled her eyes. "She blushed when she talked to you, and she couldn't take her eyes off of you. She would say yes, trust me."

His eyebrows rose. "You think?"

"Yes. *Yes*. Listen, why don't you ask her if she wants to go out while I'm here? I'll hang out with Jack."

He shook his head. "I didn't invite you here so you could babysit."

"Oh please, I know that," she told him. "But I would love some one-on-one time with Jack. He told me there's a bowling alley and an arcade on the island. I could take him bowling and we could play some video games. Maybe we could even camp in his room, like we used to do in New York."

Will smiled when he thought back to all the times he'd walked into Jack's bedroom when Georgiana was visiting their apartment in New York, only to find sheets strung from every corner, making his room into a giant tent. "He would really like that."

"Okay then, it's settled. When Elizabeth comes over tomorrow, you'll ask her out on a date." She leaned forward and squeezed his arm again. "*If* you're ready to ask her," she added. "I'm not trying to push you into it."

"I know. But I would really like to ask her. And I will." He took a deep breath. "When Elizabeth comes here tomorrow, I'll ask her out."

Eleven

"I'm sorry you and Sarah can't make it, but I'll be happy to have Sam for the day," Will told Mike Grady as they spoke on the phone Sunday morning. "Jack will be thrilled."

"Honestly, Jess will be ecstatic," Mike replied, referring to his teenage daughter. "She wanted to spend the day with a friend and wasn't happy to be stuck babysitting instead."

"That settles it, then. Sam can spend the day here."

"You're sure?" Mike asked.

"Absolutely."

They finished their conversation, and Will walked outside to find Georgiana and Jack. He spotted them walking along the border of the backyard.

"Hey," he called out as he headed over to join them. "What are you looking at?"

"Auntie G is just showin' me where some flowers are growin'," Jack answered. "See 'em?"

Will nodded as he looked at the green shoots poking up from the soil. "I guess we'll have to clean out these flowerbeds soon. Hey, I called the Gradys. Sam is going to come and hang out with us today. How does that sound?"

Jack pumped his fist. "Awesome! Can we have another squirt gun battle?"

Will saw Georgiana's eyes widen, and he grinned mischievously. "Auntie G would *love* that."

Jack looked up at his aunt excitedly. "Yeah, Auntie G, you can be on my team with me and Sam. Dad can have Mr. Bingley and 'Lizabeth."

"We'll see," she answered. "I don't know if I'm prepared for a squirt gun battle."

Jack looked puzzled. "You don't need to be 'pared, you just gotta run fast so you don't get wet."

Georgiana laughed. "Is that the trick?"

"Yeah, but it's not a trick, you just run away," Jack said earnestly. "I'm goin' on my swing." He ran toward the tree and pulled himself up on the giant black tire, pumping his small legs to get it moving.

"So what do we need to do for tonight?" Georgiana asked Will. "Do you need my help with anything?"

He shook his head. "I don't think so. I have chicken marinating, and the corn on the cob just needs to be shucked."

"How about a garden salad? Or some potato salad or something?"

He scratched the stubble under his chin. "Hmm. Maybe the market has something. You want to stay here with Jack? I'll take a ride."

"Sure."

"Alright, I'll be back in a bit." He went into the house and grabbed his wallet and sunglasses and then headed out to the Batmobile. He pulled up to the market a few minutes later, and when he heard someone call out his name, he turned to see Caroline walking toward him across the small lot.

"Hello, Caroline."

"Hey stranger, how are you?"

"I'm well, thanks. You?"

"I'm fine," she said as she came to stand next to him. "I'm looking forward to your party tonight."

He chuckled. "I wouldn't call it a party. Just a cookout, nothing fancy."

"Well, I'm sure it will be fun. I haven't been to that house in ages; I'm curious to see the changes you've made."

"Actually, I've left it alone. There wasn't anything I wanted to change."

"It's a lovely house. Have you started to stock the wine cellar yet?"

"Not yet," he said, laughing a little. "I have good intentions though. I keep saying I'm going to stop into the wine store Maddie told me about, but I haven't made it there yet."

"There are several good wine shops in town. If you ever want an escort, let me know."

He nodded once. "I'll keep that in mind."

She hesitated and then frowned. "I feel like I owe you an apology."

"Me? Why?"

"I was pretty negative about Charles's business venture the other night, and I'm sure I sounded like a shrew. I *do* have faith in him, and I know that once he sets his mind to something he's usually successful. It's just—it's *getting* him to set his mind to something. And this is huge. He's put so much money into it, with even more to follow...I would hate to see him fail."

"You don't need to apologize to me," Will said quietly, "but maybe you should apologize to him?"

"I have, we talked the next day. But I still feel badly that I acted like that in front of you. You barely know him, but you've given him so much help. I feel like I offended you."

He shook his head. "You didn't."

She placed her hand on his forearm. "Are you sure? I would hate for things to be tense between us, especially since we're just getting to know each other."

He glanced at her hand and then looked back into her eyes. "There's no tension."

"That's good, because I'd like to continue to get to know you." She squeezed his arm, then moved her hand to curl it around his bicep. "Now, I need you to help me with something." She guided him into the market and over to the deli. "I need to find something to bring tonight, and since you're here you can help me decide." She leaned into him, almost resting against him as she perused the freshly prepared foods. "I was thinking of the Caprese salad."

He peered through the glass case. "The what?"

"The Caprese. It's fresh mozzarella with tomato and basil."

"Oh, sure. Um, that sounds great. Don't go overboard, though."

"I enjoy going overboard." After ordering, she turned to him again. "So tell me, is there...anything else you need?"

He pulled his head back slightly, feeling she was a little too close for comfort—*his* comfort. Her proximity, along with what she'd just said and how she said it, made it abundantly clear what she was offering. Her fingers slid from his bicep to his forearm, where they stroked slowly up and down.

His eyebrows rose as he slowly extricated his arm from her grasp. He'd never been hit on before, at least not so blatantly. There had always been women who'd seemed a little too friendly with him, even when Anne was alive, but he never imagined they were flirting. Anne always noticed and playfully teased him about how oblivious he was.

"I'm all set, thanks." He dredged up a smile, but he felt cornered. Had he done something to give her the idea he was interested in her beyond friendship? An image of Elizabeth's face drifted into his head, her big brown eyes startlingly different from the bright blue ones facing him now.

It's her attention I want.

He cleared his throat. "I'm just going to grab some pasta salad and be on my way."

Caroline accepted her package from the man behind the counter, but her eyes remained on Will. "My offer stands," she said. "Whatever you need, whenever you need it, just...let me know." She leaned toward him and winked. "See you tonight."

He watched as she walked away and then turned to look at the man behind the counter, flushing with embarrassment when he realized he hadn't given his order yet. "Oh, sorry. I just...I need some salad. Pasta salad. Two pounds, please."

The man grinned knowingly. "Ya sure that's all ya need?"

WILL GLANCED OUT THE WINDOW OF HIS KITCHEN BEFORE LETTING HIS EYES wander to the clock. It was only just after four, but he was impatient for Elizabeth to arrive. Charles and Caroline were sitting outside at the table, talking to Georgiana.

He heard voices coming from the front porch and headed into the living room, swinging open the front door just as Elizabeth was about to ring the bell.

"Hey, everyone. Welcome, come on in." He gestured for them to enter.

His eyes repeatedly darted to Elizabeth, quickly taking in the length of leg exposed by her shorts before traveling up to her eyes. She was smiling brightly, and he smiled in return.

"I'm glad you could make it," he said to her, and then looked at his other guests. "Um, all of you. Here, let me help." He took a pan of chicken wings from Maddie and a large bowl from Elizabeth. "Follow me into the kitchen."

"I just need to warm those a little," Maddie noted, and Will placed the pan into the oven and set the temperature as she instructed.

Jane carried a brown paper bag, and Elizabeth asked her to set it down on the kitchen table. Drinks were poured, and they all went outside to the deck. Introductions were made between those who hadn't yet met, and everyone settled into chairs to relax.

"The house looks lovely," Caroline said to Will when he sat down. "You're right, there isn't much that needs changing."

"I like it the way it is"—he smiled at Maddie—"just as my real estate agent promised I would."

"Oh, you must have had an *excellent* agent," Maddie said, causing everyone to laugh.

Ed patted her hand. "The best, my dear, the best."

"It's gorgeous here," Jane noted as she glanced around the yard. "It's so spacious and private. And I love the way you can see the bay through the trees."

"There's a path from the backyard that leads down to a small beach," Charles mentioned casually.

Will's eyes widened. "There is?" he asked, and everyone laughed.

Charles grinned. "I know this island like the back of my hand, believe me."

"Is it too far to walk?" Jane asked him.

He shook his head. "No, not at all. Would you like to check it out?"

She nodded and smiled. "Sure."

They stood, and Charles glanced at Will. "Back in a bit."

Everyone was still gathered on the deck when Charles and Jane came out of the woods and walked into the backyard.

Maddie rose from her seat. "Oh, I forgot about the wings!"

"Sit, I'll get them," Will offered.

"I'll help." Charles stepped onto the deck and went into the house behind Will. He closed the sliding door firmly and turned to Will with raised eyebrows. "Did you see Elizabeth's sister?"

Will smirked at the look on his friend's face. "Obviously. I met her Friday."

"She's–she's…hmm. Jane Bennet." He shook his head slowly. "Who knew? I mean, I've heard Elizabeth talk about her before, and I know she's been here to visit, but we've never met. She's hot."

Will shrugged. "She's pretty, I guess."

"Pretty? You guess? She's drop-dead gorgeous," Charles said matter-of-factly.

Will laughed as he grabbed potholders and pulled the now steaming-hot pan of wings from the oven and placed it on the granite counter. "She's your type, I suppose."

"Maybe, but…" He frowned. "She's Lizzy's sister. And speaking of Lizzy…she's *your* type, huh?"

"Maybe," Will answered vaguely. "I don't think I have a type."

"Yes, you do, and it's Lizzy. You didn't tell me you took her to lunch on Friday."

"I didn't know I was supposed to report in." Will grabbed a pair of tongs and began transferring the wings to a platter.

"You are. Absolutely. Every move." He grinned when Will shot him a dubious look. "When are you going to ask the girl out already?"

"Funny you should mention that…"

Charles's eyebrows rose. "Uh-oh, what did I miss?"

"You didn't miss anything. Georgiana offered to babysit if I wanted to take Elizabeth out, so I'm thinking about asking her."

Charles slapped Will on the shoulder, hard enough to make him wince. "Do it, man! Today. Steal her away for a minute and ask her."

Will's eyebrows rose. "Steal her away?"

"Yes. Tell her you need help with something in the house."

"This is ridiculous." Will shook his head. "I can't believe I'm getting advice on how to ask a woman out from you."

"Why not me? I'm pretty good at it."

"Says the guy who was shot down by Lizzy."

Charles laughed. "You have a point. But hey, you could do worse."

"I suppose."

The slider opened, and Caroline walked in, carrying a glass of wine. "Do you boys need help? The wings will be cold by the time you bring them out if you keep dawdling."

"We're coming, we're coming." Charles lifted the platter from the counter, then eyed Will seriously. "Do it," he said firmly before going back outside.

Will shook his head and looked away, grinning to himself.

Caroline moved to stand in front of him. "What is my brother ordering you to do?" she asked as she set her glass on the counter.

He took a small step back. "Um, he's just trying to get me to broaden my horizons."

"Broaden your horizons?"

"Yes."

"Charles probably isn't the best one to help you do that," she advised. "I don't know if anyone's horizon should be as broad as his."

He laughed but said nothing and was surprised when Caroline stepped toward him again and reached up to stroke her fingers along his cheek and down the side of his neck.

"However, I would be *more* than happy to help in that regard."

He moved his head back, but her hand followed, and when he reached up to push it away, she moved closer.

"I appreciate the offer, but I'm not interested." He took another step back.

"You don't know what I'm offering," she told him softly, laying her hands flat against his chest.

He glanced down in surprise and then looked back at her. "I'm pretty sure I do."

They were interrupted when the slider opened and Georgiana and Elizabeth walked in, happily chatting away. Both women froze and stared at them silently, and Will watched as Elizabeth's eyes dropped to Caroline's hands, still resting on his chest. Without skipping a beat, he reached to remove them and spoke in a low voice.

"No, Caroline."

ELIZABETH'S STOMACH LURCHED, AND SHE FOUGHT THE URGE TO TURN around and walk back outside. Instead, she took a deep breath and forced a smile.

"Sorry, we just came in to get more napkins," she said. "Oh, and Ed wants to know if you have any hot sauce."

"Yeah. Sorry," Georgiana repeated.

"I'll just head back outside." Caroline lifted her glass from the counter and turned to Will. "We can finish our conversation later."

He shook his head a little, and Elizabeth heard his quiet but firm response. "It's finished."

"We'll see." Caroline smiled and winked at him before looking at Elizabeth and Georgiana. "Ladies." She made her way outside and the door closed behind her.

"Um, napkins?" Elizabeth asked again, noting the color in Will's cheeks.

"In the cabinet behind you," he answered haltingly. "I'll–I'll get them."

"No, I've got it," she answered, relieved to turn away for a moment. She took another deep breath and opened the cabinet.

"Hot sauce?" Elizabeth heard Georgiana say.

"Um, I don't have any."

"Okay, I'll let Ed know," she said quickly. "I'm going back outside."

When Elizabeth heard the slider close, she turned to face Will again. "Georgiana is very nice."

He nodded and cleared his throat. "Yeah, she is. She's great."

"She's crazy about Jack."

"The feeling is mutual. That was the biggest downside to leaving New York." He leaned back against the counter and shoved his hands into his front pockets. "Georgie spent a lot of time with him. As much as she could while going to school, anyway. He misses her."

She smiled softly. "So do you."

He returned her smile, though it seemed half-hearted at best. His eyes dropped from hers, and he shuffled his feet. She could see he was uncomfortable, but she wasn't exactly sure what she'd just walked in on, making her more than a little uncomfortable herself. Taking a deep breath, she decided to grab the bull by the horns and clear the air.

"I'm sorry if we interrupted something when we walked in."

His eyes flew back to hers. "You didn't," he reassured her. "Well you *did*, but it was a welcome interruption."

She groaned to herself. Charlotte had guessed Caroline would try to get her claws into Will, and by the looks of things, she was right.

"You and Caroline don't get along very well, do you?" he asked, staring at her intently.

"Honestly, I don't really know her all that well. I know more *of* her, I guess. Which probably isn't fair, but..." She shrugged. "She used to date someone I know, someone who I consider to be a very good friend, and it didn't end well."

"The new junior partner?"

"You remember?"

He nodded. "I could sense some tension there."

"She's never done anything to me directly, other than make some snide comments here and there." She paused; the last thing she wanted was for Will to think she was a gossipy shrew. "I'm sorry, I probably shouldn't say anything. Caroline probably has some very nice qualities—"

"But you can't think of any at the moment?" he interrupted, grinning a little.

Her eyes rose to his and she tilted her head a little. "I'm *trying* to be diplomatic. You're not helping."

"I know, I'm causing trouble. Sorry," he said, a playful smile still on his lips. It faded quickly when he spoke again. "One thing I've already learned about Caroline is that she's persistent."

"I'll take your word for it."

Her attention was drawn to the brown paper bag Jane had carried into the house. It was still on the table where her sister had left it. "Um, wait here a second."

He looked at her curiously and watched as she went outside to deliver the napkins before coming back into the house.

"I have a housewarming gift for you," she explained as she closed the door behind her.

His eyebrows rose. "You do?"

She picked up the bag and placed it on the island. "It's nothing big."

"I *love* the wrapping paper," he joked, taking his hands from his pockets and fingering the crinkled brown bag. "You shouldn't have gone to all this trouble."

Her mouth dropped open. "Forget it, I'm taking my gift and going home." She reached for the bag and laughed when he reached to stop her. They ended up holding hands, and she glanced down at their entwined fingers and then back up to him. "This seems to be happening pretty frequently."

"Mm-hmm, I know." He stared into her eyes, squeezing her fingers. "Can I open my gift now?"

"Only if you're not going to tease me about the wrapping paper again."

He smiled and raised their joined hands a little. "Can I do it one-handed?"

"I guess we'll find out."

WILL GRINNED AT THE BLUSH ON HER CHEEKS AND WITH HIS FREE HAND, he reached into the bag and pulled out a bottle of wine. His eyes scanned the label slowly and his smile grew. "Are you serious?"

"I couldn't resist. It's–it's meant to be a joke. When I saw it, I thought of when we first met and I thought…I thought you would think it's funny."

He looked at her and then back to the bottle of wine—called "Horse's Ass"—and laughed before setting it on the counter. "I love it. And I agree, it's sadly appropriate."

"It no longer applies, in case you're wondering."

He laughed again. "Thanks, good to know."

The second bottle he pulled from the bag was called "Honey

Moon," and she explained to him that the next full moon—happening tomorrow night—was known as the Honey Moon.

"Maybe we should open it," he suggested.

She shrugged. "It's up to you."

"Hmm…maybe not. I think I'll put it in the cellar."

She explained that she chose the third and last bottle solely for its splashes of color. Bright flowers in every shade of purple and pink were painted all around the bottle, and the name was etched in bold white letters across the front.

"This is nice," he said, examining it closely.

"It makes me think of summer. It's pretty."

"Which follows your foolproof method of selection."

"Exactly."

"These are all great." He set the bottle down and noted the sparkle in her eyes. "Thank you."

"You're welcome."

He turned to look out the window over the sink. Jane and Charles were chatting with Ed and Maddie, but there was no sign of Georgiana on the deck. He glanced into the yard and wasn't surprised to see his sister playing with Jack and Sam. Caroline was sitting at the table, not speaking or even looking at anyone; she seemed to be staring at the slider.

He turned back to Elizabeth. "How would you like to see the legendary wine cellar?"

"I'd love to. Will anyone miss us?"

"I don't think so. Come on." He placed the bottles back into the bag and carried it with him, leading her by the hand into the basement. He reluctantly released his hold on her as he opened the door to the wine cellar and gestured for her to walk in ahead of him.

"Wow! It's much bigger than I thought it would be."

"It would probably be more impressive if there was actually some wine in it."

She giggled. "Well, now you have three bottles."

He lifted the bottles from the bag one at a time and stored them in their proper places. Standing back, he rolled his eyes. "You're right, it looks much more impressive now."

She laughed again. "Well, it's a beginning." She nudged him with her elbow. "Everything has to start somewhere, right?"

"Right."

Everything has to start somewhere.

The words caught and held, almost as if they were a sign.

Do it.

He cleared his throat. "That's what I've been thinking lately." She looked at him curiously, and he felt the nerves in his stomach jump to life. "What I mean is, I've thought about…I wondered if…if maybe we could start. Something."

Her eyebrows lifted slightly. "Something?"

He sighed and looked down, lifting one hand to rub the back of his neck. "Sorry, that was horrible."

"Not necessarily. It depends."

He looked up at her again, surprised to see her playful expression. "On what?"

"On what the something is. Try again," she urged.

Her brown eyes were wide and expectant, and he took a deep breath. "I–I wanted to ask if you would like to go out with me sometime. For dinner." He took both of her hands in his. "Soon. Tomorrow? Tuesday?" He cringed, annoyed with himself for sounding a bit too eager.

She laughed softly. "Would this be a date?"

"Yes, of course," he answered, tilting his head slightly. "Wasn't— isn't that obvious?"

She shrugged, still smiling. "I'm just making sure."

"Yes, it would be a date." He was entranced by the shine in her eyes. "So…?"

She nodded. "Yes, I would love to go out with you."

His gaze dropped to her lips, lingering there for a moment before traveling back to her eyes. The electricity that sparked between them was instant and unmistakable. He watched as her cheeks pinked and knew she felt it too.

Her body swayed slightly toward his, and he moved closer to her, slowly lowering his head toward hers.

"Dad? Are you down there?"

Jack's voice echoed down the stairs, and Will lifted his head. Elizabeth nearly fell into him, releasing his hands and then gripping his hips for balance.

He turned his head toward the stairs and reached to hold her waist, helping her to keep her balance. "Yeah, bud, I am. Um, I'll be right up."

"Is 'Lizabeth down there too?"

"Yes, I—we're just looking at the wine cellar. We'll be—we'll be right there." He turned to look back at her, and nearly groaned aloud. Her eyes were bright, her cheeks were flushed, and she looked very kissable. And the way she was staring at him…

His thoughts were stopped short by the sound of two sets of feet pounding down the stairs, and they released each other just as Sam wandered into the wine cellar, followed by Jack.

"Aw, cool! What's this place?" Sam asked, looking around in wonder.

"It's a wine cellar," Jack said matter-of-factly. "Hey Dad, you have wine in it now. Three bottles."

Will grinned. "Elizabeth brought them as a gift."

"Oh. Are you gonna cook soon? We're gettin' hungry."

"In a few minutes. Go on up, I'll be right there."

The boys dashed back up the stairs, and he turned to Elizabeth. "Sorry about that."

She grinned. "Don't apologize, it's fine."

Without thinking, he reached up to stroke her cheek, relishing the warmth and softness of her skin beneath his fingers. He let them wander down her jaw to her chin and then back up to glide along her cheek again.

"I've wanted to do this since we were at the beach," he said, his voice rough as he watched his fingers lightly trace over her skin.

"It feels nice," she whispered.

Their gazes stayed locked, and he nodded. He desperately wanted to kiss her, but now that he'd had a moment to think about it, he decided it wasn't the right time. He didn't want their first kiss to be here, in his cellar, and he wanted to be careful not to rush things—for his benefit as well as hers.

He took a deep breath and slowly lowered his hand, reaching for one of hers. "Come on, let's go up." When they arrived back in the kitchen, he stopped her before they went outside.

"When?" he asked quietly.

"Tuesday?" she responded, her cheeks blooming with color.

He nodded and smiled. "Tuesday."

Twelve

After their company had left and everything was cleaned up, Will kissed a freshly bathed Jack good night, taking a moment to inhale his clean scent as they hugged tightly.

I'll never tire of that smell.

Georgiana went upstairs to tuck him in, as he requested. He was exhausted; he and Sam only stopped running and playing long enough to eat. The Gardiners had generously offered to give Sam a ride home, and after checking to make sure Jess would be there, Will had sent him on his way.

Will sank down onto the couch and took a deep breath, enjoying the silence for a few moments. His thoughts immediately wandered to Elizabeth and how he'd been on the verge of asking her to stay a bit longer. He hadn't been ready to say good night and would have loved more time to sit and talk with her. Smiling a little, he thought of the bottle of wine she'd given him.

Horse's Ass.

She enjoyed teasing him, and he was more than happy to let her, just for the pleasure of seeing her eyes light up.

He thought of the way she looked at him when she'd walked into the house earlier, only to find Caroline pawing at him. *No light in those eyes then.* Instead there'd been confusion and disappointment. She tried to hide it, but he'd seen it in her expression. The last thing he wanted was for there to be *any* confusion as to who he wanted to spend time with—or whose hands he wanted pawing at him.

He'd come so close to kissing her—twice—and knew the opportunity would probably present itself again on their date. If Jack and Sam hadn't interrupted, he would have kissed her. *In the cellar.* Shaking his head, he berated himself. *Nothing like sneaking away from the adults to steal a kiss. What am I, sixteen again?* He'd had to do his fair share of sneaking around back then, but those days were long gone.

Georgiana came back downstairs to join him and laughed as she sat down on the opposite end of the couch. "He asked me to read to him. I didn't even get to page six, and he was out cold."

"Isn't that great? I love that he's exhausted at the end of the day from playing so hard."

"*I'm* exhausted!" she exclaimed. "It was fun running around with the boys instead of sitting at the table with all the grown-ups."

He grinned. "I'm sure it was."

"Your friends are very nice," she noted. "Maddie and Ed are so funny. She's so chatty and outgoing, and he just sits and watches her with a look of total adoration on his face."

"They're great. I lucked out when I landed Maddie as my agent. She had a great sense for what I was looking for." He glanced around the living room. "I mean, look at this place. I never thought I would feel so at home in such a short period of time."

"It's beautiful, and I can tell Jack loves it. Oh, we're building a fort this week? Is that true?"

He groaned. "Not necessarily. The lumber is coming on Tuesday afternoon, so I told him there was a *chance* we could start it on Wednesday, but I didn't make any promises."

"Why not? I think we should do it. I bet we could get it done in one day if we set our minds to it."

"Possibly...but remember, this is me you're talking about."

She sighed. "Jack said you have the plans. We just have to follow them step by step. Maybe Charles could help?"

"No, he's got too much on his plate right now."

"That's true. Did you watch him and Jane today?"

"Not really, why?"

"The electricity coming off of them could have lit up a city! Lots of sparks there. *Lots.*"

"He mentioned he thought she was pretty."

"That doesn't surprise me. And all Caroline did was frown at them and at Elizabeth. I couldn't figure her out." Suddenly her eyes opened wide. "Oh! You have to tell me what happened with you and Caroline! I completely forgot about that."

He groaned and dropped his head back on the couch, staring up at the ceiling. "Nothing. *Nothing* happened." He raised his head again and looked at his sister. "Did it look like something was happening? God, that was embarrassing."

"She had her hands on you so *something* was going on."

"No, it was nothing," he repeated firmly. "She was trying, but I told her I'm not interested."

"Honestly, it didn't look like you were in the middle of a romantic embrace. You looked like you'd eaten something that didn't agree with you, and she looked like she was clinging to you."

He sighed. "Great."

"You and Elizabeth were gone for a while after that." She looked at him expectantly.

He cleared his throat. "Um, I showed her the wine cellar. Did anyone say anything about us disappearing?"

"I was in the yard with the boys, but I heard Caroline ask what was taking you so long." Her smile grew. "She *was* going to go looking for you, but Charles told her you had some old books you wanted Elizabeth to look at because you thought they were first editions or something."

He laughed. "Good man."

"Caroline didn't talk much after that. She kind of glared at the house until you came back outside."

"Yeah well, she made up for it during dinner, didn't she?"

Georgiana laughed and pulled her legs up and under her at the end of the couch. "She didn't shut up! She was trying so hard to monopolize your attention."

"She was also trying to monopolize my thigh with her hand," he said with a grimace. Somehow, he'd ended up sitting between Caroline and Elizabeth during dinner.

"Eww!" Georgiana groaned, scrunching her nose.

"Exactly."

"Did you get around to asking Elizabeth out?"

He nodded, and a small smile lifted his lips. "We're going out Tuesday night—if you're still willing to hang out with Jack?"

"Of course I am." She winked. "I won't even give you a curfew."

He chuckled. "That's generous of you." After a moment, he spoke again. "Not to change the subject, but you've been here since yesterday, and you haven't said anything about what's going on with you and Dad. Do you want to talk about it?"

She sighed, and her eyes briefly flickered away from him. "It's nothing huge. I just...I told him I wasn't sure about school anymore."

He frowned. "Georgie, that's kind of huge. I thought you loved school."

"Oh, I do. I love going to classes, and I've made some great friends. It's not school itself, it's what I'm studying. Everyone automatically assumed—even me—that I would study business so I could eventually take my place at DMG."

"Like me." He watched as she nodded. "You know, I never asked if it was what you wanted to do. I always took it for granted you were happy."

"I was okay with it at first. But once my classes started and I really began to understand what I would be doing, I was completely uninterested in all of it."

"Is there something else you would rather study?"

She shrugged. "I haven't decided yet. My mind has been set on business for so long... Is it selfish of me to want to do something else?"

He shook his head. "Of course not. It took me a while, but I've learned that you have to do what makes you happy, whatever's going to give you the most joy in life—even if it's not what other people want for you. Like Dad."

"He accused me of wanting to be a lay-about socialite whose sole purpose is to spend his money."

"You?" he asked, grinning a little. "A lay-about, maybe, but a socialite?" He laughed when she stretched out a leg to kick him. "No way, that's not you. Although you can *shop*. I've seen proof of it."

She kicked him again. "I'm trying to be serious," she said, even though she smiled as well.

"I know, and I wouldn't make light of it if it wasn't so ridiculous."

He paused. "You just need to take some time to figure out what you want to do. Don't let Dad push you into a corner."

"Is that what he did to you? Did you really want to go into the family business, or were you just guided forcefully down that path?"

He chuckled at her choice of words. "I really wanted to work for DMG. I wanted to immerse myself in the business and be part of the next generation to carry on with it. I never resented the assumption it was what I would do. I wanted it just as much as Dad did."

She frowned. "I don't understand. Why is there so much conflict between the two of you? I mean, for as long as I can remember you've been at each other's throats."

"It's complicated."

"But I want to know." She looked at him for a long moment. "Is it because of Anne?"

"He said it was because of Anne, but it was really because of his elitist attitude. He thought she was beneath me. The DeBourghs weren't good enough for the Darcys. He never wanted me to like her, never mind fall in love with her. And then to get her pregnant and marry her? Not in his plans for me at all."

Her eyes widened. "What do you mean, get her pregnant and marry her? Don't you mean marry her and *then* get her pregnant?"

"I—no. I mean get her pregnant and *then* marry her. You didn't know Anne was pregnant with Jack when we got married?"

"Will, I was thirteen! I was clueless."

"You never did the math?"

"No, I just—I never had any reason to even *think* about the math. I just assumed she got pregnant after you were married."

"Despite how it sounds, it wasn't what you think. Anne and I loved each other and had already talked about getting married. We were surprised by the news, but after the shock wore off, we were happy about it. Very happy." He shrugged. "We just sped up our plans a bit, that's all. Did you know her father used to work for DMG?"

"I vaguely remember that. Where did he work?"

"He was one of Dad's accountants. They grew up together in Brooklyn."

"So that's how you met Anne?"

"Yes and no. It's not like Dad socialized with the DeBourghs. I'm sure the fact they grew up together had something to do with Louis getting a job at DMG, but that's as far as their relationship went. Dad was the boss, Louis was the employee. Period." He paused. "I met Anne at a company picnic Dad made me go to. I grumbled about going, but he said it wouldn't do for the owner's children not to be there. You went too, though you probably don't remember. You were only five or so."

She shook her head. "I don't remember it at all."

"To make a long story short, I fell for her instantly." His mind drifted for a moment as he thought back to that warm spring day. "She didn't go to the same high school, but we started dating. Dad found out and forbade me from seeing her, which only pushed me to see her more. I snuck out at night, lied about going to visit friends on weekends, skipped school..." He chuckled when his sister's eyes widened. "I got caught a few times, and Dad was *not* pleased. But hey, I was a teenage boy dealing with his first case of puppy love. Is that surprising?"

"It is to me. I can't imagine you doing any of those things."

"I did them all and more. Dad was convinced going away to college would be the end of my childish romance, as he called it." He rolled his eyes. "He didn't know that while I was at Columbia, Anne was a stone's throw away at Wagner. I used to take the Staten Island Ferry to see her all the time, or she would come to see me. When Dad finally caught wind of it—from Richard, I eventually found out—he fired me."

"Richard ratted on you?" She frowned again. "Wait, how could Dad fire you? You were still in college."

"I worked at DMG during school breaks and over the summers. Dad knew what he was doing—he wanted me to worry that I'd be joining the ranks of all the unemployed graduates looking for work." His voice took on a harder edge. "And yes, it was Richard. I didn't know who'd been filling Dad in on what Anne and I were up to, but I never once suspected it was him. I confided in him, and he turned around and reported everything back to Dad."

Will thought of that day when he found out Richard was the one who'd been keeping tabs on him. He confronted his cousin, and what started out as a shouting match quickly turned physical, and Will had thoroughly kicked his cousin's ass.

"That's horrible. I can't believe Richard betrayed you like that."

"Richard is a whole *other* story, and not one I want to get into. Anyway, Anne's father ended up getting fired. He was accused of embezzling from DMG."

"He stole money?"

Will shrugged. "I don't know." He paused for a moment and shook his head. "I don't believe he did. I think Dad had Richard set it up to look that way, hoping it would drive Anne and me apart. How could I disgrace my family by dating the daughter of a man who was stealing from us? But it didn't matter. Louis claimed he was innocent, and from the way Anne's family lived, it was clear he hadn't stolen anything. They always lived very modestly."

Georgiana's eyebrows drew together, and it was obvious she was distressed by what he'd revealed. "I can't believe Dad would do that, that he would purposely hurt someone like that."

Will remained silent, well aware of what his father was capable. After a moment of contemplation, Georgiana continued.

"I know Louis passed away years ago, but where's Catherine? You don't talk about her much."

"She's in a nursing facility in upstate New York near her sister. She has Lewy body dementia. We found out about a month before the accident. I've been to visit her a couple of times, but the last time I called, her sister advised me not to come."

"That's sad."

"Anne was an only child, and they doted on her. They were very close."

"What did they think about you and Anne?"

"They were supportive. They knew how we felt about each other, even though we were both young. Louis made it clear to me that if things got out of hand, if Dad *ever* made Anne's life difficult, he wouldn't keep silent. But he didn't have to worry. Dad never got close enough to Anne to hurt her."

She smiled softly. "You protected her?"

"Of course," he answered seriously. "After I graduated, Dad relented and rehired me. I think he realized if I hadn't come begging for a job by then, I wasn't going to. When he found out Anne was pregnant, he fired me again."

She rolled her eyes. "Is that his go-to reaction?"

"Yes. But after Anne died, he wanted to hire me back again. God forbid he leave his grieving son out of the family fold. How would that look?"

"Will…"

He waved a hand. "It's okay. I understand what motivates him, and it's nothing remotely paternal."

"Why didn't you just say no?" she asked. "Why did you keep going back?"

"I *wanted* to work for DMG," he answered simply. "I knew everything about it and loved everything about it. I was lost after Anne died, and my job was something I could focus on. Plus, I knew Dad would retire someday, and it would become mine." He paused and looked at his sister.

"I know that sounds greedy, but it wasn't just the money I was thinking about. It was…it was something that was *ours*, something our family had built. I was proud of it, proud of what my grandfather started and Dad continued to build on. Part of me resented the business because of the kind of man it had turned Dad into, but still…there was something about it being a legacy, something tangible to be handed down. I wanted to be a part of that, and felt I could do the job just as well as Dad but at the same time, do it differently. Be a different kind of man."

"And maybe Jack would be a part of it someday too?"

Will shrugged. "Maybe, if that's what he wants. Dad had already started calling Jack the heir, the one to carry on after me. That's why he fired me again; I was taking *his* heir away from New York, away from his home."

"Did Dad ever express remorse or regret about Anne?"

Will gave a short, sarcastic laugh. "He did, in his own way."

He knew this was where his narration would end—there were other events that occurred between him and his father, but he wouldn't share them with Georgiana.

"Okay, enough about me and Dad. You really have no idea what you want to study?" he asked, putting the focus back on her.

"There are things I'm interested in, I just…I can't decide. It has to be something I want to do for the rest of my life, right? I'm not going to rush into a decision." She paused. "What about you, what are you going to do?"

"Enjoy the summer with Jack." *And hopefully Elizabeth too.* "You and I both know I don't need to work."

"So *you* get to be the lay-about, is that what you're saying?"

He chuckled. "I guess so." His expression turned serious. "I meant what I said before, Georgie. Our door is always open. If Dad gives you a hard time or puts too much pressure on you, you know you can come here whenever you want."

Tilting her head, she smiled a little. "I know, thanks. And now," she said, clapping her hands together, "you need to focus on Tuesday night. You're actually doing it, you're going out on a date!"

His stomach lurched, and he looked at her helplessly.

"Don't look so terrified! You'll be fine," she assured him quietly.

He exhaled loudly. "I'm just…I'm a little nervous. I've only been on one first date, and it was a really long time ago. I don't want to screw it up."

"You won't screw it up, don't think like that." She nudged him lightly with her foot and smiled. "I'm proud of you, you know."

He raised his eyebrows but said nothing.

"Hearing you talk about Anne…I know how much you loved her, and I know how hard it's been for you to do that, to just *talk* about her." She paused. "It seems to be getting easier."

"It *is* easier. It doesn't hurt as much, not like it used to. She's always going to be a part of me, and she's half of Jack." He smiled at the thought of his son. "But I'm ready to move on. I want to start living my life again. I know Anne would want me to be happy, so I'm going after some happiness. I feel like I have an idea of where to find it." He took a deep breath.

"So yeah, I'm really doing it. I'm going out on a date." A smile bloomed on his face, even as his stomach lurched again. "With Elizabeth."

"Lunch?"

"Yes, lunch. I thought maybe we could meet at his new pub or brewery or whatever it is."

Elizabeth turned and looked at Jane in surprise. "You realize it's pretty much in shambles at the moment, right? It's not open. He has no food to make lunch *with*."

Jane smiled. "I know, so I suggested getting takeout. I figured since you're going to be at work, it would be a nice way to pass the time." She paused. "Anyway, it doesn't matter. He said no."

Elizabeth walked back to the couch with a glass of wine in each hand and joined her sister. She handed Jane one of the glasses and spoke hesitantly.

"So…was it just a friendly invitation, or were you hoping for something more?" She noticed her sister paying a lot of attention to Charles throughout the evening.

"Well obviously, *something more* probably isn't a good idea. I leave in two days. If I were staying longer, though…" Jane's voice trailed off, and she smiled.

"Really?"

"Yes, *really*. We seemed to hit it off when we went for that walk." She shrugged. "What's with all the questions? I thought you liked Charles?"

"I do, he's a great guy, but…"

"But what?"

Elizabeth thought about Kate and what had happened between her and Charles just a few days ago. "Charles is a fantastic guy and a great friend, but he's a flirt. It's, like, part of his genetic make-up or something."

"He's a flirt? Or is he a player?"

"I wouldn't call him a player. He's had his share of girlfriends… including one he can't seem to end things with completely."

Jane pursed her lips and nodded. "I appreciate you telling me that. It was just going to be lunch, anyway. He's nice to look at and fun to talk to. And those eyes...phew!" She laughed when she saw Elizabeth roll her eyes. "I can't believe you turned him down when he asked you out. Come on, you know he's hot, admit it."

"He's very good looking, I have no problem admitting that."

"So why did you turn him down?"

"You know why. I hadn't been here long and was nowhere near ready to date. And I'm glad I *did* say no, because if I'd gone out with him, we might not be friends now."

"True." Jane paused for a moment and then waggled her eyebrows at her sister. "You know who else is really hot?"

Elizabeth grinned. "Yes." Her face warmed, and she took a sip of wine to try and hide it. "Will."

Jane smiled widely and giggled. "He looked so bummed out when you were leaving tonight. I swear he wanted to kiss you. If we weren't all standing there, he probably would have tried."

Elizabeth's mind wandered to their almost-kiss in the wine cellar, and she felt her stomach jump. "Maybe."

"Tell me what happened when you were in the house! I had to restrain myself from running to the slider and peeking inside."

"We just talked. When I first went in with Georgie, Caroline was kind of hanging on him. It was so awkward."

"Caroline was hanging on him?" Jane slapped her thigh. "*That's* why she kept staring at the house when you two were inside. She has the hots for him."

"Apparently. I asked him straight out if Georgie and I had inter-rupted anything, and he said it wasn't what it looked like."

"Do you believe him?"

Elizabeth nodded. "He said she's persistent, so obviously it's not the first time she's made, um, overtures toward him."

"Hmm. Well, looking at that house, I'm assuming he has money. That's a big draw for her, isn't it? She's the one who screwed over Charlotte's brother, right?"

"The one and only."

"Her reputation precedes her. So what else happened?"

"I gave him the wine, so he offered to show me the wine cellar."

"Did he get the whole 'Horse's Ass' thing?" Jane asked. "I hope he laughed about it."

Elizabeth grinned. "He did. I made sure he understood it was a reference to the past, not the present." She cleared her throat. "Anyway, when we were down there, he asked me out."

Jane's eyes widened. "He asked you out?"

Elizabeth nodded and took another sip from her glass, trying again to hide what was surely a prominent redness in her cheeks. "We're going out Tuesday night."

"Lizzy, that's fantastic! He seems so nice, and then of course there's the hotness factor."

"Oh, he's got it."

"In spades."

They both laughed, and then Jane grew serious. "So…are you ready for this?"

"Ready for what?"

Jane rolled her eyes. "Don't be obtuse. Ready for *this*—the date, the *act* of dating, being involved, seeing someone, having a relationship. All of that."

"Can I get through Tuesday night first?" Elizabeth answered, laughing a little. "I just want to make it through our date without spontaneously combusting. That's my goal. I'm already nervous, and it's still two days away."

"Are you going to tell him about Bill? Or George?"

"Well, no, not on Tuesday night! Geez, Jane, don't you think you're putting the cart before the horse?"

"I don't know. What if he asks? Are you going to ask him about his wife?"

"No! Will you cut me some slack? For all I know, our first date might be our last. We might make each other miserable and not say a word to each other the whole night."

"You? Not say a word? Pfft."

Elizabeth lightly slapped her sister's arm. "Shut up. It's possible we'll have nothing to say to each other and the whole night will suck, and we'll never want to see each other again."

"Not likely. As much as I looked like I wasn't paying attention to the two of you, I was. He stared at you constantly."

"He was observing," she murmured.

"What?"

"Nothing."

"Well, he was doing it a *lot*—whenever Caroline wasn't forcing him to talk to her, that is. She was trying way too hard. Why did he even invite her?"

Elizabeth shrugged. "They're friends. She's Charles's sister, and he hasn't met many other people."

"Introduce him to your friends, broaden his social circle."

"Once again, can I get through Tuesday night first?" Elizabeth shook her head, but smiled at her sister. "You are unbearable at times, you know that?"

"I know, but I'm looking out for you. That's why you love me. I'm pushy, but in a good way. You need to be pushed."

"I'm perfectly capable of pushing myself when the need arises."

"The need has arisen."

"So what do you want to do tomorrow night?" Elizabeth asked, decidedly changing the subject. "Maybe I'll see if Charlotte is off. I think Kate has to work."

"Smooth, very smooth. I see what you did there." Jane narrowed her eyes. "But yes, I think another night out with the girls would be fun."

"Me too."

It was quiet for a moment and Elizabeth sighed deeply, staring off at nothing. Her thoughts inevitably traveled to Will and their almost-kiss. The remembrance of it and that feeling of anticipation made her heart pound. She didn't want to share what happened with Jane, preferring to soak in those feelings a little bit longer.

"Stop, Lizzy."

Elizabeth startled. "Stop–stop what?"

"Stop being nervous. I can tell you're thinking about it."

"Oh, yeah. I know."

"Just be yourself. That's who Will likes and wants to take out."

Elizabeth nodded and smiled. "I know. I couldn't possibly pretend to be a different person. It requires way too much effort."

Jane laughed. "You're absolutely right. Will knows a good thing when he sees it."

"Thanks, Jane." Her eyes dropped and focused on her hands as she held the wine glass and slowly swirled the deep red liquid. "But do I know a good thing when I see it?"

Jane looked surprised. "Of course you do."

Elizabeth kept her eyes lowered. "That's a pretty bold statement considering my track record, don't you think?" She shook her head, unsure from where these thoughts had suddenly sprung. "What if I'm wrong about him?" She looked at her sister. "Any vague feelings about him you'd care to share?"

"I think he's one of the good guys. His sister is very nice, which says a lot, and you can see they're close—all three of them. I watched the way he interacted with Jack, and he has so much patience with him. I get a good vibe from him, Lizzy. I think he's okay."

Elizabeth absorbed everything Jane said and knew she was right. She thought back to her conversation with Will when they'd been at the beach; he said he was comfortable with her and felt like he could let his guard down, as if they'd know each other for much longer. She felt the same way; there was a certain rightness to all of it. A rightness to *him*.

"What are you thinking?" Jane asked.

"I was thinking you're right. Will knows a good thing when he sees it." Elizabeth smiled softly and lifted her chin a little. "And maybe this time, I do too."

WILL STOOD AT THE DOCKS ON TUESDAY MORNING, LIGHTLY ROCKING ON his heels as he waited to board the ferry. His eyes scanned the small crowd and finally found Elizabeth slowly walking across the parking lot. She was completely focused on a book she held open in front of her, paying little attention to where she was going.

He made his way toward her, positioning himself in her path so she had no choice but to bump into him.

"Oh! I'm so sorry, I wasn't—" She looked up and her startled expression bloomed into a smile. "Will! Hi!"

He chuckled. "Hi, yourself. Sorry, I couldn't resist. You're a danger to people, walking around with your nose buried in a book. If you're not careful, you'll walk right off the pier."

"Well, that makes me more of a danger to myself, doesn't it? Besides, I'm a good swimmer, so no worries there. What are you doing down here?" She took her backpack from her shoulder and opened it to put her book away. Before she had a chance to hoist it back up, he took it from her and put it over his own shoulder.

"I'm going to do some grocery shopping. I gave Jack the option of staying home with Georgie, and he didn't hesitate to ditch me."

"I'm sure it was a very tough decision," she said with mock seriousness.

"I'm sure it wasn't," he answered, gazing down at her.

Her dark brown eyes were bright as she looked up at him, and her growing smile was infectious. He found himself smiling back and realized they probably looked ridiculous, standing in the middle of the lot and grinning like fools. Glancing up, he noticed passengers boarding and gave her arm a little nudge. "Come on, I'll buy you a cup of coffee."

She wrinkled her nose at him as they started to walk toward the dock. "You don't want ferry coffee, trust me. I know where we can get a cup in Portland, if you have the time."

"I'm not on a schedule. The perks of being unemployed." He grinned when she laughed. "Do you have time?"

She nodded. "I always give myself an extra few minutes in case I make a detour into the bakery. It's hard to walk by when all those incredible smells are drifting outside... I don't have a lot of willpower when it comes to that stuff."

They made their way up to the top deck of the ferry and decided to sit outside in the sunshine. Will folded himself into a seat, his knees nearly coming into contact with the seat in front of him.

She chuckled. "Can you fit?"

"Barely."

"How tall are you, anyway?"

"Six-three. And a half."

"Does the half really matter?"

He was surprised when she lifted his hand from where it rested on his thigh and held her hand up to it, pressing their palms together. Each of his fingers reached at least an inch, if not more, beyond the tips of hers.

"Those things are like paws," she said teasingly. "I don't know if you can really call them hands."

He quickly entwined her fingers with his and held them securely. He noticed hers were bare of any jewelry, the short nails perfectly shaped and painted a pale pink. He turned to look at her, a gentle smile playing on his lips.

"It doesn't matter what you call them, they fit perfectly with yours. See?" He lifted their joined hands to place a kiss on the back of hers. "That's all that matters."

ELIZABETH FELT HER FACE FLUSH AND TURNED AWAY FROM HIM. THE SURGE of happiness she'd felt at seeing him in the lot had taken her by surprise.

She'd taken in his appearance—shorts, a Portland Sea Dogs T-shirt filled out admirably by a set of broad shoulders, and an old pair of Sperrys—and had nearly swooned on the spot. She was *still* trying to get her bearings and trying to accept that this tall, handsome, incredibly sweet man wanted to take her out.

"Isn't Jane leaving today?" he asked, pulling her from her thoughts. "I'm surprised she's not with you."

"Oh, well, we went out last night with a few friends, and I think she's probably not at her very best right now. She's going to meet me for lunch before she heads back to Boston."

"A crazy night out, huh? You seem okay."

She turned to look at him again, finally feeling as though the heat in her face had diminished. "I was the sensible one in the group. One, I had to work today, and two, I didn't want to feel lousy…later."

He smiled. "I don't want you to feel lousy later either."

"It would make a horrible first impression."

"First impression? We're way beyond that," he teased. "We must be at second or third impressions by now."

"Lucky for you," she said, arching one brow.

"I didn't make a very good first impression, did I?" He laughed. "And I didn't even have a hangover, I had no excuse. We don't have to rehash that, do we?"

"No, I think I've reminded you of it enough over the past couple of days."

"Right, especially with my housewarming gift," he said, still with a little smile on his lips.

"I told you, I couldn't resist. It was too perfect."

He continued to smile, but said nothing.

"What?" she asked, searching his eyes.

"I like it when you tease me."

"Oh." Her face flooded with color again.

"And I like watching you blush."

She rolled her eyes slightly and looked away, mortified at how many different shades of red she turned when in his presence.

"Uh-uh, don't look away." He tugged on her hand, and when she turned to face him fully and lifted her chin a little, he chuckled softly. "That's better."

"For whom?" she asked, though she couldn't help but grin. The warm, deep sound of his laugh caused her stomach to flip.

"For both of us. We have to get all this blushing and first date awkwardness out of the way, don't you think?"

"Wouldn't it make sense to get it out of the way while we're actually *on* our date?"

"Under normal circumstances, sure, but since we're here, we can get it out of the way now."

She bit back a grin. "Oh. Okay."

"So, what would I say to you tonight that would make you blush? Let me think." He paused for a moment, his eyes traveling over her face and then quickly down her body and back up again. "I would probably tell you how beautiful you are."

He's such a flirt. Her face flamed once again.

"See? It's working. When I tell you how beautiful you are tonight, you won't blush. It'll be old news."

She laughed outright, knowing the heightened color in her cheeks would probably be there for most of the day. "I don't even know how to respond to that."

"You don't need to, I'm moving on." He lifted their joined hands. "We've already conquered this, we're comfortable holding hands. But I was thinking... First kisses can be awkward sometimes, right?"

Her heart picked up its pace, skipping along briskly. "I'm sure they can be."

He smiled and leaned in close, reaching with his free hand to stroke her cheek. "If we were alone," he said, his expression turning serious, "I would be trying very hard right now to overcome that awkwardness." His gaze dropped to her lips, lingering there for a moment before lifting to meet her eyes again as his fingers moved to travel along her jaw. "Unfortunately, we're not exactly alone."

She shook her head slowly. "No, not exactly."

She swallowed heavily and stared into his eyes. They were a rich, deep brown, and she couldn't look away.

"You have the most gorgeous eyes." The words tumbled from her lips before she was aware she was saying them. To her surprise, his cheeks became suffused with a light shade of pink.

"You're blushing," she said incredulously, unable to stop her small smile.

He lowered his hand and leaned back in his seat, closing his eyes and shaking his head. "I'm sure I am."

"Should I tell you how handsome you look to save you from blushing tonight?"

He chuckled, and she watched his color deepen. Being teased, and then teasing him in return and making him blush, had made her feel a surge of warmth and affection. He opened his eyes again, and when he turned to look at her, a small grin lifted his lips.

"I fully expect you to tell me how handsome I look tonight," he said, puffing out his chest a bit. "Telling me now won't get you out of it later."

She arched one eyebrow playfully. "My, aren't we a little full of ourselves."

He shook his head slightly. "No, I'm not. Not really. You can tell me I am though, I don't mind."

He squeezed her hand, and his smile lessened a bit. "I don't know...I'm not...I have no idea how to do this."

"Do what?"

"*This*," he replied, "what we're doing. I'm just...I'm completely winging it, and I hope I'm not embarrassing you, or–or making you uncomfortable. Or making a fool of myself."

She'd already begun to shake her head before he finished speaking. "You're not doing any of those things." She paused and squeezed his hand in reassurance. "I'm winging it too. Please don't worry about that."

He nodded but remained serious. "Okay."

She leaned her shoulder against his and nudged him a little. "Plus, we still have to get past that awkward first kiss, right? We'll both be winging it with that."

"Oh, I won't be winging it with that," he said, his eyes dropping to her lips. "I definitely know how to do that."

Thirteen

E lizabeth stood in front of the full-length mirror in her bedroom and examined her appearance. She'd already changed her outfit twice; the first was too casual and the second too dressy. The bright floral print skirt, vivid blue short-sleeve blouse, and low-heeled sandals she wore now were just right. With a roll of her eyes, she reminded herself that Will hadn't asked her out because of her impeccable sense of style.

She'd had lunch with Jane earlier in the day, and then they'd said their goodbyes, though her sister had promised to come back in a couple of weeks. She asked Elizabeth to call after her date with Will, and Elizabeth told her she would, as long as it wasn't too late.

There was a knock at the front door, and she quickly glanced at her alarm clock. *Too early for Will*. She walked into the living room and smiled when she saw her landlord. "Hi, Maddie! Come in."

"I was just wondering if you had plans for dinner tonight. Ed is going to grill up some salmon, and we thought you might like to join us."

"Um, actually, I *do* have plans." Elizabeth smoothed her hands over her skirt. "I have a date."

"You have a date? A real date?"

Elizabeth laughed. "Yes, a real date. I know, it's surprising."

"I'm not surprised you were *asked* on a date," Maddie clarified, "I'm surprised you accepted. You haven't exactly been the queen of the dating scene since you moved here."

"I know, but you know why," Elizabeth said softly.

"I'm sorry if it sounded like I was making light of it," Maddie told her apologetically. "I'm not."

"I know you're not. It's just...I haven't felt a connection with anyone."

"And you do now?"

Elizabeth nodded and smiled. "Yes. It's–it's an odd feeling. Almost unsettling, but in a good way."

Maddie stared at her intently. "And does Will feel it too?"

Elizabeth's eyebrows rose. "How did you know?"

"The way that man looks at you? I knew it was only a matter of time before he worked up the courage to ask you out."

"What do you mean, the way he looks at me? It took him forever just to acknowledge my presence. You were there the day we met. He barely even glanced at me."

"I think you had him thrown from the very start, and he didn't know how to handle it."

"Maybe," Elizabeth murmured, smiling a little and recalling that Charlotte had said something similar.

It's possible his reticence had been some sort of defense mechanism, something for him to hide behind. It would make sense; they'd both been through a tremendous amount of loss and pain, though completely different in nature.

"I know this is a big deal for you, Elizabeth, but don't overthink it."

"I'm not, I swear. I think we've *both* been thrown, and we just need to step outside of our comfort zones and shake things up a little. And I want to do that with him. I think we're both ready to try."

"That's all it takes, a voice inside of you telling you it's time and that you're ready," Maddie said. "I think in Will's case it's especially true, but it holds true for you as well. It's not as though the two of you could have pointed to a date on a calendar and said, 'That's the day I'll start again.' It had to arrive on its own, and then it just took both of you realizing it *had* arrived. And maybe meeting each other helped move it along."

"Like fate?"

"Yes. Whatever it is, it put both of you here on this island at this particular point in your lives."

Elizabeth nodded and clasped her hands together, then unclasped them and wiggled her fingers. "I'm just a little nervous."

"That's understandable."

Elizabeth rolled her eyes. "You're supposed to tell me I shouldn't be."

Maddie chuckled. "Honey, you're going to be nervous regardless of what I say. But no, you shouldn't be. There's no reason to be nervous."

Elizabeth took a deep breath. "Do I look alright?"

"You look gorgeous. Where are you going?"

"To Island Jewel for dinner. I think he wants to stay on the island because of Jack, which is fine with me. It'll be quieter here."

"I'm sure the sunset will be lovely tonight. You should take advantage of it."

"Maybe we will. I could show him the beach at the Point."

Maddie's eyebrows rose. "Now *that's* a romantic spot."

Sighing, Elizabeth covered her eyes with one hand. "Okay, so maybe not *that* beach. It would probably sound too forward, not to mention cliché, if I suggest going to the Point to watch a sunset. It sounds like a pick-up line, and not a very good one at that."

Maddie went to Elizabeth and gently pried her hand from her face. "It's not forward. Do you want to know what I think?"

Elizabeth nodded.

"I think Will is sitting at home right now, fretting about this as much as you are. Don't put so much pressure on yourself for it to be perfect. What fun is that? If it seems like he would enjoy going to the beach to watch the sunset, suggest it. Don't plan it, just go with the flow." She squeezed Elizabeth's hand before releasing it. "Wing it."

Elizabeth smiled as those words instantly brought back the conversation she'd had with Will on the ferry this morning and how he'd talked about their first kiss. Her stomach knotted with anticipation; she was looking forward to the moment when she would finally find out how it felt to kiss him.

"That's an interesting smile," Maddie said, interrupting her thoughts. "Care to share?"

Elizabeth shook her head. "No. I think that's just what I'll do, though—I'll wing it."

∽

"THIS IS GOING TO BE A PIECE OF CAKE, YOU KNOW. IT LOOKS PRETTY easy."

Will looked at Georgiana incredulously. "Easy?" She'd taken the plans for the fort and had spread them out on the kitchen table. Jack was next to her, kneeling on a chair to gain a better view of the design.

Will placed a hand on Georgiana's forehead. She pulled away, looking puzzled. "What are you doing?"

"Checking to make sure you don't have a fever. What is it that looks easy about that?"

"It's just following directions, step by step. The wood is pre-cut, partially drilled, and labeled. We just have to match up the right screws and things. And look"—she bent to lift a small box onto the table—"this is all of the hardware. It's already labeled as to what goes where." The larger box containing the lumber had arrived, its contents now stacked against the back of the house.

"Thank God."

"Fitzwilliam, this set is designed for people just like you," she told him as she walked over to the stove to stir the ground beef browning in a pan.

Jack giggled.

"What's funny?" Will asked, poking his son in the ribs.

He giggled again. "Fitzwilliam."

Will grabbed him from behind and lifted him out of the chair and up over his head before pretending he was going to drop him, making Jack screech. "You're lucky you didn't end up with that name, pal."

Jack laughed. "Yup, I know." When his father placed him back on the chair, he looked at him curiously. "Why're you all dressed up?"

"Remember I told you I was going out tonight?"

"Oh yeah. With 'Lizabeth, right?"

"Right. Auntie G is going to stay and hang out with you."

"Where're you goin'?"

"Just out to eat."

"Why can't me and Auntie G go too?"

"Well, Elizabeth and I thought it would be nice if just the two of us could go out this time."

"Oh." Jack thought for a moment, his expression serious. "Is 'Lizabeth your girlfriend?"

From the corner of his eye, Will saw Georgiana's eyes widen and the obvious effort she was making to hold in her laughter.

"Well no, not–not really. Not yet. Maybe she will be, though. Someday." He took a deep breath. *This is not what I expected.* "Would that be okay with you? If Elizabeth was my girlfriend?"

Jack nodded solemnly. "Yeah. She's nice."

Will smiled. "I think so too."

"Can we start building the fort tomorrow morning?" Jack asked, his mind back on more important matters.

"Absolutely. Auntie G will be the boss; we'll just do what she tells us to do."

"She already told me that. She said she has to be the boss 'cause you don't know what you're doin'."

Will glanced at his sister, who burst out laughing. "Thanks, Georgie."

"Hey, you already admitted it. Jack and I will get it all puzzled out. You just need to show up."

"Yeah, Dad, don't worry." Jack patted Will's arm. "We know what we're doin'. You just need to show up."

"Oh, I'll be there." He ruffled Jack's hair. "Why don't you get washed up? I think your dinner is almost ready."

"'Kay."

Will watched Jack leave the kitchen and then took a deep breath. "That was a surprise."

"The girlfriend thing doesn't seem like a big deal to him." Georgiana turned from the stove to face him.

"I know. I just didn't expect him to ask, not when I'm about to go on my first date with her."

"Well it's over and done with, so now you don't have to worry about it." She paused and turned off the stove. "*Were* you worried about it?"

"Not really. If Jack had been older when he lost his mom and had memories of her, it might be different. He likes Elizabeth, so that helps."

"What's not to like? She's great."

"Yeah, she is." He rubbed his hands together before jamming them into the front pockets of his pants.

Her eyebrows rose. "Are you nervous?"

"Yes."

"What time do you have to pick her up?"

He glanced at his watch. "In fifteen minutes."

"So...shouldn't you be leaving?"

He nodded once. "Yes."

"Then go!"

He glanced down at his clothes. "Do I look alright?" He'd chosen khakis, a deep green short-sleeved button-down shirt, and his Sperrys.

"You look great. Very preppy, like you're headed to a yacht club."

He rolled his eyes. "Fantastic."

"I'm teasing, you look very handsome." She tilted her head. "Your hair is getting long."

He reached up to touch it self-consciously, running one hand through the thick, dark waves. "I haven't bothered to find a barber yet. Jack needs a cut too."

"He looks cute with long hair."

Jack came back into the kitchen and climbed up on a stool while Georgiana took a pan of taco shells from the oven. "Mmm, tacos. We haven't had 'em in a long time, huh, Dad?"

"Yeah, that was a good idea from Auntie G," Will said, kissing him on the head. "Be good for her tonight, okay?"

"I will. We're gonna make tents in my room like in New York."

"Have fun." He gave his sister a kiss on the cheek. "Thanks again, Georgie. Call my cell if anything comes up."

"Have a great time," she instructed lightly, "and don't rush home."

WILL PULLED INTO THE GARDINERS' DRIVEWAY AND GLANCED AT HIS watch. *Six o'clock on the nose.* He took a deep breath to slow his galloping heart rate, then stood from the cart and smoothed his hands over his shirt. Straightening his shoulders, he headed for the footpath that led to Elizabeth's cottage.

"Hello, Will!"

He started at hearing his name called out and turned to see the Gardiners sitting on their deck.

"Hi, Maddie. Hi, Ed," he said, stopping for a moment. "How are you?"

"We're just fine," Maddie answered. "We thought we would enjoy dinner outside. It's such a lovely night, isn't it?"

He nodded. "It's very nice. Um, if you'll excuse me…"

"Of course, we don't want to keep you."

As he walked toward the cottage, he heard music. He observed Elizabeth through the screen door, quietly singing along as she put in an earring.

"Knock, knock," he finally said softly. She jumped, and one hand flew to her heart. "Sorry, I didn't mean to startle you."

She opened the door. "It's okay. Come in," she said, smiling brightly.

He stood in the living room and looked around with a bemused expression. "Wow, you were right. This place is *huge*."

She laughed. "Isn't it? I'd give you a tour, but I'm afraid it would take too long and we would miss dinner."

He laughed. "It's very charming."

"It's ridiculously small, and actually, with you standing here, it seems even smaller." Her eyes traveled over him quickly. "But yes, it's charming. I love it, although the entire house could probably fit into your living room."

The walls were painted in pastel colors with white trim, and the furniture was covered in bright floral patterns. The kitchen was located in the small lighthouse-shaped structure, with the counters conforming to the curve of the walls. There were two other rooms off the living room, and he assumed one was the bathroom and the other her bedroom.

"I like it," he told her. "You're right, it's cozy."

"Thanks. It's home. Well, I'm ready. Should we go?"

"We should, but first I need to tell you how beautiful you look."

Her skirt was very pretty, sexy even, and her hair tumbled down her back in long waves. He remembered what it felt like to twirl one long strand around his finger on the beach that day, and he took in the light flush on her cheeks. "Very beautiful."

"Thank you. You look pretty handsome yourself."

His face warmed, and he glanced away from her, but not before he caught sight of her cheeky grin as she picked up her purse from the coffee table.

"Okay, now we're even," she declared. "Ready?"

He chuckled a little and nodded. "Yes. Um, we might have an audience when we leave."

She groaned. "Ed and Maddie?"

"Yes. They didn't seem surprised to see me."

"Maddie popped over a little while ago. I mentioned I had a date, and she figured out the rest on her own."

"Really?"

She nodded. "She's pretty intuitive."

"Either that, or I'm pretty obvious."

"According to her, it's a little of both." She laughed as he shook his head. "Don't worry, it's not just you. I think I'm just as obvious."

"I'm glad." He held out his arm. "Well, I guess we should get it over with."

"You make it sound like we're heading to the gallows," she teased as she curled her hand lightly around his bicep. "Come on, they're harmless."

They walked out of the cottage, and he pulled the door closed behind them. Their eyes remained on each other until they heard Maddie say something quietly to Ed.

"How was dinner?" Elizabeth asked them.

"Absolutely delicious," Ed answered, "especially since we washed it down with some of Charles's beer. There's nothing better."

"I agree," Will said.

"Don't let us keep you." Maddie picked up their plates, trying—unsuccessfully, Will thought—to appear nonchalant. "Have a wonderful evening."

"Yes, enjoy yourselves," Ed added.

Elizabeth and Will thanked them and wished them a good night. They continued down the path to the small driveway, and once seated in the cart, he turned to face her. "That was easier than I thought, although I wondered if Maddie was going to whip out a camera. I feel like we're going to prom."

Her eyes lit up and she laughed. The musical sound brought a smile to his face and made his heart thrum in his chest.

She turned to look at him, probably to say something, and before he knew what he was about, he was leaning toward her and gently cupping her face with one hand as he brought his lips to hers. He had the fleeting thought that it wasn't the right time, but it vanished quickly. He remained still, not doing much more than lightly pressing his mouth to hers.

He knew the instant her surprise dwindled away; her lips softened and became pliant under his, and he raised his other hand to cradle her face before letting it slide into the deep brown waves of her hair.

His heart was pounding heavily now, and his senses were completely overwhelmed by her—the softness of her skin, the floral scent he knew he would always associate with this moment, and the sweet taste of her lips, now moving tentatively with his.

Time seemed to stand still, and a wave of warmth spread through his body, making his hands shake. He lowered them to his thighs and drew away from her slightly, ending the kiss, and waited until she opened her eyes to look at him. Both of them were breathing erratically; he could feel the gentle puffs of her breath on his face as they stared at each other. He tried to talk, finding it necessary to explain himself or apologize or *something*.

He swallowed and tried to slow his breathing. "I–I'm sorry—" He stopped speaking when she shook her head and reached for his hands, closing the small distance between them and lifting her lips to his.

ELIZABETH KNEW WHAT HE WAS GOING TO SAY; HE WAS GOING TO TELL HER he was sorry, and she couldn't bear to hear it. As they kissed again, her hands slid up his forearms and over his biceps to his shoulders. They were a little surer of themselves now, and she silently encouraged him.

Once again, he reached to lightly frame her face with his hands, holding her as the kiss slowly and gently deepened.

A shiver shot up her spine and everything around her grew hazy and out of focus. There was only Will and this moment with him, the feel of his lips stroking over hers and the warmth of his thumbs caressing her cheeks. Even the sounds around her disappeared; all she heard now was her own heartbeat.

The thought quickly crossed her mind that she was exactly where she was supposed to be: in a golf cart in the Gardiners' driveway, kissing Will.

Like fate.

Their lips separated slowly, and she opened her eyes. His remained closed, and when she leaned back a little, he sought her lips again. They kissed once more, and she couldn't stop herself from moaning softly. The sound seemed to jostle him, and he unhurriedly pulled his lips from hers and took a deep breath before nuzzling her cheek and kissing her there.

He opened his eyes and smiled before lowering his forehead to hers and although her lips quivered, she managed a smile in return.

"Not awkward," she whispered breathlessly.

He chuckled and lightly stroked one hand over her hair, still keeping his forehead against hers. "No, not awkward," he echoed roughly. "Not at all." He sat back and looked around, then lowered his hands and took a deep breath. "Not the most ideal setting for a first kiss."

She reached up to touch his warm cheek before taking one of his hands in hers. "It was more than ideal. It was perfect."

They'd long since finished their dinner and were now just lingering, sitting and talking about everything and nothing. The candlelight and quiet piano music in the restaurant created a cozy, intimate atmosphere, making it easier to share.

When conversation turned to their families, he told her about the untimely death of his mother when he was just eleven, and how she'd died shortly after giving birth to Georgiana. Elizabeth was shocked, but before she had the chance to ask him any questions, he began to tell her about Alice Reynolds. She was something of a nanny/housekeeper for the Darcy family, and talking about her brought his smile back. He didn't mention his father, which didn't really surprise her; she knew there was some discord between them. In turn, she told him about her sisters and her parents.

"What does your father do?" he asked.

"He used to work for the MBTA, which is the public transit system in Boston. He had some medical problems a few months ago, so he decided to retire."

"That's too bad. Is he okay now?"

"He's fine. He spends his days working in the gardens around the house, or driving my mother crazy. I think he enjoys both equally."

The mention of Boston had led to a particularly spirited discussion of the merits of their home cities, and he'd let slip he was a New York Yankees fan. Of course, she'd been born into a Boston Red Sox family and was a proud member of Red Sox Nation. To pledge loyalty to any other team equated blasphemy in the Bennet household.

Now, he was intent on moving their conversation onto something else.

"Tell me something about you that no one else knows."

"That's impossible," she told him before taking a sip of wine. "I have no secrets from Jane. She knows everything about me."

"Alright, then…something Jane knows but no one else does."

She chewed her lip for a moment as she thought about what to reveal. "Oh, I know. I play the piano."

His eyebrows rose in surprise. "You do?" He sat forward again and rested his arms on the table, leaning toward her.

"Yes. Pretty well, actually," she boasted lightly. "It's not really a secret, but it's something *you* didn't know."

"So you play piano *and* sing."

"Were you listening when you came to pick me up?"

"Maybe."

"How long were you standing there?"

"Long enough. You have a very nice voice."

She returned his steady gaze, and when her face began to warm she cleared her throat. "Thank you. Okay, it's your turn."

"Oh, you want to know something about me?" She nodded. "Hmm. I don't really have any secrets."

She rolled her eyes and reached to lightly tap his wrist, but before she could pull her hand back, he weaved her fingers with his and tugged them gently.

"Okay, I guess there's my name. You don't know my real name yet."

Her eyes widened. "What do you mean? It's not William Darcy?"

"William is an abbreviated version. My first name is Fitzwilliam."

"Really?" she answered, biting back a grin. "That's–that's a unique name."

He tugged on her hand again and stroked it with his thumb. "You can giggle, it's okay. Jack does whenever he hears it."

She smiled widely and tried to focus on his words, and not on the warmth enveloping her hand. "I'm sorry, I'm not laughing, it's just...I don't think I've ever heard that name before."

"It's my mother's maiden name." He shook his head. "Do you know how much it sucked to try and learn to spell it in kindergarten? F-I-T-Z Will I am," he said in a sing-song voice, making her giggle. "I was ecstatic when my parents let me shorten it to Will in fourth grade. That's why Jack is just *Jack*, we didn't want to—"

He stopped speaking and his eyes dropped away from hers, and she lightly squeezed his hand. "You didn't want to saddle him with a long name?" she asked softly.

He nodded and swallowed. "Yes. I mean, we–we liked the name Jack anyway. It was just a plus that it only has four letters."

"What's his middle name?" She could sense his discomfort and held tightly to his hand.

"Um, it's Louis. After his maternal grandfather. My father-in-law."

"It has a nice ring to it," she said softly. "It's a very strong name."

He nodded. "It is. It's a great name. For a great kid."

∼

"WHERE ARE YOU TAKING ME?" HE ASKED AS THEY DROVE ALONG THE bumpy dirt lane. "Are you kidnapping me?"

"Interesting thought, but no," she replied coyly. "You said you wanted to see the sunset, so I'm taking you to the Point."

"Of course, the Point."

"It's not much further."

Soon enough, the lane opened up and ended in a large dirt parking lot. There were a few other carts, and when they walked down to the wide, sandy beach, they saw a small group of people further away who were trying to finish a volleyball game before the sun disappeared completely.

"This is beautiful." He took her hand but kept his eyes on the horizon and then looked up over his head. "You can already see the stars coming out."

She looked at him curiously when he sighed. "What was that for?"

He shrugged. "Just thinking."

"About...?"

He hesitated and then gave a short laugh. "A lot of things."

"Such as?" She held onto him for balance while she removed her sandals.

"Such as...I'm glad I left New York. I'm glad I brought Jack here." His eyes wandered to the ocean lapping calmly against the shore. "I love having this view, this amazing scenery, right in my backyard. I love that I *have* a backyard." He smiled at her quiet laughter and turned to look at her again. "I'm very happy you're here with me and you no longer think I'm a horse's ass."

She erupted in laughter, and the sound brought a smile to his lips. He lifted her hand to lightly kiss the back of it.

She quieted and looked up at him. "I'm happy I'm here too."

He remained silent, and his heart began to thump heavily when she moved closer to him. She stood on her tiptoes and reached up with her free hand to grasp his shoulder.

"But I would be happier if you kissed me again," she whispered, her eyes never leaving his.

He placed his hands on her waist and drew her closer before lowering his lips to hers. He kissed her slowly but thoroughly, determined not to rush. She was not shy or tentative; her lips stroked over his confidently, and they fell into a perfect rhythm. When he slid one hand up along her neck, he could feel the riotous beat of her pulse. He stroked her there lightly, and the sound of her soft gasp against his lips caused his entire body to tremble.

She drew closer and pressed against him as she reached up to wrap her arms around his shoulders, her hands sinking into his hair. He held her close and had the vague thought that he would happily stand here all night, doing nothing but this.

A cheer from the volleyball game brought them back to their surroundings. He reluctantly broke the kiss and held her against his chest as they swayed a little. His heart was still pounding heavily, and he knew she must have been able to hear and feel it, relaxing as she was against him.

Elizabeth fought to control her breathing and rubbed her lips together, licking them a little to savor the taste of him. *That was more than a kiss.* It had felt as though she was being consumed in a slow-burning fire, one that began as a small ember but steadily fanned to a bright blaze. She lowered her arms to wrap them around his waist, burrowing further into his chest, and inhaled the light scent of his cologne.

They both stood silently, holding each other and watching the sun drop into the ocean. The volleyball players began to pack up, taking their belongings and leaving the beach.

"It's going to be pitch-black here shortly," she told him quietly.

She felt the movement of his chest as he took a deep breath, and she closed her eyes, basking in the warmth of him.

"I don't want to take you home yet," he murmured.

"I don't *want* you to take me home yet."

"Where can we go?" he asked, nuzzling her hair.

She looked up at him and kissed his chin. "I have an idea."

Fifteen minutes later, they were walking across the small lot of the community swimming pool toward the playground. It was especially bright, as the previous night's full moon—the Honey Moon—shone brightly, casting long shadows.

They reached the swings and sat side by side. He immediately reached for one of the chains of her swing and pulled her toward him to kiss her. She smiled against his lips, and he lifted his head.

"Why are you smiling?" He gently pushed her away from him and then pulled her back, keeping his feet braced on the ground while hers floated underneath her.

"I was just thinking about the awkward first kiss we were supposed to have."

"We handled it pretty well, didn't we?"

"*Very* well. You said you wouldn't be winging it with that, so…I guess you were right." She laughed at his smug expression and then turned serious. "Why did you try to apologize?"

He lightly pushed her away and then pulled her back again, causing their swings to slowly twirl. "I don't know," he said with a shrug. "I feel like I ambushed you. I know you weren't expecting it."

"I wasn't. I'm glad you did it, though." She grinned. "I'm glad you couldn't wait."

"Oh, *now* who's full of themselves?" he asked playfully and pushed her away again.

She giggled. "That's not what I meant. I'm glad you couldn't wait because *I* couldn't wait."

When she drifted close to him again, he held the chains tightly. "Really?"

"Yes, really." She leaned toward him and kissed him briefly but sweetly. "I told you, it was perfect. I thought you were sorry you kissed me."

His eyes widened a little. "No, that's not what I meant at all, I just…I felt like I went too fast."

She shook her head and smiled softly.

She had so many other questions, but the last thing she wanted was to turn their first date into an inquisition. In the small amount of time she'd spent with him since he moved here, he'd only mentioned his wife twice and had hesitated each time, as if he were breaking some sort of unspoken rule if he said her name or talked about her. But it was different for him; losing your spouse because of divorce wasn't the same as losing them because of a sudden and unexpected death. It had been her choice to end her marriage, but Will wasn't given a choice. Chances were good that if his wife were still alive, he would be happily married and living in New York.

But he wasn't married anymore, and he wasn't living in New York. He was here, on this tiny island in Maine, sitting on some swings with *her*. Somehow she already knew there would be many dates to follow this one, and she knew it with such conviction that it should have made her question her sanity. She could only compare her feelings now to what she'd experienced when she'd moved to the island.

It feels like coming home.

He tugged on the chains of her swing again, continuing to pull until she was as close as she could be. "What are *you* thinking about?"

"Just that there's so much we don't know about each other," she said softly, and he nodded in agreement. "But I also think we have plenty of time to learn. We don't have to find out everything in one night, do we?"

"Of course not." He grinned playfully. "But we *could* get the basics out of the way now."

"The basics?"

"Yes. You know, the easy stuff. I'll start. What's your favorite food?"

"I have to pick one?"

"Yes."

"Seafood."

He rolled his eyes and shook her swing a little, making her laugh. "You can't say seafood, it's way too broad. That would be like me saying 'meat.' Be more specific."

"Okay, fine. Lobster. Yours?"

"The woman who lives in Maine picks lobster as her favorite food. That's a shocker," he teased. "Mine is a tie between Mrs. Reynolds' homemade mac and cheese, and a perfectly cooked filet mignon with Béarnaise sauce. Okay, favorite color?"

She let her eyes wander slowly down the front of his shirt and back up again. "Green." Her answer earned her a glimpse of his dimples and another kiss. "Yours?"

He stared at her for a long moment. "Right now, it's brown." Her cheeks flushed. "Now it's pink." His eyes dropped to her lips. "Hmm…now I think it might be red."

He tugged her toward him again, positioned the swing between his knees and reached for her hands, encouraging her to stand. She complied and now, with him still seated, they were at an equal height.

She stared into his eyes, so close to hers. "I–I think I'm changing my answer to brown."

WILL'S HEART RATE INCREASED AS HE LEANED INTO HER, STROKING HIS nose along hers before moving to her cheek and inhaling the scent of her skin. He detected a trace of his own cologne there and felt a sudden, unexpected burst of pleasure. Releasing her hands, he wrapped his arms around her waist and gently pulled her up against him. The momentum pushed his swing back slightly, and she placed her hands on his shoulders to brace herself. Without taking his eyes from hers, he brushed her lips with his in a fleeting, soft kiss.

He leaned back slightly to look at her and then repeated the action again and again, kissing her a little longer each time, keeping his eyes locked on hers. She leaned closer to him each time he pulled away, and he slowly moved his hands up her back and into her hair, groaning softly when he finally kissed her the way he *wanted* to kiss her.

Every bit of his focus was on the woman in his arms and how perfectly she fit there. He broke the kiss to catch his breath, but decided oxygen deprivation was not such a bad thing and quickly brought his mouth to her neck to inhale the sweet scent of her skin. He thrilled at the sound of her uneven breathing and at the feeling of her body aligning with his, her hands tangling in his hair and grasping it tightly. It was sensory overload and he reveled in it, feeling incredibly alive for the first time in a long while.

His hands left her shoulders and the shelter of her hair, sliding lower and coming to rest at the small of her back. He felt the heat coming off of her skin, and it would have been so easy to continue to stand there and bask in it, but he knew he needed to stop. He nipped at the soft skin on her neck, making her jump, but followed it with a light swirl of his tongue.

"Will," she said, her voice a throaty whisper.

His lips moved up her neck to the curve of her jaw and finally back to her mouth. "Elizabeth," he murmured. She sighed a deep, shaky exhalation of breath, and he kissed her again.

Finally he lifted his lips from hers and moved his hands up to cradle her face, letting his thumbs glide over her warm cheeks as he looked into her eyes.

"We–we should…" she began, before her words died and she just stared at him.

"We should stop," he finished for her.

She nodded but said nothing. Her fingers continued to play with the strands of hair at the nape of his neck until she moved her hands to his shoulders, kneading them gently.

He dropped his head to rest lightly on her shoulder, needing some time before he could stand up and not embarrass himself.

After a few moments spent holding each other quietly, he lifted his head, and she was surprised to see a playful expression on his face. "What?"

He reached behind her and grabbed the chain of the swing she'd vacated, and encouraged her to sit again. Once she was comfortable, he tugged on the chain and pulled her toward him.

"I am," he began, pausing to clear his throat before continuing on. "I am *not* sorry I kissed you in the Gardiners' driveway, and I'm not even sorry we were in the Batmobile. I am *not* sorry I kissed you at the beach, and I'm not sorry I kissed you here. I'm not apologizing for any of it."

She smiled. "I hope not. It would definitely lessen your chances for a second date." She raised her bare feet and rested them on his ankles.

"We can't have that. If we don't have a second date, I'll never find out all the other important things I need to know about you."

"Such as?"

"Your favorite type of music? Your favorite movie? Sunrises or sunsets? Dogs or cats? And the all-important question—fiction or non-fiction?" He stopped talking when she began to laugh again.

"These are things you have to know?"

He grinned and winked at her. "If answering yes gets me a second date then *hell* yes, I have to know. I want to know…"

"You…you want to know what?"

"I want to know *everything*," he said simply. "I want to know every possible thing there is to know about you."

"Everything?" she whispered.

He heard the hesitance in her voice and nodded.

"The good, the bad…and the really bad?"

He nodded again, more emphatically this time. "Yes. All of it."

He knew she understood what he was saying. *Warts and all.*

He stood from his swing and moved closer to her, lifting one hand to cup her cheek. His thumb stroked over her bottom lip and he bent to kiss her lovingly.

When he finally stood straight again, he gently pulled her from the swing and hugged her close. "All of it."

She nodded against his chest. "I–I want the same from you too. I want to know everything. Do you think you can tell me?"

"Yes," he answered quietly, his arms tightening around her. "Yes."

Fourteen

Will woke slowly, rolling to his back and releasing a long sigh. He scratched his bare chest and noticed his bedroom felt unusually cool, and he couldn't understand why until he cracked open his eyes and looked around. He was naked, only partly covered by a sheet, and all of his bedroom windows were open. The breeze drifting through them lifted the curtains, making the gauzy material billow and ripple, the morning sun creating shadows that danced and played on the walls.

The scent of something familiar floated around him, and he inhaled deeply, trying to identify it and wanting to imprint it on his memory. It was floral and decidedly feminine, and suddenly it came to him: it was *her*. It was the scent of the small indentations under her ears, the smooth valley between her breasts, and the tender skin behind her knees. Pleasure coursed through his body, and he wished for the ability to conjure up the delicate scent whenever he desired. Settling himself further into the pillow, he became lost in his thoughts and almost missed the very slight movement next to him.

He turned his head and beheld the sight of a luxurious mass of brown hair on the pillow next to his, and a grin slowly spread across his face. *It's her. She's here.*

He lifted his hand and reached out, tangling his fingers in the thick, soft waves before leisurely stroking down her bare back, following the sloping curve of her spine. Her body shifted as she woke, and he watched as she stretched, elongating each limb like a contented cat. She lifted her arms over her head and rolled over to face him, smiling languidly.

"Good morning," she whispered, sliding closer.

The sound of her sleepy voice was all it took to bring his body to life, and he rolled to his side to face her. "Good morning, Lizzy."

She was bare, the sheet only covering her from the waist down, her beautiful breasts only inches from his chest. The sheet slipped lower when she moved closer, revealing her stomach and one perfectly rounded hip. She was beginning to tan, and the warm tone of her skin was a striking contrast to the stark white sheets.

He lifted his hand and placed it on her breast, palming it gently, cupping the weight of it and watching in fascination as the peak tightened and grew under his touch. Unable to resist, he leaned forward to take it between his lips. Her arms curled around his head, pulling him closer as his tongue moved in gentle swirls and strokes, her body arching and legs tangling with his. She grasped his hair and urged his mouth to hers, and they kissed as if they were starved for the taste of each other.

He wrapped his arms around her, holding her tightly against him and kissing her hungrily until the need for air broke them apart. He stared at her lips, swollen and red, and all he could think about was making them *more* swollen, *more* red—and then she smiled again in a way that made his blood simmer. One petite hand landed on his chest and slowly moved lower, sliding further down his stomach and disappearing under the sheet.

He was beyond aroused already, and when he felt her warm hand trail over his abdomen and snugly wrap around him, he let out a low moan and closed his eyes before rolling to his back. Her hand moved at a leisurely pace, up and down the length of him, and when he opened his eyes, she was gazing down on him with a heavy-lidded, come-hither expression. Her mouth lowered to his, and his eyes lazily drifted shut as they kissed deeply. She continued to caress him, causing any and all coherent thoughts to flee and leaving only sensation in their wake. When she pulled her lips from his, he heard her speak.

"It's Wednesday." She removed her hand from his body and sat back. "It's time to make the fort."

He blinked at her in confusion. "What?"

"I said it's time to make the fort."

His eyes flew open just in time to see his forty-pound son leaping onto his bed. Jack jumped on top of him, bringing him from sound asleep to wide awake in a matter of seconds, and then he stood and jumped up and down on the gigantic bed. He launched himself at Will again, unintentionally lodging one boney little knee into his father's groin.

A loud *"oomph"* was all Will managed to grunt as pain rocketed through his body. He attempted to roll onto his side and curl up into the fetal position—something all males instinctively did when those particular body parts were violently under assault—but Jack was still perched partially on top of him with his knee dangerously close to striking again. Will reached down to protect himself, relieved to discover he was wearing boxers, and groaned into his pillow.

Jack suddenly seemed to realize exactly what had happened, and he moved off of his father quickly. "Uh-oh. Did I get you in the privates, Dad?"

Will could do nothing but groan and nod.

"Sorry, I didn't mean to. Do you want me to get Auntie G?"

Will groaned again and emphatically shook his head, grunting out a "no."

"It must hurt, huh?"

Will opened one eye and glared at his son. "Yes," he said, his voice hoarse.

"I was just comin' to see if you were awake. Auntie G is up, she said you need to get up 'cause we have work to do."

Will took a deep breath but kept his hands between his legs—just in case. "Did Auntie G make coffee?"

"Mm-hmm."

Will sighed. He could tell by the light coming into his room—the windows of which were definitely closed—that it was early. "Alright. Give me a minute." He closed his eyes again.

"'Kay."

Will felt the bed move, but when he didn't hear his son's feet on the wood floor, he opened his eyes. Jack's face was hovering over his, those bright violet-blue eyes staring at him intently and his dark hair falling across his forehead.

"Do you need some ice or somethin'?"

His expression was so serious and his question so earnest that Will had to laugh despite his agony. "No, I'm alright. I just need to catch my breath. Thanks anyway."

"'Kay." Jack leaned forward to kiss his father's cheek, and then he climbed off the bed and left the room. Will tentatively lifted his hands and stretched, grimacing a little. *That's gonna leave a bruise.*

He tried to conjure up any remnants of the dream he'd been having, but as most dreams do, it had fled from his mind almost entirely. If the steady, rapid beat of his heart and the morning wood he'd woken with were any indication, it must have been a pretty damn good one. Even though he couldn't remember much of it, he definitely remembered who had the starring role.

One date. That's all it took. One taste. Well, several tastes, actually. All fuel to fire up his subconscious.

As he'd driven to Elizabeth's house to pick her up, he'd been completely preoccupied with thoughts of kissing her. He wasn't nervous about it—not about the mechanics of it, anyway—but he was apprehensive about how it would feel, how *he* would feel. Would it conjure up thoughts of Anne? Comparisons? Would he feel guilty? The questions plagued him as he drove along, until he forced himself to stop thinking about it and instead focus on how happy he was to be taking Elizabeth out on a date.

All that worry had turned out to be for nothing. Later that night, he realized he hadn't thought about Anne at all during or after the kiss. Not once the entire night, actually, except for when he talked about naming Jack. The realization shocked him at first, but he eventually decided it was a good thing. *A very good thing.* Elizabeth Bennet was here in every way and was very quickly becoming the center of his thoughts.

After enjoying dinner and the sunset at the beach, they'd lingered at the playground for quite a while. It was nice, just talking and being playful, kissing and holding each other. There was an undercurrent of awareness between them, and it wasn't just physical; it was something far more acute, rooted in a desire to connect on a deeper level. He was certain she felt the same way; they both admitted they wanted to know all there was to know about each other, good and bad, and to Will, that confession had put them on equal emotional footing.

However, they'd *also* agreed that last night wasn't the time to delve too deeply; it was about having fun, getting past first date jitters, and making it through the evening with as little bumbling and floundering as possible. *My bumbling and floundering, not hers.* It wasn't time for them to bare their souls or dig up skeletons they'd both worked so hard to keep buried.

He thought back to the end of the evening, when he'd taken her home.

"Are you going to kiss me good night?" she'd asked as she leaned back against her front door.

"Do you want me to?" He moved closer and reached for her hands.

She nodded and smiled shyly. "Yes. Very much. Um, do you want to come in?" Her eyes darted toward the Gardiners' house then back to his face. "I mean, just–just for a minute."

He glanced over his shoulder and could see lights on in the house. "Afraid we'll have an audience?"

"Honestly? Yes. I wouldn't put it past Maddie to spy."

He smiled. "You know her better than I do, so… It's up to you."

She hesitated for only a moment before unlocking the door and leading him inside, still holding one of his hands. He closed the door behind them, and when he turned back to her, she looked nervous and apprehensive.

"Are you sure this is okay?" he asked.

She nodded. "You're just…you're very tall." She glanced around the room and then back to him. "It's like the room shrunk when you walked in. Again."

He bent his knees until he was at eye level with her. "Better?"

She laughed softly. "No. I–I like that you're tall. You just…overwhelm. A little. The room, I mean. Not–not me." She lightly cleared her throat. "You kind of take it over."

He looked at his surroundings, once again noting the colors and décor, and realized she was right; he did stick out a bit. He stood straight again and studied her expression. She was trying so hard to appear confident and composed, but he could see she wasn't, and he thought he knew why. When he'd been here earlier tonight to pick her up, they hadn't yet kissed, they hadn't crossed that line. But in a matter of a few hours things had changed, and now she was nervous; gone was the playful sprite he'd kissed on the beach and on the swings.

"I don't want you to be uncomfortable," he told her, lightly stroking her cheek.

Her eyes stayed focused on his, and she gave a barely perceptible shake of her head. "I'm not."

He wasn't completely convinced but decided to take her at her word. "Okay." He moved closer and gently tugged her toward him, inching her forward until their bodies were touching. He held her to him and swayed a little, and her arms wrapped around his waist. Eventually he felt her body soften as she began to relax.

They stood that way for a little while longer, and he kissed the top of her head. "Better?"

She nodded against his chest. "Yes."

He sighed now, remembering the kiss that followed. He'd let Elizabeth lead, let her decide how long and how deep. She was tentative at first and kept it very slow, but it didn't take long for them to become completely immersed in it. He left shortly after, with the promise to call her the next day.

And now, a dream about her. He groaned in frustration when he tried to remember the details again. The only thing he could recall was that the windows had been open and the curtains were blowing.

His thoughts traveled back to about two months after Anne had died, when he'd had the same type of dream. It was the first of several full-blown sex dreams he would have about her, and he woke from it with a painful, raging hard-on, every bit of the dream as vivid in his mind as if she'd been right there in bed with him. Not knowing what else to do and mired somewhere between an all-encompassing sorrow and the desire to experience her again, even if only through a fantasy, he relieved himself while letting the images play over and over again in his mind.

Afterward he rose from their bed and took a small bottle of her perfume he'd kept and scattered droplets of it on the pillow next to his. He fell back to sleep clutching the pillow tightly, and though he was filled with shame and more than a little self-loathing at what he'd done, he also slept better that morning than he had since she'd passed away.

Remembering it now, he didn't view it the same way as he did back then. He could look at that morning more objectively without casting judgment on himself and his actions. He'd been a man in the throes of grief, trying to cope, and he wouldn't condemn himself for doing something that brought him a small measure of peace, however temporary it had been. He pushed the memory, less clear and sharp now, from his mind. *It seems like a lifetime ago.*

It was amazing how things could change, how choosing one particular course of action—in his case, moving to Maine—could open up a world of possibilities. It was like a domino effect, with one new experience propelling him toward another. Or maybe it was something as simple as fate, a force bigger than himself that he had absolutely no control over. Something that had led him here and put Elizabeth in his path.

Fate, dumb luck, serendipity…whatever it is, I'll take it and be happy for it.

His thoughts were interrupted by the sound of Jack's feet pounding up the stairs. He came tearing down the hall into Will's room and jumped onto the bed again, though with a little less vigor this time.

"Dad, what're you doin'?" he asked, obviously exasperated. "You're not even outta bed yet! Auntie G said if you're not downstairs in five minutes, she's startin' without you."

Will chuckled. "Alright, I'm coming." He tickled Jack, making him giggle. "Let's get this fort built."

ELIZABETH SIPPED COFFEE FROM A TRAVEL MUG AS SHE RELAXED ON THE ferry. She was heading to work, though she didn't feel fully awake yet. Usually she would be raring to go, but then she usually went to bed on the earlier side when she had to work the next day. Last night had been a little different.

Will hadn't brought her home until just before midnight. They sat on the swings at the playground for a while before finally moving to a bench, and when she mentioned at around eleven that it was probably time for her to head home, he leaned toward her until his face was only inches from hers.

"Are you going to turn into a pumpkin?"

She shook her head and kept her eyes on his, forcing herself to remain serious even though a smile threatened. "No."

"Werewolf?"

"Um...only when the moon is full."

He looked up into the night sky, then looked back at her. "Missed it by one night. That's too bad," he said, smiling crookedly. "I think I might like being bitten by you."

He'd teased and charmed her, revealing little bits and pieces of himself through their conversations, even when they amounted to nothing more than silly banter. He had a playful side, something she never would have expected when she first met him. He had a passionate, romantic side too, one she became more familiar with throughout the night.

He seemed to want to touch her all the time, even if it was just his leg bumping hers as they swung next to each other or his hand caressing hers or his fingers toying with her hair. And the kisses! She enjoyed kissing him—it made her head spin in the most wonderful way—but eventually those kisses would lead to more. It would be the natural progression of things, and although it was probably too soon to think about, apprehension wormed its way into her brain.

That apprehension had taken over at the end of the night, and as they'd stood in her living room, she felt nervous. He'd picked up on the change in her demeanor instantly and had held her, his hands lightly stroking up and down her back until she finally overcame her anxiety and had relaxed enough to initiate their kiss good night.

Oh, and what a kiss. Even now, her face flushed. He'd focused entirely on her mouth, determined to find the perfect angle of his lips on hers. It had been slow and sensuous and seemed to go on forever, igniting a flicker of desire in her belly, something she hadn't felt in a long, long time. When they finally separated, both breathing raggedly, they stared at each other for a long moment until he pulled her close again.

She felt his arousal, the hardness of him pressing against her, and again, a surge of trepidation shot through her. She remained in his arms though, wanting desperately to conquer her nerves. Her heart rate had eventually slowed, and the involuntary tightness in her muscles had gradually loosened.

He'd left a short time later, giving her another brief but sweet kiss before heading out the door. She immediately went to bed, but sleep proved elusive. She replayed every little thing that happened over the course of the evening, from the moment he came to her door until the moment he walked out of it, and it was after two when she fell asleep.

When the ferry docked, she grabbed her backpack and purse, rose from her seat, and headed down to the lower deck to stand with the other passengers waiting to disembark. Just as she was walking down the long ramp to the pier, her cell phone rang. She looked at the caller ID and saw Jane's name.

"Hello," she answered cheerfully.

"You were supposed to call me after your date."

"Good morning to you too," Elizabeth said, laughing at her sister's tone.

"You said you would call me!"

"I said I would call if it wasn't too late," Elizabeth reminded her. "I was going to call you in two minutes, I swear. I just got off the ferry."

"I was worried."

Elizabeth frowned. "Really? I'm sorry."

"No, it's okay. I knew you would be alright, I wasn't too worried." Jane paused. "Okay, I wasn't worried at all. I just said that to make you feel bad for not calling me."

"You're a pain. Don't you have a classroom to clean or something? Why aren't you at work?"

"I *am* cleaning my classroom, which means I can talk on the phone as much as I want. So spill it! I want some details."

Elizabeth sighed. She didn't *want* to spill it—not all of it, anyway. Most of it she wanted to keep to herself, and Jane would probably think she was crazy if she told her some of the things she'd been thinking about. How could she possibly explain how Will made her feel or describe the intimacy and the connection that already seemed to exist between them?

"There isn't much to tell." She decided to be vague and hoped Jane wouldn't dig too much.

"Well, where did you go? What did you do? Did you have fun?"

Realizing she was going to have to give her sister at least *some* details, Elizabeth told her a few things about the evening: dinner, sunset at the point, and their visit to the playground.

"And you just talked the whole time?"

"Yes." *Most of the time.*

"What did you talk about?"

Elizabeth wavered again; she didn't want to reveal too much. "Just normal getting-to-know-you things. We talked about family and about New York and Boston. And about Jack... Oh, and I found out his real name is Fitzwilliam, not William."

"Wow, that's a mouthful."

Elizabeth laughed. "I know. It's a family name. I told him I play the piano... Just little things."

"Nothing too serious?"

"Nothing too serious."

"Did you kiss him?"

"Yes."

"Really? How was it? I mean, I don't need specifics, but just...generally."

"It was wonderful," Elizabeth said with a sigh.

"Good. Are you going to go out again?"

"We didn't make a set plan, but I think we will."

"You didn't talk about it last night?"

"Well, no, not in so many words. We just said we would talk today."

"Oh."

Elizabeth heard something odd in her sister's tone. "What's the matter?"

"Nothing, but I thought he would have made it clear to you if he wanted to see you again."

"He *did* make it clear to me," Elizabeth responded, now feeling a bit deflated. "Why are you so concerned about it?"

"I'm not concerned, it's just…the date sounds kind of plain."

Elizabeth began to silently fume and struggled to keep her voice even. "Maybe to you, but it wasn't to me. It was far from plain or boring or whatever else you might be thinking."

"I'm not trying to upset you."

Could have fooled me.

"He's very wealthy," Jane went on. "Did you know that?"

Elizabeth stopped short in the middle of the busy sidewalk, forcing several other pedestrians to veer around her. She finally moved out of the way and leaned against the brick wall of a shop. "No, I *didn't* know that, so do you mind telling me how *you* know that?"

"I looked him up online while I was waiting for you to call last night."

"Are you serious?" Elizabeth asked incredulously.

"Yes. I wanted to find out more about him. Did you know his wife—"

"No! Stop!" Elizabeth took a deep breath and tried to calm herself. "I don't want to know. I want to find out about Will from Will, not from you or the Internet."

"I didn't read anything bad if that's what you're worried about."

"I'm *not* worried about that. We've had one date, and it was…it was perfect. I had a wonderful time. But you know what? The afterglow is wearing off pretty quickly, thanks to you."

"I'm just trying to look out for you."

"I can look out for myself." Elizabeth started to walk again, feeling utterly exasperated with her sister.

"I'm just…I'm worried he might be a bit much for you," Jane went on. "The money, the son, the volatile relationship with the father, the running away from New York—he's been the subject of more than one blurb in the gossip pages. I just don't want you to get in over your head. I mean, what if he decides he belongs back in New York? Or what if you're just a rebound relationship?" She paused. "Everything I've read says he was practically a recluse, holed up in his penthouse in New York after his wife died. And it wasn't for lack of options, because he's considered a very good catch. But whenever he's been seen over the past couple of years, he was either alone or with Jack or Georgiana, and even then, it wasn't very often."

Elizabeth paled at her sister's words, not because of what she was hearing but because the words were spewing from her sister's mouth like a torrent of verbal diarrhea. "I'm glad you've become so educated on Will Darcy, Jane. I'll have to remember that when I have any questions about him. I mean, it sounds like you know it all, so why bother asking him? I'll just call you instead."

"Lizzy—"

"I'm going to hang up now. If this is you trying to look out for me, I would rather you didn't. Goodbye, Jane." Elizabeth ended the call and shoved her phone into her purse.

Tears stung her eyes behind her sunglasses, and she was furious with herself for letting them come. *I cannot let her get me upset and ruin my day.* Despite feeling sleep-deprived, she'd been on cloud nine all morning, but now she felt like she'd been through the wringer. At the hands of Jane, no less! Her sister had always been her biggest ally, especially over the past few years. But in the space of a short telephone conversation, Elizabeth felt completely undermined by her.

She thought of what Jane said about Will being too much for her. *Is she actually trying to say I'm not enough for him?* Was she telling Elizabeth she needed to lower her expectations and not reach so high?

She arrived at the library and heard the ringing of her cell phone from inside her purse. Convinced it was Jane again, she let it go to voicemail. She walked through the doors and took a deep breath, determined to have a good day. *At this point, it can't get much worse.*

WILL SAT BACK IN A CHAIR ON HIS DECK AND TOOK A SIP OF WATER AS HE stared at the nearly completed fort in his backyard. Thankfully Georgiana had taken charge, because he was completely useless. His mind would not stay on task; instead, it was more pleasurably occupied by thoughts of warm brown eyes, a pair of soft lips, and a musical laugh that made his heart race.

He'd hoped to talk to Elizabeth this morning before she went to work, but she hadn't answered her phone. It was probably a bit impulsive to call her so soon, but he wanted to tell her he enjoyed himself last night…and maybe ask her out again. Maybe invite her to dinner. *Tonight*. With him and Georgie and Jack. He wasn't sure if he should do that or not, and the last thing he wanted was to appear clingy or needy. He was neither of those things, and didn't want to scare her away by coming on too strong.

She'd appeared so confident at times, teasing him and returning his kisses enthusiastically, but at other times she seemed skittish and unsure of herself. He was sure there was more to it, and he would wait patiently until she was ready to confide in him.

"Hey!" Georgiana called out to him. "What the heck are you doing?"

"Um, taking a break."

"From what, daydreaming?"

"Shut up, Georgie."

"Dad! You shouldn't say shut up, it's not nice," Jack reprimanded his father seriously. "You're supposed to say 'be quiet, please.'"

"Be quiet, please, Georgie," Will said, trying to hide his grin. "Sorry, Jack."

"That's okay, just don't let it happen again," Jack told him, making his father and aunt laugh.

Will disappeared into the house and came out with two glasses of lemonade. "Come on up, have something to drink."

Jack and Georgiana walked onto the deck and seated themselves at the table, and both took long sips of their drinks.

"We're almost done," Jack said excitedly. "Can we get some chairs and stuff to put inside it?"

"Sure, we'll get something," Will answered. "Maybe a little table too so you can eat in there when you have friends over."

"Yeah, that would be cool. Maybe Sam can come over tomorrow, and we can play in it."

"Maybe." He turned his attention to his sister. "When do you think you'll head back to New York?"

"Why, are you trying to get rid of me?"

"Of course not. I told you, you can stay as long as you want. I just didn't know if you'd been thinking about it."

She sighed. "Actually, I have. I think I'll probably go back Friday. I feel like I left things unfinished with Dad."

Jack finished his lemonade and rose from the table. "I'm goin' on my swing."

"Okay, bud." Will watched Jack as he ran to the large tree that held the tire swing before turning back to his sister. "Don't feel like you have to rush off to make things better with Dad. He's not going anywhere."

"I know, but it's different with me. You and Dad are used to conflict. It's not like that with him and me. I don't like it when we argue. I want to resolve it instead of letting it fester and get worse."

He nodded. "I get that."

She stared at him for a long moment. "You haven't said much about last night, although you seem a bit distracted."

He gave a short laugh. "That's the perfect word for how I feel today. Distracted."

"Good distracted or bad distracted?"

"Good."

"So it was okay? It went well?"

He nodded, unable to stop smiling. "It was great, we had a good time. I didn't want to say too much in front of Jack. He doesn't miss a thing."

"Do you think you'll go out again?"

"I hope so. I want to. I think she does too. I guess we'll see." He could feel Georgiana's eyes boring into him. "What? Why are you staring?"

"I'm not, I'm sorry. I'm just happy for you. I'm glad you had fun."

"Thanks." He cleared his throat. "Maybe I'll take you and Jack into Portland tomorrow night, and we'll go out for dinner somewhere. We can just kick back and take it easy tonight." He'd already rethought his idea of inviting Elizabeth over, figuring they would have plenty of time to see each other once Georgie was gone.

"Sure, that sounds good. What time does the pool close?"

"Seven, I think."

"Maybe we can go for a swim when we finish here?"

"Great idea." He glanced at his watch and saw it was nearing three-thirty. "We don't have much more to do, right? Let's get her done."

ELIZABETH'S MOOD DAMPENED FURTHER WHEN SHE REALIZED THE CALL SHE ignored this morning was from Will. She listened to his message at least half a dozen times, enjoying the sound of his deep voice and smiling a little as she heard him trip over his words.

Hi Elizabeth, it's Will. Um, I was just calling to say good morning and to tell you I had a nice time last night. With—with you. I hope you had a good time too, and I hope we can go out again. Soon. I would really like that. So, um, you can call me back if you want, but I know you're at work, so if you can't that's—that's okay, that's fine. Um, I'll just talk to you...when I talk to you. Okay. Have a great day. Bye.

Even thinking of the message made her smile, and again she gave herself a mental kick for not looking at her phone when it rang. She thought about calling him now but decided to wait until she was out of work so she wouldn't be interrupted.

Before she knew it, five o'clock had arrived, and she was walking out the library doors and into the warm summer air. She pulled her phone from her purse, but felt a surge of insecurity as Jane's words echoed through her mind. She pushed them aside, refusing to let her sister spoil things. Taking a deep breath, she dialed Will's number and waited for him to pick up, which he did almost immediately.

"Hello, Elizabeth."

"Hi, Will," she answered, slowing her pace.

"How are you? How was work?"

"I'm fine. Work was...work. Wednesdays are always busy, but it made the time go by a little faster. Did you build the fort today?"

"We did, it's all done. Georgie deserves most of the credit, I just did what I was told."

She chuckled. "I can't wait to see it."

"It looks great. We're celebrating with a swim at the pool. Are you on your way home?"

"Yes, I'm walking to the ferry as we speak." She paused. "I'm sorry I missed your call this morning."

"I figured you were already at work. Did you get my message?"

She smiled. "Yes. I had a nice time last night too."

"Good, I'm glad. Do you want to get together again? Maybe this weekend?"

"I would like that."

"Great. Um, Georgie leaves Friday, and I want to try and spend time with her while she's here."

"You don't need to explain. It was nice of her to stay with Jack last night so we could go out. Tell her I said thank you."

"I will. I hope I didn't keep you out too late."

"You did, but it was worth every yawn that slipped out of me today."

He chuckled. "Georgie told me I was distracted."

"You were?"

"Yes," he answered softly. "I can't stop thinking about you."

"Really?" Her heart pounded madly as she slowed to a stop on the sidewalk.

"Yes. Is that so hard to believe?"

"I–I don't know. Maybe." She started walking again and headed down the cobblestone street toward the docks.

"I guess you'll have to take my word for it. Um, do you mind if I call you later?"

"Of course not."

"Okay, good. I'll talk to you tonight."

"Talk to you tonight. Bye, Will."

"Bye, Elizabeth."

She hung up and after walking a little more, she realized every bad feeling and every negative, insecure thought she'd had throughout the day had been completely wiped away by one short conversation with him, and her smile remained in place as she boarded the ferry.

∾

WILL WATCHED GEORGIE AND JACK PLAY TOGETHER IN THE POOL. USUALLY he'd be in there with them, splashing around and having fun, but he wanted them to have as much time together as possible. He had plenty of time with Georgiana at night after Jack went to bed.

He thought about the brief conversation he just had with Elizabeth. Why would she find it hard to believe he couldn't stop thinking about her? It was the absolute truth; she hadn't been far from his thoughts all day, and he had the bruised thumbnail to prove it. It probably wasn't a wise idea to let his mind drift to kissing her when he was trying to pound in a nail. He'd howled in pain and hopped around the yard clutching his hand like a cartoon character, which struck Georgie and Jack as enormously funny. He glanced down at the half-moon bruise that had formed under his nail and wiggled his thumb to make sure it still functioned.

Saturday is too far away. He glanced at his cell phone and saw it was nearing five-thirty. He had an idea and walked to the edge of the pool, squatting down to have a brief conversation with Georgie and Jack before leaving the pool and walking to the Batmobile.

Ten minutes later he was parked in the back of the lot at the docks, wondering if he was being too presumptuous and questioning whether this little gesture would be interpreted as a creepy stalker thing. It was too late to leave, at any rate; the ferry had docked, and he could see the people standing inside, waiting to disembark, which meant Elizabeth may have already spotted him. *Damn.* He hated that he was second-guessing himself; fifteen minutes ago, this had seemed like a brilliant idea.

He saw her walking down the long ramp a few minutes later, her backpack slung over one shoulder. His eyes traveled over her, taking in her pale blue sundress and the gentle sway of her hips. She wore sunglasses, so he couldn't discern where her eyes were focused, and her expression gave nothing away. He got out of the cart and waited, wondering if she would notice him, and wasn't sure she had until— she smiled. He almost looked around to see if there was someone else she could possibly be looking at like that.

"Hi," she said quietly, still smiling brightly as she came to a stop in front of him.

"Hi." He leaned in toward her and lifted her backpack from her shoulder. "Need a ride?"

The light breeze moved the air around them, and he caught the subtle scent of her shampoo or perfume. Suddenly he found himself in the middle of a fairly graphic flashback to the dream he'd had this morning. She was naked in his bed, facing him, reaching for him, stroking him... He closed his eyes for a moment, torn between wanting the recollection to play itself out and wanting it to end to save him some serious embarrassment. When he opened his eyes, she was staring at him oddly.

"Are you alright?"

He nodded quickly. "Yes, I'm fine." The erotic images disappeared, but he felt light-headed, as if too much blood had left his upper body and rapidly headed south. He cleared his throat. "I hope this is okay. Me being here, I mean. To pick you up. You said you were tired, so I thought you might like a ride home."

"Of course it's okay," she answered, still looking a bit puzzled as she took off her sunglasses and tucked them into her purse.

He gestured to the cart, and she climbed into the passenger seat. He dropped her backpack into the storage area, and once he was settled behind the wheel, he reached to take her hand. "Can I ask you something?"

She nodded but remained silent, her eyes on his.

"Why did you question me when I told you I'd been thinking about you all day? Why is that so hard to believe?"

He watched as her eyes dropped away from his. "I–I don't know. What was I supposed to say, 'of course you were'? That would have been a little conceited, don't you think?"

"It would have been right on the money," he said, chuckling a little. He stared at her for a long moment and then released her hand, only to reach up and stroke her cheek as he moved closer. "Should I have kept that to myself?" He shrugged lightly. "I've already told you, I don't know what I'm doing. I dreamed about you this morning..." His thumb brushed her cheek before moving to trace gently over her bottom lip. "And I *have* been thinking about you all day. Am I not supposed to tell you that? Am I supposed to keep you guessing?" He swallowed thickly, but his eyes never left hers. "I don't know how to do this."

"I thought about you all day too." Her admission came out in a breathless rush of words. "I–I was ridiculously upset when I realized I missed your call, and I listened to your message…eight times."

He smiled widely and leaned closer to her, until his face was mere inches from hers, and raised an eyebrow. "Only eight?"

She began to laugh quietly, but he moved to kiss her. It wasn't a passionate, deep kiss; he kept it soft and sweet, trying to be mindful of their surroundings before pulling back slowly.

"So, is that a no?"

ELIZABETH'S BROWS DREW TOGETHER. "NO? TO–TO WHAT? WHAT WAS THE question?"

His kiss had erased whatever he'd asked; as it was, she was still trying to come to grips with the fact that he'd come to pick her up. Her heart had done a funny little dance when she'd spotted him, standing barefoot next to the Batmobile, in a T-shirt and swimsuit and looking simply gorgeous.

His fingers left her cheek and lightly threaded into her hair. "The question was about keeping you guessing." His expression turned serious and his eyes left hers to follow the motion of his hand. "I don't want to play hard to get, or–or make this into some kind of game. I don't want you to wonder how I feel or what I'm thinking. I'm honest to a fault. Sometimes it's gotten me into trouble, but it's the only way I know how to be." Slowly, his smile returned. "So when I tell you you're beautiful, or when I tell you I can't wait to see you or that I've been thinking about you all day, you can believe me. Okay?"

She nodded, feeling slightly breathless. "Okay."

He started the motor and headed out of the lot, driving along slowly and holding tightly to her hand. Neither of them spoke, but the silence was welcome. Her heart was hammering in her chest, and she needed the time to absorb what he said.

They pulled into the Gardiners' driveway and climbed from the cart, and she was relieved to see that neither Maddie nor Ed were outside. After grabbing her backpack, Will walked with her to the cottage, once again holding fast to her hand.

"Is it too much?" he asked, reaching up to push her hair behind her ear as they faced each other on the small porch.

She shook her head, knowing what he was asking; he wanted to know if *he* was too much. Jane's earlier comments about him came rushing back, though Elizabeth wouldn't tell him what her sister had said or how Jane had made her feel—completely inadequate and full of self-doubt. It had nothing to do with him and everything to do with Elizabeth letting Jane get the best of her.

"No," she answered quietly, reaching up to hold his wrist lightly. "No, it's not too much. It probably should be, but it isn't."

"I haven't scared you away?"

She smiled softly and shook her head. "No." She didn't feel scared at all. Instead, she felt oddly calm.

"Good." He exhaled and nodded. "Good."

His concern was obvious and she wanted to reassure him more, but before she had the chance he spoke again.

"Um, I–I should go. I don't really want to, but…I left Georgie and Jack at the pool, and I promised them pizza tonight." His eyebrows lifted. "Do you–would you like to join us?"

She shook her head. "You wanted to spend time with Georgiana, and that's exactly what you should do."

"She would love it if you came over, and so would Jack."

She reached up to hold his face in her hands, pulling it down to hers so she could kiss him. His hands moved to her waist, and she felt them tighten as the kiss deepened. Something warm unfurled in her stomach and spread through her body, causing her to move closer and press up against him.

The action spurred him to wrap his arms around her waist and hold her tightly as they kissed again. She inhaled the faint trace of sunscreen mixed with the unique scent of his skin, and it seemed to surround her, invading her senses. Once again, he concentrated completely on her mouth, molding it to his, turning the kiss into something electric and intimate. Needing to catch her breath, she reluctantly pulled back.

He inhaled deeply, looking down into her eyes, and cleared his throat. "Is that a yes?"

She shook her head. "No, it isn't. I'm sorry." She laughed when he pouted. "Hang out with Georgiana and Jack. You and I have plenty of time, don't we?"

"We do." He leaned his forehead against hers. "I'll call you later, okay?"

"Okay. Thank you for picking me up. It was the best part of my day." He smiled widely, revealing his dimples and causing her heart to trip into a double-time beat.

"Mine too." He leaned in to kiss her again. "'Bye, Elizabeth."

"'Bye, Will. Have fun tonight." She laughed at his skeptical expression and waved when he took one last look back at her before disappearing around the corner of the Gardiners' house.

Sighing happily, she walked into her cottage. *Definitely the best part of my day.*

Fifteen

E lizabeth left work on Thursday with a spring in her step. She'd spoken with Charlotte last night and had made plans to stay at her place tonight so they could go out. Kate was invited too, but Elizabeth wasn't sure if she'd found someone to cover her shift at Trinity.

Will had called last night as well, and she'd thanked him again for picking her up at the ferry. He admitted that he'd almost changed his mind and left, and when she asked why he'd decided to stay, he told her he thought she might have spotted him already.

"I didn't have second thoughts about seeing you," he'd explained, "because I really wanted to see you. But I was worried you might be a little weirded out that I just showed up. I had these visions of you being really sweet and nice to me, but on the inside you'd be completely freaking out."

Honest to a fault, he'd said. *That he is.* She reassured him she was neither weirded out nor freaking out. "I thought it was sweet of you. It was a nice surprise."

He mentioned getting together over the weekend, and she told him the Portland Performing Arts Festival was taking place on Saturday.

"You know I'll have Jack with me, right?"

"I figured you would. It's fine, we'll have fun."

"It's just that he's never had a sitter before other than Mrs. R or Georgie. But I know I have to find someone to keep an eye on him when I want to do things without him."

She was fairly sure she understood the implication and she smiled. "Well, this isn't one of those things," she'd told him. "I know you're not just Will, you're also Jack's dad. I get it."

He thanked her, and she heard the relief in his voice.

"Jack will love it. There are all different performers. Some events are indoors, but most are outside, at the waterfront and the park."

He agreed it sounded great. They'd talked a bit longer about her plans to go out with Charlotte and possibly Kate, and his plans to take Georgiana and Jack out to dinner in Portland. He asked if she knew of a good restaurant that was kid-friendly and she recommended Quinn's Grill.

She smiled now as she walked, remembering the text he'd sent her just after she'd arrived at work today.

Good morning, beautiful

She responded in kind and marveled that he'd had her blushing over a text.

After making the short walk from the library to Charlotte's apartment, Elizabeth sat on the couch and sipped a glass of wine while she waited for Charlotte to get ready. Her phone chimed with an incoming text, and assuming it was from Kate, she checked it immediately. She was surprised to see it was from Will.

Hi

She grinned as she typed back. *Hi yourself*

What are you doing?

Hanging at Charlotte's while she gets ready. What are you doing?

Waiting for a table at Quinn's. Nice place

Try the bistro steak, it's my favorite

Maybe I will. Where are you off to tonight?

Maybe Front Row or Gritty McGee's

Sounds like fun. G leaves tomorrow morning

Tell her I said goodbye, and it was nice to meet her

I will. I had a thought

She smiled. *Hmm. Should I be worried?*

Ha. Always teasing. Would you like to join the Darcy men for a movie tomorrow night?

What's playing?

I think we're having a Shrek marathon

Charlotte walked into the living room. "Is that Kate? What's the deal, is she coming or not?"

"Um, no. It's not Kate." Elizabeth looked back at her phone and continued typing.

I would love to join you. Do you think Jack will mind?

Not at all. I'll call you tomorrow

Perfect. Have a good night

You too

When Elizabeth looked up from her phone, she noticed Charlotte staring at her.

"Why are you grinning like that?" her friend asked suspiciously.

Elizabeth immediately tried to sober her expression. "What do you mean?"

"You, over there on my couch, looking all gooey-eyed. Are you texting him?"

"Him who?"

"Don't give me 'him who.' Mr. Amazing Dimples. *That* him."

"Ohhh, him. As a matter of fact, I am."

"Really? You are? Why are you texting him?"

"He just wanted to say hi, and we sort of made plans for tomorrow night."

"You *sort* of made plans? What kind of plans? Did I miss something? Is the earth rotating in the opposite direction? Are the planets aligning?"

Elizabeth laughed. "We went out on a date. Did I forget to mention that?"

"You went out on a *date* with him?" Charlotte's eyes widened comically. "Shut the front door!" She sat down next to Elizabeth on the couch. "When? Where did you go? Why didn't you tell me?"

"We went out for dinner Tuesday night."

Charlotte held up one hand. "Wait! Stop!" She got up and walked into her little kitchen and returned a moment later with a beer. "Okay. Talk."

Elizabeth filled her in, though again, she chose to keep some things to herself—mainly how she'd felt just being with him, how it felt so right and like it was where she was meant to be. It's not that she thought Charlotte would think she was crazy; she just wasn't ready to share those feelings yet, not when she was still trying to deal with them herself.

"Wow, Lizzy. I have to meet this guy, right? He must really be something. Did you kiss him?"

"I hope you get to meet him. And yes, I kissed him." Elizabeth blushed again. "He's...it was good. He's a good kisser." She sighed lightly. "Very good."

Charlotte smiled. "That's great. There's nothing worse than a lousy, forgettable first kiss." She suddenly reached to hug Elizabeth. "I'm so happy for you. This is fantastic!"

"We're not getting married, Charlotte! It was one date." Elizabeth disentangled herself from Charlotte's arms, though she understood her friend's excitement.

"But it's *good*. You really like him, I can tell. You can't hide anything from me."

"I would never dream of trying," Elizabeth responded, rolling her eyes.

"What does Jane think?" Charlotte stood from the couch and retrieved her purse. She pulled out her phone, checking for a text from Kate. "You told her, right? She must be excited for you."

"She is, but we got into an argument yesterday, and I haven't talked to her since."

"About what?" Charlotte looked incredulous as she sat down again. "You guys never fight."

"She looked up Will online, which is fine, I don't really care about that. I just wish she'd kept it to herself. I mean, she didn't tell me much, but now she has all these theories about him. She thinks he might be too much for me. Or maybe she thinks I'm not enough for him. It's hard to tell."

"Why would he be too much for you? And why wouldn't you be enough for him? What does that mean?"

"I don't know. She thinks because he's a widower and has a son and just showed up here randomly... It might be too much. Her words, not mine."

"That's ridiculous."

"And then she read that he's wealthy."

"Oh. He is?"

Elizabeth shrugged. "I guess. I kind of had a feeling he was, but I didn't think about it much. Anyway, I stopped her before she could tell me *how* wealthy. And then she started to say something about his wife, and I didn't want to hear it. I don't want to know." She paused. "Well, that's not true. I *do* want to know, I'm curious…but I don't want Jane to be the one who tells me. It would feel wrong if I sat down someday with Will—I mean, if we ever get to that point—and he started to tell me about his wife and what happened to her, and I already knew everything. It's unfair, don't you think? Or is that stupid?"

Charlotte shook her head. "It's not stupid. I get that Jane is curious —if I'd known you were going out with him, I probably would have done the same thing. But like you said, it's your first date. Do you have any feelings about it, like whether it could lead to something? Or is it too soon?"

"I don't know." Elizabeth was still hesitant to talk about her feelings. "But we had a great time and we want to see each other again, so…that's that. Movies at his house tomorrow night, and then the festival on Saturday."

Charlotte smiled and quickly squeezed Elizabeth's hand. "I'm thrilled for you, Lizzy. Whatever happens, I'm glad you're getting out there."

Elizabeth returned her smile. "Thanks."

"HOW'S EVERYTHING GOING WITH CHARLES'S PUB?" GEORGIANA ASKED Will as they sat in a booth at Quinn's, waiting for their meals to be served. "Have you talked to him this week?"

He nodded. "He called when we were at the beach today, while you and Jack were building your sand castle. He sounded a little frazzled, but he's working on getting bids from contractors to come in and tear the place up."

"So he's starting from scratch?"

"Pretty much. There wasn't much to salvage."

The server came with their food, setting it in front of them and checking to be sure they were all set before leaving.

"Auntie G, can I have the ketchup?" Jack asked.

"Please," Will reminded him.

"Please," Jack repeated. She passed it to him, and he squirted a puddle of ketchup onto his plate with a flourish.

"I think that's enough, pal. Watch your sleeves."

"'Kay."

Conversation lapsed as they tucked into their meals. Will had ordered the bistro steak, Georgiana ordered a fresh seafood stew, and Jack opted for chicken tenders with fries and a salad.

"Good?" Will asked, watching his son dig in enthusiastically.

Jack nodded in reply and looked at Georgiana. "Auntie G, do you hafta leave tomorrow?"

She frowned. "I do. I'll come back again soon though, I promise."

"I wish you could stay a longer time," he told her quietly. "We didn't even get to play in my fort a lot."

"I know. The next time I visit, we'll sleep out there, okay?"

Jack nodded but brightened only a little. "'Kay."

Will slipped his arm around Jack's shoulders and squeezed him in a brief hug. "I'll miss Auntie G too."

They talked as they ate, and when Jack mentioned he was excited about watching *Shrek* the next night, Will mentioned Elizabeth might come over to join them. "She likes *Shrek* too," he said, and was relieved when Jack smiled.

"Everybody likes *Shrek*, Dad. Are we goin' to story hour too?"

"Maybe. Auntie G leaves tomorrow, so we'll see if we have time after we take her to the airport."

"'Kay."

They were given dessert menus after finishing dinner, and although Will and Georgiana declined, Jack chose a brownie sundae. Will ordered and asked the server for the bill and three spoons—just in case —and not five minutes later, all three of them were sharing the sundae. Will heard his name and looked up to see Caroline walking toward their table with another woman.

"I can't believe you're all here!" she exclaimed, smiling widely.

Will stood, remembering manners drilled into him ages ago, and smiled halfheartedly. "Hello, Caroline."

"What are the chances we would run into each other? This is lucky, isn't it? I was just telling Louisa about you. Louisa, this is Will Darcy. Will, this is Louisa Hurst, a good friend of mine."

Will shook the other woman's hand and noticed her blatant perusal of him.

"Nice to meet you, Will Darcy," she said, holding his hand a bit too long. "I've heard wonderful things about you, it's nice to finally meet you in the flesh."

"It's nice to meet you too." He pulled his hand from hers. "This is my sister, Georgiana, and my son, Jack."

Louisa's eyes flickered over them briefly. "Hello."

"Hello," Georgiana and Jack both replied, although Caroline was already beginning to speak again.

"We just finished dinner, and I noticed you hiding in the corner here."

"We're just getting ready to leave," Will said as he sat back down.

"Do you mind if we join you until you do?" Caroline asked, lowering herself onto the seat next to Will.

Georgiana's eyes widened but she politely scooted further into the booth so that Louisa could sit.

"Dad, I'm gettin' squished," Jack complained softly, trapped between his father's broad frame and the wall.

"We'll be leaving in a few minutes. Keep working on that sundae." Will mentally urged his son to eat faster as he paid their tab. The smell of Caroline's perfume enveloped him, and he resisted the urge to lean away from her, not wanting to appear rude—or cause permanent injury to his son.

"What are you doing after dinner?" Caroline asked, turning to Will and tossing her hair a little. "Checking out any more of the sights?"

"We're actually heading back to the island," Will responded. "Georgiana leaves tomorrow, so it's looking like an early night for us."

"Dad, I'm done." Jack pushed the bowl toward the center of the table. "I'm stuffed."

"Great. That's our cue to leave."

Caroline and Louisa both rose from the table, followed by the three Darcys. "We're ready to leave as well," Caroline said. "Maybe we can walk a little with you."

Will glanced at Georgiana, who remained completely silent. He sent her a pleading look and she responded with an expression of helplessness.

Once outside they walked toward Old Port. Georgiana held Jack's hand and walked ahead of Will, who somehow ended up flanked by Caroline and Louisa. He tried to walk a little faster but it didn't help; they only adjusted their stride to his.

Up ahead, he spotted a sign hanging from the brick facade of a building. *Front Row. That's one of the places Elizabeth mentioned.* Despite spending the evening with Georgie and Jack, she'd never been far from his thoughts. The feel of Caroline's hand as it wrapped around his upper arm startled him.

"It's a gorgeous night for a walk, isn't it?" she asked. "The air smells so sweet."

He turned to Caroline, intending to tell her to remove her hand— but as fate would have it, Elizabeth and her friends chose that moment to walk out of Front Row. They were laughing hysterically, so much so that one of them—Kate, he knew, recalling Charles's description of her —was nearly doubled over.

"You kill me, Lizzy. How you can make rejection sound so sweet is beyond me."

"She wants who she wants, and it's not *that* guy," the other woman said.

Charlotte, Will surmised, noting her myriad tattoos. He contemplated the little bit of conversation he'd just heard before being distracted by Jack, who'd spotted Elizabeth and called out to her.

"'Lizabeth! Hi!" he yelled, waving frantically.

She turned toward them, her eyes lighting up. "Jack! Georgiana! This is a surprise!"

She looked past them and looked surprised to find Will walking with Caroline Bingley. He groaned to himself while the eight of them stood there, facing each other in the center of the sidewalk as though they were in the middle of some kind of weird standoff. He watched

Elizabeth's smile disappear, only to be replaced by a look of confusion. Her gaze lowered to take in the grip Caroline had on his arm, and his stomach plummeted when he saw the question in her eyes.

"Well, look who it is!" Caroline said with false cheeriness. "It's Portland's very own version of The Three Musketeers. Out making the rounds of the bar scene, I assume?"

Will felt her hand tighten on his arm as she leaned into him, and he tried to lean away.

"We just had a lovely dinner at Quinn's," she went on. "Fabulous food. Wouldn't you agree Will?"

He stared at Elizabeth and began to shake his head a little, afraid she would get the wrong impression. "I–we–um, yes, the food was good, but—"

"You should have seen the way Jack devoured his brownie sundae!" Caroline interrupted. "I would *love* to be able to eat anything I want." Her gaze flickered over to Elizabeth and her friends. "Some of us obviously still do."

It was said under her breath, but Will heard her clearly. His eyes were still glued to Elizabeth, and he saw Charlotte nudge her and look at her pointedly. She finally pulled her eyes from his and looked at her friends.

"Oh, um, Charlotte Lucas and Kate O'Leary, this–this is Will Darcy, his sister, Georgiana, and his son, Jack," she said, gesturing toward them distractedly.

Everyone said a very awkward hello, but the tension in the air was palpable. Kate merely nodded while she looked his way, but her baffled expression spoke volumes. Charlotte was a different story; she walked right up to Will and looked him in the eyes before letting her gaze drop to Caroline's hand, still wrapped snugly around his bicep.

"Nice to meet you," she said, her voice laced with false sweetness. "I think."

His mouth dropped open, but no words came out. He pulled his arm out of Caroline's grasp only to bump into Louisa, who seemed to be crowding toward him. He glanced at Georgiana, who stared back at him with an expression of bewilderment.

"It's–it's nice to meet you too," he finally managed to mumble.

"My Dad said you're comin' to watch *Shrek* with us tomorrow," Jack interjected as he stood in front of Elizabeth. "We're gonna watch two of 'em, and I get to stay up late."

She smiled down at him. "I–I might come over. Maybe. We'll see."

It was obvious to Will that her smile was forced and she wanted to be anywhere but here, and she turned to Kate.

"Um, should we go?"

"Off to another bar?" Caroline remarked with a snide tone. "Old habits die hard, don't they?"

Charlotte looked at Caroline with clear disdain. "You should know that better than anyone, Caroline. How's the restaurant business, by the way? Or have you tired of it, like you did the legal business?"

Caroline looked momentarily flustered but recovered quickly. "I can't imagine what you mean."

With wide eyes, Georgiana looked at her brother before taking Jack by the hand and leading him toward the window of a candy store. She glanced back at Will, and he nodded to her before she took Jack inside, thankful she was taking him away.

"Oh, so Chef Michael is old news already?" Charlotte fastened her steely gaze on Will. "It doesn't take long for you to form *new* habits, does it?"

Caroline managed to appear haughty. "Still bitter about your brother? I suggest you let him speak for himself—I imagine it's quite emasculating to have your sister fight your battles."

"I think being cheated on by a two-timing *slut* is a little bit more emasculating, don't you?"

Kate stepped between them. "Okay ladies, back to your corners. Lizzy, Charlotte, let's go. I believe we have dates waiting for us."

Will's eyes flew to Elizabeth's face, and she visibly blanched as she turned to look at Kate.

Dates? He needed to talk to Elizabeth *now*. He glanced at his watch and saw they had about twenty-five minutes to make the ferry, but when he looked back up, Charlotte had already hooked her arm through Elizabeth's and was pulling her backwards.

"Good night everyone. It's been a real treat," Charlotte called out.

"Wait," Will said, finally finding his voice and breaking away from

Caroline and Louisa. "Hold on. Elizabeth, wait. Please." He reached for her wrist and tugged it gently, pulling her away from her friends so they wouldn't be overheard. She looked up at him, and her wounded expression made his heart sink. Unfortunately, he said the first thing that popped into his muddled mind.

"Do you really have a date?"

Her eyes widened, and she pulled her arm from his grasp. "Good night, Will."

She turned and walked away from him, returning to her friends without a backward glance. He watched her rapidly retreating form and sighed heavily when he saw Charlotte wrap her arm around Elizabeth's shoulders. *Dammit.* He was distracted by Jack, who came dashing out of the candy store with a bag of goodies in hand.

"Dad, Auntie G bought me candy! Maybe we can eat it when we're watchin' *Shrek.*"

"Sounds great, Jack," Will responded, his eyes still following Elizabeth.

He finally turned to face Caroline, who was laughing and talking quietly with Louisa as if nothing had happened.

"If you don't mind, I'll join you and Georgiana and Jack on the ferry," she said. "I'm feeling a bit tired and should probably call it a night."

His frustration grew, but he wouldn't speak his mind in front of Jack. "It's a public ferry, Caroline," he answered brusquely. "You can do whatever you want."

Ten minutes later, they arrived at the dock and boarded the ferry. Will hadn't said a word the entire way; he was too angry—at Caroline, yes, but mostly at himself. *Thank God for Georgie.* She'd kept Jack chatting as they made their way down the cobblestone streets to the waterfront. Caroline had been silent as well, which was fine with him; he didn't want to talk to her until they had some privacy.

Once they were on the ferry and Georgiana and Jack were seated comfortably at a table inside, Will asked Caroline if he could talk to her alone.

"Of course," she answered, and followed him outside.

He walked to the railing and looked out at the dark bay and toward the lights in the distance that marked the entrance to Great Diamond's harbor. Caroline stood next to him and lightly placed her hand on his arm.

"Don't," he said calmly, moving away from her.

Her brows furrowed. "I'm sorry. You–you look angry."

"I *am* angry." He sighed and tried to get his words straight before he blurted them out. "I'm trying to figure out why you feel you have the right to be so familiar with me. Have I led you on somehow?"

"Well, I–I thought maybe you were attracted to me. You–you were staring at me that day at the pool, and—"

"That day at the pool?" he interrupted. "Two weeks ago?"

"Yes."

"I'm probably not the first man who's looked at you, right? But since then, have I given you any indication I want to get to know you as more than a friend?"

She sighed quietly. "No."

"And didn't I tell you on Sunday that I wasn't interested? I thought I'd made myself pretty clear."

"I—you did."

"So why do you hang all over me when you see me? I have no interest in you other than as a friend."

"It's Elizabeth, isn't it?" she asked indignantly. "You're interested in *her*."

"That's none of your business."

"My brother asked her out, did you know that?"

"Yes."

"Do you know anything about her? She's loaded down with baggage. Why would you want to deal with that? From what I understand, you have enough of your own."

He glared at her, his anger rising steadily. "Don't push it, Caroline. You don't know me or anything about my life, so don't stand there and talk to me about *baggage*. I'm sure you've got a few suitcases of your own."

She moved closer to him. "You're awfully wound up, and I don't want to argue with you. I know some great ways to let off steam, and

I'm guessing it's been a while for you, right? Since you've...been with someone?"

His eyes widened. "Are you...are you propositioning me?"

"You're so tense, and maybe a little...frustrated?" Her head tilted. "Why don't you let me help you with that? No one has to know. It can be our little secret." She placed her hand on his stomach. "I think you'll find I'm quite adept at my own type of therapy."

He felt like he was in the middle of a bad dream, and when he looked down at her hand, he suddenly felt the urge to laugh. He took a step back and watched her hand fall away and then leaned back against the railing. Closing his eyes, he fought to remain somber.

She seemed determined to misinterpret his every action and expression though, and stepped closer to him again. "This is easy, Will. No strings attached. No deep, committed relationship. Just full-on sex. Two adults giving each other pleasure."

"Friends with benefits," he said drolly, unable to look at her. "Is that it? Is that what you're offering?"

"Yes, exactly. Good friends with *excellent* fringe benefits."

"Giving each other pleasure." He repeated her words, still amazed he was one of the people participating in this bizarre conversation.

"Yes. And believe me, you'll feel pleasure. Several times over, if I have my way."

That did it, he couldn't contain himself any longer. He dropped his head and quietly chuckled, but eventually his mirth subsided as his anger resurfaced. *This has to end now, before she embarrasses herself—and me—further.*

"Here's the thing, and you need to listen to me." He faced her again. "I'm not interested in having a friend with benefits. The whole concept of it is completely unappealing to me. Call me old-fashioned or a prude or whatever, but my answer is no. I'm not interested in *or* attracted to you. At all."

Her mouth dropped open, and in the lights surrounding the deck, he could see her face flush crimson. He felt badly, but it was brief; he needed to be blunt.

"I'm sure there are a lot of guys who would jump at the chance to have an arrangement like that with you." He shrugged. "I'm just not one of them." He saw he'd rendered her speechless, and decided it was time to walk away. "I'm going back inside. I'll see you around."

THE CROWD AND PULSING MUSIC INSIDE THE CELLAR, A LOCAL CLUB, WAS just what Elizabeth needed. She sat alone at one of the bar tables while Kate and Charlotte danced with each other to the pounding music.

Of course, she tried to pretend seeing Will with Caroline wasn't a big deal, but she felt slighted. More than slighted, she felt ignored and insulted. They faced each other in the middle of the sidewalk, and he acted as though he hadn't spent most of Tuesday night kissing her, whispering in her ear, charming her, and making her feel things she'd never felt before.

Not thirty minutes before that, she'd been telling Kate and Charlotte how romantic the date had been, how sweet and attentive he was, how much she enjoyed being with him and kissing him...and then he'd treated her as if she were a stranger. No sign of familiarity, no smile, *nothing*. Why didn't he just walk up to her and hug her? Or flash those marvelous dimples, just for her? Or kiss her?

Then again, why didn't I do the same?

She wondered how he would have responded if she'd just walked right up to him and given him a kiss, right in front of Caroline and everyone else. She frowned, knowing she would have been doing exactly what Caroline was clearly trying to do—stake a claim.

What made her angry were the first words out of his mouth when he pulled her aside—she couldn't believe he'd actually asked if she had a date. It wasn't "let me explain" or "this isn't what it looks like." Instead, he questioned *her*.

She'd laid into Kate a little bit for saying they had dates. "You could have said we needed to leave. You didn't need to say anything about dates. That was a little bit childish."

"I know and I'm sorry, but I was pissed off."

"Caroline is a complete bitch," Charlotte chimed in. "We all know she gives it out freely to anyone with a fat wallet."

"I'm sure it's not like that," Elizabeth said. "I'm sure it's just nothing."

Remembering how her friends had looked at her then was painful. *Pity. They feel sorry for me.*

It had been her idea to come to the club, just to avoid talking about it anymore. What good would it do? She was sure she would hear from Will, that he would text or call when he got back to the island; he wouldn't leave things the way they stood now. At least she hoped he wouldn't. In any case, she wouldn't call him. He asked for time with his sister, and she was determined to let him have it.

The only thing she wanted from him was honesty—and patience—if they were to move forward. Her thoughts were interrupted by the feel of two large hands grabbing her shoulders from behind.

"Hey, Lizzy!" John Lucas came around in front of her and planted a kiss on her cheek. "Where's the rest of the terrible trio?"

"Hi, John. I didn't know you were coming." She rose to give him a hug and gestured to the dance floor filled to capacity with gyrating, jumping bodies. "Your sister and Kate are out in that throng."

"Come on, let's go find them." He took her by the hand and pulled her along behind him.

It didn't take long for them to locate Charlotte and Kate. John gave each of them a kiss on the cheek and soon they were dancing in a tight circle. Elizabeth loved John like a brother, and he and Charlotte were very close. It didn't surprise Elizabeth when Charlotte confronted Caroline tonight; Charlotte never passed up the opportunity to get a dig in when she could, especially since Caroline had treated John so poorly.

After dancing to a second song they wandered back to the table, and John casually draped his arm around Elizabeth's shoulders. He was naturally affectionate, and although it took some getting used to, she learned it was just who he was—a giant teddy bear.

More than one pair of female eyes rested on them—mainly on him —as they stood there, looking every bit like a young couple out on the town. John was handsome, with the same flawless chestnut-colored skin as his sister—minus the tattoos. His curly black hair was cut short and close to his head, which only served to show off his dark eyes and the small diamond studs he wore in his ears. At over six feet tall and well-built, he could wear a suit or a pair of jeans equally well.

"Where's Isabelle tonight?" Elizabeth asked him, referring to his newest girlfriend. Lately she couldn't keep track of them.

"Gone," Charlotte answered for her brother with a roll of her eyes. "Complained once about his long hours at work and found herself out on her ass."

Elizabeth frowned. "I liked her! She was nice."

"I liked her too, but I have a very, *very* important job with very random hours." He puffed out his chest. "These women get what they get and they shouldn't get upset."

Elizabeth and Kate burst out laughing while Charlotte only shook her head.

"C'mon, Lizzy, we're going back out there," he said.

She only had time for a quick sip of her beer before she was pulled back into the mass of people. He twirled her around and then attempted to dip her, with nearly disastrous results. He held lightly to her waist and came up behind her, keeping a respectable distance between them, and began to loudly sing nonsensical lyrics in her ear, and she couldn't help but laugh. She spun around and danced away from him and then watched as he approached two young women who were making no secret of ogling him. She laughed at their expressions; both were obviously appalled and probably assumed she was his girl-friend. She gestured as if she was pushing him over to them, letting them know she was not with him. Their expressions altered instantly, and all three were soon smiling as he became happily sandwiched between them.

She started to walk off the floor but Kate and Charlotte were making their way back and made sure to keep her with them. Soon enough, the three women were dancing together again, laughing and enjoying themselves, and Elizabeth forced Will Darcy from her thoughts for the rest of the night.

Sixteen

Friday morning was unlike any morning Will had ever experienced as Jack's father. It seemed his son had been replaced during the night by a back-talking, stubborn clone. After spending most of the morning bickering, they had another confrontation over breakfast.

"I don't *want* eggs," Jack said, crossing his arms over his chest.

Will sighed and tried to keep a grip on his patience. "Fifteen minutes ago, you told me you *did*."

"I changed my mind." Jack defiantly pushed the plate away.

"Well, unfortunately for you, the eggs can't be put back in the shells." Will slid the plate back toward his son. "Eat."

"No."

"Jack Louis—"

Jack pushed the plate away once more and crossed his arms again, his expression as challenging and stern as could be. "No. I don't want them."

"Jacky, come on. Your dad just made those for you," Georgiana intervened gently. "They're nice and cheesy."

"I said I don't want them, and *don't* call me Jacky, that's a baby name." He turned his glare on his aunt.

"Fine," Will said, scowling as he snatched the plate from the table. "I'll eat them. You can have cereal or go without breakfast."

Jack rose from the table. "I'm not hungry." He stalked out the sliding door and closed it loudly behind him before running down the steps to the backyard, heading straight for his fort.

Will sighed and shoveled a forkful of eggs into his mouth,

grimacing as he took a sip of coffee to wash it down. "I can't believe he eats these, they're awful."

"He loves them," Georgiana remarked. "Usually."

"He doesn't love them today. He doesn't love *anything* today. Getting up, getting dressed, having a normal conversation... It's been one battle after another. Maybe I take it for granted that he's so easy. He hardly ever argues with me."

"Something is obviously bothering him. But wow, does he ever have the Darcy scowl mastered! He looks just like you when he does that." She arched a brow. "And not for nothing, but you're not in the best mood either."

Will frowned and grunted.

"I'm not criticizing, I know why *you're* grumpy. Do you think he's upset I'm leaving today?"

Will closed his eyes. "Oh, of *course* that's it. And here I thought he was cranky from going to bed so late. I'm such an idiot."

Georgie was right; Will *was* grumpy. He felt unsettled and on edge, and would remain that way until he could talk to Elizabeth.

"You're not an idiot. You're a great dad," Georgiana said softly.

"Thanks. I'm trying..." He sighed heavily.

"Do you want me to talk to him?"

"No, I'll go. Um, maybe we can leave early and walk around Portland before we go to the airport."

She nodded. "Okay."

He went outside to the fort and knocked lightly on the door, and when it swung open he ducked inside.

"What's going on, Jack?" Will asked as he sat cross-legged on the floor.

Jack shrugged but said nothing.

"Come on, I know something is bothering you. You skipped your cheesy eggs, so it must be something serious. You can tell me anything, you know that." He watched as a tiny tear slipped from one of Jack's eyes.

"I don't want Auntie G to go back to New York." Jack's voice was filled with sadness. "I want her to stay here." More tears followed, making wet paths on his pink cheeks. "It's not fair."

Will pulled him into his lap and hugged him close as tears sprang to his own eyes. "I know you're going to miss her. I will too. Maybe we'll see if she can come back in a couple of weeks and bring Mrs. Reynolds with her. Would you like that?"

"But that's far away. She said she's havin' a summer vacation too, like me. Why can't she stay more?"

"Because she misses her friends, and she misses Grampa and Mrs. Reynolds."

"But when she goes back to New York, she's gonna miss us."

Will nodded as he lightly rubbed Jack's back. "She will, just like she always tells you on the phone, right?"

"Mm-hmm."

"No matter where Auntie G is, she's always going to be missing someone."

"When we lived in New York, she got to see all of us, and she wasn't missin' anyone."

Will's hand stopped. "Do you want to go back to New York, Jack? Did you like it better there?"

Jack shook his head. "I like it here. I like our house and the ocean and all the trees and our yard and the fort. We don't have all that stuff in New York." He sniffled and settled further against his father's chest. "But sometimes I miss Auntie G and Mrs. Reynolds."

Will held him close. "I know you do. I do too."

They were silent for a long moment until Jack spoke again, his voice almost a whisper. "Sometimes I pretend Auntie G is my mom."

Will's vision blurred with a rush of tears. "You have a mom, she's just...she's not here with you. With us. But she loved you more than anything in the world."

"And she loved you too, right?" Jack's violet-blue eyes were still wet with tears as he stared up at his father.

"She did." Will smiled sadly. "We're pretty lucky guys, aren't we?"

"Yeah."

"We don't want to make Auntie G feel bad about leaving. It's okay to tell her we'll miss her, but we want her to be happy for the last couple of hours she's here, right?"

Jack nodded and dropped his eyes. "I don't want her to be sad."

"Should we go back inside and start the morning all over again?"
Jack wiped his eyes and smiled a little. "Yeah."

ELIZABETH HURRIED INTO WORK, RUNNING SLIGHTLY BEHIND SCHEDULE.
Charlotte hadn't set her alarm for the correct time, and they'd both
ended up scrambling to get out the door. She rushed into the library,
miraculously only fifteen minutes late.

"Mary! I'm here," she said quietly as she walked behind the
counter to her desk. "Sorry. I stayed at Charlotte's, and we both
overslept."

Mary raised an eyebrow. "More drinks with umbrellas?"

"No, no drinks with umbrellas. I stuck with beer and only had a
few. A children's library is not the ideal place to nurse a hangover."

"I wouldn't know," Mary said primly, offsetting her words with a
roll of her eyes and a smile.

Elizabeth sat down at her desk and frowned. "Ugh, I just realized
it's the last Friday of the month. I need to review the publisher's
announcements. I have a bunch. What about you?"

Mary typed rapidly on her keyboard. "Just a few. I'll email them to
you."

On the last Friday of every month, Elizabeth read over the emails
that came from several domestic and international publishing houses,
alerting bookstores and libraries as to what each house would be
releasing the following month. Mary was responsible for finding the
pre-release reviews from independent sources, and from there the two
women were able to compile a list of new acquisitions they wished to
make. It wasn't quite as tedious as it sounded; she liked being privy to
the new books being released.

She logged into her computer and started looking through her
inbox, highlighting the announcements to print. "There aren't many. I
should be able to have a list ready pretty quickly. Are you looking at
reviews?"

"Yes. We'll cross-reference later."

"Okay."

"Are you reading for story hour?"

Immediately, Elizabeth's mind conjured up Will's face. "Um, I'm not sure. If I have time. Who do we have for assistants today?"

"Just Jill."

Elizabeth sighed. "What about volunteers?"

Mary nodded toward an elderly man standing next to one of the long shelves of books, using a small feather duster to clean them. Elizabeth looked at the man and then looked back at Mary.

"Hubert," they said simultaneously.

"He's a sweet man, but it takes him entirely too long to read a story." Mary shook her head. "The kids get impatient."

"I know. And Jill is just the opposite." Elizabeth laughed softly. "She gets so nervous she flies through it, tripping over every other word and turning red as a tomato."

"I guess that leaves you. You're the best, and the kids love you. They're all scared of me."

"No, they aren't," Elizabeth argued halfheartedly. "They just don't know you. You have to make yourself more approachable."

"I don't *want* to be more approachable. I want to stay behind my little desk. *You* are the approachable one."

"Hm." *Not last night, apparently.*

Sighing, she forced her attention back to her work, determined to keep her mind off of Will.

SAYING GOODBYE TO GEORGIANA AT THE AIRPORT WASN'T AS TRAUMATIC AS Will had expected. Jack was stoic, though the dampness in his eyes and the quiver in his chin gave him away. Georgie was emotional too; she hugged Jack for a long time and promised she would be back soon. After she walked through the security gate, she turned to give them one last wave and then disappeared into the main terminal.

Jack was silent as they drove back to the parking garage, and Will decided to let him be, knowing he would come around eventually. It happened sooner than he thought it would; his son's eyes lit up at the sight of the golden arches of a McDonald's, and Will immediately pulled into the parking lot. They sat in the sun at a ridiculously uncomfortable metal picnic table while they ate, and Jack quickly began to perk up. *The healing properties of chicken nuggets and fries.*

"I bet 'Lizabeth is gonna read today," Jack said as they finished up their lunch. "And how come she said she didn't know if she was watchin' *Shrek* with us? You said she was comin' over."

Will frowned. "When did she say that?"

"Last night. I told her we were watchin' 'em and I got to stay up late, and she said *maybe* she was comin'. She said *we'll see.* When you say 'we'll see,' it just means no."

Will sighed as they got back into the truck. He'd been so distracted by the mention of her date, he'd forgotten all about her answer to Jack's question. On top of that, he'd been a coward today. He knew he needed to call her and should have done so last night, but by the time they got home and he put Jack to bed, he was grouchy and confused and completely embarrassed by his own behavior. Even Georgiana had called him out on it.

"What were you thinking?" she'd asked him last night as they sat outside on the deck.

"What do you mean, what was I thinking? Wasn't it obvious there were no productive thought processes occurring in my brain during that short period of hell?"

"Caroline is devious," Georgiana said. "You know that, right? I mean, I've seen my share of soap operas. She's like the diabolical villainess of the quaint small town, trying to seduce all the rich men, and stopping at nothing until she gets what she wants."

Will turned to look at his sister. "You watch way too much television."

She ignored him. "What happened to you? It was like you swallowed your tongue. You barely acknowledged Elizabeth! What the hell was *that* all about? You *just* went out on a date with her two nights ago. You said you had a good time—"

"I did, I had a great time."

"Well, you could have fooled me. You might as well have been strangers standing there! She didn't look happy when she walked away."

"She wasn't. You're right, I was a total idiot." *A horse's ass.* "I asked her if she really had a date."

"Oh, good grief, Fitzwilliam! Of *course* she didn't have a date! It's *so* obvious her friend said that to make you jealous. She was being protective! Didn't you see the look on Elizabeth's face? She was mortified."

"Maybe because it was supposed to stay a secret."

"You *are* an idiot. She was just as surprised to hear that as you were. You should call her or at least text her."

He looked at his watch. "It's too late."

She looked at him doubtfully.

"Hey, maybe it's not too late for you and your New York friends, but it's late for us Mainers. Plus she's staying at Charlotte's. I don't want to interrupt her time with her friends."

"Or interrupt her date."

"Shut up. You know, I was going to tell you how nice it's been having you here," he teased, "but now...maybe not."

She smiled. "I've had fun. And I *will* be back soon. I might just make this place my summer getaway."

He saw her expression become more contemplative. "What are you going to say to Dad about school? Have you decided?"

"I know what I'm going to say, but I still don't know what I want to do." She paused and looked away. "There's one thing I've been thinking about, but...I'm still not sure." She smiled. "You'll be the first to know."

"If things get rough between you and Dad, you can always come here."

"I'll come back, but not because of that. I have to stand up to him, not run away from him." Her eyes widened. "I don't mean...I'm not saying *you* ran away. If I were you, in your situation, I probably would have done the same thing. Your life is far more complicated. I'm just a kid trying to figure out what to study in college."

"I know." She didn't realize how often he'd wondered if he *had* run away.

"I'll go home," she continued, "and say what I need to say."

"Good for you."

"But I still think you should call Elizabeth."

Now, as he turned onto the road that wended along Portland's waterfront, he reprimanded himself again for being a coward. He'd thought about texting her, but could two people really have a proper conversation with texts? *Well, they probably could, but not the conversation we need to have.*

"Hey, Jack, I have an idea. Why don't we park the truck and take a walk? We'll go to Mr. Bingley's pub to say hi, and then we'll go to the library."

ELIZABETH RETURNED TO THE LIBRARY AFTER TAKING A SHORT WALK during her lunchbreak, and immediately spotted Will standing near the playhouse. He smiled at her, and though she didn't return it, he headed in her direction.

"Hi, Elizabeth," he said softly.

She looked him up and down impassively. "I'm sorry, have we met?"

He frowned. "Okay, I deserve that. I don't blame you for being upset." He moved closer to her. "I know I was a jerk last night. It probably won't be the last time, but I'll always own up to it when it happens." He shrugged. "Which might be frequently, knowing me."

Her resistance lowered. Slightly.

"I just want to talk to you," he said in a low voice. "Please?"

"Oh, fine," she huffed and led him over to a corner of the room where they could have some privacy. She turned to face him and leaned against a small desk. "I'm surprised you're here."

"Jack wanted to come, so…"

"Oh, *Jack* wanted to come?"

"Yes, but–but I did too. I want to explain about last night. It's not what you think. Or what you…what you thought." He looked away from her as the words came steamrolling out of his mouth. "Caroline just…she showed up at our table with that other woman, and they just *stayed*. I didn't invite her, and we didn't eat together. She made herself comfortable while Jack ate dessert, and then they followed us out. I didn't plan it, I had no idea—"

"Will."

"—that she was going to be there," he continued, as if she hadn't spoken. "And she's like a bad case of static cling, she just *sticks*. I couldn't shake her off. Between her and her friend, I felt like the meat in a sandwich, they were *surrounding* me, and—"

"*Will*," she repeated, finally drawing his eyes to hers. "I know you weren't with Caroline last night."

"You do?"

"Yes. I could tell by the look on your face." She tilted her head a little. "It was obvious she intruded on your night with Georgiana and Jack."

"You're not...you're not angry?"

"Not anymore, but I was last night. It was like you didn't even know me. You didn't smile, you didn't—" She paused and pulled her eyes from his. *You didn't kiss me.* "I wish you had approached me, at least. It was very awkward."

"I know, and I'm so, so sorry. I can't apologize enough." He reached down to hold her hand loosely in his. "I was caught off guard, and I was so worried about what you were thinking that I couldn't...I couldn't *move*, I didn't know what to do."

"I was embarrassed, especially since I'd just been talking about you to Charlotte and Kate. And then there you were, with Caroline..." She shook her head. "I felt foolish. When you finally pulled me aside, I was so relieved. Until you opened your mouth."

He looked away from her with a contrite expression. "I didn't know what to think when your friend—"

"Kate."

"When Kate said you had a date. It threw me."

"She wanted to get under your skin."

He smiled sadly. "She'll be happy to know she succeeded. But how was I supposed to know that? We haven't discussed *this*." He squeezed her hand gently.

"We haven't had the opportunity to discuss *this*," she reminded him, squeezing back. "Maybe I should have just walked up to you and kissed you."

He grinned. "That would have been nice."

"I wish now that I had, but I'm just...I'm not that confident. Not yet. And not knowing what we are or what we're doing..."

She noticed Mary standing near the counter, looking at her and pointing to her watch. The kids were gathered in the reading area, waiting patiently for Elizabeth to join them.

"I have to go."

"I know." He looked over his shoulder and then turned back to her. "I'm truly sorry. I would really like it if you came over tonight, and I know Jack would too. Will you consider it?"

She sighed, knowing she was about to give in. "How could I turn down the chance to watch *Shrek* with the Darcy men?"

"Great." He smiled, and she clearly heard the relief in his voice. He glanced over to the group of kids again. "Um, the natives are getting restless. I'll talk to you after you're done."

She watched as his gaze dropped to her lips and she felt his thumb stroke over her wrist, shooting little jolts of electricity up her arm. She squeezed his hand one more time and then walked over to her desk, picked up the book Mary had chosen, and tried to gather her wits.

Elizabeth took the ferry back to the island after work and then walked home. Will had offered to pick her up at the dock, but she declined; she needed the walk to clear her head. She accepted his offer of a ride to his house though, and he and Jack were there at six-thirty to pick her up. He also offered to take care of dinner, and to her surprise, he'd picked up a scallop and risotto dish from the market, unaware it was one of her favorites. He'd given Jack his dinner earlier, but waited to eat with her.

They sat out on the back deck, talking quietly, enjoying dinner and the wine he'd chosen—the bottle of "Horse's Ass."

"I thought it was appropriate," he said dryly as he raised his glass. "Here's to never being deserving of another bottle."

"One can always hope." She raised an eyebrow as she toasted with him.

"I might be a lost cause, so let me apologize in advance for all the horse's ass moments that are sure to come, and again for the one last night."

She laughed and shook her head.

"I mean it," he said seriously. "I'm sorry I made you feel that way. The last thing I want is to hurt you or make you feel humiliated."

She could easily read the question in his eyes, so she leaned forward and kissed him. "Apology accepted."

"Thank you." He lifted her hand and lightly kissed the back of it. "Do you want to go for a walk?"

"Sure."

He rose from the table and took her hand, leading her down the steps to the backyard. Once they were on the lawn, he wrapped his arm around her shoulders, pulling her up against him and turning to kiss her head. It was a small gesture, but one that made her full to bursting with happiness.

"I want to walk down the path where Charles went with Jane." He glanced up at the sky. "We'll still have light for a little while."

"Okay." She wrapped her arm around his waist and realized they fit together perfectly. The warmth coming from his body made her want to burrow against him further.

Jack trailed behind them, but once they found the path, he bolted past them. It didn't take them long to reach the rocky stretch of sand.

"I had no idea this was even here," Will said. Jack had already removed his sandals and was wading into the calm, flat tide. "Hey Jack, don't get too wet."

"I won't." Jack hopped down the beach, going from one foot to the other and sending up small splashes of water.

Elizabeth and Will hung back, enjoying the view from the edge of the woods. "It's rocky, but it's nice," he noted. "I wonder if I could have it cleaned or something. Can I just get rid of the rocks?"

She shrugged, still enjoying the weight of his arm around her shoulders. "I don't know. You could check with Maddie, she might know about those kinds of things." She could feel his eyes on her, and she smiled a little.

"Why are you grinning?" he asked.

"You're glaring at me," she teased.

"I'm *staring*. There's a difference."

"Mm-hmm, I know. You used to glare and now you stare, right?"

He turned her to face him and wrapped his arms around her waist. "No, I was always staring. Admiring."

The tone of his voice perfectly matched the warmth in his eyes, and when he leaned to kiss her she met him halfway. She sensed his hesitance and raised a hand to cradle his cheek, kissing him more confidently, and he responded to her silent encouragement.

"Hey!" they heard, causing them to separate. They looked down into the face of their five-year-old spectator, his expression a mixture of disgust and curiosity. "You guys are kissin'."

Will nodded. "Yes, we are."

"Oh." Jack looked away and frowned as if deep in thought, and then looked back up at his father. "*Now* is 'Lizabeth your girlfriend?"

Will grinned widely. "Yes."

"Oh. That's good," Jack responded before meandering away.

Elizabeth's eyebrows rose, and she tried very hard not to be overcome by the sight of Will's dimples and the declaration he'd just made.

"I guess I don't have a say in this," she said softly, but he wasn't listening; he was already in the process of kissing her again, his lips tracing along her jaw to her neck before meeting her lips again. His hands stroked up her back and into her hair, then traveled down again to rest on her hips. She leaned further into him, craving more contact.

He groaned softly and slowly broke the kiss, catching her bottom lip in his teeth and tugging it playfully before leaning back to look at her. "I really, *really* like kissing you," he said, his voice noticeably rough.

She smiled widely. "Of course you do."

He laughed heartily and pulled her into a hug. "Of course I do, exactly, but I should probably control myself in front of my son."

They stood that way for a moment longer and watched Jack play until Will called him over so they could head back to the house.

"Yeah, time for *Shrek*!" Jack exclaimed as they walked down the path again. "Shrek is the best ogre. Dad, why were you laughin' before?"

"Elizabeth was being funny."

"Oh. Hey, 'Lizabeth, know what's funny?"

"Hmm," she said. "I give up."

"My dad's name. It's *Fitz*-william. Like soda, soda fitzes."

"Fizzes," Will said drolly. "Soda *fizzes*, Jack."

Jack giggled. "Yeah, I know, I was just makin' a joke."

"You're a regular comedian." Will grabbed him from behind as they entered the yard and swung him around wildly, to Jack's delight.

"Put me down, *Fizz*-william!" Jack yelled, only causing his father to twirl him faster.

Elizabeth watched them play, and a smile bloomed on her face. She loved being here with them, loved seeing this side of Will, so playful and loving with Jack. It filled her with warmth and something else, something she couldn't quite define. *It's a feeling of completeness, of belonging*, she decided. *Something I could really get used to.*

WITHIN HALF AN HOUR, THE THREE OF THEM WERE ENSCONCED ON THE couch in Will's living room watching the movie. Jack was already in his pajamas and insisted on sitting between them with a giant bowl of popcorn in his lap. Elizabeth tried to focus on the movie, but her mind kept wandering to Will.

Of course, he wasn't helping; he'd draped his arm along the back of the couch and was lightly but deliberately rubbing her neck, sometimes letting his hand wander up to massage her scalp. It was all she could do not to drop her head forward and moan.

About an hour into the movie, Jack asked for it to be paused so he could use the bathroom. As soon as he left the room, Will reached for Elizabeth and pulled her toward him, making her squeal.

"You're sitting here now." He settled her snugly against him. "I'm getting jealous of my own kid."

"Your kid wasn't rubbing my neck."

"I certainly hope not." He looked down at her and gently pushed a piece of hair off of her cheek. "He had grand plans of watching two movies tonight, but I don't think he'll make it beyond this one." He leaned forward to lift their glasses of wine from the coffee table and handed her one, and then Jack came charging back into the room.

"Hey!" He stopped in front of the couch. "Where am I gonna sit?"

"On the other side of Elizabeth," Will answered. "Shuffle your feet, lose your seat."

Jack sighed. "'Kay."

Will started the movie again, and Elizabeth stretched her legs out next to his, resting her feet on the coffee table. She grinned when she realized her feet only went as far as his calves, and when she noticed the size of his feet she giggled quietly.

"What's funny?" Will whispered.

"Your feet."

He looked at his feet and then back at her. "My feet are funny?"

She nodded. "They're huge. I could easily sail across Casco Bay in one of your shoes. You could put the ferry out of business."

Jack leaned forward and shushed them firmly, making them both laugh guiltily.

"Sorry, Jack," she whispered.

Not long after, she felt Jack's weight settle heavily against her, and she could tell by his even breathing that he'd fallen asleep. She nudged Will and nodded toward his sleeping son.

"I knew he wouldn't make it." He stood from the couch and leaned down to give Elizabeth a kiss before hoisting Jack into his arms. "I'll be right back."

She nodded and when he left the room and headed upstairs, she took the empty wine glasses and the bowl and walked into the kitchen.

Will came back downstairs a moment later. "He's out cold. I don't think he's ever slept as well as he does here."

"Really?" She leaned against the counter as she dried her hands. "Maybe the noise of the city kept him awake at night."

He shook his head. "No, it was pretty quiet in our apartment. I think it's just the air here. He's always outside running around, or we're walking in Portland or swimming... It's non-stop." His eyes traveled to the bowl and glass she'd just washed. "You didn't have to do that. You could have just left everything in the sink."

She shrugged. "I didn't mind. I left your wine glass. I wasn't sure if you wanted more."

"I do want more." He took the towel from her hands and tossed it onto the counter, then stood in front of her and placed one hand on either side of her body, caging her in. "Just not more wine."

Her heartbeat immediately sped up, and she felt a warm flush moving up from her chest to her neck. He placed his hands on her waist and without skipping a beat, lifted and turned her, placing her on the island. They were nearly at an equal height, and he stood between her knees, his hands resting beside her thighs.

"Do you know what I thought of a little while ago?" he asked her quietly.

She shook her head.

"I realized I can't drive you home. I can't leave Jack here by himself, even if it's just for twenty minutes."

"It's okay, I can walk. I don't mind."

"I'm not going to let you walk home, not in the dark. It's too late."

She rolled her eyes playfully. "It's not even ten o'clock. There will be plenty of people out and about."

"It's not late *now*, but who said anything about you leaving now?" He moved in closer and kissed her lightly before pulling back again. "By the time you leave, it *will* be late."

"Oh, really?" She suddenly felt breathless.

"Well, not *scandalously* late, but later than it is now. Ten o'clock is like…" He stopped talking to kiss her again, a little longer this time. "It's like, middle school late. Not grown-up late."

"So how am I getting home?"

"Well… I thought I would just keep you here."

Seventeen

E lizabeth's eyes widened and her mouth dropped open slightly. "I–I...but I can't... Do you mean—"

"I'm just teasing," he interrupted softly, leaning closer to her. "You can take the Batmobile and bring it back in the morning."

She sighed and shook her head a little, and he watched her color rise as she looked everywhere but at him. He reached up to stroke her cheek and gently tugged on her chin, encouraging her to look at him.

"Do I make you nervous when I say things like that?"

She gave a barely perceptible nod. "A little, yes."

"I'm sorry, I don't mean to."

"I know."

"Why do you get nervous?"

"I don't have a very good track record as far as relationships go," she admitted, her face pinking further. "And as far as being physical, having...having that type of relationship with someone, with a man, I don't have a lot of experience." She paused and took a deep breath. "And the experiences I *have* had weren't always...pleasant."

He stared at her, completely fixated on her body language and her words. He moved his hands to her shoulders and felt her trembling. "Are you afraid of me touching you like this, or kissing you?"

"No. I *love* kissing you." She leaned forward and did just that, and he kissed her back tenderly. They broke apart and she reached up to stroke his cheek. "It's just that I know what will follow...eventually, and when I think about it, I start to panic. Just a little."

He continued to massage her shoulders, understanding a little more what was at the root of her nervousness. Little did she know, he was nervous too—he just hid it better.

"But eventually is not right now; it's not tomorrow or even next week or next month," he said. "It's whenever *you* decide it is."

He leaned toward her and kissed one corner of her mouth. "In the meantime"—he kissed the other corner—"we can just kiss"—his lips slid to her jaw—"as much as you want."

He moved in closer and continued at a slow pace, letting his hands drift from her shoulders until one was at the nape of her neck, the other gently cupping her cheek. When his lips moved back to hers he noticed she'd stopped trembling, but before he could think on it further—he was getting to the point where he could hardly think at all —she took control of the kiss.

When she bit his bottom lip and then sucked it lightly, his knees nearly buckled. Her arms wound around his neck, and they kissed— for how long, he couldn't say, because he completely lost track of time. He moved his hands back to her shoulders and then down her sides until they rested firmly on her hips, anchoring her to the counter. She had no idea what she was doing to him, this woman in his arms, who'd just admitted to having very little experience with men and was acting on pure instinct. She was sexy and playful, and he was completely drowning in her.

He slowly moved his hands up her sides until his thumbs lightly grazed the sides of her breasts. She tensed, a barely perceptible tight- ening in her muscles, and he felt the way she lost the kiss. She pulled away from him, both of them gasping for breath, and her eyes dropped to her thighs, which were tightly gripping his hips. She pushed against his chest, and he immediately dropped his hands to the counter and backed away from her slightly.

"I'm sorry," she murmured as she pushed further away from him, crossing her arms over her chest and looking away.

He moved his head until he caught her eye and tried to slow his breathing. "Why are you sorry? For what?" He watched as her eyes quickly flickered down below his waist before rising to his face again. "You're not apologizing for my physical state, are you?" Her eyes darted away from his once again.

"Elizabeth, look at me." He waited until she did. "That's nothing to be sorry about." He thought about their date and knew she must have felt how aroused he was when he was kissing her at the end of the night. "It's not the first time this has happened."

"I'm not a tease," she whispered as her eyes filled. "I'm sorry if–if I led you on. Kissing you is…it's perfect. I got carried away."

"I love kissing you too, and I would never think of you as a tease." He knew, then, that she was possibly dealing with bigger issues; someone had hurt her, this beautiful woman in front of him. He raised his hands to cup her face and stroked her cheeks with his thumbs. "It's not very late. Do you want to sit and talk?" She looked at him warily. "Just talk, I promise."

"Okay." Her wide brown eyes stared up at him. "Maybe we should talk."

He held her hand as she hopped down from the counter. "Where would you like to sit? We can go out to the deck or sit in the living room again…?" He looked at her expectantly, waiting to follow her lead.

"The living room is fine."

She walked in ahead of him and sat in the overstuffed chair. He guessed she wanted to maintain some distance between them, so he settled onto the couch. Just as he was thinking it didn't feel right for her to be so far away, she spoke.

"I can't sit over here. I want to sit with you."

She moved to the couch and leaned against him, resting her head on his shoulder. The silence lengthened, with only the sounds of the crickets and the light summer breeze coming in through the open windows.

"It's so odd," she began haltingly, "to sit down with the intention of having a discussion about a very specific thing, something you know you could go on and on about…and yet, not have the slightest idea how to begin. I don't know where to start."

"How about if I ask you some questions?" His arm was wrapped around her, and he let his fingertips trace a pattern on her shoulder.

"Okay."

"Okay." He cleared his throat and kissed her head. "So…you were married?"

She nodded. "Right out of college."

"You must have been about twenty-two or so?"

"Mm-hmm. My ex-husband is a year older. We went to the same college and met during my freshman year. He was a nice guy. Very sweet and thoughtful, but a bit of an introvert." She paused. "It's hard to reconcile that man with the man I eventually divorced. They are distinctly different."

"How long were you married?" he asked, feeling a mixture of curiosity and dread.

"Not long. I filed for divorce at fourteen months."

"Wow."

She looked up at him. "How long were you married?"

"I thought we were talking about you."

"We are, but I'm curious. Why can't we talk about both of us?"

"We can. I was married for almost three years." *Nine hundred and ninety-nine days, to be exact.* He'd committed the number to memory, though he hadn't thought of it in a while.

"Were you together for a long time before that?"

He nodded.

Her eyes dropped, and she pulled his free hand into her lap, wrapping her fingers around his. "Were you happy? Did you have a good marriage?"

"Yes, I think so," he answered somberly, his mind rapidly sifting through random memories of Anne. "I mean, it wasn't perfect, but it was good. We loved each other."

She lightly traced over his fingers before lifting his hand and pressing a kiss to his palm. "I'm so sorry you and Jack lost her," she whispered, lowering their joined hands to her lap.

He was nearly rendered speechless by the compassion in her voice. "Thank you." It was silent for a long moment, and he waited patiently for her to go on.

"Our marriage was good for about six months, but then things slowly started to change," she finally said. "*He* started to change."

"In what way?"

"It was little things at first. Wanting his laundry done a certain way, or being picky about the way things were arranged in the kitchen cabinets. He used to say, 'labels out, Elizabeth,' as if he was reprimanding a child. I used to roll my eyes, and he would just stare at me…" She fell silent, and when he lightly squeezed her shoulder, her eyes went to his. "Sorry."

"It's okay."

"I didn't know he'd lost his job." She focused on Will's hand, running her fingertips over the back of it and tracing the paths of his veins. "He left the house every morning as if he were going to work, but he wasn't. I still don't know what he did all day." She shrugged. "I knew something was wrong, but when I tried to find out what was going on, he became more and more closed off. Eventually, he made me feel like *I* was the problem. I needed to look better, dress nicer… He said his days were stressful and coming home to a clean home, a hot meal, and a smiling, beautiful wife would make everything better. But it only got worse. The condo was never clean enough, the meals were never tasty enough, and I was never even *close* to good enough. Too heavy, ugly clothes, too much makeup, not *enough* makeup…"

Will kept his expression blank, determined to hide his astonishment. *What the hell was wrong with that guy?* Elizabeth was as close to feminine perfection as a woman could be, in *every* way. She was smart, witty, kind, loving, compassionate, affectionate, beautiful…and sexy as hell.

"And then it became all about my friends," she continued. "*They* weren't good enough, they were bad influences or losers…it just went on and on. But I had to have my friends, I–I needed them." She frowned. "I felt like I was slowly drowning, but I was so afraid of giving up. I thought that whatever it was, whatever was eating at him, I could fix it."

"What did your friends think? Did you talk to them, or to Jane?"

She shook her head. "I was embarrassed. He'd told me so many times it was me… When you hear something enough, it's only a matter of time before you start to believe it."

Will muttered a curse under his breath and when she looked up at him, he saw that her eyes and cheeks were wet. He lightly grasped her chin and bent to kiss her cheeks, following the salty tracks before lightly brushing his mouth across her eyelids. They fluttered against his lips and she sighed as her body relaxed into his.

"Thank you," she whispered.

He remained silent and held her close, waiting for her to continue.

"Sometimes I could get away. I'd go out with Jane or a friend, but I'd always be checking my phone or looking over my shoulder. Bill would call and demand to know where I was, or tell me to come home. When I finally *did* go home, he would ask if I was out whoring. He would get right in my face…"

He felt her shudder and reached for her hand, and she hooked her fingers through his and squeezed them. "Did he ever hit you?" he asked, afraid to hear her answer.

"No, but he would threaten to. He would raise his hand, and then laugh when I flinched. It got to the point that I cringed whenever he came near me. He'd become so…so *menacing*, so intimidating. And I think he enjoyed it; he enjoyed making me fearful. If–if the things in the kitchen cabinets weren't all facing the same way or the bathroom towels weren't folded properly, if–if my clothes were wrinkled or the laundry wasn't done, if dinner wasn't ready…it would start all over again."

Will took a deep breath and tried to slow his thrumming heart. He didn't know what was wrong with her ex as far as putting a clinical name to it, but he knew what *he* would call it: *Cowardly. Weak.* What kind of man intimidates and terrorizes a woman and gets his kicks from it?

"Is that why you pushed me away earlier?" he asked.

"Yes. No." She shrugged and shook her head. "I don't know. I'm sorry."

He kissed her temple. "Please stop apologizing. You have nothing to be sorry for."

I'm not ready for this conversation to go further, Elizabeth thought, and they both fell silent again.

She'd already told him so much; the last thing she wanted to talk about was her dearth of sexual experience. It was one thing to talk about Bill and her marriage, but talking about how clueless and help-less she'd felt in that particular area was entirely another, especially since Will was coming from a marriage of love. He hadn't been headed for divorce when his wife died, he'd been happily married. It was safe to assume the physical relationship he'd shared with Anne was miles apart from the one she'd shared with Bill. The physical aspect of her marriage was just another horrible layer, one lousy part that contributed to the whole rotten sum.

Still, she knew the moment of truth would come. Her physical response to him couldn't be denied; she felt things with him she'd never felt before, things that made her crave more.

"I was stupid," she finally whispered.

"Hey." He squeezed her hand. "Please don't do that. Don't beat yourself up. You were confused and afraid, not stupid."

"I *was* stupid. I stayed with him for *eight months* after all of this started happening. Eight months of feeling humiliated and inadequate and scared."

"But you took the steps to end it."

"Well, I had *decided* to end it...but Bill ended it himself."

He frowned. "What do you mean? What did he do?"

"He was away on business—that's what he told me, anyway—so I made lunch plans with a friend. I didn't know Bill had come home early, and when I walked into the condo with George, Bill overheard us talking. He heard George begging me to leave, and he came downstairs with a gun. He grabbed me by the hair... George lunged at him, and the gun went off."

Will gently scooted her onto his lap and wrapped his arms around her. The calmness of her voice belied the shaking of her body, and he stroked his hands soothingly over her back.

"Were you hurt?" he asked.

She took a steadying breath. "No, but George was shot. Bill went to prison, and I started divorce proceedings as soon as I could.

"Was George okay?"

"He healed, slowly but surely. Bill always thought there was something more going on between us. He never believed we were just friends," she explained, almost desperate for Will to know the truth.

"Are you still friends?"

She shook her head. "No. Too much happened between us after." *That's a conversation for another time.*

"I'm sorry. For all of it, for everything you went through."

"I'm not a–a submissive person," she said firmly. "I'm not weak. At least, I never thought I was. But after everything happened, I questioned myself constantly. Why did I let him do that to me?"

"You're not weak. You didn't *let* those things happen to you. Your ex-husband is the weak one. You're a strong woman. Seeing who you are now, it would be obvious to anyone who knows what you've been through. Your ex-husband had psychological issues, none of which can be blamed on you."

She pulled back to look into his eyes. He was being so sweet and supportive, but she knew she had to give him the opportunity to bow out gracefully before things went further. Jane's words about him being too much came back to her, but she wondered if maybe the opposite were true.

Maybe I'm too much for him.

She reached up to stroke his cheek and felt the new growth of whiskers there. "I won't hold you to what you told Jack tonight."

He frowned. "What did I tell Jack?"

"The girlfriend thing. I appreciate you wanting to make an honest woman out of me." She smiled sadly and tilted her head. "I'm sure the last thing you expected was to hear all of this. If you want to take a step back, it's okay." It hurt to say it, but he needed to know she had no expectations.

"So I'm supposed to just walk away now?"

His indignant tone caught her by surprise. "I just...I wanted to tell you it's okay if you decide it's too much to deal with, or that *I'm* too much. I would understand."

He stared at her before leaning forward to kiss her, his brown eyes warm. "You *are* too much. You're too beautiful, too kind...too everything. Everything *good*." He hugged her close. "I'm not going anywhere. You're not the only one who's trying to start over."

She settled against him and felt a wave of relief, but with it came a niggling surge of curiosity. "Will?"

"Mm-hmm."

"What happened to Anne? Was she sick?"

He shook his head. "We were in a car accident. Our car was T-boned by a guy who ran a red light, and she took the brunt of the hit. She held on for a couple of weeks, but her injuries were too severe."

She sat back to look at him. "How old was Jack?"

"He was two. Almost two and a half."

WILL PAUSED AND PONDERED HOW SURREAL IT FELT TO BE TALKING ABOUT the accident. Surprisingly, it was very matter-of-fact, almost like telling a story about someone else's life, and he wondered if this was how the healing process worked; if looking back on those days would be more and more like looking back at a series of blurred photographs.

"She'd insisted on driving, and she had this little hybrid car…it didn't stand a chance. I couldn't get past that for the longest time."

"You felt guilty?"

He nodded. "If we'd taken my truck, I would have been driving… Maybe there would have been a different outcome. Maybe I would have taken a different route, maybe the damage wouldn't have been as great…"

"But you didn't know what would happen. It was out of your control."

"I know, and you're absolutely right." He nudged her a little. "Just like I'm right about you not being stupid. Or weak."

She stared at him. "Okay, fair enough."

"It took a while, but I worked through it. I know I'm not responsible for what happened."

"I can't imagine what it must have been like for you, struggling with grief and guilt, and through all of it, trying to be a daddy and raise a little boy."

It was strange, but he knew she truly ached for him and for Jack and for everything they'd been through. She turned to face him, and his eyes drifted closed as her warm, soft lips scattered kisses across his cheeks.

It was then that he realized that what they were slowly and carefully building was going to last. He could feel it in his gut, in his soul.

He reached to hold her face and kissed her deeply, wanting to express with actions what he wasn't yet ready to say, although he felt very sure of himself.

He held her face in his hands and kept his eyes trained on hers, his heart pounding heavily. "I'm ready to move forward, and I want to do that with you. Are you ready to move forward with me?"

She nodded. "Yes."

Elizabeth woke on Saturday morning to the ringing of her cell phone, and she rolled over to check the caller ID. *Jane.* They hadn't talked since Wednesday, and she knew they were both holding out, waiting for the other to call first. She reached for her phone, knowing she needed to get the conversation over with.

"Hello."

"Good morning, Lizzy," Jane responded, her voice subdued.

"Hi."

"How are you?"

"Great. You?"

"I'm fine." Jane sighed. "I'm calling to tell you I'm sorry. I shouldn't have said a lot of what I said, and I don't blame you for being upset. I would have called you sooner, but I thought maybe you needed a little time to calm down and think about everything."

Elizabeth reached up with her free hand to rub her eyes. "Everything?"

"Yes, everything we discussed."

Elizabeth's hand fell back to the bed. "Do you mean everything you *told* me? We didn't really discuss much."

"Okay, then, everything I *told* you. I should have waited before I said anything to you about Will."

"Waited for what?"

"Well, to see if anything was going to come of this."

"This, meaning me and Will?"

"Yes."

"So if you saw that Will and I were developing a real relationship, you would have waited to drop your bombs then, is that it? Or if it *didn't* work out and he dropped me like a hot potato, you wouldn't need to say anything at all, right? Well, except for I told you so."

"You make it sound like I'm intentionally trying to hurt you," Jane responded, sounding offended. "I told you I'm just trying to look out for you. I'm sorry if you see it differently."

"But I don't need you to look out for me! I do fine on my own. All I want is for you to be *happy* for me. Is that too much to ask?"

"That's not fair. I've *always* been in your corner, you know I have. But you know nothing about Will Darcy!"

"I know enough. And I hate to say this, but you were with Stuart for a long time, and you didn't know him at all."

"Low blow, Lizzy."

"It's *not* a low blow." Elizabeth forced herself to speak calmly. She didn't want this to turn into a shouting match. "How do you think I felt when you said that Will was too much for me? And is that what you really meant? Do you think he's too much for me, or do you think I'm not enough for him?"

"Both," Jane answered, her voice softer now too. "He's a very sought-after man. Filthy rich and in line to inherit everything from his father when the time comes. I'm not blind to who and what he is, but you seem determined to be. He's not some hick who'll be happy living on that little island. Right now he's in love with the place, but that's because it's a novelty. But what about this winter, when you're knee-deep in snow and he's restless?" She paused. "That lifestyle, the people and money he left behind in New York... I honestly don't believe he would turn his back on all of that, for life on an island in Maine."

"Life on an island in Maine *with me*. That's what you *really* mean, right? You think he'll just grow tired of all of this and head back to New York without looking back? That he'll miss it so much that he'll just...go?"

"I'm sorry to say it, but yes, that's what I think. I think he's crushing on you, the cute librarian from the quaint little island. But honestly, how long do you think you'll be able to hold his attention?"

Elizabeth felt bitterness well up inside of her. She thought of the conversation she'd had with Will last night and about everything that had happened after, and she shook her head. "Part of me understands why you see it that way, and I know you feel like you're being helpful and protecting me, but *I* don't see it that way. I don't see *him* that way. Do you remember when we talked not too long ago, and you asked me if I was dipping my toes in the water?"

"I remember."

"I told you I hadn't found any waters worthy of my toes, and we laughed about it. But now I *have* found the waters. I wish I could explain it to you. There's something between Will and me, something special. And it's not one-sided." Elizabeth didn't want to say more than that about his feelings; they were private, and his words from the night before were held close to her heart. "Can you try to be happy for me?"

"I am, Lizzy. I hope it works out. I hope Will proves me wrong."

"So I guess we'll call a truce then?" Elizabeth offered, although she wasn't sure if they'd resolved anything. She glanced at her alarm clock and saw it was almost eight-thirty. "I have to run. We'll talk soon?"

"Sure. Soon."

They said goodbye, and while she showered, Elizabeth replayed their conversation. She was still angry, though less so than she was a few days ago. Mostly she was disappointed that Jane was choosing to view Elizabeth's budding relationship as one destined to fail.

Instead of dwelling on it further, she focused on the day ahead. The sun was already streaming through her windows and the sky was a beautiful cerulean blue—perfect weather for the arts festival.

She thought back to the previous night, how she and Will had ended up stretched out on the couch, talking a little bit more but avoiding anything serious. They'd kissed—a lot—and she felt as though it hadn't been enough.

Lying next to him had made her hyperaware of his body—the way it fit alongside hers, the smell of his skin, the rough timbre of his voice as it vibrated his chest under her ear… It led her to wonder whether the hair on his chest would feel coarse or soft, and what the skin at the small of his back would feel like under her fingertips…

Her thoughts had definitely strayed, and although she wasn't ready to jump into bed with him by any means, she was ready for things to move forward.

Their discussion had briefly turned serious again when Will had teased her about dragging her into a piano bar so he could hear her play, and she'd mentioned she used to have her own piano. It was a vibrant pink upright her father had bought her for her eighth birthday and had been her most prized possession. She'd taken meticulous care of it and practiced regularly.

"Why don't you have it now?" he asked.

"About seven months after I got married, it was gone. I'd been out shopping with Jane, and when I got home…no more piano." She'd tried to act as though it wasn't a big deal. "Bill sold it. He said we needed the money. He advertised it online, and when he found out I was going to be gone for the day, he arranged for the buyer to come and pick it up. I thought it was strange he let me go shopping without a fuss. Once I got home, I understood why."

He stared at her, sadness etched in his deep brown eyes. "I'm so sorry."

"It's okay, it was just a piano. A piece of furniture."

"Elizabeth, come on." He kept his eyes glued to hers. "It must have hurt."

She'd given in and nodded, resting her chin on his chest as she looked at him. "It did. It hurt a lot. I think I mourned that piano for longer than I mourned my marriage."

That remark, although not intended to be funny, had struck her as such, and she giggled, which in turn caused Will to chuckle, and the seriousness of the moment dissipated as they hugged each other and laughed quietly. They spent the rest of the night tangled up on the couch, doing nothing more than kissing and talking about random, inane things.

It was one of the best nights of her life, and she wouldn't have traded a single minute of it for anything.

Eighteen

Will's cell phone rang as he stepped out of the shower. Thinking it might be Elizabeth, he wrapped a towel around his waist and quickly walked into his bedroom, leaving a trail of water behind him. He was surprised to see Sarah Grady's name on the caller ID.

"Good morning, Sarah."

"Good morning, Will. I hope it's not too early to call."

"Not at all. How are you?"

"I'm fine, thanks. Sam has been pestering me to call since Thursday, and I meant to last night, but it slipped my mind. He would love for Jack to come over today if you don't have other plans."

"We're going to the arts festival in Portland; we were planning on spending the day."

"Oh, I forgot the festival was this weekend! That's okay, I'll just let Sam know you're busy."

"Well, why don't I ask Jack? He's been wanting to play with Sam too."

"Do you want to call me back?"

He looked down at the growing wet spot on the floor as water dripped down his legs. "Sure, give me five minutes."

After getting dressed, he called for Jack to come upstairs.

"Yeah, Dad?" Jack answered as he came down the hallway.

"Mrs. Grady just called. Sam would like you to go to his house to play today."

Jack's eyes widened. "He would?"

"Yes. But I told her we're going to the festival in Portland."

Jack visibly deflated. "Oh yeah, that's right."

"But I think you should decide what you want to do instead of me deciding for you."

"You do?"

"Yes. It should be your choice."

Jack frowned. "Are you gonna be mad if I play with Sam instead of goin' with you?"

"Would you rather play with Sam?"

"Kinda. I like playin' with him."

"I know you do. If you would rather go to Sam's house, it's okay."

"And you can go to the festival with 'Lizabeth?"

"Yes, if you're okay with me being off the island for the day."

Jack shrugged. "That's okay."

"I'll call Mrs. Grady back and let her know. You need to get dressed and brush your teeth. Elizabeth will be here in a little while to pick us up."

"How come she's pickin' us up? Are we gonna drive Vixen?"

Will chuckled. "No, she drove the Batmobile home last night."

"Oh. Can I pick out some toys to take to Sam's?"

"Sure, but not too many, okay? I bet Sam has plenty of things to keep you busy."

Jack hurried to his room, and Will called Sarah back. "He would much rather play with Sam than go to the festival. I don't think it was a tough decision."

She laughed. "I don't want to ruin your plans for the day."

"No, it's fine. Do you want me back at any particular time to pick him up?"

"What time were you planning originally?"

"Probably around dinnertime."

"That's fine. He can have dinner with us. We're just having pizza."

"Are you sure you don't mind?"

"Not at all. When are you leaving for the festival?"

Will glanced at his watch. "In less than an hour. I can drop him off on the way to the ferry, if that works?"

"Sounds great, Sam will be thrilled. I'll see you in a little while. Oh, have Jack pack his bathing suit and a towel in case we go to the pool."

"I'll do that. Hey, quick question—does Jess do any babysitting?"

"She does a *lot* of babysitting, especially during the summer. Are you trying to find someone for Jack?"

"Yes."

"I'm sure she would love to watch him. It's helpful if she knows a few days in advance, just because she books up pretty quickly when the summer residents are here. She has a lot of repeat business."

"I'll be sure to make my reservations far in advance."

They ended their conversation, and Will finished getting ready. He was a little bummed that Jack wouldn't be with him today, but at the same time, he was thrilled to spend the day alone with Elizabeth.

He'd had a hard time going to sleep after she left the night before, as he kept replaying everything she'd told him about her ex. What she'd been through was heartbreaking, and even though she'd opened up a great deal, he knew there was probably more she hadn't told him.

She'd pushed at him and backed away when they were kissing in the kitchen, and although she hadn't really been forthcoming about why she'd done that, he had some theories. *If that bastard was as controlling as she said, I can only imagine how he treated her in bed.* The thought had made him speculate wildly and had kept him awake for a long time.

It had felt so good to lie next to her on the couch. She was all softness and curves and fit against him so perfectly; he'd been in a constant state of semi-arousal, and it was all he could do to keep his hands in respectable places.

They ended up drifting off, her head tucked under his chin and one arm thrown across his stomach. His arms were wrapped around her, and their legs were tangled, his much longer ones propped on the armrest at the opposite end. It was a quick nap, and when he woke he kissed the top of her head to gently rouse her. She stretched against him, and semi-arousal quickly accelerated to full arousal. When she looked up at him with those sleepy brown eyes and a soft smile, memories of the dream he'd had about her came rushing back.

He pulled her up higher on his chest and began to kiss her, softly at first but then deeper when she responded so willingly. He kept the kisses slow and sensuous, taking the time to really learn how to kiss her the way she wanted to be kissed, the way she *liked* to be kissed. His hands moved slowly up and down her back and her hands clutched at his shirt, bunching it in her small fists, but he knew it wasn't from nervousness or fear. She was feeling what *he* was feeling, an intoxicating mix of excitement and desire.

Eventually they stopped and just stared at each other, both nearly gasping for breath and smiling like fools. Seeing her smile like that did even more to assure him that this was all...good. *Very, very good.* It was after midnight when she finally left in the Batmobile, and as promised, she texted him when she arrived home safely.

He did mindless tasks this morning while he waited for her to show up, full of anticipation for the day ahead and eager to spend more time with her. His feelings for her ran in an endless circle; the more he saw of her, the more he wanted to see. The more he knew of her, the more he wanted to know.

And the more I touch her, the more I want to touch.

ELIZABETH STEPPED OUTSIDE INTO THE BRIGHT SUN WITH A SMILE. SHE WAS looking forward to the day, and had asked Will what he and Jack would be most interested in seeing. He'd mentioned the puppet show and magician, but other than that he was leaving it to her to decide where they went and what they saw.

She'd packed her work clothes in a small bag and had texted Kate this morning to ask if she could crash at her place tonight, since they both had shifts at Trinity. Both Kate and Charlotte were always gracious about letting Elizabeth stay with them when she worked at the restaurant, as the ferry didn't have a late trip to the island.

Will and Jack were waiting patiently on the front porch when she arrived at their house. Will walked around to the driver's side of the cart, and before she could move to the passenger seat, he leaned in to give her a warm kiss and reached up to stroke her cheek.

"Good morning, Elizabeth."

A zip of awareness shot straight up her spine. "Good morning." Sighing happily, she moved over and turned to Jack, who was holding his backpack and waiting patiently for a place to sit. "Hi, Jack, how are you today? Looking forward to the festival?"

"I'm not goin' to the festival, I'm goin' to Sam's," he answered excitedly as he climbed onto Elizabeth's lap.

She glanced at Will, and he shrugged as he drove the cart out of the driveway. "Sarah called this morning to invite him over, so I left it up to him."

"And you picked Sam over puppets and magicians?" she teased Jack, tickling his waist lightly. "Are you *sure* you don't want to see the ballet dancers and the jazz band?"

He giggled and scrunched his nose. "I'm sure. Sam has two new Transformers, so I'm bringin' mine, and we're gonna have an epic battle with the Autobots and the Decepticons. And I got my swimmin' suit too. Dad said we might go to the pool."

"Okay, I *guess* that sounds like fun," she conceded, pouting dramatically for good measure and making Jack laugh.

Although she liked the idea of having Will to herself all day, she would miss Jack. Just as she was getting to know Will, she was also getting to know his son. If she and Will were going to make a go of something together, Jack would be a very big part of it. She loved watching them together; seeing Will as a loving, gentle father was incredibly attractive.

"You can show Dad all that stuff, he's really excited. He kept walkin' up an' down the porch, up an' down, up an' down before you came over. When I do that he always tells me to sit still."

She laughed and peeked at Will.

"Thanks, Jack," Will said, shaking his head.

When they arrived at the Gradys', Sarah and Sam came outside to greet them. Jack jumped out of the cart, and after shouting his goodbyes, the two boys disappeared inside. Elizabeth could see the curiosity in Sarah's expression, and was sure she was wondering if anything was going on between them. The three of them made small talk for a few minutes, and Will reconfirmed that Sarah didn't mind having Jack for the entire day.

"It's fine. The two of them play really well together. Go have fun, enjoy the festival."

Will smiled. "Thanks, I appreciate it. Call my cell if anything comes up."

They said goodbye to Sarah and headed to the dock. Once parked and on the ferry, they settled into a pair of seats on the top deck, enjoying the warm sun and the light breeze. Elizabeth smiled when Will wrapped his arm around her and pulled her close before leaning in to kiss her.

"You look pretty today. Well, you look pretty *every* day," he corrected, winking at her.

"Thank you. You look very handsome yourself." His striking good looks still caught her off guard sometimes, and today he looked especially gorgeous in a pair of khaki shorts and a short-sleeved button-down shirt, which he'd left untucked.

"How did you sleep?" he asked.

"Really well. I was out as soon as my head hit the pillow. How about you?" She turned to look up at him as he pulled a pair of aviator glasses out of his shirt pocket and put them on, making her stomach do a little dance.

"It took me a little while to fall asleep, but I slept great."

She looked away and lowered one hand to his thigh, absentmindedly moving her index finger in a figure-eight pattern and letting it glide through the sprinkling of hair there. "Were you thinking about what we talked about?"

"A little."

She turned to look at him again. "I'm sorry if what I told you is bothering you. I don't want you to dwell on it."

"I said I was thinking about it *a little.* Mostly, I was thinking about how perfect it felt to fall asleep with you curled up against me on the couch. And how it was even more perfect to wake up holding you and kissing you. I could have stayed there all night just doing that."

She smiled at him as she recalled what her last thoughts had been as she was falling asleep last night. "Great minds think alike."

THE FESTIVAL WAS CROWDED, JUST AS ELIZABETH SAID IT WOULD BE. THEY wandered the cobblestone streets of Old Port, stopping into a few shops and watching various street performers and musicians. A magician on a crowded street corner caught her eye, and Will's eyebrows rose when the man took Elizabeth's hand and urged her to move to the front of the crowd.

He never spoke a word but made her giggle when he made a big show out of making a single red rose appear from thin air. Bowing dramatically, he made as if he was going to present it to her, but at the last minute he looked at Will and handed the rose to him and then gestured toward Elizabeth.

Feeling slightly embarrassed, Will handed her the rose with a little flourish, and the small group of spectators clapped and whistled.

As they walked away, Elizabeth held the flower to her nose and inhaled deeply. "You weren't too mortified by that, were you?"

He chuckled and rolled his eyes. "Oh no, not at all. Why would you say that?"

While she broke off most of the rose's stem and reached behind her to affix it under the elastic of her ponytail, he took the opportunity to let his eyes travel over her once again, as they had many times already. She looked bright and fresh in a light denim skirt that fell to mid-thigh, a coral-colored top, and sandals.

"I don't think I've seen you turn that pink before," she teased as she adjusted her hair. "I'm used to *me* being that color when we're together, not you. But I've heard that real men can wear pink, so…"

"Keep it up, Ms. Bennet, keep it up." He squeezed her hand as they set off down the street.

"Do you think Charles is at the pub today?" she asked. "We're pretty close by."

"Probably. He's there all the time. I've barely spoken to him this week."

"We should stop in, maybe we can drag him away for lunch."

"Good idea."

They walked the two blocks to the pub and saw that the doors were open and workers were milling about inside. Charles was standing at a table near the bar and looking over some papers with another man.

"Hey, what's a guy gotta do to get some service in this place?" Will called out over the din of voices and machinery.

Charles's head snapped up, and his face broke out in a wide grin. He said something to the man at his side and slapped him on the back before making his way over to Will and Elizabeth.

"Hey, guys, what's up? Checking out the festival?" He gave Elizabeth a kiss on the cheek and shook Will's hand.

"Yes," Elizabeth answered. "It's always a good way to kick off the season."

"It's the official start of the summer in Portland," Charles told Will. "You'll notice it on the island too. By this time next week it'll be mobbed."

"Can you take a break?" Elizabeth asked. "We were thinking about grabbing some lunch and thought we could talk you into joining us."

"Definitely, I'm starving. Hang on." Charles found the man he'd been talking to earlier and had a quick conversation with him before joining Will and Elizabeth again. As they walked toward the door, he looked down at his clothes, spattered with paint stains and sawdust. "Um, can we go someplace really, really casual?"

Elizabeth grinned. "I think we can manage that."

The three of them ended up getting sandwiches from a food truck near the pub, and then Charles led them to a magnificent stone fountain surrounded by benches. Because they'd wandered so far from the festival, they had ample space to sit.

"So, no Jack today?" Charles asked as they ate. "You two are wandering the streets unchaperoned?"

Will nodded. "He got a better offer from Sam and ditched us."

Charles's cell phone rang. "Sorry," he said before answering it. "Hey there. I'm sitting by the fountain on Prescott, having lunch with Will and Elizabeth," he said to the person on the other end of the line. His eyes flickered to Will. "Um, I guess, yeah." Another pause. "Okay, sure. Bye." He cleared his throat. "That was Kate. She's on her way with Charlotte."

Will groaned to himself. *Great.*

Ten minutes later, the five of them were sitting on the benches and chatting about the festival and Charles's pub. Will felt like he was under a microscope; Kate and Charlotte watched him closely, and when he wrapped his arm around Elizabeth's shoulders and kissed her temple, they blatantly stared.

He cleared his throat and pointedly ignored them, turning to Charles instead. "Have you thought of any names for your beers?"

"Wouldn't you rather know the name of the pub first?"

"Oh, yes, I want to know!" Elizabeth said, sitting up straight. "What is it?"

Charles stood and lifted his arms. "I am the proud owner of Black Rock Brewery," he announced, to which they all responded with cheers, whistles, and a round of applause. "Thank you," he said, bowing deeply. "Thank you very much."

"Great name," Will said, still clapping. "Now sit down and brainstorm some beer names."

"So, what's the deal?" Charlotte asked Elizabeth as she glanced at Will, who mostly had his back turned to them while he talked to Charles. "You're looking very cozy and cuddly with him. Did I miss something?"

"Yes. And I'm not talking about it now, for obvious reasons," Elizabeth said firmly, keeping her voice low. "Later."

Charlotte huffed and turned to glare at Kate.

"Don't look at me. I'm as clueless as you."

Elizabeth hadn't told Kate she was coming here with Will when they'd texted this morning, because it would have led to a phone call with Kate asking a million questions.

"You're *both* clueless," she stated quietly. "Everything is fine. It was a misunderstanding, and we straightened it out. Okay?"

The two women nodded. "Okay."

Will's voice drew her attention. "So, your IPA is Diamond IPA. That's a good one," he noted, nodding thoughtfully.

"Yeah, but the rest have me stumped," Charles said. "I want them to have names relating to Maine, or at least to the Portland area."

"What else do you have for beers?" Elizabeth asked.

"I have a stout, a lager, and a blonde ale."

"What about Black Rock for the stout? Can't one of the beers have the same name as the pub?"

Charles shrugged and nodded. "Yeah, maybe. Black Rock Stout sounds alright."

She arched a brow. "Gee, try to contain your enthusiasm."

He laughed. "I like it. I'll add it to my list...which now has one name on it."

They batted names back and forth and within fifteen minutes, Charles had some credible suggestions: Diamond IPA, Lighthouse Lager, Black Rock Stout, and Casco Bay Blonde were the top contenders.

"This is the most productive lunch I've had in a while," Charles said after thanking everyone. "I've got to get back to the pub. Maybe I'll see you all later." He spoke to the group but glanced furtively at Kate. She smiled but said nothing more than a quick goodbye.

Elizabeth noticed Kate's eyes were focused intently on Charles as he walked down the street, and seeing that Will was attempting to make small talk with Charlotte, she went to stand next to her.

"Do you want me to see if I can crash at Charlotte's place tonight instead? I don't want to put a crimp in your plans."

Kate shook her head. "We don't have any plans, though I can tell he's hoping we will." She chewed her bottom lip. "You can stay. If you don't, I'll let him come over. I have no willpower where he's concerned, and I have to work on that."

"So why did you call him?"

"Charlotte and I wanted to see if he was at the pub. We wanted to check it out."

Elizabeth lifted an eyebrow but said nothing.

"That's the only reason I called. Really."

"Okay."

"I'm going in a little early tonight," Kate said, changing the subject. "Jen wants me to go over the new inventory system with her, so I told her I'd meet her at three. I'll leave the key under the mat outside so you can get changed before you come in."

"Great, thanks. I'll see you around four-thirty."

Kate and Charlotte said goodbye and headed toward the festival, leaving Will and Elizabeth alone once again.

"I take it you and Charlotte are good friends?" he asked, a grin tugging at his lips. He wrapped his arms around her, pulling her against him as they stood next to the fountain.

She groaned and dropped her forehead to his chest. "Oh no, what did she say? Did she threaten you?" She took a deep breath and inhaled the scent of him, which immediately took her back to the previous night.

He laughed softly. "She just wanted to know a little bit about me, that's all. Mostly, she wanted to know if my behavior on Thursday night was the norm for me, or if it was what she referred to as 'a one-time moronic aberration.'"

She laughed into his shirt, completely unsurprised Charlotte would confront him and demand an explanation. "I swear, I didn't put her up to it."

"I know. I assured her it *was* just a moronic aberration, but I also told her there was a good chance I would be doomed to repeat it occasionally."

"She really is a very nice person. She's just—"

"Protective?" he guessed, kissing the top of her head.

She heard him inhale deeply and knew he was smelling the rose in her hair. "Yes, protective. She's like another sister to me. Kate too."

"It's nice to have people looking out for you."

"It is. Charlotte's a good friend." She stood on her tiptoes to kiss him lightly. "I'm sorry if she came on too strong."

"She didn't. And I don't blame her. I didn't make a very good impression on Thursday night." He frowned slightly. "I'm still kicking myself for it."

"It's over and done with. Can we just forget about it?" She smiled. "In fact, didn't you ask me just last night if I would move forward with you?"

"I did, and I want to do that."

"But we can't if you're stuck on Thursday night." She squeezed his waist and shook him a little. "Right?"

"Are you always this persistent?"

She shrugged. "When I see something I want, I suppose I am." A blush crept up her face as she realized what she'd just said.

"And you want me, is that what you're saying?" He grinned widely, revealing his dimples.

She nodded mutely, staring into his twinkling eyes.

He lowered his head until it was next to hers. "I'm sorry, I couldn't hear you."

"You're awful," she said quietly, although she couldn't stop from smiling.

"That's not what you *said*."

She shook her head, unable to think of a clever response.

"Alright, I'll stop." He kissed her cheek and then her lips, lingering there for a long moment, and when he finally pulled away he stared into her eyes. "Just to make it clear, if it isn't already... I feel the same way, Elizabeth. I want you too."

THEY SPENT MORE TIME EXPLORING THE FESTIVAL, FINALLY STOPPING TO watch a local band Elizabeth was familiar with. Will stood behind her with his arms around her waist, and she would have been perfectly content to stay there, wrapped in his embrace and swaying to the music. When she realized it was nearing three o'clock, she knew it was time to head to Kate's so she could get changed and spruce up a bit for work.

Will asked if he could walk her there and then to work before he went back to the island, and she texted Kate.

Is it okay if Will goes with me to your place and hangs out while I get ready for work?

You're not going to dirty up my couch or anything, are you?

Elizabeth laughed. *I'm going to pretend you didn't ask me that*

It's fine. My apartment's actually clean, so have at it. Not literally!

Ugh. Thanks, Kate. See you soon

They made their way to the apartment, holding hands and walking slowly, both of them sad to see the day coming to a close. Will sat on the couch and waited patiently for Elizabeth while she changed. She donned her uniform of black pants, white dress shirt, and black shoes, and after brushing her hair out, she put it into a ponytail again and carefully reattached the rose. The last thing she did was apply a tiny bit of make-up, though as her summer color deepened she wouldn't need it.

When she emerged from the bedroom, his eyes quickly traveled over her, and he frowned. She looked down at herself and then back at him. "What's the matter?"

"Nothing, I'm just bummed you have to go to work. I wish we could go out to eat or something."

She smiled sadly. "Me too."

His eyes dropped to her mouth. "How long before you have to be there?" he asked as he went to stand in front of her.

"About thirty minutes."

"And how long does it take to get there from here?" He moved closer.

She looked up at him as he towered over her. "Um...fifteen minutes. Give or...give or take a minute or two."

He reached up to lightly trace his fingers along the line of her jaw and down the slope of her neck to where it met the collar of her shirt. "I've been waiting to kiss you all day."

She laughed, though it came out as more of a breathless sigh. "You *have* been kissing me all day. Not that I'm complaining."

"Not the way I want to kiss you." He lifted his other hand so that he was cupping her face gently. "We have a few minutes, don't we? I can't think of a better way to pass the time."

"Me either. I think your idea is—"

Her words were extinguished as his mouth met hers. He kissed her top lip, her bottom lip, and the corners of her mouth; light, teasing forays designed to torment. Her lips parted as he deepened the kiss and she wrapped her arms around his neck.

He groaned, a low sound that came from deep in his chest, and his hands fell from her face to wrap around her waist, caging her tightly to his body. They swayed together, and suddenly he was moving them toward the couch, lowering himself to sit and pulling her across his lap.

Kate's text regarding the couch crossed Elizabeth's mind but quickly vanished, driven away by his attention to her. Their kisses grew longer and more passionate until they were straining against each other, her upper body twisted and pressed against his and her legs hanging off his lap.

She felt one of his hands as it slowly began to slide up from her waist to her breast, and instinctively she stiffened. His hand immediately stopped and began to travel back to her waist, and she pulled away and looked at him, breathing heavily.

"It's okay... I want you to touch me," she whispered as she stared into his brown eyes, their irises so dark they nearly looked black. She felt the warmth of his hand as it slid under her blouse and trailed up her side, then felt the slow movement of it over the material of her thin, lacy bra, cupping and stroking. She sagged against him, sighing into his mouth as she kissed him again.

She was lost in a haze of sensation, but wanted to feel him the way she'd imagined last night. Reaching for the bottom of his shirt, she pushed her hand underneath it until she finally came into contact with his warm skin. He continued to kiss her but she wanted *more*, wanted his mouth and his hands kissing her and touching her everywhere.

That thought brought the reality of what they were doing—and more importantly, *where* they were doing it—hurtling into her mind. She broke the kiss and sat back slightly, looking at him while his eyes were still closed. His lips were parted and he was breathing heavily, and after a few lingering caresses, his hand slid out from under her shirt.

She suddenly became aware of the hardness pressing into her hip, and she backed away a little, putting some space between them. His cheeks were flushed and when he opened his eyes, the way he looked at her... In that moment, she thought he absolutely *had* to be the sexiest man on the planet.

And he wants me.

It amazed her, and she knew without a doubt that she wanted him too, wanted to give herself to him and feel the pleasure those eyes promised.

She relaxed against his chest and rested her head on his shoulder as their breathing slowly returned to normal.

"Are you alright?" he finally asked as he toyed with her ponytail.

She nodded. "Yes."

It wasn't completely true; although she'd just acknowledged the strength of her attraction to him, she wasn't sure she'd handled it all that well. *Asking him to touch me? Practically begging him?*

"Hey," he whispered. "What's wrong?"

She swallowed. "I just...I don't want you to think that I'm..."

She sighed, not knowing how to explain it. In the past, whenever she'd drummed up the courage to express her desires or try something different during intimate moments with Bill, he'd shut her down and told her she was behaving too aggressively. And as she'd already told Will, when you heard something enough, it was only a matter of time before you started to believe it.

"Did you enjoy what just happened?" he asked, his gaze roaming her features.

She nodded.

"I did too." He lightly touched her cheek. "I won't rush you, Elizabeth, but I'll follow your lead and your cues. If you ask me to touch you, I'm going to touch you. I *want* to touch you. Constantly."

"I want to touch you too."

"I'm glad. Help yourself." She laughed, making him smile. "Don't be embarrassed or feel like you're doing something wrong. This is all part of moving forward. I want to earn your trust in every way, emotionally *and* physically. Anything that happens between us is under your control, okay?"

She nodded again. "Okay."

He stared down into her eyes as she tangled her fingers in his. "Are you ready to go to work?"

She sighed. "I guess."

He chuckled and nudged her a little. "Um...I just need a minute."

"Oh, okay." She quickly removed herself from his lap. "Thank you."

"For what?"

"For understanding...and for being so patient. For waiting."

"You don't need to thank me, Lizzy." He rose from the couch and kissed her lightly. "You're worth waiting for."

WILL PICKED UP JACK AS SOON AS HE ARRIVED BACK ON THE ISLAND, AND listened to his son's steady narration of the day's events all the way home.

Jack wanted to play a board game before he went to bed, but Will couldn't concentrate; his mind kept wandering to Elizabeth and their day together, especially the time spent at Kate's apartment. Just thinking about it caused a riot of feelings, not the least of which was arousal and excitement, so he decided he was better off thinking of something else. It wasn't long before Jack's bedtime arrived, and after tucking him in, he grabbed a bottle of water and headed out to the deck.

As he sat and listened to the chorus of crickets and tree frogs in the yard, his mind traveled to his sister, and he wondered how her return home had been. He went back inside to grab his cell phone, and although he didn't really expect her to be home on a Saturday night, she picked up on the third ring.

"Hi, Will!"

"Hey, Georgie, how are you?"

"I'm great, how are you? What's up?"

"Not much. I just put Jack to bed and thought I'd check in." He sat down on the couch in the living room. "Are you in the middle of anything?"

"No. I went out last night and didn't get home until this morning, so I figured I'd lay low tonight."

"This morning, huh?"

"You know how it is in the city. We New Yorkers stay out later than you Mainers, remember?" she teased.

"Mm-hmm. You're being careful, right? Not walking around alone?"

"I'm always with friends, and we're usually hanging out at someone's apartment. No clubs for me yet. So what are you up to? No hot date tonight?"

He chuckled. "Not tonight. Elizabeth and I spent the day together though."

"So everything is good with you guys?"

"Yes. All good."

"I'm glad. Did she join you for the *Shrek* marathon last night?"

"Yeah. Jack conked out before the end of the first one."

"Was he okay after I left? He seemed alright. If he'd cried, I think I would have lost it."

"He was fine. A little quiet, but he snapped out of it once we went to McDonald's."

She laughed. "Replaced so easily by fast food."

He grinned. "I told him you would visit again soon, maybe with Alice."

"We'll work something out."

"Have you had a chance to talk to Dad?"

"Yes, and actually, it went surprisingly well. He was very accepting of what I had to say."

"That's great. What did you tell him?"

"The truth. I said I wasn't interested in being involved in the family business in any capacity. I thanked him for the opportunities DMG has given me and told him I respect what he's done with the company and how he's built it up, but that I would make his life a living hell if I had to work for him."

Will laughed. "You said that to him?"

"Yes. He got a kick out of it," she responded, laughing a little as well. "He really seemed okay with it. And I think I've decided what I want to study."

"And?"

"I'm going to apply to either a Physician Assistant program or a Nurse Practitioner program, I'm not sure which one yet. I have to do a bit more research."

"Wow, Georgie, that's great. And honestly, I'm not surprised. You were always into that science stuff. Have you told Dad?"

"Yes, tonight at dinner. He wasn't surprised either. And he gave me his blessing."

Will's eyebrows rose. "He wants you to be happy. Maybe he's finally realizing what makes *him* happy isn't necessarily what's going to make his kids happy."

She sighed. "He asked about you and Jack."

"Oh yeah?"

"Yes. He wanted to know how you're doing."

"What did you tell him?"

"I told him you're both happy, and that you have a beautiful home and seem content and more like the old you."

He smiled. "I *feel* like the old me...but different. Does that make sense?"

"I think it does. I know what you mean." She cleared her throat. "He asked about Elizabeth too."

His eyes widened. "He asked about Elizabeth?"

"Yes. He wanted to know if I'd met her. Did you tell him about her?"

"No. Jack mentioned her on the phone, so of course Dad tried to antagonize me and get me to talk about her. It didn't work. I don't want him to know a thing about her." His sister remained silent, and he sighed heavily. "What did you tell him, Georgie?"

"I...he spoke about her as if he *knew* about her. He knew she was a librarian—"

"I told him that much. We were arguing and I let it slip."

"He said that he thought Jack liked her, or something like that, and I told him that you both did. I told him you took her out while I was there, and that you were fond of her."

Will groaned into the phone.

"He made it seem like *you* talked about her! I thought maybe you told him...ugh. I'm sorry, Will."

"It's fine," he said calmly, although he was incredibly annoyed—not with his sister, but with his father. *Manipulative bastard.*

"He seemed genuinely interested. I didn't say much, but I said enough, I guess."

Will knew she was beating herself up. "Don't worry about it, G.

You just happened to be the most convenient way for him to get information. I'm sure he'll be digging around and trying to find out more."

"Why can't he just be happy for you?"

"I wish I knew."

"Do you think he'll leave it alone?"

"I don't know." *Fat chance.* "Time will tell, I suppose."

They talked a few minutes longer, and she apologized again. He reassured her she had nothing to be sorry for, and reminded her that somehow, their father always found a way to get what he wanted.

But not when it comes to me. Never when it comes to me.

Nineteen

Richard Fitzwilliam settled his lanky six-foot frame into his seat on the plane, cursing every second of the hour-and-twenty-minute flight he was about to take from New York to Maine. It was entirely too early, his head was pounding from his overindulgences the night before, and the flight attendant wouldn't give him anything to drink until the plane took off. *A little hair of the dog would go a long way.*

To top it all off, he would have to take a *boat* to an *island* in order to find his cousin. As if he didn't have better things to do the day before July Fourth! And it was a Sunday, at that. He should be back in New York, sleeping off this raging hangover and getting ready to celebrate America's independence with a sweet bottle of tequila in one hand and an even sweeter redhead in the other. *But no.* Instead he was doing his uncle's bidding, just as he always did.

Robert had wanted him to go to Portland over a week ago, but Richard convinced him it made more sense to go when it was closer to the Fourth; he could use the excuse of being concerned for his cousin's welfare and state of mind. After all, the accident had happened on the Fourth, although Anne had held on for another two weeks or so.

Tough little bitch.

They'd never gotten along well—he thought she was an ice queen who wasn't good enough for his cousin, and she thought he was a pandering ass-kisser who couldn't be trusted.

She had me pegged.

Darcy usually slipped into a funk around the anniversary of when Anne had ungraciously clung to life by a thread, keeping her husband suspended in a hellish limbo. Every year, during those fifteen days, Darcy crawled into an emotional black hole. The only one who could get through to him was Jack; Darcy would do anything for that kid, and Jack was the only thing that kept him from going off the deep end for good.

Things between Richard and his cousin weren't the best at the moment, but what else was new? They managed to be civil, at least, until this last blowout between father and son. *But really, Darcy, what the hell? Maine?*

Richard *still* didn't get it and couldn't begin to understand the motivation behind it, but for right now, he would pretend that he did. He would show concern for his cousin, play with Jack, and tell Darcy that his new home was just *perfect*, that the clean, exhaust-free Maine air was remarkably invigorating, the view of the ocean absolutely enthralling.

Two hours later he was standing curbside at the Portland airport, trying to find a cab. Unlike New York, where cabs were a dime a dozen, Portland seemed to have only one cab company, aptly named Yellow Cab. Finally one pulled up, and the aging driver climbed out and put Richard's suitcase in the trunk as he climbed into the backseat.

"Where ya headed, friend?" the driver asked politely.

"I need to get to the boat that takes me to…some island in the bay." He thought for a moment as the driver just stared blankly into the rear-view mirror, waiting patiently. "Emerald Isle? Is that one of the islands around here?"

The driver laughed. "Son, if you're lookin' for the Emerald Isle, you got the wrong airport. In fact, you got the wrong continent. Now, if you're talkin' about an island with a gemstone in the name, you got to be talkin' about either Little Diamond or Great Diamond."

"That's it!" Richard snapped his fingers at the driver. "Great Diamond Island."

The driver pulled his cab away from the curb. "That's a pretty little place. You'll need to take the Casco ferry over there. She goes back and forth pretty often."

"How long does it take?"

"Forty minutes, give or take. Nice trip. Where ya from?"

"New York." Richard groaned. *Since when do cabbies make polite chatter?*

"I knew that weren't a New England accent ya got there. You're not a Yankees fan, are ya?"

Richard raised his eyebrows and returned the man's stare in the mirror. "As a matter of fact, I am."

The man chuckled. "Well, best keep a lid on that, if ya know what I mean."

Richard had never been so happy to see the end of a cab ride in his life. He climbed out while the driver retrieved his bag from the trunk and paid him the fare as well as a hefty tip. *Maybe that will help him retire before I need a ride back to the airport.*

He relaxed on the ferry and read over some reports Robert had given him, paying no attention to the people or scenery around him. When it was time to disembark on the island, he noticed a small shuttle bus in the dirt parking lot, parked alongside a lot of golf carts... And that's when he noticed there were no cars. At all.

Oh, this just gets better and better.

He approached the driver of the shuttle, who was waiting patiently for customers.

"How are you today?" Richard asked, smiling widely.

"I'm fine, sir, how are you?"

"Great, thanks. I'm hoping you can help me. I'm looking for my cousin; he moved here not too long ago with his son. I wanted to surprise him, but I'm afraid I lost his address. Would you happen to know Will Darcy?"

The driver smiled. "Mr. Darcy bought the Millers' old place on Old Dock Lane. I'll take you right there, just as soon as I see if anyone else needs a ride."

They waited another five minutes or so, and when it was clear no one else needed the shuttle, the driver headed out.

"Your cousin grabbed himself a nice spot of land, with a view of the bay to boot. Wasn't on the market long."

"I've heard it's quite lovely," Richard replied drolly.

His mind had already drifted away from the inane conversation of the driver and back to how he would explain his unannounced visit. He had to convince his cousin he was there on a peacekeeping mission and *not* a reconnaissance mission. His uncle had made his expectations clear: Richard was to find out all there was to know about his son's new life and the people in it.

Especially Elizabeth Bennet.

THE WEEK SINCE THE FESTIVAL HAD PASSED IN A BLUR FOR ELIZABETH. There was work, time spent with friends, and plans made with her sisters. Lydia had called to talk about visiting and had made it a point to say she and Jane would be coming together. They agreed the best time for a visit would be after July Fourth, when Jane's summer school class had a small break.

Elizabeth wanted things to return to normal between her and Jane and thought some time together might be just what they needed. She also wanted Jane to have the opportunity to get to know Will a little better, so she could see for herself how off-base her assumptions were. More than that, she wanted Jane to see how happy Will made her. But she wouldn't force it; if Jane still clung to her opinions, Elizabeth would have to let it go. The most important thing was that *she* knew Will's true feelings.

For the most part, though, the week following the festival had consisted of a lot of time spent with Will—and when not spending it *with* him, she spent a lot of it *thinking* of him. Sometimes it was just the two of them, but most of the time they were with Jack as well. Will had decided to call Jess Grady, and she'd babysat Jack twice so they could go out at night and enjoy some time alone.

They'd stayed on the island the first time, getting takeout from the market and eating at her place while watching a movie. Their original plans of having a picnic at the beach had fallen by the wayside when a rainstorm rolled in.

The second time they'd gone out, just a couple of nights ago, Will came to the library to meet her after work. They walked around the bustling streets of Portland, always busy on a Friday night, before heading to The Land Room. It was small and intimate, and it was usually impossible to get a table without a reservation, but they lucked out and enjoyed an incredible dinner before slowly working their way back to the ferry and then to her house.

They'd ended up tangled together on the couch, and after kissing for a long, long time, she sat up and looked at him, gloriously sprawled out underneath her with one leg braced on the floor.

Without saying a word she began to slowly unbutton his shirt, the only sound in the room their heavy breathing as her trembling hands did their work. When she was done, she spread the shirt wide and stared at his chest before touching him. He stayed perfectly still, letting her explore.

Her fingers traveled over the contours of his muscles and traced over the slight indentations of his ribs. His skin was hot, and she finally found out what the hair on his chest felt like—it was soft, not coarse at all. She glided her hands over his pounding heart, and her eyes rose to his. Their dark heat pulled her in, silently encouraging her and making her feel bold.

She moved her hands to her own buttons and began to undo each one. Strangely, they'd stopped shaking, and as they moved down the front of her blouse, she saw the heat in his gaze intensify. He reached to still her hands, and she read the question in his eyes.

Are you sure?

She was. She'd grown used to the feel of his hands on her and craved his touch, so much so that just kissing him would make her ache. Her fingers continued their work, and he lowered his hands and watched with rapt attention as she parted her blouse and unclasped the front of her bra in one fluid motion. She stopped then and let it hang open, still partially covering her.

His eyes moved from her chest to her face, and he stared at her for what felt like forever. He finally reached for her but not for her exposed skin; instead, he cupped her face and pulled her down to kiss her. Her bra parted further, and they both groaned when her bare breasts came into contact with the warmth of his chest.

Everything after that was a blur to her senses. It was the feel of his hands on her body, so gentle and tender as he touched her. It was the scent and taste of his skin as she finally bent to kiss his chest, and the heat of his mouth on her as he did the same, trailing warm, damp kisses over her breasts, lingering there before moving up her neck and back to her lips.

When she thought back to that night, the one thing that stuck in her mind was his expression. He'd gazed at her as if she were the most exquisite woman he'd ever seen, whispering how beautiful and desirable she was—and by the end of the night, he'd had her convinced.

When you hear something enough, it's only a matter of time before you start to believe it.

Even so, before he'd left, she'd felt a surge of uncertainty at what she'd instigated and encouraged.

He'd read her like a book and reassured her that he saw her actions as a sign of her bravery and trust of him, which meant the world to him.

Besides those two date nights, they'd spent a day at the beach with Jack. This time, she had no qualms about jumping in and joining them as they played, though she made sure to give them some time alone.

She worried that Jack would feel like she was intruding on his time with his father, though he never seemed resentful of her presence. He was happy and engaging, and she made it a point to interact with him as much as possible—not because she felt like she had to, but because she enjoyed talking to him. He was energetic and silly, but also very smart and well-spoken.

She was pleasantly surprised when Jack asked her to go rock hunting with him at the beach. Off they went, leaving Will to watch after them. Jack was determined to find bits of the twisted black rock that lined the cove. She loved the conversations she had with him as they were more like little adventures—she never quite knew where they would end up. He mentioned visiting the "Nature Museum" in New York, which she assumed to be the Museum of Natural History, and she took the opportunity to ask him about the city.

"It's loud." He was focused on the sand, keeping an eye out for the elusive rocks. "There's lots of people everywhere. I liked when my dad took me to the park. We went to the castle all the time."

"The castle?"

"Yeah, there's a castle in the park. You didn't know that?" he asked with a note of disbelief in his voice.

"I didn't know that." She bumped him playfully. "I've never been to Central Park. I've never even been to New York."

His eyes widened. "Wow." He paused for a moment. "I've never been to Massa—where you're from."

She smiled. "Massachusetts. And see? Now we're even." She remembered, though, that he *had* been to Massachusetts with his mother and father when he was very little.

"Maybe we can go on a trip," Jack said. "My dad knows all the fun places in New York, and you can show us all the fun places where you lived."

She smiled. He was talking about the three of them planning something together, and granted, he was just a young boy, but his words struck her just the same.

"I like Maine better than New York," he went on, and this time he looked up at her.

She smiled. "You do? How come?"

"I like havin' a yard and I like drivin' around in the Batmobile and ridin' on the ferry." He shrugged and simultaneously reached up to push his bangs out of his eyes. "And my dad was sad in New York. He's not sad here."

This time she was speechless, and even more so when, after declaring their search was over, he took hold of her hand. He began to talk again as they made their way back to Will, this time about the Central Park Zoo and his favorite animals there.

She understood more than anything that Jack was the center of Will's existence; there was no such thing as an exclusive claim to Will. She shared him, and just as her feelings were growing for Will, she realized they were growing for Jack as well.

Besides those particular times, she and Will had managed to see each other every day or night, even if it wasn't for anything special. During those hours together, they'd talked endlessly, sometimes about serious things—he'd finally discovered her penchant for a good debate—but sometimes about silly, mundane things. There wasn't anything they hadn't touched on, from politics and the state of the world to pop culture and sports.

Sometimes he would show up with Jack to give her a ride to the ferry in the morning, or she'd swing by his house to pick them up if she'd driven the Batmobile home the night before. A couple of times he'd been at the ferry to pick her up in the afternoon when she'd returned home. Every night ended the same way no matter how it began—with the two of them tangled up in each other, kissing and touching and slowly working past her apprehension and timidity. She set the boundaries, and he left it up to her to decide how far she wanted to push them.

Now, as she stood in his kitchen making breakfast for the three of them after walking over early Sunday morning, she felt wonderfully at peace. She commandeered Jack as her assistant chef and they cooked French toast and bacon, talking of everything important to a five-year-old boy: Transformers, swimming, dogs—he wanted one—and what he imagined his school would be like. He was in charge of dipping the bread into the batter, so it ended up getting a little messy, but he liked helping out.

They ate breakfast on the deck, and when Elizabeth was finished she sat back and closed her eyes, letting the sun warm her face as she drank the last of her coffee. Will reached for her free hand and she held his hand tightly.

"Dad, I'm done. Can we play catch?" Jack asked. "The gloves are in my fort."

"After I clean up the kitchen, okay?"

"Alright. Do I hafta help?"

"You helped cook, so you're off the hook for clean-up. Just take your plate and glass inside and leave them on the counter, please."

"'Kay." Jack rose from the table and did as he was asked, then came back outside and ran across the yard to his fort, where he disappeared inside.

Elizabeth's eyes were still closed, but she could feel Will's gaze on her and she smiled. "You're staring."

"Yup."

Her smile grew, but she remained silent.

"What are you thinking about?" he asked.

"You. Us. Friday night, in particular."

"Reaaallly. And what part of Friday night were you thinking about?"

Her smile grew. "*All* the parts," she answered vaguely, leaving him to wonder.

Actually, she was thinking about how she was learning to read him and beginning to understand what he was thinking and feeling by his facial expressions. And to be honest, she was *also* thinking about being on the couch with him and how his lips had felt on her skin... Just thinking about it, reliving it, gave her that now-familiar feeling down low in her stomach, almost like butterflies, but far, far better.

"I've been thinking about all the parts that involve *your* parts," he said quietly, and this time his voice was very close to her ear.

Her eyes opened, and when she turned to him, his face was even with hers, making it all too easy to kiss him. He reached up to hold her face with one hand, deepening the kiss, and something inside her completely softened.

The entire morning was an ideal moment in time, and in some ways, it felt more intimate than their cautious forays into the physical part of their relationship. Cooking with Jack, eating with the two of them, and sitting here with Will while Jack played in the yard... She was becoming a part of his life, a part of *their* lives, just as they were becoming a part of hers.

He lifted his head from hers with a small sigh. "I've got kitchen duty."

"I'll help you." She reached up to glide her fingertips over his jaw, tracing over his morning stubble. *This must be what he looks like when he wakes up.* Her cheeks flamed at the thought.

They cleared the rest of the dishes and brought them into the house, and she laughed when he lifted her and sat her on the island.

"What is it about me being up here?"

"Better vantage point for kissing. No bending means no crick in my neck." To prove his point he kissed her, at first just lightly teasing but then deepening it, causing her to sway forward. When he stopped he looked down at her legs, mostly bare because she wore shorts. "Easy access to...very soft skin."

Will's fingers trailed up and down the tops of Elizabeth's thighs, and he watched her response, drawn to the way her eyes softened and became almost drowsy looking. They'd made such strides this week, not just physically but in every respect. They were sharing themselves completely, and for the first time in a long time he felt...whole. It was almost as if little pieces of him that had been scattered to the wind were starting to knit themselves back together.

The skin of her neck called out to him, and he moved to stand between her knees. He nearly groaned out loud when her legs hooked loosely around the backs of his thighs, and her arms wrapped around his shoulders. He bent to her, kissing the spot where her pulse pounded. Her heart was beating rapidly, and after giving a lot of attention to that little patch of smooth skin—one that had become his favorite—he moved back to her lips.

She clutched at his hair, holding his head in place so he couldn't pull away. His thumbs traced small circles on her inner thighs, moving higher until he slid his hands under her shirt. He began to stroke over the thin material of her bra, and her legs tightened around his, making her slide further to the edge of the counter until their bodies were as close as could be.

They both sighed into the kiss, completely absorbed in each other, neither one hearing the sliding door as it opened. Will vaguely heard the clearing of a throat and then a familiar voice.

"Pardon me, I don't want to interrupt."

Elizabeth jumped and pushed at Will's hands, trying to get them out from under her shirt, although her legs were still wrapped tightly around his hips. Will turned his body away from the intruder but only because he couldn't face him; his gym shorts would do little to hide his...condition, something his cousin—because he *knew* it was his cousin—would certainly notice. He glanced at Elizabeth apologetically and gently eased her legs away from him. Thankfully, the blood that had pooled in his groin was now beginning to circulate again through the rest of his body.

"Richard," Will said flatly, finally turning his head to look at his cousin, though he still kept Elizabeth captive on the counter. "What a pleasant surprise."

"I *knew* you would think so." Richard grinned widely. "Are you going to introduce me to your...friend?"

Elizabeth stared at Will, her cheeks a brilliant pink. "I need to get down, please."

He nodded and backed away from the counter, holding her hands to help her down, and then he wrapped his arm around her shoulders to hold her close. "Elizabeth, this is my cousin Richard. Richard, this is Elizabeth."

"Just Elizabeth?" Richard asked, a glint in his eye. "No title? Not... girlfriend?" He looked around the kitchen, still cluttered with dirty dishes and pans. "Or maybe housekeeper?"

"Girlfriend." Will felt a prick of annoyance. "Not that it's any of your business. You just got here, and you're already pissing me off."

Richard ignored him and extended his hand to Elizabeth. "It's nice to meet you, Elizabeth the girlfriend."

She shook his hand. "It's nice to meet you too."

"Why are you here?" Will asked.

"Why am I here? I came to check on you and see how you're doing." He made a big show of looking around the kitchen and peeking under the table. "Where's my FCOR? I would love to see him."

Elizabeth looked at Will in confusion, and he rolled his eyes. "First cousin, once removed." He turned back to Richard. "He's outside."

Richard looked out the sliding door and glanced around the yard. "Where?"

"Probably in his fort," Will answered.

"A *fort*?" Richard asked incredulously. "Ah, there it is. I think I'll go check it out and say hi...if you don't mind."

"Go right ahead."

As soon as he was gone, Elizabeth buried her head in Will's chest. "Oh. My. God. That was mortifying."

He wrapped his arms around her. "I'm sorry. I had no idea he was coming. What the hell could he possibly want?"

"Maybe he's just here to visit and see how you're doing, like he said."

He shook his head. "I wish I could believe that, but I know Richard.

He always has an agenda." He watched out the window over the sink as Jack came out of the fort and gave Richard a hug. Even when the two cousins were at their worst with each other, Richard always treated Jack well. *Even though he couldn't stand Jack's mother.*

"I should go," Elizabeth said, stepping out of his embrace. "I'll help you clean up first, and then I can walk home."

"No, please don't go. I want you to stay. We're supposed to spend the day together."

She stood on her tiptoes and kissed him lightly. "It's okay."

"No, it's *not* okay. I didn't invite him. I don't really want him here, and I'm not letting him chase you away."

"He's not chasing me away, but he's obviously here for a reason. And we're still going to John's barbecue tomorrow, right?"

"Of course we are, I wouldn't miss it."

"So we'll be together all day. And we get to watch the fireworks tomorrow night from the beach...and maybe we'll even make some of our own." She wiggled her eyebrows playfully.

He grinned. "Are you flirting with me, Ms. Bennet?" He reached for her hips and pulled her close.

She shrugged coyly. "I guess you'll have to wait until tomorrow night to find out."

He sighed loudly and shook his head. "I don't want you to leave."

"And I really don't want to, but I think it's the right thing to do. I'll feel like I'm intruding if I stay." He opened his mouth to argue but she lifted a finger to cover his lips. "I know what you're going to say, but it won't change how I feel."

He kissed her finger and then pulled her in for a hug, breathing in the scent of her hair. "Okay. I don't want you to feel uncomfortable, and you shouldn't. *He* should. But I understand." He kissed the top of her head. "Why don't you take the cart, I'll get it back later."

"Thanks, but I'll walk. It's nice out. But first, I'm helping you clean. Come on, let's get it done."

They worked to straighten up everything, and he drifted into silence as he thought about the woman next to him and how much she was coming to mean to him. They were truly becoming a couple, both of them learning how to just *be* with someone again. As he'd thought to himself many times before, it all just felt right. There was no other way to explain it.

He thought back to Friday night, and his mind immediately conjured up the image of her straddling his thighs as she slowly unbuttoned her blouse and unhooked her bra. He was shocked enough that she'd unbuttoned *his* shirt, never mind her own. The sight of her bared skin was enough to put him over the edge, but the taste of her was something else altogether; the flavor of her skin was intoxicating, and he was instantly addicted.

It had been a feat of self-control to slow things down, but he was afraid of overwhelming her. He'd seen her confidence flagging, the passion in her eyes replaced by self-recrimination. He wanted to alleviate her worries and sought to reassure her that she'd been brave to take that first step, and what they'd shared was nothing short of beautiful. *She* was beautiful.

Her voice jostled him from his thoughts. "Where'd you go?" She looked at him curiously as she wiped down the counter.

"I wasn't that far away." He smiled softly. "I just took a short trip back to Friday night."

Her response was interrupted by the sound of footsteps on the back deck. Jack opened the sliding door and flew in, followed by Richard.

"Dad, you didn't tell me Richard was coming!" Jack said. "He said he's gonna stay here for a couple days."

Will glared at his cousin. "I didn't know he was coming, Jack. I'm even more surprised to hear he's staying."

Richard appeared baffled. "I thought you'd be thrilled to have me! But I've only been here thirty minutes, and you're already itching to send me packing." He winked at Elizabeth. "Nice guy, huh?"

Elizabeth remained silent, and Will was grateful; it was obvious Richard was trying to bait her.

"Oh, tough crowd, tough crowd," Richard said, shaking his head. "I was only planning on staying a few days, just through the holiday. I know this one can be tough for you, and I just wanted to see how you're coping."

"Can I talk to you privately?" Will asked, his eyes drilling into his cousin's.

Richard frowned. "Yeah, sure. Um, where...?"

"My office, down the hall." Will glanced at Elizabeth. "Can you wait just a few minutes? This won't take long."

She nodded. "Of course. Jack and I will go outside."

"Thank you." Will gestured for Richard to leave the kitchen ahead of him, and as they walked down the hall, Richard peeked into another doorway.

"I'm relieved to see you have a guest room. I was beginning to think I'd be relegated to sleeping in the fort."

"If I have my way, you'll be sleeping in a hotel in Portland," Will said as they entered his office. "Or better yet, back in New York." He closed the door and took a deep breath before turning to face his cousin. "I don't know what you're doing here, but if you think you can convince me you're here to check on me, you're more of an idiot than I thought you were."

Richard's eyebrows rose. "Man, cuz, you are strung *tight*."

"Only since you walked into my house."

Richard stared at his cousin for a long moment. "Oh, now I see." He nodded toward the door. "That one's taking care of you, huh? Did she finally get the stalled Darcy engine revving again?" He removed his suit jacket and hung it over the back of a chair before sitting down and making himself comfortable.

Will folded his arms across his chest. "Screw you, Richard. You don't see anything but what you want to see, or what my father *tells* you to see."

"Hey, I know what I walked in on. I saw *that* with my own eyes. If I'd shown up five minutes later, I'm sure I would have been treated to an even *better* show. A word of advice, though: kitchen tables serve that purpose far better than kitchen counters. It's a height thing. Didn't marriage teach you anything?" He snapped his fingers and grimaced. "Oh, that's right, you were married to Anne."

Will moved toward Richard and rested his hands on the arms of the chair, looming over his cousin and causing him to tilt his head back to meet Will's eyes.

"I'm going to pretend those words didn't come out of your mouth," Will said. "The only thing that's saving you from getting your teeth knocked out the back of your skull right now is the fact that my son is right outside that door."

Will knew it wouldn't be much of a battle; they'd fought before, and Richard had always been on the losing end. Will had about four inches and at least fifty pounds on him.

"Tell me why you're here. You have five minutes." Will straightened and backed off slightly to lean against his desk.

Richard sighed and looked down at his lap. "You can believe what you want, but I'm here for the reason I said—to check on you."

Will shook his head. "Bullshit."

Richard raised his eyes. "It's not bullshit, Darcy. Don't you remember what it was like? What *you* were like?" He leaned forward in the chair. "For the past two years, you've disappeared for the two weeks after July Fourth. Physically *and* mentally."

Will remained silent.

"At least in New York, Mrs. Reynolds could check on you," Richard went on. "Sometimes you would talk to Georgie, so at least I knew you were alive. But now you're in *Maine*." He sighed. "Look, no matter what's happened between us in the past, we're still family. And let's face it, there aren't many of us left."

"I'm fine, and I certainly don't need you playing mother hen," Will replied, his voice low. "And of course the Fourth of July is difficult. Do you think I haven't thought about the accident? I can't *not* think about it, it's just…part of the holiday. But things are different this year." He paused and shook his head. "I'm trying to move on."

Richard stared at him for a long moment. "I can see that. And despite what you think, I'm not trying to intrude. I didn't call you first because I *wanted* to catch you by surprise. I didn't want to give you the chance to prepare for my arrival. Plus, you probably would have found a way to ban me from the island if you knew I was coming."

Will raised his eyebrows but said nothing.

"I only want to stay for a couple of days." Richard looked around the office and then gazed out the windows toward Casco Bay. "You've got a nice place here. Jack seems happy. I just want to make sure you're okay, then I'll turn tail and leave."

Will narrowed his eyes, considering his request. "A couple of days, and then you'll leave? That means you're out the door on Tuesday morning."

"Right. Tuesday morning, I'm gone."

"I've made plans. There are things I was planning on doing today. And tomorrow," Will said. "I'll have to get some things squared away." He paused and stared at Richard again. "I need to make one thing very clear though."

"And that is...?"

"If I let you stay, it's on *my* terms. I'm telling you right now, Richard, don't push me. Watch your mouth, and watch your step with me and with Jack." Will paused. "*And* with Elizabeth. You won't get any second chances. One strike, and you're out."

Richard nodded. "Fair enough."

Without another word, Will walked to the door, letting Richard know their conversation was over. His cousin rose from the chair and grabbed his jacket, and both men proceeded back to the empty kitchen. Through the sliding door, Will saw Jack on the tire swing with Elizabeth spinning him in slow circles, smiling at him as he obviously rambled on and on about something.

He instantly calmed and felt the tightness that had settled in his chest begin to loosen. She looked toward the house, and when she saw him standing at the door, she tilted her head and gave him a reassuring smile. His heart thudded in his chest as he smiled back.

I'm falling in love with her.

The realization and certainty of it didn't hit him like a thunderbolt. It didn't take his breath away or make him feel as if he could leap tall buildings in a single bound. It just...was. His heart *did* do a funny little dance in his chest, however, and he waited patiently for it to resume its normal rhythm.

The timing couldn't have been worse for the revelation as far as the company he kept. So instead of doing what he wanted to do, which was go outside and kiss his girlfriend senseless, he just stood there and stared at her as she turned her attention back to Jack.

"My God," he heard Richard say from somewhere behind him, "you can't take your eyes off of her."

"I'm going outside," Will said simply, ignoring his cousin. "I told Jack I would play catch with him."

He left the house and went straight to Elizabeth, fully aware his cousin was watching, and bent to give her a soft, lingering kiss.

"Are you okay?" she asked.

"I'm fine." She gazed at him for a long moment, her eyes probing his, and he bent to kiss her again. "I'm good. Really."

Sighing, she wrapped her arms around one of his. "Walk me to the end of the driveway."

"I don't want you to leave, Elizabeth."

She squeezed his arm. "I know you don't want me to leave, but I don't want to add tension to an already *unbelievably* tense atmosphere."

"You won't. If anything, you'll keep me calm and less tense."

She smiled but was resolved. "If something changes and you're free later, call me. I'll be home."

"Alright." He turned to Jack. "I'll be right back, buddy. I'm just walking Elizabeth out to the road. We'll play catch when I get back."

"'Kay. Bye, 'Lizabeth. See ya later," Jack called out.

"Bye, Jack. Have fun today."

"'Kay."

As they walked toward the driveway, Will glanced at the house and saw that Richard was still standing at the slider watching them, and he sighed.

"I feel lousy, like I'm blowing you off. I wish you would at least let me drive you home."

They stopped at the end of the driveway, and she turned to him. "It's my choice to leave. You're not sending me away, I'm sending myself. And it's just for today."

He pulled her close and wrapped his arms around her. "Richard wants to stay until Tuesday morning. I don't really want him to, but I think we need to hash some things out."

"So what does that mean for tomorrow? Should we change our plans?"

He shook his head adamantly. "No, no way. Nothing is keeping me away from you tomorrow. He can hang around in Portland while we're gone."

"Why doesn't he just come with us?"

His eyes widened. "To John's party?"

She nodded. "John won't care. And I know you'll be wondering what he's up to while we're gone. I'll even call John to make sure it's okay."

"The only thing I care about is how *you* feel about it. Nothing else matters."

"Then we're even, because all I care about is how you're going to enjoy the day if you're preoccupied with your cousin." She tilted her head. "It's your decision, Will. Whether he comes with us or stays here makes no difference to me as long as you and Jack are with me."

He smiled down at her. "You're being possessive."

She leaned back but remained in his embrace, placing her hands on his biceps. "Am not!"

"Are too." He chuckled. "Me Lizzy, me want William and small boy with me," he grunted.

"Shut up." She gave his arms a playful shove. "And so what if I want William and small boy with me? So what if I *am* possessive?"

"I didn't say it was a *bad* thing," he answered, pulling her close again.

He bent to kiss her and she leaned into him. After a long moment, he pulled away, kissing along her jaw to her ear before lifting his head.

"I love that you feel that way," he said roughly. "I will gladly be possessed by you. I'm pretty sure I already am."

She blushed and rose up on her tiptoes to kiss him lightly.

"Are you sure you don't want a ride home?" He reached up to caress her cheek with the backs of his fingers. "I'm sure Jack would love to go for a drive."

She shook her head. "No, I'll walk. Just call me later, okay?"

"Of course."

He frowned, and she kissed him again. "Stop, I'm fine. *We're* fine. Absence makes the heart grow fonder, right?"

His frown deepened to a scowl. "I always thought that line was a crock."

She giggled as she pulled out of his embrace and began to walk backwards, away from him. "Me too, but it sounded good, didn't it?"

He smiled but said nothing.

"Bye, Will." She wiggled her fingers in a wave as she got further away. "See you tomorrow."

"Bye, Lizzy."

He took a few steps toward her, nearly ready to give chase, but he saw her eyes suddenly flicker toward the house. He turned and caught movement in one of the front windows. It didn't surprise him to see Richard standing there, and he wondered how long he'd been watching them.

But he really didn't have to wonder; he already knew the answer.

He's been watching us the whole time.

Twenty

Elizabeth took her time wandering home, soaking in the warm morning sunshine. It was obvious Will wasn't thrilled by Richard's unexpected appearance, and her thoughts alternated between sweet ones of Will and decidedly curious ones of his cousin. She wondered at Will's animosity toward his cousin, and knew he would tell her what was at the core of it after Richard was gone.

Richard came off as snarky and a bit rough around the edges, and physically, the men couldn't have been more different. Richard wasn't quite as tall or broad or muscular as Will—nor was he as handsome. Where Will was all dark, wavy hair and dark eyes, Richard was just the opposite, with short blond hair and hazel eyes. *No familial resemblance at all.* She was surprised at Richard's nonchalance when he'd walked in on them and maybe just a *little* insulted by his question as to whether she was Will's girlfriend or his cleaning lady.

As embarrassed as she was to be caught sitting on the kitchen counter practically wrapped around Will, she'd loved every moment of that little interlude. The past couple of weeks spent with him had awakened things in her she'd resigned herself to never experiencing or feeling. Maybe it had been pessimistic for her to feel that way at the age of twenty-six, but she never imagined someone would come along and sweep her off her feet.

And that's how I feel. Thoroughly swept.

She was disappointed their plans for the day had been disrupted, although they hadn't really planned anything more than a lazy day with Jack. She'd been tempted to stay, and Will had made it abundantly clear he'd wanted her to, but she would have felt like a bug under a microscope. Tomorrow would be different; there would be plenty of other people around, and she was sure she would feel less...scrutinized.

Thinking of the party at John's reminded her to call him. She dialed his number and he answered quickly.

"Hey, Lizzy! How are you?"

"Hi, John. I'm good, how are you?"

"Excellent. Getting ready to do some last-minute shopping for the party tomorrow. You're not calling to cancel, are you?"

"Of course not! I'll be there. Do you need me to bring anything?"

"Just yourself. I actually decided to have the whole thing catered this year."

Her eyes widened. "Are you serious?"

"Hell yeah, I'm serious. Why not? I can afford it. They cook *and* clean up. That's huge. Remember how miserable we were cleaning up last year?"

She laughed. "I remember it very well."

"Hey, I heard from my little sister that you're bringing a couple of guests. Anyone I know?"

"No, but you'll meet them tomorrow. And that's why I'm calling—would you mind if I brought along a third?"

"Of course not, you don't even need to ask."

She smiled. "Great. Thanks, John."

"No problem. I'll see you tomorrow?"

"See you then. Bye."

An hour later she was at the pool, after easily talking herself out of cleaning. The thought of lounging in the sun for a little while was much more appealing.

Many of the chairs were already full, the warm day drawing plenty of families for a swim. Elizabeth saw the Gradys swimming together and felt a twinge of disappointment that the Darcys weren't there too, but she managed to give a bright smile and a wave when Sarah spotted her and shouted a hello. Seeing a few vacant chairs near the deep end, she claimed one and spread out her towel before taking off the shorts and tank top she wore over her swimsuit, and then settled in with a book.

She had her earbuds in and music playing softly while she read. A shadow fell across the pages and glancing up, she was surprised to see Caroline.

"Hi, Elizabeth," she said cheerfully. "Mind if I join you?"

Elizabeth's eyebrows rose as she pulled out the earbuds. "Why on earth would you want to join me?"

Caroline sighed as she sat down on the end of the chair next to Elizabeth's. "Because I was hoping to apologize to you for that whole fiasco outside of Front Row. I'd had a little too much to drink, and I was probably a bit overzealous with Will. I hope you didn't think too much of it. I don't know what came over me, honestly."

Hm, Elizabeth thought. *I know what came over you.*

"Anyway," Caroline continued, "he made it clear to me he's not interested in me at all. *Painfully* clear." She gave a contrite smile. "It was pretty embarrassing, and I won't be setting myself up to have it happen again."

"Good to know." Elizabeth didn't believe for a second that Caroline was feeling remorseful for how she'd behaved. *It's just another tactic.*

"So, how are things with the two of you?" Caroline asked. "I didn't cause too much of a problem, did I?"

Elizabeth smiled benignly. "Not at all. It was nothing."

Caroline frowned. "I doubt it amounted to *nothing.* The look on your face that night spoke volumes."

"What's your point?" Elizabeth's patience was wearing thin. "Are you really so desperate to have your ego stroked? Or are you trying to intimidate me? Either way, you're wasting your time. And I know the last thing you *really* want to be doing right now is making nice with me. Whatever your game is, give it a rest. I don't want to deal with it or with you."

She stopped and took a deep breath. *Wow, that felt good.*

Caroline abruptly stood and glared down at her. "The last person I would need to stroke my ego is *you.* I have plenty of men to do that for me, thank you very much."

Elizabeth smiled brightly. "Great! Why don't you go find one?" She put her earbuds back in and returned to her book, not even paying attention when Caroline stormed off.

She sat for a while and stared at the pages of her book, but didn't read a single word. Endorphins were pumping through her body, lighting her up from inside. She felt strong, as if she could go off and conquer the world…and it was a spectacular feeling. *All because I stood up to Caroline.*

It had taken a lot for her to get to this point, to feel as though she could stand up for herself and not be pushed around. Years ago it was the norm for her, but her short union with Bill and her subsequent relationship with George had decimated her confidence and self-assurance.

Standing up to Caroline was necessary; she was clearly trying to sabotage Elizabeth's relationship with Will. Then again, if Caroline approached her like that about *anyone* Elizabeth loved, whether it was Will or Charlotte or Kate or anyone else, her reaction would have been the same. Caroline needed to be put in her place.

Her breath caught as she rewound her thoughts.

Anyone I loved.

She took a deep breath and gazed off into the distance as her thoughts swirled wildly. *Am I in love with Will?* She sifted through the memories they'd already made together, alone and with Jack. A kaleidoscope of butterflies took flight in her stomach and her heart began to race.

It's just a physical reaction. A wonky stomach and hammering heart do not equate to falling in love.

She swallowed roughly as the butterflies persisted and even increased, making her feel almost nauseous. She sighed again and smiled.

Who am I trying to kid?

～

"WHAT'S FOR DINNER?" RICHARD ASKED AS HE OPENED THE CABINETS IN Will's kitchen and searched for something to eat. "I'm famished."

Will smirked from his seat at the island as he slowly sipped a beer. "Whatever Jack and I decide you're going to treat us to."

Richard chuckled as he started rummaging through the refrigerator, his back still turned to Will. "Man, do you ever eat? There's nothing here."

"I need to go shopping, but I have to wait until Tuesday when the freight boat can deliver the groceries."

Richard stood straight and turned around. "Freight boat? Man, Darcy, how much food do you buy?"

Will chuckled. "The boat brings groceries over for all the island residents. They do it once a week. There's a market here on the island, though, remember? I pointed it out when we were sightseeing today."

Richard nodded as he stood across from Will and leaned his elbows on the granite counter-top. "Yeah, I remember. I think." He paused, a slow grin spreading across his lips. "So, how well do you know that blonde we talked to? What's her name?"

"Caroline. And I would've been happy to drive right past her, believe me."

Richard raised his eyebrows and took a long pull from his beer. "I didn't ask you to stop."

"Jack would have wondered why I ignored her when she was waving to us, and he's a little too young to understand the phrase 'conniving bitch.'"

Richard laughed. "So you *do* know her well."

Will rose from the table and took his empty bottle to the sink. "Well enough."

"What are we talking about? Did you fuck her?"

Will spun around and glanced toward the living room where Jack was engrossed in a movie. "Keep your voice down. And *no*, I didn't."

"But I bet you could have, right? She has that look."

"What look?"

"You know, *that look*. She looks like she would be a handful, and not necessarily in a bad way."

"She won't be *my* handful."

Richard's eyebrows rose. "In any case, if you hadn't stopped to say hello, you wouldn't have known the brunette was down at the pool. That one really does it for you, huh? She's cute."

Will glared at his cousin. "Her name is Elizabeth." He felt a surge of annoyance. "Do you always refer to women by their hair color?"

"Sometimes it's easier. And you didn't answer my question."

"And I'm not going to. Mind your own business."

"I hate to break it to you, Darcy, but we're family. You are my business."

Will shook his head as he turned back to the sink and let the remark slide.

He'd been very pleased to find out Elizabeth was at the pool, though he could tell Caroline was practically gritting her teeth when she'd told him. Without giving it another thought he drove straight to the pool, ostensibly to show it to Richard, who only rolled his eyes at his cousin's ruse.

Richard opted to stay in the cart, but Jack went with Will into the pool area. Elizabeth had been resting with her eyes closed, earbuds in and a book lying open across her stomach. Feeling mischievous, Will encouraged Jack to dip his hand in the water and flick the cool droplets onto her face. She sat up with a start, but when she realized it was them, a smile spread across her face and lit up her eyes. It made his heart skip a beat, and for a moment, all he could do was stare and smile in return. Jack spotted Sam and dashed off to talk to him, so Will sat down on the end of Elizabeth's chair.

He'd apologized again for ruining the day, but she refused to hear it, telling him to shush. He leaned in to give her a soft kiss, lingering there for only a brief moment. Unfortunately, the pool area was crowded, and he was sure Richard was watching them. As much as Will didn't want to hide his relationship from his cousin, neither did he want to make it fodder for Richard's overactive imagination.

When she giggled, he looked at her curiously. "What's going on with you?"

"Nothing, I'm just happy to see you. How did you know I was here?"

"A little bird told me."

"Hmm. You saw Caroline?"

He nodded. "She waved me down. Jack and I are giving Richard a tour of the island."

"And she actually told you I was here? I can't believe it."

"Mm-hmm, she did. And she looked a little irritated... Did you talk to her at all?" His eyes narrowed suspiciously, although he was still grinning.

"Yes."

"And?"

"And, nothing. It was a quick conversation. We didn't have much to say to each other." She tilted her head slightly. "I guess you could say we came to an understanding."

He rested his hand on her calf and squeezed it gently. "You look pretty pleased with yourself."

Her reply had been a barely perceptible nod, as she was studying his hand. He turned his attention to it as well as he lightly caressed her leg, up to her knee and then to her thigh, transfixed by the smooth feel of her skin.

"You're so warm." His eyes met hers.

"And getting warmer," she'd whispered before leaning forward to kiss him again.

Sighing, Will shook his head a little to bring himself back to the present. He rinsed a few glasses and plates before loading them into the dishwasher.

"So, what, now you're daydreaming too?" Richard asked.

"I was just...thinking about dinner."

"Are you sure you're doing okay?" Richard asked after a moment. "I mean with the anniversary coming up and everything?"

Will finished in silence, making his cousin wait for an answer. He'd been anticipating this and knew Richard would bring it up again. At least he hadn't brought up DMG or anything to do with the company. Will didn't want to know what was going on with his father's business; right now, he was enjoying blissful ignorance. He reached for a towel and dried his hands before turning to face his cousin again.

"What do you want me to say? Do you want me to hide myself away for the next two weeks just to make you feel like you didn't waste your time coming up here?" Even as he said the words, he had a feeling deep in his gut that there was another reason for Richard's sudden appearance.

"Of course I don't want you to do that; what the hell kind of question is that?" Richard took a deep breath. "Look, you and I both know your wife and I never saw eye to eye. Just the same, Darcy, *you* loved her, and I saw what her death did to you. I wouldn't wish that on anyone."

The kitchen was silent for a long moment as the men retreated into their thoughts. Will was the first to speak again, but he kept his voice low; the last thing he wanted was for Jack to overhear their conversation.

"I know you wouldn't, and I appreciate your concern." *Though I still don't believe it's genuine.* "Like I told you before, it's not like I haven't thought about the accident lately. It's impossible not to. But it's different now. It's like it took place during another lifetime. I still wish to God it never happened...but it did." He ran one hand through his hair and rubbed the back of his neck. "The thing is, it's not just the way I *see* it that's different. It's *me* that's different. And a lot of that has to do with being here."

"And the brunette...she probably has a lot to do with it too, right?"

"Her name is Elizabeth, Richard. Can you use her proper name, please?"

"Sorry. Elizabeth probably has a lot to do with it too, right? What's the deal with her?"

Will shrugged. "We're having fun. We like each other." He purposely made it seem as if his relationship with her was just a casual, flirtatious thing, although it meant so much more. "We've only known each other for a month or so. It's nothing serious." His stomach flipped as he said the words, but he would *not* confide his true feelings to his cousin.

Richard eyed him shrewdly. "You sure about that?"

"About how long we've known each other?" Will asked slyly. "Yes. I moved here on the fourth of June. I met her that day. Tomorrow is the Fourth of July. Do the math."

"Not about that, you ass. About it being fun and casual. I mean, if it *isn't* serious and it's just about you getting laid—finally—then I'm all for it."

Will stared at his cousin but didn't say a word.

"You *are* getting laid, aren't you? At least tell me that."

"No, I won't tell you that." Will looked away and shook his head. "It's none of your business."

"When are you coming home?"

"When am I coming home? Back to New York, you mean?"

"Yes, back to New York, back *home*. When is this self-imposed exile going to end?"

Will looked at him incredulously and couldn't help the laugh that escaped him. "Did my father tell you to ask me that?"

"No, *I'm* asking. How long do you plan on staying here?"

Will shrugged, still smiling a little. "Maybe forever."

Richard rolled his eyes. "You know as well as I do that you won't last a year on this rock."

"I wouldn't be so sure about that. I like it here. If my father and I ever end up working things out, if he ever pulls his head out of his ass, then we'll see what happens. I could certainly work from here. Right now, I don't plan on going anywhere. I've met people. Good people." *Elizabeth.* "Jack has made friends, and he loves it here. I've already enrolled him in kindergarten at the local elementary school."

Richard's eyes widened. "You're sending him to *public* school?"

"Absolutely." Will enjoyed his cousin's shocked expression. "Most of his friends will be there, so why would I send him somewhere else?"

Will watched as Richard shook his head in disbelief.

"Why are you finding it so hard to believe I could be happy here?" Will asked, genuinely curious. "Did you even bother to really soak in the scenery when we drove around today? It's beautiful, it's quiet, the air smells good… Didn't you notice any of that?"

"Not really. All I saw was a lot of empty space, too many golf carts, and not a single golf course. It's just dull. Boring."

"You and I might come from the same family, Richard, but we're completely different men."

"Obviously."

"Jack is happy here." Will tried one more time to drive his point home. "*I'm* happy here. Right now, that's all that matters."

❧

ELIZABETH WOKE EARLY MONDAY MORNING, BUT INSTEAD OF RISING immediately as she normally did, she curled onto her side and thought about the two very different phone conversations she'd had the previous night.

The first was with Jane. It started out well enough, with them discussing Jane and Lydia's upcoming visit. Elizabeth asked about Jane's summer class, and Jane told her a couple of funny stories about her students. Elizabeth hesitantly relayed small details of the time she'd been spending with Will and Jack and mentioned that her Sunday plans with them had been thwarted.

Jane asked what happened, and Elizabeth told her of Richard's unexpected arrival. Jane was appalled that Will had "ditched her" for his cousin, and as many times as Elizabeth tried to stress that it was *her* idea to disrupt their plans, Jane wasn't hearing it; to her, it was further proof that Will would eventually choose his previous life and the people in it over his new one.

If Jane had been standing in front of her, Elizabeth likely would have throttled her. These feelings of tension between them were odd and unwelcome, and so she decided she would no longer share even the smallest details concerning Will with her older sister. It wasn't an easy decision to make. She *wanted* to tell Jane about her growing relationship, and it hurt deeply that Jane was being so close-minded. But Elizabeth resolved to move forward and embrace the rediscovered self-confidence and new-found happiness she was feeling.

After that, their conversation had become stilted and awkward. They agreed to be in touch before Jane's visit and abruptly ended the call.

Thankfully, Elizabeth had Kate and Charlotte in her corner. Her friends embraced her relationship with Will and were truly thrilled for her. They were happy *she* was happy, and because of Jane's attitude, Elizabeth was all the more grateful for her friends' unwavering support.

Her second phone conversation, with Will, followed shortly after Jane's. He'd sensed that she was in a bit of a funk, but she hadn't relayed anything to him about her sister's call. In Elizabeth's mind, talking about Jane's suppositions and theories would lend them a certain level of credibility, so she kept them to herself. Instead, she told Will she was simply missing him. *Which was the truth anyway.*

"I talked to John about bringing another guest, and he said it was fine." She heard him sigh on the other end of the phone. "What's the matter?"

"I hate that Richard will be tagging along, that's all. I shouldn't care because I still get to spend the day with you and Jack. There will be other kids at the party, right?"

"Oh yeah, a bunch. John has a huge yard, so there's plenty of room for them to run around. Sam might even be there, now that I think about it. I think John and Mike know each other."

"Jack will be psyched if he is." He paused for a moment. "I missed you today too. My cousin's company doesn't compare to yours."

She laughed. "Hmm, I should hope not. Did you have time to talk more? I'm not prying, I just…I could tell you both needed to get some things off your chests."

"We did."

"Good."

"I'm glad I got to see you at least once. And in your bathing suit, at that. I should have offered to rub lotion on your back."

"Or on my legs." The memory of his hand on her calf made her face warm.

"Mm-hmm, there too."

She sighed now and rolled onto her back, thinking about the day ahead and deciding she needed to get up and out of bed so it could begin.

Will, Jack, and Richard met Elizabeth at the ferry just after noon. Maddie had been nice enough to give her a lift to the dock, and the men arrived just as Vixen was pulling into the small dirt lot. Will greeted Elizabeth with a warm kiss and then said hello to Maddie and introduced her to Richard. After saying goodbye, Maddie drove off as they all boarded the ferry.

"Now *that's* a golf cart," Richard noted as they walked up the long ramp. He and Jack walked ahead of Will and Elizabeth, who were holding hands. He turned his head to talk to them over his shoulder. "If you're going to get stuck driving one of those ridiculous things around, that's the one to have." His attention focused on Elizabeth. "No cart for you?"

She shook her head. "I like to walk. I have a car in Portland, but I don't use it much."

"What do you do when it rains?"

"Oh, we have these crazy things here in Maine called *umbrellas*. They're pretty handy."

Will grinned and squeezed her hand.

"Funny girl," Richard said flatly.

They headed up to the top deck, where Jack picked their seats and they all settled in comfortably. Richard never looked away from his phone and barely spoke. Will was annoyed, but only until he realized he didn't need to worry about what would come out of his cousin's mouth.

Since Jack was busy peering over the railing and down at the waves, Will was able to focus on Elizabeth. They talked quietly for some of the trip, other times just sitting silently with their eyes closed, letting the sun warm them. Will had his arm wrapped around her shoulders, pulling her up against him snugly. Her hand rested comfortably on his thigh, and her fingers traced lazy circles on his knee. She frequently turned and lifted her face to his, silently asking for kisses, and although he was enjoying every single one, he was a bit surprised at her lack of shyness around Richard. It was almost as if something had changed during their time apart. As much as he wanted to ask her what it was, he knew now wasn't the time.

And maybe I shouldn't ask her at all. Maybe I should just go with it.

After all, it wasn't as if something was wrong. In fact, it was all very right.

THE PARTY WAS IN FULL SWING WHEN THEY ARRIVED, AND TRUE TO Elizabeth's word, there were a bunch of kids for Jack to play with. Sam wasn't there, but it didn't matter; he was gone in a flash.

A giant dunk tank sat in the back corner of the yard and currently John was the "dunkee." He sat in the tank in a pair of shorts, waiting patiently while a boy of about eight or nine years tried to hit the target with a baseball. After two attempts the boy was successful, and John dropped into the water with a loud splash.

When he climbed out, Elizabeth waved him over to join them. He laughed with the boy who'd dunked him and gave him a high five, then grabbed a towel and began to dry off as he made his way through the crowd to where she stood with Will and Richard.

"You made it!" He jokingly made to hug Elizabeth.

"Uh-uh." She playfully pushed him away. "Back off."

He smiled and looked first at Richard and then at Will. "Who are your friends?"

"This is Will Darcy, and this is Richard—" She frowned and then laughed. "I'm sorry, Richard, I just realized I don't know your last name. Are you a Darcy too, or…?"

"Nope, not a Darcy." He shook John's hand. "Richard Fitzwilliam, Will's cousin."

"Nice to meet you, Richard. John Lucas." John then turned to Will. "Good to meet you, Will."

"I've heard a lot about you, John. It's good to meet you too."

Elizabeth noticed the way the men maintained eye contact while shaking hands, and she groaned to herself, knowing exactly what John was doing. *He's checking to see if Will measures up.*

"All good stuff, I'm sure," John finally answered, releasing Will's hand. "Elizabeth couldn't possibly say anything bad about me."

She rolled her eyes. "Let's not push it."

"Hey, I thought you said you were bringing an extra?" John asked.

"Richard *is* the extra."

"My son, Jack, is here too." Will nodded toward the group of kids who were running across the yard. "He's already mixed in with that crowd."

"How old?"

"Five."

"Nice. Fun age."

"Where's your sister, by the way?" Elizabeth asked. "And Kate?"

"Charlotte's here, you just have to find her." John scanned the crowd. "Kate and Charles should be here soon."

Will and Elizabeth glanced at each other wearing identical expressions of surprise.

"Well, if you'll excuse me, I hear dry clothes calling my name. Go grab some food and have a drink. There's a bar set up over there." He pointed to another area of the yard. "I'll catch up with you in a little while."

John walked away, and Elizabeth turned to Richard. "So you're a Fitzwilliam, which makes your father Will's mother's brother?"

"Yes," he answered, his eyes traveling over the crowd.

Will looked at Richard and then at Elizabeth before shrugging. He loosely wrapped his arm around her and leaned down to kiss her. She stared up into his eyes, getting a bit lost in them. He bent to kiss her again, and when he pulled away, she sighed and leaned against him.

"Am I going to have to deal with this sappy shit all day?" Richard asked, bursting their bubble of intimacy. "I would rather sit in the dunk tank."

Will gestured toward it. "Go for it. I'll be first in line to sink you."

"Actually, *you* should be in there." Richard looked Will up and down. "You could probably use a good cooling off." His attention went to his phone when it chimed.

The sound of a woman's squeal of glee reached them, and before Elizabeth knew it she was being spun around and pulled into Charlotte's arms.

"Lizzy! I'm so glad you're here!" She released Elizabeth and turned to Will, winking at him and smiling slyly. "Hi there, Will."

He smiled. "Hi Charlotte. How are you?"

"I'm great. Isn't this fantastic?" She glanced around at the crowd. "I was hoping the good weather would hold. It looks like it'll be clear for the fireworks tonight too. Are you staying for them?"

Elizabeth scrunched her nose. "I don't think so."

"Oh, come on! You have to stay!"

"I'm not sure if they scheduled a late ferry, and I don't want to be stuck in Portland. Will has Jack, plus his cousin is visiting. We'll just watch them from the island."

Charlotte looked behind Will and nodded toward Richard in amusement. "Is that the cousin?" He'd barely glanced up from his phone when she joined them.

"Yes, that's him," Will said. "Pleasant and engaging as always."

Charlotte walked over to Richard and planted herself in front of him. "Hello there."

Richard glanced up and did a double take. "Hi."

"Charlotte Lucas." She extended her hand.

"Richard Fitzwilliam." He briefly shook her hand and then dropped his eyes back to his phone.

Charlotte's eyebrows rose. "Um, are you always this crazy at parties? Because you should probably rein it in a bit. You're scaring the children."

He looked at her again. "Excuse me?"

She leaned forward to peer at his phone. "What are you doing, streaming porn or something?"

He frowned as he pulled his phone away. "No, I'm not streaming porn! Who the hell are you?"

Elizabeth turned her face into Will's shoulder, trying to conceal her laughter.

"She just *told* you who she is, you idiot," Will chimed in. "Why don't you put that thing away?"

"Exactly, you're at a party. Have you ever been to one before, or is this your first?" Charlotte asked, her voice sugary sweet.

He smirked and leaned closer to her. "Honey, I've been to dental appointments more exciting than this."

Instead of responding to him, Charlotte turned to Will. "*Now* I see the family resemblance. You both suck at first impressions."

Elizabeth couldn't contain her laughter any longer, and it bubbled out of her.

Will glanced at her. "You're laughing at *me*, you know. I'm so glad you find my flaws humorous." It was obvious he was trying to keep a straight face but was failing miserably.

Richard went on as if Will had said nothing and leaned in toward Charlotte. "I may not give a good first impression, sweetie, but believe me, I leave a *hell* of a lasting one."

Charlotte's mouth dropped open, and she looked at Will. "Is he for real?" She turned back to Richard. "I'm curious, do lines like that really work on women? I mean, other than for comic relief? And that little thing you're doing, with your eyes?" She wiggled her finger in front of his face. "Is that, like, a smolder or something? How's that working for you?"

Richard pulled back a little, a glint in his eyes and a small smile on his lips.

Elizabeth heard Will groan softly, and she turned to him. "What was that for?"

He shook his head. "There is nothing my cousin loves more than a challenge, and to him, Charlotte is throwing down the gauntlet. I can guarantee you that in his mind, this is some twisted form of foreplay."

This caused Elizabeth to giggle, which made Will laugh as well, causing both Charlotte and Richard to look at them suspiciously.

"Anyway," Charlotte continued, "my point is that you should put your phone away and try *talking* to people. *If* you're not too sophisticated for that." She glanced at Elizabeth. "I'm going to see if John needs help with anything. Let me know when Mr. Lasting Impression here is in the dunk tank so I can take a shot."

Richard's eyes raked up and down her body, pausing briefly at the intricate angel wings tattooed on the expanse of skin above her breasts, before traveling back to her vivid green eyes. "Hate to see you leave but love to watch you walk away."

This time, Will's groan was louder, and Charlotte strolled away, laughing and shaking her head.

"What was her name again?" Richard asked, staring after her as she disappeared into the crowd.

"If you can't remember, I'm not telling you," Will answered, laughing at his cousin's flustered expression.

Two hours later, the party was still going strong. Charles and Kate had shown up, and Richard's reaction to the two of them was almost comical. Elizabeth watched the way he studied Charles, taking in his longish hair, board shorts, mostly unbuttoned short-sleeve shirt, and sandals, and it was easy to read his thoughts.

He thinks Charles is a joke.

When Richard looked at Kate, however, his reaction was quite different. His eyes widened slightly, and he looked her up and down, not even bothering to hide that he was doing so. Kate looked at him oddly, obviously perplexed, before turning her attention back to Elizabeth and Will.

They made small talk for a while, and then Jack came trotting over to them. He'd rarely been with his father today, though Elizabeth knew Will had kept a close eye on him. Jack had been happily playing and running with the other kids and seemed to click especially well with a young boy named Thomas. Not only that, but he'd also drawn the attention of a young girl named Zoe. Elizabeth knew this because Jack was now complaining to Will that Zoe kept chasing him.

"Ask her to stop, but do it nicely. Say please," Will advised. "I'm sure she'll quit if you ask her to."

Jack only rolled his eyes, which were barely visible, Elizabeth realized, under his long hair. Will noticed as well.

"Hey, how about a trip to the barber tomorrow?" he asked Jack.

Jack's shoulders sagged dramatically. "Yeah, can we go? I'm so hot with all this hair, and it's always in my eyes." He looked at Elizabeth, pushing his hair off of his face at the same time. "Girls must hate havin' long hair."

"Oh, it's not so bad." Elizabeth grinned. "We tough it out."

"I want to get mine all buzzed off like a soldier."

Will smiled. "We'll see." They watched as Jack ran off to play again with the other kids.

Toward the end of the afternoon, Elizabeth stood by herself, watching Will as he weaved his way through the crowd to the bar. She'd had a few beers and was feeling the beginnings of a pleasant buzz, and decided now was a good time to switch to water. Her eyes moved from Will to the dunk tank where Charles sat, waiting patiently as Kate tried to hit the target. She succeeded, and Elizabeth laughed when Charles climbed out and made a beeline for her, wrapping her up in his arms and getting her soaked in the process.

I'll have to find out what's going on with them later.

"Having fun?" a voice said from over her right shoulder. She turned to see Richard standing there, sipping some sort of cocktail.

"I am. It's a great crowd." She glanced up. "And there isn't a cloud in the sky, which means we'll see a good fireworks show." She dropped her eyes to his. "How about you?"

He shrugged. "It's alright. There are worse things I could be doing today, I suppose. With worse people."

She remained silent, inwardly thinking—again—that he was more than a little arrogant.

He cleared his throat. "Listen, I want to thank you for helping Will."

Her eyebrows rose. "Helping him?"

"Yes. You know, taking his mind off of everything. He really needs that, especially now."

"What do you mean? Why now?"

He stared at her. "He didn't tell you about the accident?"

"The accident that killed his wife? Yes, he told me about that."

"Did he tell you it was three years ago *today*? It happened on July Fourth."

Her stomach sank. "No, I...no," she answered, suddenly feeling rattled. "He didn't tell me when it happened."

"She held on for a couple of weeks, but the poor thing just couldn't handle it. She was too fragile, I guess." He sighed and shook his head. "We all thought he was going to go off the deep end. Anne was his entire world, you know? Since he was sixteen, it was her and *only* her."

She nodded, completely unsure of what to say, or whether she should say anything at all.

"He's never even had another girlfriend or anything," he continued. "Well, there was this one woman, she—" He stopped abruptly and grimaced. "Sorry, it's not a story for mixed company. Anyway, around this time of year, he tends to sink into a depression, I guess. He used to go off into his own world for a couple of weeks, just him and Jack, hiding away." He shook his head sadly.

"Of course, Jack didn't know what was going on, he was too little. But the rest of us...we would all be waiting on pins and needles for the anniversary to pass, wondering if Will would come out of his cave mentally intact."

"He–he seems better. He seems okay. Th–this year, I mean." She tried to process everything he'd just said and was determined not to let him see how much it had shaken her.

"Well, yes." He leaned toward her and smiled. "*That's* why I'm thanking you." His voice was low, and his gaze dropped to her breasts and then wandered down further before coming back to her face. "You *do* seem to be a cure-all, Ms. Bennet. He says you two are having a lot of *fun* together, and believe me, it's just what he needs—a no-strings-attached relationship to get him back in the game again. When he goes back to New York, he'll be a new man."

She stared straight ahead and caught Will's eye as he walked toward them with two bottles of water. He smiled at her from a distance, and with every ounce of determination she had, she took a deep breath and smiled back.

"I'm glad I could help."

THE STORY CONTINUES…

Sanctuary: Volume 2

"It's not as though the two of you could have pointed to a date on a calendar and said, 'That's the day I'll start again.' It had to arrive on its own, and then it just took both of you realizing it had arrived. And maybe meeting each other helped move it along."

Will Darcy and Elizabeth Bennet have unexpectedly found each other—and a slice of happiness—on a tiny island off the coast of Maine. With wonderful friends surrounding them and a passionate new love in full bloom, life is moving forward; they're planning a future together as a family of three with Will's son Jack, and the lazy days of summer are looking exceedingly bright.

But while some relationships are slowly and painstakingly being rebuilt, a long-kept secret, finally revealed, threatens to tear others apart.

***

Sanctuary: Volume 3

She studied him in the gray, dreary light of the morning, and her heart ached as she wondered how she was going to tell him that once again, the past was forcing its way into the present.

Will Darcy and Elizabeth Bennet are deeply in love, and together with Will's young son Jack, they are looking forward to their happily ever after on the shores of Great Diamond Island.

For Will, the future has never looked brighter: he's wild about Elizabeth, has found a best friend in Charles Bingley, and his new consulting business is slowly gaining momentum—as is his fledgling relationship with his father.

Elizabeth, too, is deliriously happy: she's crazy about Will and is embracing her role as Jack's "new" mom, she loves her job at the Portland Children's Library, and is looking forward to having her younger sister Lydia settled close by.

It seems they've left their troubled histories behind and are heading into the future as a blissful family of three. But can anyone *truly* forget—or escape—a past that is determined to reassert itself? Can a new love withstand the many forces that seek to destroy it?

ACKNOWLEDGMENTS

I owe tremendous gratitude to the friends I've made via the world of Jane Austen, but especially Heather, my remarkably patient sounding board and incredible tech wizard; Mariana, who has been a constant source of encouragement since my writing journey began; and Jan, whose beta skills helped me grow as a writer. Thanks also to Sarah, for being a tireless cheerleader of this story, for keeping me calm and providing a pain-free editing experience.

Thanks to Elizabeth and Gail, who encouraged me when I made the decision to wade into the self-publishing waters, answered my many questions, read my manuscript and gave invaluable feedback; and to April and Laura, who also read my manuscript and offered their honest, insightful opinions.

Huge thanks to my besties, my *sistas*, Jenn, Kristina, Nicole, and Sylvia, who had no idea that I'd been quietly writing novels for years, but when they found out, were incredibly excited for me. Your steadfast encouragement and unbridled enthusiasm bolstered me more than you could ever know.

And last but by no means least, a heartfelt thanks to Timothy, Cameron, and Owen, who always keep me laughing and whose faith in me never wavers. xo

ABOUT THE AUTHOR

Cat Andrews has always been an avid reader, but didn't discover Jane Austen until her love of a certain British actor led her to the BBC's 1995 production of Pride and Prejudice, because she just had to know—why all the fuss over this Darcy guy? What followed her viewing of that glorious miniseries was an inhalation of and immediate fixation on all of Austen's novels, though Pride and Prejudice remains her favorite (and that certain British actor will always be, to her, the quintessential Darcy).

Her discovery of Jane Austen Fan Fiction opened up a whole new world, and thus began her addiction, and months and months of sleep deprivation, as she immersed herself in JAFF. After reading a modern Pride and Prejudice variation that she fell in love with, she was inspired to begin a cautious but earnest foray into the world of writing.

In real life, Cat has spent thirty-plus years working in healthcare. She is a confirmed thalassophile and enjoys life on the shores of Cape Cod, Massachusetts, where she grew up, fell in love with her own Mr. Darcy, and raised a family. More often than not, you can find her at the beach with a book in her hand and her toes in the sand.

Sanctuary is her debut novel.

Website: catandrews.com

facebook.com/cat.andrews.583
goodreads.com/cat_andrews_author

Made in United States
Troutdale, OR
07/19/2023

11413471R00224